NOVELS BY THE SAME AUTHOR

Novels

OUTSIDE MAN

THE BIG TIDE

14 DAYS IN JULY

THE NORMAN

FEENEY'S LAST

Feeney's Part

Feeney's Part

Marc Heberden

Camerado Press

Cover Design: Joyce Eileen
Dark Art Studios

Author photo: Sultan, Washington - 1982

ISBN: 979-8-9906870-6-6 (Camerado Press)

www.cameradopress.com

In memory of Pete Steffens

FEENEY'S PART

Life is not a spectacle or a feast: it is a predicament.
— George Santayana

Part 1

The Gathering Storm

Apologies to Winston Churchill

Chapter 1

Curiosity

PATRICK FEENEY didn't like going down into his basement. It was a place for storing and losing things that no longer had any use, or never had use to begin with. But if he did go down there, he never sat in any of the old, nearly discarded armchairs or the sofa, which had been arranged as though it were a place people might gather. But most of all he avoided, as though cursed, going anywhere near the dozens of dusty old boxes stacked into what had once been a fruit room, where the faintly fermented smell of apples and damp wood still lingered.

Yet there he was, sitting in one of the old armchairs, watching his son Jack kneel on the rug in front of him, setting out boxes and bags stuffed with papers, manuscripts, letters, envelopes full of photos, and bales of newspapers tied with twine. Feeney hadn't opened any of those boxes in over twenty years. Roughly Jack's age. The contents were much older than that. They were things he had once been intimately involved with, but which now seemed they belonged to someone else's life. What was back in that fruit room resembled that: other lives.

Jack picked up one of the newspaper bales and nodded happily. "I knew I could find them."

"You're not planning to read any of that?"

"Why not?"

"Why not?" Feeney said, staring at the bundles. "First, dead news. There's nothing in old newspapers except for historians. Local historians. Very local."

Jack looked at the newspapers. "And second?"

Feeney looked at his son. Feeney's hair, now graying and thinning, had once been flaming red where Jack's was a light brown with golden highlights. And Feeney's skin, although the freckles had faded, had the same matte tone that Jack had beneath his freckles. And Jack's dark hazel eyes—golden in certain light—were the same. Steady, large—sometimes soft, sometimes penetrating. But where they resembled each other was in the quiet stubbornness that meant arguments Feeney might make about this business of rummaging around in his past, weren't going to get far.

"Because only a few things were worth writing about. Most of it is filler."

Jack ran his finger over the knot of one of the bundles. "It was just to take a look. You wrote about everything, right?"

Feeney nodded. "It was a small-town paper. I didn't have much choice. But you're not going to see anything there that's of use. The world has changed too much. There aren't as many community papers as there used to be."

"They're coming back."

"I've heard that. But not in the same way."

"You don't know. They are coming back."

"And that's what you want to do?" Feeney stared at his son. "You want to work on a small-town paper?"

"Not forever," Jack smiled. "But it could be interesting."

"Oh, it would be interesting. I can guarantee that. And maybe more so than in my day."

Jack looked at the bundle, and then back at his father. "You've never told me about any of that."

"You'd get bored."

"Well, hey," Jack smiled. "Why don't I go get a couple of beers and see for myself?"

There was nothing for it and Feeney slumped back in the armchair.

Most men, when described by what they did, can be summed up in a word. A banker. A teacher. A fireman. An engineer. A politician. A farmer. A truck driver. A scientist. Life being what it is—full of the rich pageantry of love, family, mortgages, economics, and the pressures of ambitions or expectations—the wisest course is to keep their way of making a living simple. Learn one skill and, if they're lucky, develop it to the point where they won't have to do it and can manage and direct others to do it.

But Feeney's life didn't resemble that, except in its share of life's pageantry. He had taken on so many different occupations, some by choice and some by necessity, there was no one word to describe what he had done. And though he knew he was different in that sense from most men, he wasn't bothered. He rarely reflected on any of that, preferring to think what he was doing rather than what he had done. It was rarely that he found himself confronted with such things.

And one of those rare occasions had arrived.

While Jack went upstairs, Feeney looked at the bundles of newspapers. As he did, time went reeling back to days that seemed impossibly distant from the life he was living.

Another universe.

Chapter 2

But First

WITH Jack sitting in another armchair, beer in hand, looking at him expectantly, Feeney tried to think how he could explain to his son about the life and the times of a very different Feeney—a man who had been living at a long-distant moment in one of the soggier counties bordering Puget Sound in the state of Washington.

Jack, who had been born and raised back east, didn't know much about Washington State. During the last two years of his high school, they had lived out on San Juan Island, part of the island group sitting at the northern end of Puget Sound. Because of the lack of nearby mountains, it was much less wet than the actual Puget Sound counties, and quieter... being less prone to the social and economic upheavals that rolled up and down the mainland counties surrounding Seattle.

The county where Feeney had worked as a reporter—Snohomish—sat squarely in the middle of those Puget Sound counties on the east side of the Sound, stacked from south to north like the keys of a piano. Their western edges were broken by a messy border of cliffs, beaches, salt marshes, tidelands, and port towns along the inland sea, while their eastern edges were cut off sharply by the watershed crestlines of the Cascade Mountains.

Most of those counties were shaped by a single river system. Each river began far up in the alpine meadows of the Cascades—places difficult enough to reach that few people saw them—then trickled, runneled, gathered, and finally rushed its way down through deep forested canyons, growing larger with every tributary until it spread out across foothills and farmland before emptying into the Sound.

Those rivers had provided the earliest settlers with their first access into what had once been an impenetrable forest of cedar, fir, and spruce standing right down to the waterline. For a time they also served as the only practical link between the small pioneer settlements along their banks.

Over time the rivers and their scattered settlements created natural territories, and when Washington became a state those territories evolved into counties. It was a simple arrangement and, for once, a logical one—something settlers in the American West had not always been concerned about when carving up the land.

What his son could not easily understand was that the world he had been living in looked stable. In fact, so stable that no one in that corner of Washington State realized how close it stood to changing forever.

As for the time, Feeney had been living there during the opening years of Ronald Reagan's presidency, when a wave of patriotic nostalgia seemed to be washing across the country. After the upheavals of the 1960s—Vietnam and all that—a good many Americans were willing to believe that the turbulence had finally passed.

Feeney himself had grown up through those years and had come to suspect that vague, chaotic dreams rarely carried anyone far. Instead he had settled into the habit of living life day by day. What he considered a pragmatic discovery was the sort of realization that often arrives naturally when a young man finds himself holding down a job and facing real responsibilities.

But if Feeney had settled into a conventional mindset, that did not mean he possessed an easily settled nature.

Other lives he would lead later would show little evolutionary connection to the ones he had lived before.

Feeney's movement through different lives—along with the dissatisfaction that tended to settle over him after a few years of doing anything—was partly due to the fact that he had been unmarried.

He had known love—knew well what it felt like to be head over heels in love—and he had known the quiet tragedy of watching it slip away. He had hoped he might feel that way again someday, and the next time it might not vanish.

But if he could admit that much in those days, he could also admit he had begun to feel he had very little to offer anyone in the way of a secure hearth and home.

Nothing much different from a hobo, really.

A question of worth.

And so that was young Feeney, newspaperman, living alone and already carrying a dissatisfaction with both himself and life.

But this was not the place for complete honesty. And certainly not with Jack.

What Feeney could remember was—setting his personal life aside—he had focused hard on the job at hand, little realizing how the small world he inhabited stood on the brink of major change.

On the surface, the world he lived in still resembled the one his parents had known.

Despite wars and social upheavals, everyday life had not altered for several generations. Communication still required time and effort. If the telephone rang and no one happened to be nearby, the call went unanswered.

You were not in constant contact with the world. There was no invisible cloud of communication swirling around you—news, messages, friends, family, an unceasing stream of information you neither asked for nor needed. Continually… inside.

You could go out the door and simply be… outside.

Truly outside.

Where the world was something to be explored and discovered. The world—and the people in it—were out there, in the Outside.

And if you wished to say something important, you sat down at a desk and wrote a letter.

If you needed information, you consulted books or encyclopedias.

People read.

Everyone read.

Newspapers, of course, but also magazines—Life, National Geographic, Time, Sports Illustrated—and the others that accumulated on coffee tables and bedside stands. Books came from libraries or bookstores or through the Book-of-the-Month Club. Having reading material around the house was a household necessity.

And newspapers stood at the center of that world.

If you wanted to know what was happening in your town—or in the wider world—you needed a newspaper. Big cities often had two, three, even four competing papers, each scrambling to uncover the news of the day: the vital, the strange, the amusing, the scandalous, or the worrisome.

Newspapers eventually grew so large they had to be printed in sections—news and opinion, business, sports, home and garden, travel and entertainment, classified advertisements. They offered more than needed but allowed readers to choose what mattered to them.

And that brought it back to Feeney.

He was a newspaperman.

That was his occupation, his profession, perhaps even his vocation.

Newspapermen ran the gamut from daily hacks churning out routine copy to the greats: Ida Tarbell, Lincoln Steffens, H. L. Mencken, Edward R. Murrow, John Hersey, Walter Lippmann, William Shirer... and, in Feeney's own time, Carl Bernstein and Bob Woodward.

Feeney knew well he did not belong among the latter.

But he hoped to hell he was better than the former.

His work consisted of chronicling—on what Edward de Vere called that 'petty and day-to-day pace'—the life of the place where he lived.

And the most important thing he could bring to the job was perspective.

His task was not merely to report what happened, but to try to understand what it meant.

Or at least that was what he told himself.

Because he believed he had that perspective—as much as anyone in town—he assumed he could see what was coming around the bend.

Which meant he did not expect surprises.

But at that particular moment, in that corner of Snohomish County, nobody realized how close the world was to changing forever.

And even if they had known… what could they have done?

People rarely turn their lives upside down in anticipation of change. Even those who sense change approaching continue living exactly as they always have.

Most people cannot live with the idea of uncharted waters.

Which is why a conservative instinct tends to prevail when times appear stable. It is simply the easiest way to live.

At that moment Feeney's world still appeared stable. America, a little groggy from the upheavals of the 1960s, had voted itself back to sleep.

People were sleepwalking.

And that made Feeney's job delicate.

Because he lived in a world where people managed not to know things unless they were forced into their faces.

Which created a problem for him.

Because getting into people's faces was exactly where he and his boss disagreed about what defined a newspaperman.

Feeney got into people's faces.

Sometimes that was simply honesty. But it had made him a little blind to the possibility that life—or the world—or other people— might get into his face.

Feeney decided the best way to explain things to Jack was to start with the day his tranquil world as a young newspaper editor— after six months settling into a routine—suddenly exploded.

Chapter 3

Where Things Have to Start

BRILLIANT, white morning.

The screen door—a minor resistance against something just outside on the porch. A peripheral flick of consciousness downward… quickly ignored. Another flick towards The Stalker, but the coast was clear. It was way too early for that.

He stepped onto the porch.

The sky dazzled cloudless and the silhouettes of tall Douglas firs behind the houses across the street cut the dawn's rays from the long yard, but there on his front porch they shone through directly as though led there by an obscure plan linked to skyward signs and solstices. A morbid mind could form from that an omen, even a talisman auguring of better things.

But not.

There, simply, was a bright place to step out into. A gentle welcome to the day. To savor. To enjoy. To breathe deep of the fresh morning air.

Birdsong…

He was being stubborn about this.

Because he knew.

He'd seen it.

As usual, he was alone in the morning quiet of the weekend, often up at such an early hour, although rarely this cheerfully. But in that odd way Life sometimes has of suddenly pouncing, all grinning and optimistic, joyful and vibrant and full of vain hope and silliness, an indescribable vitality had flooded into his body the moment he had woken, bringing with it an urge of—well, maybe not creation or motivation—but something.

Something to do.

Something to accomplish.

Maybe even… things.

He had barely blinked his eyes into focus before hurtling himself out of bed as though electro-prodded with strange enthusiasms. Which was still with him now, despite… it.

And there he stood—bathrobe loosely tied, coffee mug grasped and steaming—on that paint-peeling wooden porch, shards of split paint etching into his bare feet, bare legs cold in the morning air. Staring at nothing and everything while maintaining a resolution not to let it happen.

Above his head a wild dance of hair spun and tossed, orange and red filaments tracing like a collision of sub-atomic particulates, floating outward and forming a resplendent sunrise of their own.

He needed a haircut.

The Dawn.

Not that Feeney had either the temperament or any good reason to become enraptured by Life's bounty. And especially not in the morning. But there it was… an awkward sense of contentment which he was determined to hang on to for as long as possible.

Weird.

Subversive.

But accepted, for once.

The proverbial gift horse.

He grinned, although the deliberateness of it made it feel more like a grimace, and took a sip of his coffee—which wasn't too bad.

Things were just OK.

Forget reality; let Poetry hold sway…

Which it did for all of another thirty, pitifully joy-drunk seconds, each one a bit more desperate than the last, the object at the edge of his vision stubbornly ignored, before he finally gave in and looked down at the thing lying next to his right foot.

He stared at it.

Took another sip of coffee.

And then—despising how easily that familiar feeling of jaded normalcy came sinking back into his body—admitted that war had been declared.

On his doorstep.

On him.

Chapter 4

Life Gets In

WAR. In his face. And in a big way.

Of course he had noticed it… birdsong aside. Right from the moment he'd stepped out onto the porch. Not directly, but in the way people, when noticing changes in the immediate environment, attempt to adjust. By trying to ignore it.

The thing was there, and several chary neurons, deep back behind a hazy disavowal, had recorded, analyzed, and yielded to what it was—and could be nothing but trouble, and this for two very simple reasons. The first was that it had no business being there, either solicited or unsolicited. And the second was that it contained absolutely everything that concerned his life.

He leaned down and took closer stock of the folded paper lying there on the porch.

It was the Snohomish Star.

The largest paper sitting between Dean Parker's mighty newspaper empire up-valley and the rest of the county down-valley to the port city of Everett.

Feeney wondered if the Star had been delivered by error. But as it unrolled in his hands, a supplement fluttering to land flat on the porch, revealed the new Snohomish–Lake Stevens–Monroe–Duvall–Sultan supplement to the Star. Or in other words, the whole goddamned county, minus Everett.

Feeney stared at it. Donald Jansen, its publisher, had evidently had some commercial epiphany explode like a big bang in his greedy little mind and had decided: to hell with the creeping nibbling he'd been pursuing into other papers' coverage areas for the past twenty years. He'd just get it all over with, once and for all.

Feeney picked up the supplement. It was fat, but not surprisingly. Jansen would have had to come out with all guns blazing.

It was only paper, covered in the most ephemeral form of printing known. But in his hands it felt like he was holding the entire county there. Every town, city, sprawling development, strip malls, farmhouses, companies, shops, clinics, dealers... every potential advertiser and reader outside Everett, including Feeney's current or hoped-for advertisers and readers.

But what he was holding was a newspaper war.

And he was having a hard time believing it.

His fingers, sensitized to the personal affront he was holding, began to smudge halos of gray ink and exasperated sweat into the grainy newsprint.

Anyone who worked on a newspaper had heard of them, but few had experienced them. Some had been legendary, especially in the big cities, and some of the old-timers would talk about them with a certain amount of wizened pride not unlike the way the more talkative veterans of real wars might do.

Feeney didn't feel a stirring of heroic notions or a thrill. He felt more like he was being mugged.

Star Wars—the original movies having come out by then—was Feeney's first tangible, sour thought... and Donald Jansen was Darth Vader.

And no, Feeney wasn't exaggerating the importance of this. In terms of newspaper encroachment, this was about as subtle as D-Day on Omaha Beach. Except this wasn't the good guys.

This was a betrayal of an unwritten code. Maybe not outlawed. But the sheer, callous, and wanton mayhem it set loose was breathtaking. It was the sort of thing you expected of land developers, not small-town newspaper folk (the perpetual wars and carnage of big-city newspapers he considered another planet).

Normally, while there is always a certain amount of news coverage overlap between county papers, there was a nearly universal agreement not to put one's foot too far afield. Everyone had their own garden plot. Their own advertisers. And the readers those advertisers wanted to reach.

Far down, at the western, tideland edge of Snohomish County, the big daily newspaper in Everett printed not only all the main national and state stories but also offered local coverage—or at least coverage that made sense to its readers, mainly focused on Everett and its main employment concerns.

Those concerns meant, lately, the new naval base Everett's favorite son—former Herald journalist Senator "Scoop" Jackson—had managed to bestow on the town… and, perpetually, All Things Boeing, connected to the big plant to the south at Paine Field.

The Everett Herald did cast an eye towards the rest of the county, but that was with a tempered approach. The farther inland it went, following the roads and highways winding out and away from the tideland sloughs and deltas of the coast, making their way further up into the lumpy, logged-off foothills and then up into the tangled high valleys and ravines of the Cascade Mountains to the east, the coverage dwindled with the size of the towns until, finally, it died off.

The demography of the county was simple: the farther from the coast, the smaller everything got.

Heading inland on State Highway 2 out of Everett, first came Snohomish, an old farming and former logging town. Jansen's small but prosperous daily, the Star, had—until that moment—given the town the exact news its readers expect, with half the town working for Boeing. It also covered all the Snohomish doings as well as into the neighboring towns planted here and there on the soggy farmlands to the north and south of town.

Another ten miles inland on Highway 2 came another former farming and logging town, Monroe, where Feeney's boss, Dean Parker, kept his office on Main Street and produced three local weeklies. One, called the Ledger, covered the small towns down towards Snohomish and Everett that the Herald and the Star tended to pass over. Another, called the Post, was for Monroe itself. And then the last, the paper Feeney edited, was the Skykomish Register, situated further up-valley at Sultan, covering not only that town but everything else going from there up into the Cascade Mountains.

Feeney's job, nearly a journalistic monopoly, was to cover all those towns and semi-towns planted on or near that highway as it climbed ever steeper until it came out at the top of Stevens Pass, where the ski resorts ruled and where all things Puget Sound at that longitude ended and all things Eastern Washington began.

The three newspaper organizations—Everett, Snohomish, and Monroe—consisting of what was left of the several dozen other papers that had come and gone in that area—had managed for more than a hundred years to stay pretty much out of each other's hair.

This, evidently, had just come to a brutal end.

Feeney knew well the publisher of the Star. He envisioned Donald Jansen's fat, red face and hard, suspicious eyes, a cigar poking straight out of a tight mouth which always had a sly turning up at the corners.

"You bastard."

Feeney didn't yet open the supplement, but now held it in one hand, fanning the air with it as though its only worth was for waving away flies.

Leaving the porch, he walked down to the sidewalk and turned to walk up his street in the direction of Main Street. As he went he looked at the porches of neighboring houses. Sure enough, on each walkway or porch lay a copy of the Star supplement. Feeney knew he could get in his car and drive all over the area that morning. . . down to Duvall, or up into Sultan or Gold Bar, and he would see the same thing.

Innocuous, not.

It was a classic opening gambit. Smear it out everywhere and see where it stuck.

Whether it succeeded, though, depended on more than personalized news coverage alone.

Feeney stopped there on the sidewalk, took the supplement in both hands, and opened it up. He wasn't looking at the news coverage, his eyes barely registering the articles. He was looking specifically for one single thing.

He turned exactly two pages.

And there it was.

The depths of treachery he expected.

Confirmed.

"Fucking bastard."

There, occupying the same place it did in his own paper, was the full-page shopper's advertisement for the Safeway store in Monroe.

That lousy supermarket, with its barely existing fresh fish, meat, vegetables, fruit—anything—sections, was one of the largest advertisers in all of the down-valley Parker papers and the single most important one in Feeney's up-valley paper.

Feeney's normally large, well-humored, interested, curious, and trusting eyes now narrowed to slits.

Safeway's local manager, Joel Myer, had evidently felt there had been nothing to lose in going for one hundred percent saturation. Feeney could understand. Of course he could. What store manager could refuse a deal like that? Especially a conniving, hen-pecked (Feeney had his sources), insecure, middling-ethics, anti-union skinflint like Joel.

It wasn't even a question of temptation resisted. For Joel it would have been a no-brainer to hitch a cheap ride on an undoubtedly cut-rate opening price.

Local papers be damned.

Whatever had been left of Feeney's birdsong dawn disappeared. As had the weekend. He was now at work.

He turned to make his way back to his house, his mind quickly realizing that his professional world had changed. He was no longer a newspaper editor simply working on a community newspaper. He was now the editor of a competing paper.

He took the rolled-up supplement and swung it like a truncheon. It wasn't hard to imagine what his subconscious was taking a club to.

Feeney could honestly say he had never been complacent about the copy he had written. He had never believed he had a captive, placid audience providing a comfortable little arrangement of steady subscribers, newsstand sales, and advertising. But he had never killed himself, either. Now, though, he knew he would have to start killing himself. Figuratively. Before Jansen did, literally.

His news copy would not only have to be complete, factual, informative, and pertinent, but would now have to glow with inspiration. To glow in Monroe, or Sultan, or on up into the mountains, was going to take some work.

Feeney's mind snarled at the thought. Style wouldn't count for much. The glowing inspiration would have to concern itself with how many of the glowing faces of the town he could cram into each glowing issue. And that would take a lot of footwork.

But he had a couple of advantages. The first was that he knew the territory. And the second was that he had the words.

Always the words.

Feeney never suffered from writer's block. He was a reporter, and words came out of him like hot and cold running water, ready to mix to whatever temperature was needed. That was mostly a blessing at those times when he had half a dozen dull town meetings to write up on deadline. But at other times it was like some sort of verbal, neurotically uncontrolled disease which could neither be cured nor even restrained.

So the problem wasn't going to be the words, but where they went and what they had to do. Writing now would be like throwing mud upon an eroding dike to stop the leaking loss of subscribers.

He wasn't going to be a reporter or an editor anymore. He was going to be a human barrage. And he would now have to produce thousands of words with no purpose other than to counter the thousands of words that were going to be flung from the other direction.

Feeney could only hold on to one small shred of optimism in all this. Because of Feeney's advantage of territorial proximity, Jansen would have to shell out for a full-time stringer up there for as long as the war lasted. Feeney knew most of the journos down there. He couldn't imagine any of them agreeing to come up-country.

He unrolled the supplement and flipped through the pages. His instinct was right. Most of the stories could be picked up through press releases or a phone interview. Even the photos were stock.

Feeney took another look at Joel Myer's ad. The squint in his eyes became thoughtful. It wasn't fresh. It was a reprint of last week's ad. So, on top of the rest, Jansen hadn't even set his advertising staff to creating one.

All that was comforting, but Feeney knew it wouldn't last, and his face went black with painful, lousy thoughts.

The sun no longer shone, let alone brought him cheerful, semi-poetic feelings.

He slapped the supplement shut and glared at the front page. His eyes ran down to the bottom of the page and then back up, and then caught something that made his lips curl in disgust.

To add insult to injury, Jansen, with an eye towards advertisers, had set dead center in the volume and date box in the nameplate an announcement that 5,000 copies had been printed and distributed.

Not just printed.

Distributed.

It was crass. But Feeney had to admit it was effective.

He turned onto his walkway to his apartment. He was suddenly freezing in his old terry-cloth bathrobe... the drafts and vapors of the chill, sunny air biting into his flesh like a swarm of pin-sized piranhas.

In his now paranoid state of mind, and wary of other disasters near and far, he glanced as he walked toward his porch at the neighboring house belonging to Brian and Melinda Williams, expecting in his pessimism that—why not?—that particular discomfort should be added to his day.

But no.

The Stalker hadn't manifested itself.

Or herself, to be precise.

Feeney let out a puff of relief. At least there was that.

He pulled open his screen door and went into his house and stood there for a moment. Then he tossed the supplement into a chair and walked into the kitchen and started messing around with his Mr. Coffee maker.

20

Getting out the filter and a can of MJB, he imagined his boss up there in his tony rambler on the hill above the racetrack. At any moment Dean would be wandering outside and discovering the paper on the immaculately swept imported Arkansas flagstones of his porch.

Feeney nearly doubled the amount of coffee he spooned into the filter, imagining his boss's face looking at the Star supplement for the first time.

For a slightly portly man in his late forties, Dean Parker had a cherubically young face despite the heavy bluish cast that even immaculate shaving could not efface. When he was in a good mood he could look outright pleasant. Jovial. Cordial. Affable.

Feeney was now long past being fooled by that pleasantness.

Parker, at bottom, was a complete cynic. But, to Feeney, an interesting one, because in his deep cynicism—which he was aware of—he was convinced no one could be as cynical as he was. Which meant Parker's self-assured sense of superiority to, and acrimony towards, his fellow man led him often enough to get caught off base.

People who are sure the whole world's out to get them have a hard time believing it ever will.

Feeney imagined that cheery, jolly, convivial face turning red as a tomato, steam coming out of his ears like in a cartoon.

It was Saturday. But it might as well have been a Monday.

While Mr. Coffee was bubbling away, Feeney went over and sat on his overstuffed TV chair.

Waiting for Parker to call.

21

Chapter 5

The Beguine Begins

THE phone call was exactly what Feeney expected.

Feeney picked up the phone, hearing the outraged noise even before it reached his ear, then said hello. For form.

"... guessed. That goddamn son-of-a-bitch. That son of a bitch. Every fucking door on the block, right? I'm looking across the street. Every porch. Right? You too? Damn it. And goddamn Joel slid right in, neat as a pig in a blanket. Pig in a poke. Pig... oh, never mind. You see that? God fucking damn it. I have half a mind to do a health inspection story on Joel's dump. Fucking store smells like it's been permanently fungicided. And we know why, right? What do you think of that? Huh? Should have done it years ago anyway. What?... Oh, yeah, right. Probably shouldn't do that. But, fuck... Have you looked at this thing? What do you think? I think it's a piece of shit. Nothing to worry about. Just a big bluff. Huh? Yes, yes... I know, yes. We can't take this goddamn thing lightly. I'm going to go see Joel. I'm sending the girls up and down the streets on Monday morning. Got to nip this thing in the... What?... Oh, I know. But... What?... Why the hell would he do that? That would cost him... yes, I know... but not at first... He would? He WOULD? Goddamn him, I guess he would. Well, he can try, but we've got him. He doesn't think so, but we've got him by the nuts. The nuts. That son of a bitch... OK... well..."

The phone went dead. Feeney listened to the dial tone buzz, hung up, and went into the kitchen. Mr. Coffee was wheezing out its last sighs. Feeney grabbed the container of Quaker, shook out half a cup of rolled oats into a saucepan, added a cup of milk and a handful of raisins, and set it on the stove on low.

The phone rang again and he went back out to the living room. This time he didn't bother with hello.

"... yeah, so that won't happen. So, here's the deal: I want you to go see Joel... Yeah, I know what I said, but I want you to do it. Good cop, bad cop. What?... I don't know... Me? No, maybe not me. You'll be better at that... No, no, I'm not saying you're better at being an asshole... What?... Oh, a joke. Yeah, OK. Funny. Very funny. Anyway, you go and... What?... Well, I don't know. How the fuck would I know? Figure something out, goddamn it. What do I pay you for?... What?... Oh, for god's... Look, just get over there, and fast. We can't let this stand, right? We have to react and make sure he knows we know, you know? So you go over there and let him know we know... Yes, I know he probably knows that. That's not the point. But, you know, don't bang on his desk or anything... No, no, I know you're not the desk-banging type. But, you know, talk to him in a way that it's obvious we don't like it... What?... Yes, I know it's obvious already that we wouldn't like it. But make it obvious it's obvious. And then, and then... God, what a mess... Me?... Well, for one thing, soon as I get down there this morning I'm going over to Town Hall. Brendan's put me off too damn long—publishing his legal notices, but not giving us the time of day. And look at what's happened. He thinks he's all smart getting elected as a Republican mayor in a town that's Democrat. Or... yes, or was. No, it is. Well... the county is Democrat from here down to the coast... Well, Everett is. Yes, I know, up there with your area, I suppose. It gets more conservative as you get farther up... Yes, I do keep that in mind. I've lived here all my life, what do you think?... Oh... Oh, what the hell! Doesn't matter. What are we talking about? This is the thing: we have to hammer on this thing. You got that? Hammer on it! You go see Joel. The girls will handle Main Street. . . What? Up there? Well, I don't see... OK, OK... I'll send them up there. But you'd better not make more waves in that pond up there. No more waves. Keep the editorials down to a dull roar. Quit lighting fuses... Oh... Oh, c'mon. I didn't say that... Yes, your job… that's… that's… Oh, OK… never mind. Never mind. Oh, fuck it. That bastard really knows how to ruin someone's day. Yeah… yeah right…. What?… Oh, so sorry. So fucking sorry… What?!… Oh… another joke. Quit joking around, Pat. This is serious. It's time you got serious about things for once in your life… What?… Oh fuck, I don't have time for this. Just go see Joel and kick his ass or something…"

The phone went dead again. Feeney hung up, left it there, and then took the receiver off the hook.

In the kitchen, he pulled the oats off the stove and went to take a shower. A long shower, letting the hot water run over him like a curtain.

With his oats and coffee at the kitchen table, he looked through the supplement, circling the articles he was already doing, but could do better, putting big frames around the articles he hadn't done but now would have to, and making notes about things Jansen's staff couldn't know yet. And after a while he felt himself getting irritated. Dean had been right. It was a piece of shit. But the quality wasn't what annoyed him. It was Jansen's low opinion of what the readers would put up with.

Feeney could point with pride to quite a few issues he'd produced. But in all honesty, he had produced not a few bored and lazy issues. And, looking at the supplement, he could see that Jansen had made a calculation and was putting out the minimum he thought necessary. He didn't have to do much better than Feeney's worst. Feeney sat back in the chair, staring into space.

It was insulting, of course, to have another professional show you, in no uncertain terms, what he thought of your work. And it was exhausting. Because, regardless of what happened, he could not allow his paper and the supplement to exist on the same level. Regardless of whether anyone noticed. He had to force Jansen to invest in reporters. And to do that Feeney not only could not let his guard down—he would have to turn cartwheels. Week after week. Month after month. For however long this went on.

He stood up and imagined everything… Jansen, the supplement, his own paper, his office, all the meetings, the writing,

Parker, advertisers, his days, evenings, weekends, papers spitting out of the press up in Marysville... and there it was like a wall in front of him. He took a breath and, with a growl, pulled his shoulder back and hit out at an imaginary punching bag.

But that wasn't all. There were other things.

That town. The life he was living. It just...

After his shower, and after getting dressed, he shook the sheets back over the bed and saw the elastic hair thing fall to the floor. He picked it up and looked at it, and immediately felt depressed.

It was part of everything else, and he could see that complacency wasn't going to cut it anymore.

He was going to have to think about things. His job, his life, and all the rest.

Chapter 6

Bad Cop

MONDAY: rain. Not heavy, but just the usual Cascade drizzle that could go either way. When Feeney came out his door to go to the car, he looked to the west. Like everyone else who had grown up in the Puget Sound, the first instinct is to look in that direction. If there was any lightening of the sky, it would perhaps let up. If it was all gray, that was the day.

The sky was all gray.

He got in his car and started it, as always with a swaggering contentment to hear its deep rumble. It was only an old, '74 Vega. But after blowing out the ridiculous aluminum four-cylinder engine, he and his best friend—in best-friend fashion—had done the equally ridiculous thing of cramming in a V-6 motor from a Monza, creating a race car out of a lemon. But as with all best friend barn projects, there were a few quirks they'd been unable to figure out, including the ventilation system. He wiped his hand to clear some of the humidity from the windshield, set the defroster to max, and took off.

Up the misty street to Main, where he turned, drove through the downtown with its original brick or wooden false-front commercial stores and offices, one red light in the middle of all that and then on beyond past the gas station, the tired strip mall, a cafe, the bowling alley, the tire store, and the Department of Transportation sheds and warehouses with their snow removal equipment, towards the highway intersection.

He got nearly to the highway intersection before he remembered.

He frowned at himself, turned around at the gas station, and headed back down Main to the light, where he turned right and went up to cross into the big parking lot attached to, in those days, the town's big-box store array: a Safeway, a Pay-'n-Save, a Lamont's, and an Ernst Hardware, all good Northwest chain stores and all, save Safeway, still owned in those days by Monte Lamont Bean, Seattle's most discreet businessman.

He went into the Safeway, walked back into the beer and wine section, then through a side door into part of the storage room where he went clunking up some steel stairs to a catwalk spanning a line of suspended offices with windows looking out over the main store. He came to the open door at the end, spotted his prey, and walked in without knocking.

Impolite as that was—he could have phoned first—he hadn't wanted to give the store's manager, Joel Myer, a chance to prepare.

When Myer looked up to see who was striding into his office, he nearly rolled his eyes. He was a small man, with black eyes, a black mustache, black wire-rim glasses, and thin black hair. Even at rest he looked harassed. Hanging on to a thin wish of optimism, he made what was supposed to look like a surprised smile.

"Hey! Pat! Buddy! Howya doing?"

"Cut the shit, Joel." Feeney looked around the cramped little office.

Myer slumped back in his chair. "Really?" he sighed.

"You expected roses?"

Feeney took a chair and moved it to where it was exactly lined up across the desk from Myer, and then slowly took a seat, settling into it comfortably, as though he was going to be there a long, long time.

Myer watched him doing that.

The room went quiet for a moment.

Then, almost defiantly, Myer said, "I don't expect anything, to be honest."

Feeney gazed impassively at Myer for long enough that it became rude, then blinked his eyes slowly and cocked his head to the side.

"You cannot be that fucking naïve."

Myer now did roll his eyes toward the ceiling. But strangely, he felt relieved. He'd been living with this for several weeks, and with it finally all out in the open, he could handle this. He was a businessman, after all. And so was Feeney. It would be hard, but they'd get through this. Things were back to normal. All the cards on the table. He looked back at Feeney with a companionable air. He could feel sympathy. They'd always pretty much gotten along.

"It's not what you think it is, Pat."

"It isn't? It's not what I... think... it is?"

Feeney unrolled the Star supplement, opened it out flat, and carefully turned the pages until the Safeway ad appeared.

It was only a full-page ad. But there in Myer's office, it looked like a billboard.

Feeney took a moment to look intently at the ad, nodding at this or that item, the way a man might inspect something he already understood too well, and then glanced up over it at Myer.

"I don't know. Maybe I'm mistaken, but what I think it is—you correct me if I'm wrong, Joel—is that you've gone and agreed to place the Safeway ad in the Star. I don't know... I just don't know... how I got that fucking impression."

"Yes... yeah... but it's not like that."

Feeney looked concerned.

"What exactly is it... like?"

Myer's mustache twitched toward a smile.

"I'm not stopping the Parker ads, Pat, if that's what you think. This was just an offer, you know... that was impossible to say no to."

Feeney brought his knuckles to his jawline and did the Marlon Brando thing with a wheezy "anhhh," but then dropped his hand and said, flatly:

"How impossible? What'd Jansen do, cut the price in half, or... ha ha ha... free?"

"That's not any of your business."

"It's exactly my fucking business, Joel."

Feeney slowly folded up the paper and laid it softly on Myer's desk. He leaned forward.

"This whole thing is my business. I mean, what have we done for you? Let's remember. We set up a running ad with you. We go over it every year. The ad staff comes here every other week to get your specials and take the photos of the products and sets up the ads so they go out on Thursday so all the shoppers will have it before the Friday evening and Saturday morning shopping rushes. And four times a year, for the big holidays, we give you a double-page spread. At no extra cost. And, as well, we always set up the paper so that all our social news stories, with pictures of the kiddies, or group shots of the garden club, book club, Knights of Pythias, or whatever it is that people in the town like to cut out and keep... are always on the verso of your ad. And... what else? Oh, how we've given you little story boosts... employee of the month, or the redesign of the parking lot, or how you expanded your fucking designer wine selection to reach out to the diversifying upscale population. And we haven't raised the price in years."

Feeney stopped there, putting a quizzical look on his face.

Myer put his hand out onto the Star as though trying to make it somehow disappear.

"I couldn't say no, Pat. And... they did run it for free."

Feeney raised his eyes and nodded.

"No shit? Free. Imagine that. What a huge, amazing surprise."

"What was I supposed to tell him?" Myer said. "No?"

Here ensued a short but richly layered staring contest.

Then Feeney said, "Uhhhh... yeah."

"Are you kidding me? A guy comes in telling me he's going to pass out a free, full-page ad in a paper... a one-time shot for all I know, all over half the county?"

Feeney's expression, somewhere between controlled patience and astounded pity, didn't change.

"A one-time shot. A one-time shot. Oh, yeah, that makes sense. He'll put this out, with free ads, just once. To... hmmmm... provide

birdcage paper to half the county. And he let you get it for free as…
I don't know… what? A public service? Your ad? An ad, by the way,
which we paid our ad staff to build…"

"OK, OK… yeah, I guess you've got me on that. But you could
see, if you're honest at all, how I couldn't really turn this down."

Feeney looked at Myer for a moment, and then shrugged.

"Don't wheedle me, Joel. And don't pretend that you don't
understand what Jansen's up to. He's trying to move in, and he's
going to come in just like this, guns a-blazing, making it really, really
easy for advertisers to go with this. And it'll sound great: three, four,
five times the readers for the same price. And over time, as you and
other advertisers begin making more permanent decisions,
negotiations will have a whole new aspect, and Parker will see
revenue falling, and there will be cutbacks. First in column inches.
Then in pages. Then in coverage. Then in staff. And you know that.
And then it all becomes a new ball game."

Myer, more comfortable with business discussions than
recriminations, frowned and held his hands up as if to say, what are
you worrying about?

"But you've got your subscribers, he doesn't."

Feeney shrugged.

"For now, Joel, yes. But that doesn't have anything to do with
anything. And… of course… he doesn't care about the subscribers.
Except in terms of the numbers."

Joel shook his head.

"What do you mean he doesn't care about the subscribers?
That's what it's all about. The readers, right? He can't beat you on
local coverage and the revenues from subscriptions."

Feeney's patience act was wearing thin, but he persevered for
the moment.

"That's interesting, Joel. I would have thought that you, as one
of our main advertisers, would have had a fairly good understanding
of what keeps us going."

"Subscribers, of course."

"Subscribers? No. Subscribers barely cover the paper and ink.
Everything else—the rent, the lights, the insurance, the salaries, the

equipment… my fucking lunch—is paid for through advertising."

He pulled the supplement out from under Joel's hand and waved it in the air.

"And that is what this is all about. And you've just gone and given Donald Jansen everything he wanted, with no sense of responsibility or care on your part. You just handed him the keys to the kingdom. Fucking hell, Joel, you should have asked him to pay you!"

Myer stared at Feeney.

"Would he have?"

"Oh, for god's sake. Are you kidding me? Irony, Joel. Irony. But, who knows, now that I think about it, maybe he fucking would have. He's that much of a pirate."

"I'm sorry, but I've got a business to run. Like yours. And it's a complicated one and it's all I can do to see it works and I can't spend my time wondering or worrying about other people's businesses."

"Fair enough." Feeney nodded. "But you know… you knew… us being businessmen and all that… that there was no way I could not come up here and… how do I put this?… let you know that we know that you know, etc. But also, to make something else clear that maybe you hadn't yet got around to deciding you knew as well. And that something is that all this will have an effect."

Myer's eyes widened slightly, but Feeney went on.

"No, no… it's not that bad, Joel. We'll just have to adjust to this situation for a while, hopefully not forever, but who can say? But it does mean that there's just now a tarnished sense to what passed for our past business dealings. And deal. Not so much a question of trust, per se—although I'd like to put it like that just between me and you. But… you know… setting that aside… you know what I'm trying to say?"

Myer nodded.

"Sure."

Feeney got up.

"OK, I'm done. But… look… Dean told me to come in here, be an asshole, and lean all over you. He was pretty angry this weekend, and I can sort of agree with him. I hope I didn't come off

31

that bad, Joel. But do me a favor, right now. Pick up your pen and write something down for me..."

Joel looked at him for a second, then, with a conciliatory smile, picked up a pen and pulled a notepad over.

Feeney began, with pauses for Joel to get it.

"Patrick Feeney told me today... that once Jansen thinks he's beginning to clear us out of town... and he's sure you think he's going to be the only paper you will have to advertise in... No, I'm serious, Joel, write... he's going to talk about how many subscribers he has, his bigger staff, the more people you'll have coming into the store... and how it would only be reasonable... only reasonable... to pay this slightly higher price per month."

Feeney paused while Myer finished.

"Good. Now date it and put it in your top drawer there."

Myer, good-humoredly, did all that.

"Anything else this morning, Pat?" he said, as he closed the drawer.

Feeney shook his head and turned.

"No, Joel, that's all. Have a good one," and he walked towards the door.

But the moment he got there, he stopped and turned around.

"Just one last thing. That ad there... that's the ad we designed for you, with our layout, our photos. It's very clever, but I can see Jansen's staff took a clean copy, reshot it, set that up at the print shop, and sent it through the rollers. He not only ran that ad for free, he ripped off our back shop. Don't let that happen again."

And he walked out.

Myer listened to Feeney's shoes retreating down the catwalk and then down the stairs. When there was finally silence, Myer gave a little laugh and picked up his pen and turned to his books again.

But then something in his face changed and he looked back up at the open doorway.

For a long moment he stared into it.

Chapter 7

Patterns and Ruts

GOD, drift was difficult to break out of.

Feeney stood naked in his cold, plasticized kitchen, having breakfast. The doorway opened straight out into his living room with its eight-foot picture window, but his drapes were pulled shut so he didn't have to worry about The Stalker. His breakfast had consisted of three cups of black coffee and all his thinking had produced was an unwitty epigram: Formica is despair in an industrial format.

It was a bad epigram and a worse breakfast, which, at that moment... with a flickering acknowledgement that his lifestyle could become bad for his health... wasn't doing what he wanted to do by jumpstarting his energy. Flat... he felt flat.

For several weeks he'd been working from seven in the morning until ten at night to come up with story ideas, to go get the information, interview someone, take pictures, call people... while at the same time fending off Dean Parker, who seemed to have an uncanny instinct for when he was at the office. And it all felt like floundering, and the more he was out running around like this, trying to be everywhere at once, the more he felt like he was nowhere and nobody. Hours driving around in his car, hours pounding the typewriter at the office or back at his house... he was barely breathing. And worse, it made him think of something he'd felt since the first day he'd come to that town.

He was lonely.

But not just lonely. Really lonely. Which he had been ignoring by way of a lazy, pointless, makeshift relationship with a divorcee named Beebee. Before this Jansen madness had descended on Parker, and to some extent Feeney, there had been some semblance of a social element in his daily rounds. He could go by the Post and chat at the front desk with Marlene Carter, Dean Parker's Miss Moneypenny, or with one of the three ad girls, or the typesetter lady. Or stop by a city hall or fire station and share some jokes with a town employee. Or go pretend to have a social life sitting at some bar. But this brief period had revealed to him the shallowness of all that, and he realized that all the time he had been living and working there in that town, he might as well have been living in a closet.

Feeney stared at the coffee maker. There was still an inch in there and he could go for a fourth cup, but he felt his stomach lurch and went to open the fridge.

Something.

Anything.

There was half a rubbery block of what Safeway called cheddar cheese and he grabbed it out, cut off a piece. He turned back to the counter, thought, and then pulled a slice of whole wheat bread from a package. He looked at the two things, pulled open the fridge again, saw nothing that could meld them together… no mayonnaise, no mustard, no luncheon meats… then shut the door and opened his cupboard. There he stared:

Blackberry jam. Peanut butter. A can of baked beans. A package of macaroni.

Peanut butter won. He grabbed it, pulled a knife from the drawer and started making… something. What could he do about it? His social life? It wasn't something you just went out and "did."

He lived alone. He pretty much worked alone, and when he was around any of the other staff members there was no vibe that anyone wanted to see anyone else after work or on the weekends. Expanding the social circle. In Parker's outfit, people fled for home after work. The closest people to his own situation were Parker's other, down-valley, reporters, Tom Wickmore and Greg Stafford, two hard-working family men. Feeney liked both of them and got along with them, but on the few times he'd accepted hanging out with either one, a backyard barbecue or two, the contrast between the Family Life and his own would become too oppressive. Worse, their wives began to get that look in their eyes that meant a blind date was in the offing. For married women, the temptation to try to get all their single acquaintances hooked up was irresistible, and they didn't spend time thinking there might have been a reason those people were single in the first place.

Feeney looked at his cheddar cheese and peanut butter sandwich and took a doubtful bite. My god, he thought as he chewed, you can do anything with peanut butter. But suddenly he reached for the coffee pot

He could wonder: was it only married life that made towns like that livable? There was no doubt that being a family man carried with it all the family activities... or distractions... that would dilute the feeling of being alone. Kids. Home improvement projects. Clubs you needed to join. Other married families you met through the school. School sports. Family vacations. Shopping trips. Board games.

And a boring, foothills small town just became background noise. An accessory.

Maybe he was being lazy?

There was plenty of what the town didn't have, down in Seattle. Museums, exhibits, libraries, parks, beaches, real restaurants, theaters, cinemas, concerts, professional sports, gyms. Working, single women.

But it might as well have been on the moon.

Certainly, for any particular evening it was.

Come the weekend, after the week's bombardment of town antics, Saturday and most of Sunday became a pattern where he'd drift away in a dreary, sofa-bound state of recovery. Or else he might go for a drive. But to do something in the way of improving his mind or his health or his spirit, or actually meet some engaging, intelligent, lively, generous, honest, lovely, single... woman, which was more likely down in Seattle than up there, took too much energy. Although up there there was one he sometimes thought about—the ever-lovely...

But he quickly put those thoughts aside as impossible. The centuries of fatalistic pragmatism borne by his forebears ran deeply in his blood.

Drift.

Pretty bad.

Feeney finished the sandwich, or more precisely choked it down, and drained the coffee cup. Number four. His stomach now felt better, but he knew he'd abused it. Again. He knew at some point his stomach would just throw in the towel.

Feeney walked out into the living room.

Not that his house would help much, either. If an interior decorator was to write a descriptive theme for it, it would be Don't Bother. Cheap furniture in America tends to morph through five main countenances, some just being a progression: bargain basement, rental units, trailers, student housing, junkyard... His living room he kept tidy. He was hopeful in that way. But the actual furniture, a couch with a matching coffee table and an overstuffed armchair, was about as ugly and cheap as you could get.

The rest of the room consisted of a couple of floor lamps, the small TV set in the corner, and on the long wall three shelves where sat a motley collection of books, mostly novels and histories, an old stereo and turntable, and whatever records he still had from his college days—those being the ones that hadn't been stolen by a guy who'd gone around behind Feeney's back telling everyone he was his "best friend." Feeney had made a lot of good friends along the way, but there had been a time he'd been easy-going to the point of being indiscriminate. Which had cost him, in more ways than one. There had even been a moment... brief, but real... when he'd come closer than he ever had to putting his hands on the guy. Close enough he'd felt it in his arms. It hadn't happened. But the fact it had crossed his mind at all told him something about where that easy-going nature had gotten him. Luckily, the guy hadn't touched Feeney's precious Beatles albums, which he'd had since he was a kid.

Anyone walking in there might not have found much to look at, but it wouldn't have made a particularly bad impression. The place where it all fell apart was back through a doorway into what, for all Feeney could think, had been a sort of dining nook, connected by another doorway into the kitchen, and also a door out to the back where the carport was.

Feeney did indeed have a fairly good-sized dining table in there, but would never have used it for entertaining. As such, it had become a second office, half the table used as a cluttered dumping ground. Not a lot, but enough to have reached the critical mass needed for pilings of this sort to survive. In the midst of all that sat a heavy, non-electric Remington typewriter. It would only be a couple of years before the office revolution Jobs and Gates were already fomenting struck, but for Feeney at that moment, that typewriter was the creation point where everything he thought about was produced.

He walked into a small hallway where there were two doors. He had two bedrooms. One held his bed, a dresser, and a closet. The other was just lined or piled with boxes containing the remnants of his previous lives. For Feeney, boxed-up memories didn't contribute much to daily life… but they were part of his past, and it was the only past he had, and some of it had been good and, just in that, he held onto those things almost like a talisman for better days. He walked back out into his living room and stood there. And the first thing that came into his mind was Beebee.

Beebee—her legal, ex-married name, Dogohl, always being mispronounced as Dole—had told him one morning, staying way longer than she usually did, that the only room in the house that looked like he lived there was his living room. The rest looked like either a motel or a storage box.

"Not very Home and Garden," he had conceded, not caring one way or the other. Except that, as ever with Beebee, she could always find a way to make him aware of things he normally wasn't aware of.

He did like Beebee, even if she did amuse herself with psychoanalyzing him, which he found impertinent but not irritating. As a matter of fact, not being irritated seemed the gentlemanly thing to do. Beebee's whole social and economic lifestyle had built itself around the recent wreckage of her marriage. And given the rawness of that, Feeney figured it was only natural for her to be looking for faults in men. Even men she wasn't interested in. Like him.

She had two young children. She was seven or eight years older than him. And she was looking for the sort of man who didn't mind an instant family, maybe divorced and at least experienced with being around kids. Which Feeney was definitely not. And she especially wanted someone who did not want any more kids, ever. Which Feeney was definitely... absolutely... unsure about. She'd informed him, literally on their first date, that she was getting her tubes tied. The decision obviously had nothing to do with him, she said, but she wanted him to know it anyway. And it put a strangely serious note into what they both could see was going to be an otherwise unserious relationship. As if it ought to matter.

Feeney had never thought about kids, not for one second. He was still struggling with the idea some woman would ever find anything worthy about him, in the first place, let alone see him as a father. But Beebee's absolutism suddenly did cause him to think about it. And it wasn't about impossibilities. He could handle that. For Feeney, impossible was something you lived into. Something that happened, or didn't, and you made your peace with it either way.

What didn't sit right with him was the idea of closing a door before you even knew what was on the other side. But also, that you couldn't express your feelings about it. It slightly pissed him off she could inform him of something so personal and important, in this way, without knowing a damn thing about him, as though her fate was somehow something he was a participant in. And that set the tone for just about everything else with her. Fate.

He did believe in fate, although he often wondered about what his particular fate would end up being. And suddenly... incredibly... she had managed to make him think about kids. This was something he would discover that Beebee was good at. Creating confusion out of nothing. Or making him contemplate making decisions about things that didn't even exist.

Why she had bothered to even tell him that, caused him to think about her more than he normally would have. He tried to imagine the different reasons. Some sort of challenge? He couldn't believe that… daring him somehow. Sharing? Sharing is caring? He didn't have the impression she was imagining things with him, or it was some petty, subterranean revenge on fertility and maleness. He would learn she wasn't petty. But it was definitely in the category of too much information. In the end, he decided she just felt he seemed like he could be a good enough friend, to know something like that. Which was, in fact, a test of some sort.

All this she had explained to him the first time they had been "out" with each other together, meeting for a lunch snack in a bar nearly down by Everett. As far away from her workplace and colleagues as they could get, and still let her get back to work on time. Which set the tone for everything from there on out.

And in that first meeting, which might have normally been an opportunity for getting to know each other, all they had talked about, other than her fallopian tubes, was her name. And as the clock ticked along, and as he ate the thing from the bar menu and drank a beer, he just listened and she seemed satisfied with whatever it was about him that seemed suitable. And they became from then on… something.

Suitable enough. And comfortable enough. But about as compatible as a baseball and a tennis racket. Mostly, he discovered, he was just an opportunity for her to talk about anything but what was bothering her.

"What's obvious," Beebee had gone on concerning his furniture, "is that you're sure not stuck on things like style." She'd pursed her lips. "That can be good or bad."

He'd felt the analysis coming, but didn't mind. "How might it be good?"

"Oh," she'd said with indifference, "just means you're not stuck in any ruts."

"This doesn't look like a rut?"

Beebee had looked at him from behind those Slavic eyelids and then back at the room. She had a goddamned genius for vagueness, which was also part of the reason he hadn't called her lately. At best, she was fun to be around. At worst she just made him feel even more lonely, as most pointless relationships did.

39

Feeney was now standing there alone in his living room, looking at his furniture with a blank hopelessness, and he suddenly grimaced. Personal, furniture-based analysis aside, all Beebee could ever mean was an endless waste of time.

This was not a good morning.

Here he had been, day after day, working himself into the ground... his necessity was to concentrate on that.

But instead of that making him feel he was fulfilling his duty to himself and his work, it was flattening him and making him conscious of himself in ways Beebee couldn't even imagine.

Making him think not of who he was and what he'd been... but of what he might become.

Working and living in a place where a man still young could sit around and discover, one fine day, he was no longer young at all.

Chapter 8

People Prefer Legends

FEENEY knew the town of Sultan had been named after an Indian chief. That is to say, a Native American chief. Or an important man. Or something.

For early settlers in the area, this was a popular thing to do, naming after the people who had been there before. That, of course, is an old tradition for folk. Roman invaders did it all the time. What could be a better triumph than to name a place after the people you'd wiped out?

But, in a slightly more charitable light, the settlers didn't see it as a form of trophy display. They told themselves it was homage, which was more accommodating to their religious sensibilities.

For many people, years and years later, this inspiration even took on a nostalgic, burnished glow of community and kindness— theoretical as it might be—as though within the naming was proof of early bonhomie and shared, general good. It wasn't much different from the myths and legends which had sprung up around Plymouth Rock back east, culminating with traditions where turkeys and pumpkins got involved.

The way natives and whites have looked at each other has changed many times... going right back to the beginning. At the time Feeney was working, natives were thought to have been peaceful, nature-loving people, who had been run over by merciless hordes of white American settlers. Well, that last had been true. But as for the natives, there in the Puget Sound as elsewhere, there had been nothing peaceful or bucolic about their ways of life. Long before settlers had shown up, tribes had warred upon each other for thousands of years, killing, stealing food stores and material, kidnapping women, expanding their territory, and on some occasions nearly wiping out other tribes. And even after settlers arrived this went on for quite a while. The newcomers became aware of the tribal feuds and vendettas, and grew unsure who the next victims of a raid might be. Themselves, or the tribe next door. Which went on until there were so many settlers that the question was finalized by sheer numbers. And then the legends began, along with the ever-changing viewpoints.

In Feeney's day, most of the people of Sultan had no idea where the name came from or anything else about the town. Nobody, these days, goes around shaming the descendants of Vikings for what their forbears did 1500 years ago. History happens and then people just get on with it. Or, anyway, that's how most people dealt with those things, which were done by those people, in those days.

Old Sultan John, for that was the name of the native chief, would have understood. Because if there was anything that could be said about the original natives in the area, if you knew anything about them at all, it was that they were pragmatic. In fact, they were so pragmatic that years later, when they began to reclaim their natural rights of use in the region, they would run legal circles around their immigrant-sprung, late-comer neighbors.

In the days Feeney was up in those foothills, the Puget Sound had all the trappings of a long-settled world. But in fact, the towns had only been inhabited by white folk, or whoever else had come along with them, for a little over a century.

Some people, with settler grandparents or great-grandparents, were dimly aware of the first pioneers. But almost everyone else, with such scattered and diffuse roots, was not much interested in whatever happened more than a generation back. That was a complacent form of ignorance, but mainly it was a pragmatic form of indifference. Most people went about their lives as though whatever was there had always been there. Nothing could be further from the truth.

The whole Puget Sound area didn't really get going until the 1850s, when people like Doc Maynard—a footloose medical man originally heading for the gold fields down in California—got sidetracked. It's a good story and bears repeating to show how the history we read in books, which seems like a series of predictable events and developments, is mostly just an accumulation of opportunism, accidents, close calls, mistakes, and dumb luck.

Doc, who had managed to get hired as a physician onto a wagon train heading for California, ended up following a respectable widow lady into the Willamette Valley in Oregon, where he went about convincing her to marry him despite her brother's dislike and distrust for him. A dislike and distrust which probably would have been even more severe if it had been known that Doc's real wife—whose reputation had already caused Doc to have to move more than once—was back in Saint Louis waiting for news. But that part of the story has been told elsewhere, and better. How, from a single, isolated spot where Doc Maynard built a log cabin for his lady love down on a lonely point in Elliott Bay, a spot given to him by Chief Seal'th and the Duwamish tribe—soon hardened and spread into landing points and then settlements for other newcomers. If one cabin was there, it was like a magnet for other, slightly less intrepid newcomers, and after a while the settlements began moving inland, pushing up into that densely forested land of huge Douglas firs, western hemlocks, and spruce. And then industry came mostly by way of sawmills, which almost instantly transformed settlements into towns. And as the giant trees were slowly cleared from the hillsides and skidded down to the waterfront where they were sawed up into lumber and shipped down to California, farmers went into those logged-out areas where the natives, along with their neighbors—the deer, elk, bears, cougars, lynxes and beavers—were squeezed aside, and began to grow their oats and corn and run their pigs and cattle in among the immense, slowly rotting stumps.

This was a general pattern up and down the Sound and nobody thought about it—except a few early historians who marveled at how wonderful it all was. As for the generations that followed, things were just taken for granted. Or, if anybody did think about it, it seemed to the civilized European American mind that since the Stone Age people who were there didn't seem intent on or even capable of developing things, it was just a case of Manifest Destiny.

Way down in the flatlands of the county the Snohomish people had been living there since the end of the last ice age, ten thousand years before, when the mile-high glaciers had finally melted back to the north. They had fished the halibut, salmon and sometimes even a whale or two, and hunted the deer and elk which were nearly as plentiful as the rabbits.

When the settlers came in, calling that area Snohomish, of course, the natives got pushed into the muddier parts of the land, off in the sloughs and waterways of the delta, where they gave up hunting and just stuck to their fishing traditions. Higher up on the Snohomish River were related tribes, branching tribes on the branching river systems. One of those branching rivers was the Skykomish, and at the junction of that and another small tributary, the native people had a village. These natives were called the Sdodohobsh people, who were a subgroup of the Snohomish people. Already stuck with an unpronounceable name, they were also considered low-class by the Snohomish for being mean and isolationist, but whatever traces of how that was is lost to history. And all that remains is Sultan John, a name which will be returned to shortly.

That river junction was where the town of Sultan now stood, and where Feeney's newspaper was based. Despite more than a century of existence, it was still a small town, with a past based on logging and a minor gold rush that literally didn't pan out.

The main street, at one time nearly flourishing, was now quieted by the presence of the highway bypass, built in the 1960s, which took cars past the town in a little over a minute and a half.

For amusement Feeney would sometimes ask townspeople if they knew the origins of the name of the town.

People always love to speculate on obscure questions, and Feeney had discovered the town's origin was about as obscure a thing for most of the inhabitants as you could get. And so their speculations were always wrong.

Early on, Feeney would listen to the fanciful efforts, smile, and then provide the answer. But he stopped when he realized people didn't like what they heard.

The extravagant guesses came, of course, from how the name of Sultan was indeed an oddity in the region chock-full of obviously Indian or settler names. Some people assumed it had to do with wealth. That a man could come there in the settlers' days and feel like a sultan by just living there. Others thought it had to do with railroad men, who when bringing through the rail spur over Stevens Pass, named it after the engineer who had created it back in the 1890s. Railroad folk, the locals liked to say, always had a habit of setting themselves up like pashas—which was true it, should be said. Others said it had something to do with the gold rush that had almost materialized up there and evoked the type of wealth the starry-eyed gold miners hoped to find. Although the true wealth generated by the rush came with merchants providing the miners with everything from picks, shovels, tents, ropes, hammers, nails, saws, shirts, jeans, boots, beans and whiskey to—in some towns— beyond the bars, restaurants and flop houses… more discreet social arrangements.

Only very rarely did one of the townsfolk in Feeney's time get anywhere near the truth: that like Seattle, the town was named after the chief of the Skykomish tribe. But unlike Seattle, which was named by Doc Maynard after his friend, Chief Seal'th, Sultan's name sprang out of the imaginations of gold miners.

The chief's name had been Tseult-tlan. People, after all, can only do so much with a name like that, and however his name was pronounced in the Skykomish way, anything even coming close wasn't likely to last long.

It doesn't take much to imagine what people and society were like up there in those days. And learning native language subtleties wasn't high on the list of things people were doing. In about 1870, the settlement suddenly had a population explosion with hundreds of miners moving in. The natives and the miners were no doubt a bit astonished with each other, but were also relieved to discover they could co-exist. And the miners, with all that subtle good humor they were known for, quickly renamed Chief Tseult-tlan, Sultan John, and used it to name the river running alongside the settlement.

As far as the settlement went, dumb luck, or opportunity, then arrived in the form of an enterprising young man named John Nailor.

Nailor wandered into the area and saw the opportunities of a stable and growing population without any local conveniences, set up a store in 1880 to serve the miners, and incidentally claimed the entire area for himself—something the miners themselves hadn't thought of doing—and noticing what people were calling the river, decided to call the unnamed settlement that.

This was also about the time the railroad was being built, mostly by Chinese workers, and right about the time Nailor opened the store the influx of Chinese began to settle. But by 1885 they were cleared out and the town became a good, God-fearing American town despite being sunk deep up there in the still heavily forested foothills of the Cascade Mountains.

Whatever happened to Chief Tseult-tlan and the Sdodohobsh people isn't too clear. The general impression is that, with the unremitting arrival of more and more settlers, the tribe eventually decided to pack up their things and go down and move in with their cousins, the Snohomish, at the delta of the big river.

In time, of course, old chief Tseult-tlan was as forgotten as the Chinese, or the miners and their dreams of gold, and even the earliest loggers who for decades on end cut down so many trees that even that supposedly sempiternal livelihood had all but dried up.

After people die, they are mainly known and remembered by their children and to some extent by their grandchildren. Great grandchildren generally know of them by way of anecdote. But beyond three or four generations, and especially in those communities where moving around becomes an immediate concern, the past quickly becomes an anonymous river speeding its weight of water down to the sea. Even in those places which try to make remembrance. It was the sort of thing Feeney often thought about when he was digging through old newspaper files.

Feeney had been thinking about that, and Sultan's history, on the short drive up from Monroe. Wondering if he could run a story or a series of stories about the early days. If no one had run that in the last ten years, it would be as if fresh. And those were exactly the sorts of stories Jansen would never be able to commission.

When he got into town, he pulled off the highway into the Skykomish side riverfront park and drove across a small and empty gravel parking lot to say hello to Sultan John, who had recently returned to the land of his ancestors. Just before Feeney had come to town the locals had decided they, too, wanted more history to the place. A local artist was unearthed and commissioned to create a 13-foot statue of Chief Tseult-tlan and a plaque was forged evoking how well respected he was by miners who in those days were scraping bare all the salmon spawning grounds in the Sultan River.

The statue of an emaciated-looking Indian wearing both a loincloth and what resembled bell-bottom jeans, holding a spear in one hand and a dangling fish in the other, stared impassively back at Feeney as though waiting for Feeney to explain who he was and what he was doing there.

Feeney supposed the idea was Realism. As for the plaque, it barely explained anything, which on one hand didn't do much to restore any real sense of history about the area. But on the other hand, at least nobody was claiming there'd ever been some sort of Thanksgiving Dinner down on the muddy banks of the Skykomish.

He already had half a dozen stories in mind by the time he headed over to his office.

Chapter 9

Home

ONE day when Feeney was hanging around in Dean Parker's lobby, making exceedingly small talk with Marlene, he accidentally revealed to her that sometimes when he said he was going home, he meant he was going to his office. After she'd stopped staring at him over her reading glasses, she tilted her stylishly coiffed head.

"Well, that's a new one."

"I suppose," he admitted. "But it's not what you think."

"I'm not thinking anything, Pat. I know better."

Feeney, who tended to be cryptic—he liked to think it was enigmatically interesting, although later he realized it mostly made him irritating to people—had learned that Marlene didn't appreciate the way he left things dangling. "It's just a thing that got started. I was sitting in there one day with Mrs. Hagy typing away, and the mail came in and she noticed I had all my personal bills delivered up there. And she said why aren't they delivered at your home, and I said: home is where the bills are."

Marlene had the delightful ability to fall into uncontrollable giggles at not much of anything, sometimes supplying more humor to something than it deserved. And his little aphorism certainly didn't deserve that much appreciation, but he'd been gratified by her response. Generally, she eyed him skeptically most of the time.

"At least," she'd said, once the giggles subsided, "it's nice to know you don't call Bedossa's that."

Feeney smiled, then cringed, suddenly wondering what sort of impression Marlene had of his social life.

His pause made her suddenly frown. "You don't. Don't tell me…"

Feeney let her hang a second, and then said, "Of course not."

Marlene nodded, then pushed the back of her hand at him, and he scooted out the door to his car and headed up the highway.

Feeney's office occupied one half of a cinder-block building set along the side of an Albertson's parking lot. It was basically one big room divided in two by a six-foot-tall divider. On the far side were the accounting books and filing cabinets, a layout table, a labeling machine, recent editions, a desk for Mrs. Hagy the typesetter, and plants she'd brought in and stubbornly took care of—watering them each week while giving him a baleful look.

Behind that was a small hallway leading to two doors. One opened into a storage room for archiving notes and back copies of the paper. There were actually over forty years of back copies there, which people could come in and look through or buy. Anything older was taken down to the library in Monroe, where they were bound and microfilmed.

The other door opened into a small room with a toilet and a sink, which he kept locked because it was also where he stored the more important finance records and the cash register after hours.

Back out in the main room and facing the door was Feeney's office.

When people came through the door, they confronted, at a distance of about fifteen feet, Feeney's desk, with, often as not, Feeney sitting behind it. He had no private space, buffer, barrier, or secretary.

Early on Feeney had set up a defensive array of three chairs on the public side of his desk which kept people from walking up and looming over him. Just to fill things in, he'd also set up file cabinets which he didn't use, and a small table with a coffee maker, which he did. When there was any coffee in it that wasn't over five hours old, he would offer a cup to customers.

He didn't have any decorations on the walls, except a large poster of Whidbey Island that Mrs. Hagy had put up over her typing desk. At one time he did have a large pin board where people could put up posters and announcements, which surprisingly they did. But that eventually became an annoyance, so he moved the board to the outside wall of the office facing the parking lot, to avoid having people constantly coming in, standing around, making conversation, and sometimes drinking his coffee. He let that pin board be edited by whoever needed to find space there, otherwise he never touched it and so it was covered with a motley variety of announcements: plays, musical events, church notices, school calendars, town hall schedules, lost and found notes, and services people were offering. While it was still hanging in his office, he didn't let people put up job offers because at one time his front office had begun to look like an employment department with out-of-work people standing around... again, drinking his coffee—asking questions, borrowing pencils and paper, and generally being too social. And sometimes even asking if they could use his phone. But now that it was outside, he let people put up whatever they wanted.

Feeney knew his office was plain, despite Mrs. Hagy's efforts, and he liked it. Having a mind easily distracted, he didn't need his working environment to contribute to it. In any case, being ostentatious or decorative seemed out of place in a cinder block office building.

Down in Monroe, surrounded by ornate, glass-doored bookcases and walls hung with autographed photos, awards, and other gilt-framed memorabilia, Dean Parker sat in a luxurious leather chair behind a resplendent oak desk that had belonged to his father and that had probably been with the paper nearly from the start. Up in Sultan, Feeney sat in an old wooden roller chair with a barely forgiving vinyl pad behind a battleship-gray steel desk.

On top of Feeney's desk was a not too dingy, green writing pad upon which sat his electric typewriter, a telephone, a Rolodex, and a mug full of pens, pencils, scissors, and a letter opener. The rest of the desk was covered with piles of paper. He left a little space on the other side of the typewriter for walk-in customers to set things down or write a check.

That morning, like hundreds before, Feeney came in, threw his jacket onto Mrs. Hagy's chair, got the coffee pot going, and then pulled all the material—letters, notices, bills, and payments—from his box... a big wad of mail—and took it over and dumped it on his desk. And as the coffee began to percolate, he pulled a letter opener from the mug and started ripping at envelopes. He no longer called this opening his mail, but purgation.

For this operation he had two containers, one on each side of his chair. To the left was a cardboard box where—once stories were written—he would take his notes, date them, staple them, and throw them in. Reporter housekeeping. Regardless of the importance of the story, it was necessary to keep all notes, just in case a disgruntled member of the public, a lawyer, or Parker, needed to see them. Feeney's stories were almost never of the earthshakingly investigative sort, but it was standard policy and, in fact, a written clause in his contract. It usually took half a year to fill the box, at which point it would be folded shut and archived for five years.

To the right was a 50-gallon plastic garbage can which received, after a cursory look, all the announcements, letters, advertisements, notices, public relations brochures, and whatever else people thought he might find interesting to send him.

He went through all that, tearing and slashing with his opener, and it usually took half an hour. Most ended in the can, but Feeney would expertly pan out the useful things—some of public interest, some because they appealed to him. He had a soft spot for forestry and fishing department notices, advice columns from the Department of Motor Vehicles, good housekeeping tips, the occasional recipe, and perhaps some corporate news which might actually generate a job or two. And he kept anything from any local group or organization. The 4-H Club, the Masons, the Gardening Club, or Library Guild. God forbid he missed those.

Finished, Feeney dropped the letter opener back into the mug, got himself a cup of coffee and sat back down, reached for a notepad and began writing notes to himself:

1. Repaving main: everyone hates the mayor.
2. State inspection of the Sultan bridge: next year, no more logging trucks.
3. Fish hatchery: sports fisherman vs the Indians...

51

always a controversy, even the most even-handed report will rile everybody up.

4. Weird noises from the high school principal? Something about inappropriate heating/insulation?
5. The logging show failures of the past three years... rumors...
6. Gold Bar elections, and a criminal investigation into... something? What?
7. Four simultaneous restaurant openings between Sultan and Skykomish. Good news or bad timing or...?
8. The new regulations for court cases and the need for juries... judge, lawyers, mayor commentaries.
9. Signs of life in the home building market, some jobs down at the port and the lumber mill?
10. A prison extension down in Monroe, costs, rumors of payback, security?
11. Beautifying Sultan? Tourist attraction? Merchants Association?
12. Changing face of the local population: the highway spur being built down to the towns on the western side of Lake Washington in Seattle.

Feeney looked over that list, looked around the room hopelessly, and then started another:

13. How local produce was encouraged at local supermarkets.
14. How locally owned and operated newspapers held communities together.
15. Your newspaper's front page, 25 years ago. Look how long we've been here providing you with community news.
16. Your newspaper's front page, 50 years ago. See?
17. Your newspaper's front page, 75 years ago. See? See?
18. What your local supermarket (Safeway) does to keep prices down.
19. Three local businesses.
20. Four local businesses.

52

21. Three local businesses.
22. Several local artisans, workers, contract companies.
23. Historical nuggets: half a dozen stories from the past.
24. Police Blotter. Chief wants more than cop shop? God.
25. He flipped the page and began another:
26. Photos of kindergartners being taught how to square dance.
27. Photo of garden club wall-hanging projects. Photo of senior Bowling Club.
28. Photo of junior high girls' and boys' cross-country teams, boys football team, stamp collectors club, math club.
29. Photos of high school sports teams, girls and boys.
30. Photos of merchants association picking up highway trash
31. Photos of town council members inspecting Riverfront Park (photo with Chief Sultan)
32. Photos of parents of 3rd-grade class helping with the books program.
33. Photos of picnickers at the park (twice).
34. Photos of kids jumping off Sultan Bridge (5 bucks and an angry call from Parker)
35. A dozen or more photos of wedding anniversaries.
36. A dozen or more photos of weddings, birthdays, worker of the year, month, week, school achievements and honors (spelling bees, clubs).
37. Photos of the fire department personnel in action (make sure always recognizable). Police department. Sanitation department. Town Hall. School Board. Merchants Association. Rifle Club. Archery Club. Stable Club. Gold Miners Club. Bird Watchers Club. Book Club. Boy Scouts. Girl Scouts. Brownies. Cub Scouts. Baby contest contestants.
38. Photos of kindergartners.
39. Photos of first graders.
40. Photos of second graders.

41. Photos of X graders, etc., etc., etc., etc.

Feeney tore the three sheets of paper from the notebook, pushed his typewriter forward into the public space, and set the three lists side by side. Three months' worth of feature stories, business promotions, people. These were the three pillars on which a local newspaper built interest, subscriptions, and advertising.

And to what result?

They would still be bleeding to death.

Jansen was constantly whittling away at their advertising, they had lost several hundred subscribers, and some of the town organizations were beginning to send information to Jansen's staff as well as to Feeney.

Feeney stared at the lists. The photos guaranteed that several hundred extra papers were sold per week as families bought up copies for their relatives or home archives. But those sales didn't make up for the lost subscriptions, and within the next two months, when Parker had to make public his subscription figures to advertisers, it would be embarrassing.

Because, simply, there wasn't that big story.

The one that only they could do up there.

The one nobody else could do.

Nothing.

He had nothing.

Chapter 10

Social intercourse

FEENEY stared at the lists. Nothing on them was impossible; it was all just time-consuming. But it was also dead boring. Nothing was worse, he thought, than to know exactly what one would be doing for the next four months.

He looked out the big windows to the parking lot, idly wondering if he wanted to tackle any of the things from the lists. And then he stood up, grabbed his coat, switched off the coffee machine and the lights, went out to his car, and drove out onto the highway, heading east up the mountains toward Stevens Pass.

He passed each of the up-valley towns east of Sultan as he went up the highway, their city halls, fire departments, schools, businesses. Just a few miles east was the town of Startup, where the highway had wiped out whatever there might once have been of Main Street. Then a few more miles to Gold Bar, which in those days was comparable in size to Sultan but had an amateurish town council making Sultan's seem almost competent in contrast. Farther up, he passed the turnoff to Index, which at the time still had a few of its historic buildings and hadn't come to grips with how it was a ghost town. After that came Baring, which anymore was just a name, with a small general store made for highway traffic. And after quite a few miles the farthest-flung town of Skykomish which sat over on the other side of the river, so distant from the others and insignificant that Feeney felt like he had landed on Pluto every time he got out and walked around its windswept streets and wide-spaced buildings.

It did possess one oddity, though, that often brought him up: a four-year high school where about twenty students benefited from a teaching staff of six full-time teachers, and managed to field football, basketball and track teams during the year. Feeney would go to watch their games sometimes, if only out of morbid curiosity.

Beyond Skykomish was the long highway climbing up to the top of the pass, but approaching Skykomish, Feeney suddenly slowed and turned off toward the bridge to the town so that he could turn around. Beyond Skykomish was the long, climbing road on up to the ski area at Stevens Pass which didn't have town structure at all but was one of the dozen or so snow-based commercial fleshpot ski resorts in the state built to drain whatever expendable income the bored and modish had lying around in the winter months. On occasion, Feeney would go up there to see if there were any new runs or accommodations, but there was nothing up there for him. As far as his readers went, none of them cared. And as with most days, neither did he.

As he trundled his way past the few remaining buildings from Skykomish's mining days, he decided to stop at the old hotel, which now sported a small store. Local politics were nasty up there in that town, and the hotel itself was caught up in some of that. Money was passed from pocket to pocket... county money, railroad money. Feeney didn't really want to get himself involved in all that, although from time to time he considered writing about the hotel's supposed resident ghost, the Blue Lady, one of the town's "seamstresses" back in the gold rush days, who'd been murdered by a jealous miner.

Inside the store he spotted a copy of the Snohomish supplement on the coffee counter.

All the way up here.

Of course.

He picked it up and looked at the nameplate where Jansen now announced 10,000 printed and distributed.

He looked up absently at the lady behind the counter, a middle-aged woman with pigtails named Karen who might or might not have been the owner of the hotel. He had never asked. But she knew very well who he was and what he did.

"They left a stack of those, Pat. They're for free so people took a few, but I ended up throwing the rest out after a while. It'd be a good idea."

Feeney opened up the paper, looking at Joel's ad. It was still there, although now he could see that Jansen had slightly modified the items. Maybe there was a deal?

He looked up at Karen. "What?"

"You should think about it, doing that."

"Doing…?"

"Distributing your paper for free, too."

Feeney's mind was silent as a tomb as he drove back down the highway. He just watched the trees and traffic pass as he dropped in altitude, going past all the same towns in reverse order, then through Sultan, and on back down to Monroe. Evening coming on fast.

It wasn't that he was in a contrary mood, but he should have gone straight home. As it was, he drove over to Bedossa's and went in, passing the restaurant into the cocktail lounge.

It was the biggest lounge in the area, with a dancefloor and stage where bands played live music.

He had never before wandered in there on a Monday night and he was shocked by how full the place was. It was always amazing to him how hard-up local singles were for company and conversation… even with boozy strangers.

Feeney wandered behind all the backs seated on stools at the bar, not recognizing anyone, finally spotting a place at the farthest, darkest end. He took a seat, occasionally tried to get the attention of one of the busy barmaids, and looked out across the crowded tables and booths. There was no band, but a jukebox produced an underlying soundtrack to all the voices.

Feeney knew well the six places the lonely or bored could go to there up valley. Sultan had a smallish cocktail lounge at a restaurant called the Harvester, and a dark, warehouse-like dance bar lit mainly with fluorescent beer signs. Monroe had a bowling alley, two regular bars on main street—one being the biker bar—and Bedossa's, there on the highway, which during the day was a sort of Mediterranean American restaurant. In the evening it became the place, it was where people hoped to meet someone new. Hope being the key word, because nobody was ever new in there.

Disco had only just recently died off. An unused mirror ball still hung out over the dance floor. But the bar's patrons, while no longer wearing leisure suits, still managed to look disco-esque with designer jeans, tight leather jackets, and carefully blow-dried hairstyles. Even if during the day they worked at auto parts stores or in construction outfits.

Feeney didn't own any casual dress-up, out-on-the-town clothes. He did have a leather jacket and slacks which he wore most days to work, and he had a couple of suits he'd put on when he had to interview a state senator. But nothing specifically for socializing.

He realized, even on a Monday evening, looking around the room at silky dresses and expensive denim, people were taking their socializing seriously. He looked back at the barmaids, none of whom he recognized and none who had noticed him, waited another minute, then got up off the stool and headed for the door. The last thing he was going to do was drink alone at a bar full of people.

Before going home he stopped at the video store, rented a Clint Eastwood movie, a Nick Nolte movie, and a fairly new science fiction thing with some guy named Harrison Ford. After that he stopped at the 7-11 and got a six-pack of Rainier, a chicken burrito, and some chips.

At home he had just settled to watch a movie or two, or three, the burrito in one hand, a beer in the other, when the phone rang.

"You shouldn't drive with your lights off."

"Oh... hi... what?"

"When you were leaving Bedossa's."

There was no background noise of voices or muffled music so Beebee was most likely at her house.

"I must have been distracted."

"No luck down there?"

"You weren't there, no."

"I thought you said you didn't like to find me in the bars."

"If I remember, that's where you found me."

"And if you'd seen me down there... with friends?"

Feeney sighed. "I would have asked you to dance?"

A small laugh. "Why do you hate dancing?"

"I don't," he said. And it was true.

"You just need to practice."

"Practice?"

There was a bit of a pause.

"So… any particular reason I shouldn't come down?"

"Please be joking. It's Monday."

"Don't be a sourpuss. I can just call it a night, too."

Feeney sighed. "I've got some movies."

"All right. Have you had anything to eat?"

He looked at the burrito.

"No."

It would be half an hour before Beebee got there. He cracked open the can of beer. She hadn't followed him so he knew what she'd done. She'd gone in, herself, to look around.

He took a sip of beer.

Didn't matter. That was Beebee.

Another sip.

A reflection.

And then he got up to go change his shirt.

After all, it was sort of a date.

Chapter 11

Recording Democracy

FEENEY went to Town Council meetings as though a doomed convict. Lately, the meetings had become an open-season war zone and he despised petty politics, but it took his mind off Jansen.

He wandered into the city hall, ignoring the looks from the meeting-goers, and went into the council room where he took his habitual place off to the back and the side. The wooden council table, old, battered-looking but supposedly historic, stood raised on a two-step dais facing a half-dozen rows of vinyl-padded steel chairs. The place was packed, standing room only. As always.

Feeney pulled out his notepad, but for the first half hour barely wrote anything. Anymore, the mayor, council members, and the town lawyer hunched their backs and got through the council's business quickly without drawing fire from an audience crouched at the ready to blast away at anything.

Feeney had early on learned that included in that anything was the newspaper editor who, by virtue of a job description forcing him to attend, was therefore identified as one of them. He didn't feel nervous, knowing that, but he was aware that calamity was a possibility. For that he'd adopted prudence as the best course of action. Low-key was not the term for Feeney's presence. He was invisible.

Feeney's predecessor, Kirby Seager, had once been so foolhardy as to stand up and declare there was too much bickering taking place, that certain elements should have the good grace to let the council and the police chief get on with their jobs.

It hadn't come out as Kirby had meant it. All that he'd wanted to say was it seemed reasonable to let the newly elected council and mayor have a go at it for a while. If, eventually, it was clear they weren't doing a good job, then everyone, including the town's paper, would have a clear right to start criticizing. That was his idea of how democracy should work. Evidently, it wasn't a commonly held opinion. And as well, the way he said it sounded to just about everyone in the room that he was suggesting they just shut up. Even Kirby had that impression, about two seconds too late, and by the time he tried to clarify himself, the place erupted.

Being a sort of high point in town council lore, several people, with unconcealed delight, had told Feeney how Dean Parker had been obliged to show up at the next meeting to defend an all but tarred and feathered editor. Not long afterward, Seager quit. Or something.

There was no doubt Parker despised the bush-league politics of the small towns up valley, and especially those of Sultan. But he disliked even more the idea that the paper might become an issue in itself, and thereby lose subscribers and advertising. Feeney could recall being amused by Parker's insistence on the need to keep a low profile. He was no longer amused, although he'd come to see the meetings as a form of entertainment. Cloaked in calculated innocuity, he watched the action, took his notes, and silently admired how well this haywire form of local democracy shot itself in the foot every blessed Tuesday night in the Sultan Town Hall. To Feeney, the meetings now had all the trappings of a classical tragedy. No matter what piece of business came up, an immutable sequence of events followed which no one was able to change. All the actors knew their parts and knew how it would always end.

There at the center of the table sat Charles Peace, the mayor, with an expressionless mask on his otherwise fine, teacherly face— although an occasional wary glance would flash around the room from beneath lowered eyelids—shuffling through the order of business, while the six council members, three on either side of him, stared glumly at whatever papers they held. Not one of them looked like they wanted to be there and in fact they all seemed to shrink visibly the moment they sat down. Feeney thought they looked like a tableau vivant of the Seven Dwarfs doing the Last Supper.

There was one other addition to the scene, sitting down at the far end of the table and playing the role of deus ex machina: the elegantly rumpled and equally martyr/prosecution-complexed town lawyer, Newton Powell, who under normal circumstances had no need to be there. Trouble was, normal circumstances now included a plethora of wild lawsuits brought against the town by various discontented parties. The suits ranged from accusations of unfair hiring practices or criminal mishandling of funds, to sexual harassment. The result was that most of the town's discretionary budget was now tied up in various courts up and down the valley. On that point, he took delight in pointing out at every meeting that he didn't know how in the hell there could be any money mismanagement or unfair hiring taking place, since there was no money left anyway thanks to all the lawsuits. He always said it in a bored, sarcastic voice even if he didn't feel it, but he was a small-town lawyer and knew that was the way small-town lawyers always had to sound. Sometimes, a job is more of what you seem to be doing than what you should be doing.

Powell's job, now, was to seem to be there for informational purposes. But in fact, he was acting simultaneously as the town's main witness for defense, and as a sort of judge, sardonic and unyielding, formally pointing out for the record at each interruption that there was an ongoing obstruction of government taking place.

This put Feeney firmly on the spot. Although he disliked the main fomenter of civic unrest, a former councilman named Dick Brahnler, who had refused to gracefully accept the fact he had been very badly beaten at the polls, Feeney could not hold the council blameless, either. If they had not actually mismanaged things, their utter lack of diplomacy had made things worse.

A doughtily stubborn bank officer, Helen Steinman, and a remarkably uninformed real estate broker, Paul Higgins, had done the most damage early on, engaging in furious shouting matches with Brahnler or one of his cronies. Several council meetings had descended into brawls. Then came the lawsuits.

62

With the room chattering away in open discourtesy, the council came to order. There were three points of business to take care of. The first was to select among bids from paving contractors to resurface some street over by the high school. Two of the bids were from county companies. One was from a large Seattle firm and, quite naturally, it was the lowest.

The council seemed to cringe. Peace announced the obvious award. A voice rose out of the audience. "Point of order, Mr. Chairman."

Feeney didn't even look.

Dick Brahnler, a short, stocky man with a meaty face and pudgy hands, stood up, waving one of those hands in the air. Feeney watched Powell theatrically roll his eyes as Charles Peace asked what Brahnler wanted, explaining as he did so that calling out "point of order" did not then, or ever, make any particular sense.

"Well, once again," Brahnler started, ignoring Peace, "we see how what few town funds there are are being flushed on down the valley."

"You should know," Helen Steinman said.

Brahnler frowned. "I just wish, for once and for all, you people would try to think about what you are doing."

"And what are we doing, Dick?" a heavy-set councilman named Tom Scragg said. "You want us to give the contract to Jerry or Pete," he nodded at the two local contractors, "even when they don't have the equipment or the men to do the job?"

"They would get them," Brahnler said.

"Sure, and it would cost us more money."

"Jerry said he would pay for the paving machine himself." Brahnler had now waved his arm around to point at one of the contractors, whose face turned red.

Scragg looked right at the contractor. "I'm sorry, Jerry, but you know you didn't even get your bid in on time for us to legally accept it."

"An extension was filed," Brahnler said.

"And anyway, we don't have discretionary funds to shore up local economy initiatives. We don't have the carry-over budget from the last fiscal year. And you," Scragg maintained eye contact with the contractor but shook his finger meaningfully towards Brahnler, "know why."

The contractor just nodded his head and shrugged his shoulders. It was plain he knew that he had not been in the running.

Brahnler made a disgusted sound and looked around at his cohorts, a dozen or so locals who seemed to be there for the sole purpose of making Peace and the council feel uncomfortable. They were enjoying themselves immensely, and on cue, all shook their heads in perfect unison at yet another display of incompetence.

It went like that all the way to the end of the meeting. The council announced an action, Brahnler got up and called his point of order, resulting in the usual exchange of semi-veiled insults, then came the dogged council vote, duly closed by Powell intoning some legal explanation as to why the action was unimpeachable.

It all made for a dismal spectacle but at least, by following the order of business with some determination, Charles Peace got them through it once again.

This particular evening, to Feeney's dismay, Brahnler had got himself so worked up that he decided to fold the newspaper editor into his disgruntled resentment. Out of nowhere, he suddenly stood up and held aloft in his stout fist a copy of the Snohomish supplement. Feeney stared benignly at Brahnler, although mentally he was stabbing him to death out behind the dumpsters with a dull skinning knife.

"Just to say," Brahnler said loudly, as if Feeney maybe wasn't paying attention or suffered from some form of deafness, "that at least now, we can all hope to get some decent reporting here up valley."

It was singularly rude, even for Brahnler. Everyone in the room had suddenly turned to look at Feeney.

Feeney looked back at them, and then back at Brahnler and shrugged, holding up his notebook and looking quickly to the left and right. It was obvious that he was the only reporter in the meeting room.

"You'll notice Feeney here doesn't make speeches," Brahnler

said to his friends. "At least the paper learned something, after Seagull." Brahnler was one of those people who liked to make up funny names for people. He got a few chuckles, but not enough to convince Feeney that anyone felt one way or the other about him.

Feeney breathed out, "Seager," but no more. Although he never would have admitted it, Brahnler was right. The newspaper would never again be heard to say anything at those meetings except to ask a few questions. And generally, not even then. Feeney asked most of his questions after the meeting, or by phone the next day.

The meeting came slowly to an end and Feeney was relieved to find that he was able to get away practically unmolested except for one of the Brahnler Bunch who came up to him in the hallway wanting to know if he really was the editor of the newspaper.

"Yes," Feeney kept walking towards the exit.

The man pulled up closer alongside him. "You don't look like no editor, Red."

Feeney grimaced at the hated nickname and then looked more closely at his interlocutor, a big, bearded man wearing a lumberjack shirt with the sleeves rolled up to expose an immense pair of biceps. The look in the man's eyes hovered between dislike and distrust, and Feeney felt himself get angry. The man didn't know him from Adam, but was willing to come swarming all over him.

Feeney nodded and said out of the corner of his mouth, "Because I don't look like Perry White?"

"Who?"

Feeney went out the door, straight over to his car, and got himself out of the parking lot onto the road. He got himself about half a mile down the road before it came out.

"Fuck off, asshole."

Another mile, and then he told himself not to be that way.

That fellow. He had his troubles... was probably in hock up to his bull neck struggling to feed his family.

His way of addressing someone like Feeney—someone who had an occupation alien to anything the man knew—seemed hostile.

It was a manifestation of desperation.

Feeney, therefore, was being aggressive and unfair.

Chapter 12

More social intercourse, but not really

HE stared at his scotch. "Or else," he mumbled to himself, "he was just an asshole."

How many times had Feeney done this?

Mulling over the possibility that he was a transplanted misanthrope, with the transplantation not taking hold and being rejected as though it were an incompatible foreign body. Unable to easily and naturally make friends with regular folks.

How many times? That could be answered easily. These sour reflections about his social failings came as punctually as a calendar cycle, always after the Tuesday town council meetings, which had now evolved into him having a post-meeting drink at Bedossa's.

If someone had been bent on assassinating Feeney and wanted to establish a pattern, it would not have taken much work.

Even his thoughts repeated themselves.

And so he got around to the next, perpetual reflection: that as dismal as the meeting had been, what was worse was what was waiting for him the next day.

A stultifying experience is one thing. But to have to write about it meant reliving it. But not just writing about it.

Given free rein, he would have blasted that meeting into minute pieces of worthless irrelevance, revealing the petty-mindedness at play. But, no, not only would he have to retrieve the memories of that fratricidal playground brawl, but he would have to extract only the elements of the town business, boring to anyone who wasn't there, and gloss it all over in the manner imposed by Dean Parker:

don't report any of the divisions, antagonisms, or disagreements.

No mention would be made of the disappointments of local contractors with the latest bid awards. When it came to writing the truth about what went on, he was caught between a rock—the town's seamy, chaotic animosities—and an even harder place:

His employer. Who felt the slightest whiff of the truth was a sure way to lose readers or, worse, get the paper sued for slander.

It was enough to make a man drink.

"You know, Patrick," Marsha said as she brought him his second and, she knew, last scotch. "You wouldn't be such a bad-looking guy if you just smiled more often." Being a good bartender, she didn't expect a comeback.

"I didn't come in here to smile." He made a smile.

Marsha, whose family name of Armagh was about as Celtic as it was possible to get, was the only barmaid he knew down there and, when he wasn't lost in his Town Council thoughts on those Tuesday evenings, he spent the rest of the time admiring her work.

It was a job consisting of dealing with the public, continually and smoothly, and he admired the ease with which she did it. Especially considering who she had to do it with.

Regardless of whoever else was in the place, the barstools were generally occupied by a line of forlorn-looking middle-aged men who spent most of their time trying to vie for her smallest attention. There was no doubt: she was an attractive woman. What he admired most was how smoothly she fended off the insinuations and invitations coming her way, without offending anyone, or seeming to take any offense herself. It could get outright heavy-handed, depending on the steadily eroding sobriety. But even then, it was remarkable how she managed. He thought it amazing she had any reserves of friendliness left, whether professional or otherwise.

It was for that that Feeney could almost feel honored by her having singled him out.

She looked at his smile and laughed. "Not even close. You don't look happy at all."

"I am. But it's on the inside."

And she was gone.

He looked at his glass, jiggling the ice contemplatively. Too bad, he didn't have her adroitness for social interactions.

Which brought him back to the council meeting. But once there, his doubts about his own social awkwardness faded into insignificance. The real shock of the evening had been seeing the Star waved around.

And then, mixed in with everything else he had already been thinking before Marsha's visit, he realized he had an opening there—one still unexploited—that might let him push back against Jansen's attempted coverage. But it would have to be done carefully. He couldn't go scandal rag.

Brahnler made him realize that sooner or later Jansen would try to get reporters up there. But for a while, it was doubtful Jansen could get anything on a daily basis. Jansen's reporters could only parachute into the main news stories generated by the county or city governments. Things they'd only pick up by reading Feeney's reports.

Evidently, they hadn't started that yet.

But Feeney knew the personalities involved, and that was something those reporters couldn't pick up on.

He couldn't report on the antagonisms directly, but he could begin interviewing people to pull out stories about what those antagonisms were based on. That contractor, for instance. Why was it so hard for locals to compete with the Seattle firms? There were no unions up there. Equipment rentals were the same. Was there a different calculation going on? Maybe the feeling that since contract awards were so rare, there was more desperation in the estimation, trying to make as much as they could out of it?

But... the problem was still there.

He had to find the thing. The story.

At best some community issue of wide and long-term interest, generating strong attitudes and emotion.

Where could that come from? What was shared up there?

Just a few years before, the national economy had tanked. It was part of the reason Carter had lost. And all that had hit the housing market hard, causing the mills down in Everett to slow to a crawl, which in turn put the entire county into a sclerotic standstill.

Nobody was buying anything new; no new shops were opening and in fact many were closing and people were moving away. A political snake-oil scheme named trickle-down economics—based on the idea that making wealthy people wealthier meant they would share that wealth by creating jobs—had been sold effectively, collecting votes from these very people, who would never see a job or paycheck come of it.

Feeney wasn't about to light that pyre. Nothing made people angrier than to show them they'd got scammed. The politicians, of course, camouflaged that shame by making it all seem as though it had been the patriotic thing to do.

Feeling patriotic takes the sting out of feeling stupid.

Although it was late, when he got home, he did not go inside right away but wandered around the yard, distracted and thinking. At first, deep in thought, he walked the narrow circuit: up one footpath toward the alley, around the carport at the back, then down the other path again toward the front yard.

But as the things he was outlining in his mind at Bedossa's became clearer and more detailed, his pacing widened. Each turn carried him farther down the yard until every loop brought him nearly to the sidewalk.

Big long loops.

Down and back, down and back...

And he had just turned, down by the front sidewalk, when some small movement made him glance upward. He looked toward the second-story window of the house next door. He couldn't be sure, but it seemed the curtain there had moved.

He cursed himself.

Already it was bad enough to be wandering around his yard like Childe Harold in search of enlightenment.

Looking to the normal world like an idiot.

But now he had been caught at it by The Stalker.

He let go of whatever thoughts he'd been entertaining, shuffled across the dry grass to his porch, went into the house, and pulled the drapes shut.

Chapter 13

The Crime Stopper's Notebook

HE didn't have many people come to his office, maybe two or three on a good day, and he almost never had anyone from Parker's staff come by except on the rare occasion when one of the down-valley reporters might be roaming around up there and drop in to get a free coffee. His only real work-related presence came on Tuesdays when Mrs. Hagy came to typeset stories and press releases. Within only a couple more years she would be migrating to DTP, but there she still typed up nearly all the copy on a special typewriter, blazing away at nearly 180 words a minute without mistakes.

But this was a Thursday, it was raining, he'd been there alone all morning and expected it would remain that way for the rest of the day, and he was in the mood to do nothing. After the morning routine he'd spent the time contemplating the Star supplement which had been delivered, with its ever more stultifying frequency, onto his porch that morning. Feeney had looked through the paper, circling new ads from retailers and shops in the upper valley, and saw the Safeway ad had a format different from the one Parker's ad staff had created.

In the first few months of Jansen's onslaught Dean Parker had talked about nothing but advertising. It had become almost obsessional. No matter what other subject was introduced, within a minute Dean would bring it back around to the injustice of life and how ad sale losses were killing him through death from a thousand cuts. But lately it had become a banned topic, as though to evoke it was to invite more of it. Everyone knew, of course, what was happening. It was embarrassing. It was hard to tell how many people in the public were paying attention, but if they were it was obvious just by comparing the Star supplement to what was no longer in Parker's papers. It was the smaller ads: an auto parts ad here, an electrical store ad there. But even if for the moment it was only subliminal, it was there to see. And eventually, Feeney knew, it would burst into the public's mind that Parker's newspapers were failing. And in the same way that nothing succeeds like success... nothing fails faster than something that seems to be failing.

That was why the most ominous thing was how subscription renewals were slowing.

Renewals usually ticked along from month to month with little variance. It had been like that for years, even decades. People renewed their subscriptions with a near automatic regularity. They were sent a note two weeks before the renewal date, and back came the slip with a check. This month alone, though, fifty renewal notices had gone unanswered.

It wasn't a lot. But it was something.

The public, of course, wouldn't be aware of it. Parker didn't print distribution figures in his banner the way Jansen did. But Feeney knew that, eventually, it would become a known thing if only through word of mouth of people mentioning they had dropped their subscription.

Those were the things Feeney had been mulling over that morning. There was something even more bothersome than the ad sales and subscription renewals.

The front page of the supplement still sported the main news stories generated by Jansen's staff down in Snohomish, but there on page three Feeney found himself looking at specific coverage for town hall meetings in Monroe, Sultan, and Gold Bar.

As he read the one for Sultan he'd felt a cold, creeping sensation come over him.

As an article, it wasn't inaccurate. But it was weird.

Despite how he knew he'd been the only reporter at the meeting, the article was written to give the impression it had been reported first-hand. All the agenda items were noted, but—more importantly—there were quite a few words devoted to arguments and comments from townspeople. But what was worse was the mention of an item concerning bids about the high school that hadn't been talked about at the meeting. Something fairly important about renovations and costs which might, in fact, lead to asking for money. It wasn't much, just a sentence or two. But that was real news. Anything that had to do with needing to generate money through a municipal bond was a big public issue. And Feeney, sitting there in the meeting, hadn't heard a thing about it.

Just a sentence or two, but it had shocked Feeney into a quiet half hour of contemplation, staring out into the steady downpour in the parking lot. Creepy wasn't the word. It just didn't make sense.

And yet it made too much sense.

There weren't a dozen different ways that throwaway nugget of information could have ended up in the supplement.

So the question was: who was the source?

Maybe the town? Someone had wandered into town hall and picked up on it? He doubted it. This wasn't the sort of thing you learned by leaning across counters, especially if you weren't known. Discretion was a commodity most small towns relied upon, if only to keep the public sniping to a minimum. So... someone who knew... and probably someone who had gotten the information down to Snohomish, rather than someone from Snohomish finding out about it.

Feeney's eyes narrowed with a sudden thought, a suspicion.

The rest of the morning passed with him balancing the letter opener across his fingers, dipping and tapping it meditatively on his desk pad as he stared out through the glass front of the office. After a while, his thoughts shifted from strategies for unmasking sneaks to running in neutral. The day was still early and he was already burned out.

His mind disconnected.

Fragments of blank verse. Dithyrambic. Or sometimes decasyllabic. Occasionally poetic, though more often than not sourly obscene.

One's amusements.

He had so much to do and he had no intention of getting started.

The rain was getting fuller and it had gone dark outside. The faulty hydraulic closer held the door slightly ajar and let in a steady whisper of the rain falling on the parking lot. He could also hear the tinkle of his next-door neighbor's wind chimes. Claudine's Knick-Knack Shop. He thought about Claudine, wondering if she was sitting over there, on her side of the cinder block wall, staring out at the rain like he was, and contemplated going over and having a chat. But only for half a second. He knew what such a conversation would consist of. Hard-bitten as she was—a knick-knack shop was never going to be a gold mine even in the best of times—no matter how gloomy Feeney was feeling, she could outdo it.

He stared at the lot and realized it was a pretty lousy parking lot considering how much it rained up there. Badly graded for drainage, more than half the lot was covered with lake-sized puddles, within one of which his car sat with its tires in water up to the hubcaps. Far away on the other side of the lot stood a two-story wood-shingled medical office. Dental Medical. Which bought maybe two ads a year. Down at the edge of the highway squatted a restaurant: The Delicate Egg. Which never bought any.

Feeney stopped tapping the letter opener and looked at his watch. 11:12.

What to do...

The run across the lot half-drenched him and he stumbled into the overheated but well-padded comfort of the Egg. He thought he could see the back of someone's head in the kitchen behind the order bank but there was nobody at the counter. The place might as well have been empty. He took a seat and grabbed the menu, stared at it, which was a waste of time for two reasons. Nothing on the menu was interesting, and they all shared one thing: Feeney had long since quit trying to eat them while driving. And he always ordered the same thing.

The waitress, a local girl named Kim, never showed up to ask his order in less than five minutes—normally ten—although she would get miffed if he ordered at the counter. Tips being a thing.

Kim, in her spiffy yellow uniform matching the yellow band she wore in her yellow hair, finally came and he ordered his shake, burger, and fries. And then eternity began. At one point he had decided he would never come back to the Egg again without a book. But he never did, and so also had that exact same thought every time.

Finally his order came. He got things unwrapped and set out and picked up the cheeseburger to take a bite—the last bite he would manage with only two hands—when the police chief came through the door.

Feeney's heart sank.

The chief had come looking for Feeney. Feeney's car out there in the lot, the empty office with the door unlocked and the lights burning, and the near midday hour had been an obvious set of clues for the town's professional peace officer.

Chief William Spencer was resplendent, as usual. It was always a bit of a shock to see all that peace-officer regalia embodied in one person. Even from a distance he was a sight, his immaculately tailored uniform having a rather beautiful two-tone scheme of blues, like a Steller's jay.

As nice as that was, Feeney was more impressed with the chief's hip-hugging gun belt which supported, alongside a gleaming array of brass cartridges, a variety of small shiny black leather boxes which, to Feeney's mind, probably contained much, much more than fingernail scissors and Band-Aids. And, of course, hanging from the right hip in a perfectly polished woven black leather holster was what Feeney guessed to be the largest possible caliber handgun the service allowed. Not one of your dainty semi-automatic affairs, but a regular Götterdämmerung cannon. Blue-black with a dark handgrip made of some exotic endangered species of wood. Ten years on, Dirty Harry was still a thing.

After all that was the man.

Regulation haircut: short, black and parted on the left. Regulation mustache: trimmed ultra-thin. Tall, erect frame: held stiffly. And the dark eyes, in the surprisingly soft face: at once shrewd and confident.

Spencer, casting those eyes around the emptiness of the Egg as though each detail of the place had significance, finally let them settle on Feeney with what seemed like some sort of personal satisfaction. Feeney set down the burger and grabbed a handful of napkins. Spencer always made a point of shaking hands.

"Got a minute?" Spencer let off squashing Feeney's knuckles and slid into the booth. Kim appeared like magic. "Coffee, please," he said to her, and she disappeared.

Feeney smiled and opened his mouth. Kim reappeared and set a steaming cup of coffee in front of the police chief.

"Thank you," Spencer handed her exact change and looked back at Feeney.

Everyone at the Egg knew the chief only had coffee when he came there, and had it poured and ready for him from the moment they spotted him pulling up in his cruiser.

The inarticulate gloom he'd encountered off and on all morning floated down onto Feeney again.

In spite of everything: the badge, the gun, the creases, the spotless demeanor—as well as the chief's salient political life in that town which Feeney truly did feel was coming under an unjustified and crude attack by the local yahoo crowd—there was no getting around the fact that the chief could be a regular ass.

Applying his amateur form of psychology, Feeney guessed that Spencer was the ultimate product of what would happen when you took a guy who looked, despite his six-foot-four frame, like he'd been a bit of a nerd, then put him first in the marines where he'd attained the rank of master sergeant, and then in the Washington State Patrol, where he'd been an honest-to-God State Bull.

Feeney did not like, and was often dismayed, at this knee-jerk reaction he had to the chief's presence. But he couldn't help it. Every time, every blessed time, Spencer came up to him, it was always with a sort of official/unofficial, hale-fellow-well-met, life-is-just-a-grind, routine. He never did it with anyone else. Which meant that he'd figured those were Feeney's main qualities: flippant and discontented. And even though Feeney could admit that, yes, he could indeed inhabit either one of those moods, he didn't like someone framing his entire personality in that manner. And so, with sardonic rancor, instead of trying to temper his reactions so the chief might see him in a different light, Feeney would often find himself responding in ways even more crass than Spencer would have expected.

"Hell of a day, huh?" Spencer said.

Feeney nodded. Class clown. "Some days are shit; others are worse."

Spencer grinned, with a glint of disapproval. Grouchy negativity wasn't the thing. Marine training stressed a grimly good-natured Semper Fi, even when it came down to banal small-talk about the goddamn weather.

Feeney could see that if he'd ever been in the Marines, a fantastic idea in itself, and had found himself with Spencer for a drill sergeant, his goose would have been much more than just cooked.

Feeney stared at the grin and stifled a sigh. "So, what's up, Bill?"

Not surprisingly, most of what was up bordered hard on bullshit. Spencer, under constant public criticism from Brahnler, was always looking to scare up some free publicity, figuring that by keeping a regular series of articles about the department in the paper, he could sway public opinion. One week it was a kitchen safety checklist, another was about public awareness of medical aid, and yet another on pet-owners' rights. Spencer was no idiot and always went for the solar plexus of community issues.

This time, though, he surpassed himself.

Feeney was asked to do an article on a new fingerprinting and/or crime detection kit the department had purchased.

A suitcase full of Dr. Detecto tools.

It had cost almost six thousand dollars, and Spencer wanted the town to know all about it, with the official explanation for how useful this would be for crime enforcement in the community, before Brahnler got wind of it at the next council meeting.

Weakly, Feeney agreed to do it though he harbored no conviction that the kit was worth anything. All detective work, as he and Spencer both knew, was normally taken care of by the County Sheriff's office. In reality, Spencer's main job was distributing speeding tickets out on the highway, breaking up fights downtown on Friday and Saturday night, and rounding up stray dogs. But Feeney let it pass. One reason was because there was no way he could refuse the story, and the other was because he secretly felt he owed the chief a favor. Two weeks earlier, Feeney had dashed Spencer's hopes by refusing to start up what the chief wanted to call, embarrassingly, a "Crime Stopper's Notebook."

Spencer had figured it to be a weekly column concerning the public and the local police, full of topical issues and information. Feeney had felt ill just considering it. As it was, he did almost nothing on a regular basis. But to do a weekly column, and on the local police, and with a cartoon name to boot, had been too much to even contemplate.

He might have gone along if Spencer had made it a sort of press release, meaning that he or one of his inferiors would have produced it. But the compromise fell apart if only for the fact that every one of Spencer's hand-picked minions down there at the department was either too lazy or too illiterate to manage it.

Hence, an agreement to do an article on the Mr. Wizard Sleuth Kit.

Feeney dragged out his notebook, Spencer rattled away for ten minutes, and the deed was done. Or almost done. Feeney always knew better than to put his pen away before the chief left. There was always the Parting Shot, and the chief always waited to see that Feeney got it down, verbatim.

Spencer stood up, smoothing his impeccable uniform, and said with an introductory voice, "It's not always easy, you know, to come into a town and earn the trust of the people…"

Feeney inwardly winced. Spencer always liked to harp on how they were both outsiders.

"…But that's our job," Spencer went on. "And regardless of the difficulties, we're here to serve and to protect the citizens in this community." He glanced at Feeney's note-taking and, satisfied, swelled to his finish: "And I, as principal peace officer in this community, as a taxpayer and family man as well, feel a personal responsibility to maintain the closest possible liaison between the public and myself. My door is always open."

It took half a minute for Feeney to finish scribbling all that out even though he knew there was no way in hell he would print it. But when he finished, he looked up and smiled.

Spencer nodded, turning on his heel. "Anything you need to know," he said, "just drop by."

"I will, Bill," Feeney called after him, but Spencer had already gone out the steamed-over front door.

Feeney stared for a moment, pulling absent-mindedly the tray with his lunch back in front of himself. Then he looked down at it.

He got up, dumped the contents into the garbage, went out and ran up to the Albertson's and got a poor boy sandwich from their luncheon aisle, ran back down to his office, and sat down at his desk.

While Spencer had been droning away, a secondary thought had been threading its way through his mind.

Maybe it wasn't a bad idea, after all, to do that Crime Stopper's Notebook. But it would have to be on one condition: Jansen's reporters wouldn't have access to the same material.

Feeney smiled grimly. Parker wouldn't like it much... giving free space for politicians, or quasi-politicians such as the police chief, to advertise themselves. But he would agree to it once Feeney explained the reason for it.

But that wasn't all. It had taken more than an hour before the realization of what he'd been looking at earlier hit him. Munching on his sandwich, he picked up the Star and read the town hall meeting article again. And then he set down the sandwich and picked up the phone.

Chapter 14

Glimmers of a Hunch

TWO men were talking next to a big Ford pickup as Feeney pulled into the town hall parking lot. Feeney knew them both. Dan Winters was one of the town's project-committee members; Gary Spotley worked in maintenance. Winters gave him a wave. A general contractor with a fairly good reputation, he was friendly enough to Feeney, even though he was under the wing of Brahnler, who had never shown Feeney anything but distrust, if not outright animosity. Spotley, a dark and sullen fellow, Feeney tried to avoid. Feeney got out of his car and nodded at both of them. But he really only knew Winters well enough to speak to him.

"How're things, Dan?" Feeney knew Winters only did minor assessment work for Peace and never had much information about town activities. But Feeney had made a new resolution, to be at least cordial with anyone he crossed paths with.

"Going along, Pat." Winters was one of those men who never seemed to have any reason to smile, but didn't frown much either. He would just stare at people with expressionless eyes which would occasionally give a slow blink to show he'd agreed with something. But he also did that when he didn't agree. After only a minute, it could feel like sinking in quicksand.

"I hope Peace isn't taking up too much of your time," he said, "what with those three houses you've got going up upriver."

"Not too bad," Winters blinked. "I like helping him out. And it's interesting to be on the other side of the bids."

"As long as it doesn't put you in a tough spot."

Winters narrowed his eyes. "Not yet, it hasn't."

Feeney nodded, as though there could never be anything untoward in the conversation. "Nothing you need to worry about, Dan, as far as I'm concerned. But some people would try to say otherwise. You know that."

Winters's face was impenetrable, but what he said wasn't. "I hope so."

Spotley, who'd made no sign of interest in anything up to that point, suddenly pushed his chin back and forth, and nodded in agreement. "They'd better not, you know."

Feeney looked at Spotley, but just couldn't bring himself to answer. Even though he came from elsewhere, the small-town system had made him aware of both these men. Winters, hardworking and respected despite his age, had married a woman named Shelley who was six or seven years older than him and who had three kids. It was a setup, Feeney thought, guaranteed to make a young man grow up fast. As for Spotley, he seemed reliable enough regardless of his dark nature. And although Feeney avoided him, he too was known. And more than Feeney would have wanted. He had a wife named Paloma, who everyone called Paulie, and they had two small children. The general impression was of a man who had a happy home. Which was just as well, Feeney thought, considering how he had by pure accident seen pretty, dusky, dark-eyed Paulie Spotley on two separate occasions with two different men down in two different cocktail lounges in the business district of Everett.

Feeney didn't go down to Everett much, and it also meant he wasn't the only one who'd seen it. It wasn't fair to Spotley, but Feeney had a hard time not thinking certain things every time he ran across him, and it led him not to talk much to him.

Feeney looked back at Winters. He didn't usually pick parking lots as places to make points, but he realized this was a rare chance to show one of Brahnler's friends that he meant to be neither a foe nor a punching bag. Just someone trying to do his job.

"You know how some people might take it."

A small frown. Feeney was getting through. "Yeah…?" Winters said.

"You were at the last council meeting, same as I was. No stone unturned."

"People have a right to ask questions."

"That's exactly right. Absolutely," Feeney nodded. "But, you see, I have to report on everyone's questions. Everyone's point of view. So that people can see all sides. If I only reported one side, where would I be? In somebody's pocket, right?"

Winters was staring at him again. Feeney could see that explanations about the ethics of journalism weren't something he'd have defined as being of much pertinence to him. So Feeney decided to see what would happen if he brought it to a more personal level. "What I do worry about, though, are aspersions."

"Aspersions?"

"Oh... maybe not aspersions. Calumny."

"Calumny?"

For half a second Feeney thought maybe all this was going over the contractor's head, but then Winters did something totally unexpected. He grinned.

"Oh, you mean, Dick."

"Among others. But, yes, that does include your buddy."

Winters shook his head. "He's OK, Pat. He means well. But I know what you mean with the... aspersions. He was walking a fine line the other night."

"You can say that again."

"Dick just thinks the town needs to look after its own first. That's all. You look around, most of the people hired for municipal positions came from somewhere else."

Feeney could have countered that nobody in town had been qualified for the jobs with the school district, the fire department, the police department, or even some of the staffing at the library and the town archives. Fact was, most of the people with higher qualifications and educations, the kids, moved away. But he wasn't looking for that sort of debate. "I understand that. But no matter how many points he's got, he's also got to watch it. Newton is two snaps away from hitting him up for slander."

"I'm aware."

"But is he? Asking questions is a civic duty. But if it's just axe-grinding, after a while it's hard to tell if the questions have any worth or not. I mean, I try to follow up on the questions and comments, but when it's every fucking thing on the evening's agenda I sometimes don't know where to start and, to be honest, just throw in the towel."

Winters nodded. "I can understand. But the main thing... talking about aspersions and being aware and all... I can guarantee you that everyone is aware of everything down here. This isn't Seattle, or Olympia, or Tacoma for that matter. Where are you from again?"

"Seattle." Feeney could have been honest, and said Pullman, but he didn't like people there in that small town knowing he was also a small-town guy at heart.

"It ain't like those places. Here, we're aware. And lately, really goddamned aware." Winters leaned forward a bit. "Right?"

"Sure, Dan."

Winters nodded, not unfriendly, and on that looked over at Spotley and then turned to walk away. Spotley also turned, giving Feeney a last look over. Feeney nodded at him.

"Gary."

Feeney watched them go, and then stood there in the parking lot for a moment, contemplating Winters's last obvious insinuation about something. There were times, Feeney knew, when people said things—offhand comments—that had the strange whiff of being more than filler.

He now looked over at the town hall. It was a bland wooden structure; the town had never had a town hall that looked like one. But even so, it was the place where the town's business, mostly done publicly but sometimes privately, took place. It was bound to have its secrets. Feeney walked toward the building and went inside to find the man he was really there to see.

Charles Peace never meant to become mayor. He was just a community-conscious guy who got involved in local efforts and organizations in his twenties, along with his wife, when his children had entered school. At first, he'd figured he would do that for a few years, until his kids were grown. His wife's involvements didn't even make it past the elementary-school stage. He joined everything: town activities, school board activities, sports activities, club activities. But, as happens with anyone who has a natural knack for keeping things like agendas, meetings, and tasks straight, and for mollifying the picayune infighting between anyone else involved in such things, he was soon being named chairman to this and that.

The inevitable then happened when he was asked to run for city council. He did, not giving it much thought. And once elected, he never turned back. Whatever private time or hobby time he might have had disappeared, and after eighteen years of town politics the usual effects of attrition had raised him to mayor.

The first time he'd been elected to the four-year office, nobody had opposed him. Peace was such a fixture in the community that to have run against him would have been like running against a fixed element of the town itself.

The second time he faced Dick Brahnler, who'd served for one four-year term on the city council. Brahnler, who'd been convinced that the presence of a dozen or so friends at every meeting represented a fair sampling of the town's sentiments, was surprised and embittered to be so thoroughly destroyed by Peace at the last election, with nearly seventy-five percent of the vote going against him. And worse, having lost that election, he'd also given up his spot on the town council. It was partly for that reason that Peace had gotten Dan Winters to work on one of the town's building-project committees.

Peace wasn't a Machiavellian politician, keeping friends close and enemies closer. He honestly believed this was the way to heal wounds, and to also get younger fellows like Winters active in the community. Building for the future, and all that.

Feeney took a step up onto the porch at the back of the town hall but then stopped when the back door opened and Charles Peace walked out.

"Hello there, Mr. Editor," he said. For half a second Feeney thought Peace was going to put his hand out and shifted his car keys into his left hand. But Peace's hand stayed put.

83

The Mr. Editor thing was a running joke Peace made every time he spotted Feeney, and Feeney had just taken to offering it back. "Mr. Mayor... we've got a meeting, you know. You're not running away, are you?"

"I wouldn't do that, Pat. Just thought we might go down and get some fresh coffee." He jerked his thumb over his shoulder. "The pot in there's been going for three hours now."

They walked down main street to the bakery and went inside. At some time the building had once housed a restaurant, and when it was converted to a bakery, they'd kept some of the booths along the side and at the front. Peace pointed at one of the booths.

"I've got this. What do you want?"

When Peace came back, he sighed as he slumped into the bench seat opposite Feeney, pushed Feeney's coffee over toward him, then ran his hand back over his thick gray hair. He was a handsome, scholarly-looking man, but beginning to show his years. "Saw you talking with Dan, out there," he said, taking a bite of a maple bar. "Hope you weren't jazzing him too much."

Feeney gazed at Peace. The mayor was an accountant with an amorphous company down by Everett called Bigelow-Crown which provided, among other things, shipping logistics, rental equipment and office supplies all up and down the Sound. Feeney had at one time wandered into the company office in search of a story, it having once been one of the oldest businesses in the county. But the original owners were long gone and it had become just another ambiguous company. Feeney had even heard a rumor they might have been involved in prohibition running. It was surprising to find out how many of the old companies in the area had been, back in the day. And it was so long ago nobody worried about it, or felt any shame. In fact, it was often a subject of local lore, almost looked upon with pride—there had been no gangsters involved in the Puget Sound. But, no, nobody knew anything, and Feeney wasn't about to chase down retirees. Another loose end, of which the county was full. But Peace might know something. Feeney had never thought to ask him. Given his scrambling around for news items, it might be something to follow up.

"Jazzing?" Feeney said. "I don't jazz people."

"Don't tell Betty that," Peace said, giving him a benevolent look through his round, steel-rimmed glasses.

Feeney felt a smile coming on and took a long sip of coffee. Betty Hoffman, Peace's secretary over at the town hall, had let slip the fact that the town—meaning Peace—was highly unconvinced about a recent Merchant's Association proposal. For Feeney it had been like gold, resulting in a fat thirty column inches full of bitter recriminations from everyone involved. For Peace it had been embarrassing but what really irked him was that it had all come about because of two minutes of unguarded office banter. He now knew better.

Feeney set his cup down. "Is that another reason we're here? Betty's pissed off at me?"

"Oh, no, she's over that."

"She wasn't quoted. And you said straight to me it was true."

"Yes, but she sees herself as having got you started." Peace let out a short laugh. "And she can't figure out how it happened."

"You know, sooner or later, I would have heard about the proposition. I mean, come on, painting the whole downtown in shades of red and brown?"

Peace rotated his coffee cup with the fingers of both hands. "Why don't you just tell me why you wanted to see me?"

Feeney pulled his notepad out of his pocket.

"The Snohomish Star supplement."

"Yeah… OK. How's that going?"

"Well, I'll leave that to your imagination, Charles," Feeney got out his pen. "But there's a thing here I think we both might want to remember. Right?"

"If you say so…"

Feeney nodded agreeably. "Yes, I do. You know how it goes. We all just go along, doing our jobs, and we take it for granted sometimes that things are always what they will be. Like the Merchant's story. You just reacted, told them how you felt and then went on to other things. And I reported that, and then went on to other things. And you honestly didn't think anything about it at the time, did you? I mean, when you spoke to them?"

"No," Peace said, a somewhat patient tone coming into his voice. "I didn't. At least, not until…"

"Yep… not until." Feeney wrote B.? or C.? in his notebook, and responded to Peace's tone. "This fits together, Charles. I'm getting there. I mean, I don't need to tell you what the supplement represents, but I don't want the main things getting lost in the shuffle of the day-to-day. And that, regardless of anything else, you also know where the coverage up here comes from."

"How could I forget that," Peace said, now with a sardonic tone coming in.

"So, you are pissed off."

"I'll admit it," Peace shrugged. "But not now. No, not really."

"But you were…"

"I guess."

"OK. That's fine. And it's normal. So, here's the deal: good, bad or ugly, nothing has come closer to my reporting in the Register, even though that damn supplement's been around for months now. And you have to admit, you can't complain about the way the town meetings are reported, despite the heavy seas. We've been totally fair, which means—and you know it—anything even remotely fair tends to make Dick look a bit bad. You know it. We treat him fairly, too. And he digs his own grave."

"Yes, that's true. And thanks for that, Pat."

Feeney looked up quickly. "Oh no, you don't. Don't do that, Mr. Mayor. Don't you start thanking me for anything. I'm just doing my job. Nothing else."

"I have to admit, the Register's been some mighty good reading lately. You know, before I went to work for Crown, I did some leg work for Old Man Gig when I was in high school. He had a couple of reporters who wrote nearly like it was literature. Sort of reminds me of it."

"Lately…?"

Peace finished off his maple bar, washed it down with the rest of his coffee, and then looked over to the counter and waved his hand. A pot came out and his cup was warmed up.

"You said you had a point to all this…"

"Yes," Feeney went on. "Coverage. You get it. Whether you like it better lately or whatever, you've always gotten it. We normally give you as much coverage as we can. Based on an understanding of how all this works. Town government doing its business, the local paper doing its business. Sort of a… partnership… but without actually being one, if you see what I mean."

"Sure… a natural synergy."

"Right. Synergy. So… Jansen's got the Star supplement all over the place, including up here, and… yeah… he's doing what he's doing and that's just all part of Life's Rich Pageantry. But…" Feeney hung on the word to make sure Peace saw the crux of the matter was at hand. "I noticed this." From the notebook he pulled out a clipping of the supplement's article about the Sultan town hall meeting, with the pertinent sentence circled, and the words bids, high school, renovations and costs underlined. He pushed it over to Peace, who picked it up and looked at it, and went on: "Now, I don't remember that being in either the meeting's agenda or its minutes."

Peace pursed his lips. "Oh, you mean the…"

"Yes… Charles. I mean the…"

Peace shook his head. "Now, hold on here. That… that was a completely offhand thing, Pat. Some stringer came around, and it was something that was… you know… buzzing around the office that morning."

"Another little slip from Betty?"

"Maybe. Yeah."

"And you got pissed off with me about it getting out you didn't want the town painted brick red?"

"OK, OK. You're right. But… no big deal, right? It all evens out. You got a story from her, and the Star got some information about a tentative bid. Which will be dealt with at the next meeting. So, nothing to get twisted up about."

Feeney gave Peace a long look, and then said evenly, "I'm not getting twisted up. But, goddamn it. You know damn well, the Star isn't up here by accident. There's nothing innocent about why they're on everyone's doorstep, and you know as well as anyone else what they're up to. And what they're up to encroaches on a local business, the local newspaper. No… no… I know what you're going to say, but the local paper *is* a local business. I swear, I was just talking about that the other day. Like newspapers just… exist… like the air? But they don't. They have to be made to work, and be sold, and get support as a commerce, selling a product."

"Competition…," Peace said, with a shrug.

"Competition, Charles? Is that what you call it? Well, OK… you want to look at it like that, let's look at it. On one hand, you've got a business, a newspaper, been covering this area for over a hundred years… editors stretching nearly back to the so-called gold strike. In all that time, the Star has almost never come up here unless there was some outright disaster, like when the Masonic Grange up in Index burned to the ground. You barely got three inches last year for the elections. And you call that competition."

"Well, Jansen's a county boy. His family has been down there in Snohomish right back to the stump farms. You've been here, what, about a year and a half?"

Feeney stared. "What? What's that got to do with it? Jansen could be related to the sasquatches for all I know, but that doesn't mean he's more deserving of being considered the better product."

"Sasquatches," Peace chuckled.

"Are you even listening to me?"

"Of course."

"What I'm saying is… although I don't have a clue what all this," Feeney pointed at the clipping, "is about. Those words make it clear it's a big story. Maybe the biggest story of the next month or months. Bids? The high school? Are you kidding me? That's just an accidental slip of office gossip, totally meaningless, which you… or Betty… didn't think needed to be shared with the actual town paper? You let it go straight down to the guy who's hell-bent on putting Dean out of business?"

"Well, if you put it that way…" Peace frowned.

"Look," Feeney was finished with it. "I'm not asking for preference. I won't ask you for that. I had to do that with a few advertisers, but that's a commercial thing…"

Peace smiled. "I think I heard about that… Joel…"

"Oh, yeah," Feeney nodded, "Joel's no doubt trying to get everyone to think he's an innocent bystander. I don't know what he's telling people, but innocent he isn't. He's got contracts with us, with liens and guarantees, which he's been circumventing through the acceptance of free advertising—and I'm not so sure it's free anymore—in a medium in direct conflict with the one he's contracted with."

Peace looked uncomfortable. "We can't not talk to the Star people."

"Of course not. Ethics and fairness and all that."

"Right, ethics and fairness."

"Fine. We're good." Feeney took the clipping back and put it back in his notebook. "But between you and me, ethics aren't maybe as clear-cut. Ethics seems to have some slippery definitions, these days. What's ethical for Jansen, or Joel, or me or you, seems to be based more on point of view rather than a sort of general, agreed-upon foundation. You should know, if anyone, how this works. If all we needed were ethics to govern people's dealings with each other, we wouldn't need government. Would we?"

Feeney gave Peace a long look and saw the mayor had nothing to say to that. Who did? But Feeney had only said all that to prepare the terrain. He nodded at Peace.

"Look, I'm not down here asking you for exclusivity. I can't do that. But what I can ask for is that you, or Betty, or whoever else, provides in a timely manner within the same news cycle the same information anyone else is getting. And I'll do the rest. I don't want to read about my own beat in some other paper."

Peace had a serious look on his face. "Are you saying that every time something comes up, in or out of meetings, or if someone from the Star is up here, that we're supposed to ring you up? Sounds like you want us to work for you."

"No, no. Not at all. From here on out, you're going to be seeing me much more often than before." Feeney put his finger on where the clipping now was. "Because there's a story here, I'm guessing, and you're going to tell me about it now. And regardless… I know about bids and schools… these things tie in with a lot of other things, and I'll need to be coming back to you about it."

Peace leaned back against the bench of the booth. "This is now an official interview?"

Feeney picked up his pen. "Yep."

Peace smiled. "In that case, I think I'll have… I think I'll need a doughnut."

Chapter 15

Archaeology

DEAN'S down-county paper, the Ledger, reported more than a hundred non-renewals for that month. Since they were geographically closer to Snohomish, that could be expected. But it was still unfair. The Ledger had always provided much more local coverage for those towns than Jansen's ever had. Dean was right in saying it was like treason, like losing your high school girlfriend to the guy she said she'd always hated.

Dean was always good for coming up with metaphors, and that wasn't the only one he'd thrown out that morning in yet another epic phone tirade. For the most part, once Feeney had caught the main informational gist of the rant, he hadn't listened. But Dean had finished with a final, unexpected fillip:

"Pat, I need you to come up with something. Something we can do, up there, here, and down at the Ledger. Impact. Impact."

Oh, sure, Feeney had thought. No problem. Just give me a minute and I'll get back to you.

Half an hour later, he threw his pen onto his desk and stood up.

"Oh, shit," he said to the office. "Give me something." He spread his arms wide and turned, as though talking to each wall in turn. "Come on. Out with it. Give me something."

He stretched and walked over to the accounting side, looking at the books and the label machine, circling once, then back to the business side.

Nothing.

Just nothing.

Though he had thought that Peace had a huge story to tell him about the school, the mayor just hemmed and hawed until Feeney had finally given up. There was something. But he hadn't got it yet.

Then he turned and walked back into the hallway. Just stretching his legs. And he opened the storage room door and walked in, turning on the dim light bulb hanging between the racks and shelves.

With the gloom unused places tend to accumulate, the storage area seemed to Feeney like a dried-out Egyptian tomb full of dust, obscure relics, and long-dead people.

The question that had been turning in his mind ever since Dean's phone call was a simple one: how really bad were things?

Dean wanted him to come up with… something. But Feeney was fed up with this Chinese water torture of dripping bad news. He wanted to know exactly how bad things were. He needed to be aware.

He thought part of the answer was back in there.

He stared at the progressively yellowing stacks, each representing five or six copies per week… about three hundred copies to a stack for each year, going back twenty-five years—the length of time high school reunion interest remained alive. Normally, Feeney didn't think about any of it.

But suddenly… something.

On a rack back in the corner sat, not bundles, but archive boxes, holding darkened, crumbling copies going back into the mists of time. Everything in those boxes had been microfilmed, and better copies had been treated against disintegration and bound into full-sized books down at the library in Monroe. But a few copies were still here, if only for being left behind and forgotten. Early on, Feeney had spent an afternoon looking through newspapers from a hundred years before, seeing how the paper had evolved from an isolated frontier newspaper barely able to report on anything beyond a day's ride by horse, to a growing entity where national and international news was provided, and then slowly slipping back toward only local coverage as the big dailies became available.

Feeney stood there for a moment, eyeing those shelves. But he wasn't interested in the issue archives. He was interested in the account ledgers.

It was an inkling... but...

Sultan had always been a small town. After the gold rush wore off and people left, the town settled into a population of less than six hundred souls in 1910, a number that barely rose from one decade to the next. Every ten years, maybe another hundred people would be added, about half of whom would have been the local children. And that went on for the next sixty years. Then, in 1970, with the development of the state highway system, commuting became a way of life, even that far out from Seattle.

At the moment, the town was barely over fifteen hundred people, but with the way the Puget Sound area was growing, with highway spurs coming up from down south where, among other things, those new outfits were popping up down on the northeast shore of Lake Washington... companies tied in with computer outfits and giants like IBM. It was hard to imagine what those outfits would eventually do, but from his contacts, he knew they were the fastest-growing game in town down there, bringing in people from all over the country.

And that was what made this newspaper war so frustratingly obvious. If Feeney knew the area was on the brink of a population explosion, Jansen did so as well.

It was like a horse race, in terms of who could establish the best hold on the territory.

Jansen, of course, could have just sat down there and expected to see things grow around him, just as Dean Parker could. But Jansen had decided to jump all over the thing and see if he couldn't set himself up for major empire building.

Feeney flipped through the pages, glancing at the cramped entries noting long series of dates and renewal invoices. All the way back, the paper had always held a strong position in the community.

He took the ledgers out to his desk, got another cup of coffee, and began writing down monthly renewal figures. When he was done, he sat back in his chair and stared.

Over all the years, the monthly renewal rates remained the same, no particular month standing out.

No month stood out.

Feeney shut the ledger for the previous year, got up, walked over into the side shop, and looked at the current ledger to see what Mrs. Hagy had noted for the past month's renewals. Out of the two hundred or so renewals he would have expected, there had been only a hundred and fifty.

Feeney walked back to his desk and sat down.

If knowledge was power, he thought, the only power this particular knowledge gave him was the power of prediction.

In about a year's time, a lot could happen. A lot of unexpected things.

But by the looks of things, one thing looked fairly certain.

This time next year, he was going to be unemployed.

Chapter 16

The Short Straw

THE Snohomish Star supplement had just announced a print run of 15,000 copies. Feeney felt numb. Spurred on by Parker, he was nearly writing his fingers to the proverbial bones. All the writers were, and yet they were still struggling.

Other than the usual stories, he'd come up with a few ideas which stabilized the renewal rate. The cheesiest ones gave in to the love people had of finding themselves in print. Not that he'd ignored that tactic. He was doing it now practically to excess, packing more and more townspeople into the pages—mug shots, group shots, action shots, sports pictures—so parents had something to buy and keep. He was proud of his feature articles. He was inspired. But he knew a good clear picture of a dozen first graders playing with hand puppets sold three times the papers, and nailed the re-ups.

Renewals were up and down, but the ads were getting shakier

What he needed was that one big thing that Jansen's supplement couldn't cover.

He still hadn't found it.

His interview with Peace hadn't panned out with specific information. Schools always needed money. Bonds were always being developed. And though this was a new one, Peace had skated around the edges of it. In the end, Feeney was left with a dangler.

This was a typical problem for small-town papers. Everything came in fits and starts, and often there was no real news. Reporters working on the big dailies down in Seattle had it easy in comparison.

They had drawers full of big stories: corporate corruption, government kickbacks, council decisions affecting entire neighborhoods... with the processes for those going on for months and months, full of shouting-match meetings, demonstrations, editorials, and letters to the editor.

Feeney sat at his desk looking over his list of ideas. In terms of the writing ideas, he was most of the way through them and knew, any day now, he would be starting over with them again, repeating them with slight changes. The one good thing was that with the schools all going full swing, he could always go by there to get photos of students.

"God," Feeney sighed.

The phone rang with Greg Stafford on the other end.

"Hi, Pat. What're you up to?"

"Seriously?"

"Got some time free?"

"Let me check my calendar."

"Meet me at the Harvester at four."

If there was such a thing as a standard American restaurant, the Harvester was it. Just off the highway at the far end of Sultan, it was open from five in the morning until two in the morning of the next day—the late-night part mainly just to keep the lounge open. There was nothing on the menu that was unrecognizable: burgers, hot and cold sandwiches, beef, chicken or turkey plates, and attempts at lasagna or spaghetti for those who wanted to pretend they were having an actual dinner. The only reason Feeney ever went to the Harvester was that he knew he would always find some town official or employee in there.

Stafford was sitting in a booth by the front windows. Spotting Feeney, he stood up and nodded toward the doorway into the cocktail lounge. There was no one in there, but they took a table away from the bar, which brought the barmaid out to them.

Stafford ordered a double Canadian, Feeney a beer. Feeney looked Stafford over. A bit over forty, a bit overweight, with thick dark hair just beginning to go a bit gray at the temples, the reporter normally had a cheerful look on his face. Here he had a day's worth, or more, of stubble and dark lines under his eyes.

"So, what's up, Greg?"

Stafford relaxed his tie and opened his collar. He looked over toward the bar, watching the barmaid pour his whiskey.

"Just wanted to see you before Dean does."

Feeney went into reporter mode. "Yeah?"

"Parker's merging the Ledger with the Post. It'll be called the Post-Ledger."

Feeney nodded.

"He's also merging the staff. Leslie will take over the social stuff and the ad girls will do the puff pieces."

He nodded again.

"I'm shutting the office down next week. Tom's already moved."

Feeney nodded once more.

A silence stretched so long Feeney decided Stafford wasn't sure what to say next.

"And the main reporting?"

"That'll be Jimbo."

Jimbo was a beefy young man named James Sweetwater, who had graduated from Green River Community College with an AA in accounting. He'd mainly gone to school in hopes of getting an NCAA scholarship somewhere in baseball, got hired by Dean for an internship to cover the school sports for all the papers, which had evolved into a regular job.

"Jimmy? He could barely cover the cop shop. That doesn't make any..." Feeney's eyes widened. "Wait a second. When you said Tom's already moved...?"

Stafford nodded. "I meant, as in out. We're both out."

"But we're getting whacked? Dean's blowing up the coverage quality?"

"He says the margins left him no choice."

"It isn't that bad yet."

"You're not feeling it yet up here."

"I'm feeling it."

"Not like us. We're in Jansen's backyard. Our coverage always

97

did slop over into his and he's just tearing us apart. His staff's right on top of us. You know he's made way more headway into Dean's area than into yours." Stafford leveled a black look at Feeney. "So far."

"I didn't know it was that bad down there. Up here, Jansen's only thrown the occasional stringer."

Stafford nodded. "We've really been feeling it. No matter what we did, the Star was beginning to mirror everything."

Feeney felt embarrassed. He hadn't really been paying attention to the Ledger's articles as compared to the supplement's.

"Was it renewals or the advertising?"

"We flat-out lost point sales, and renewals were going down fast. But it was really the advertisers. You know, we only had a sort of bow tie from the top to the bottom of the county, between Monroe and Snohomish, and our ads came from either one of those towns. With the supplement, there was no reason for advertisers to have to choose anymore on the west side, and the Monroe advertisers got the same deal. We just got squeezed. We've known for months. Tom, you know, was always going to be the iffy one. For me, I thought at worst I'd just move over to Monroe. But Parker's decided to save both salaries."

"Sorry."

Stafford shrugged. "It makes sense, of course. Once you shut down the Ledger office and fold it up into Monroe, you can go with stringers and get the same thing. Anyway, I wanted you to hear it from me."

"When's Parker going to make the big announcement?"

"I'm rolling out two last issues, this week's and then next's, with the final issue of the Ledger announcing the merger and how great it will be and all that."

"But... Jimmy? Seriously?"

Stafford smiled for the first time. "Dean did ask me if I wanted to string, but you know how bullshit that would be. I'd work my ass off for a feature a week, and get paid thirty bucks."

"Yeah... no," Feeney shook his head, and then frowned. "He pays thirty? I pay fifty for puff pieces."

98

Stafford swallowed off the rest of his drink, caught the bartender's eye, and then gave Feeney a look.

Feeney shrugged and, with the barmaid watching, Stafford wagged his finger at himself and Feeney.

"So, is this fucked up for you?"

"When I got wind, I called Duggan. I'll start in a couple of months. And since I'll get unemployment, we'll be OK for Christmas."

"Olympia?"

"It's a step up," Stafford nodded. "I might have done it years ago."

"I didn't know that."

"Yeah, but… the way it went… there were the kids and school and all. But Mary and I talked and she now likes the idea. Believe it or not, the kids too. Finishing high school in Olympia. They think it's better for college. Mary, of course, will have to go back to teaching in a junior high for a couple of years. You know…"

Feeney did. All teachers coming new into a district always went into the junior highs. "Sounds OK. When I first saw you, I thought you looked depressed."

Stafford grinned. "Exhausted. I hope you never have to write the final issue of a hundred-year-old newspaper. But… here's something funny. Want to know who else offered me a job?"

Feeney didn't need three seconds. "No shit?"

Stafford nodded. "He's got balls, you have to give that to him."

"Can you imagine working for him?"

"Sure, if he paid double. Double what Olympia is paying."

Feeney was suddenly dying to know what Olympia was paying, but just said, "Even so…."

"Yeah, true."

"Did you actually talk to him?"

"Yeah. I just told him straight up I wouldn't work for a man who had just put me out of one job. And then I told him he must have a pretty low opinion of me, thinking I'd suddenly be part of his effort to put everyone else I know out of work, too."

"Yeah, right."

"Can you imagine? Knowing Jansen, he would have sent me up valley as well."

"No doubt. What'd he say?"

"He said it was just business, and everyone would see it that way."

Feeney laughed. "That's Jansen all over. He expects everyone to just accept whatever he does, where winner takes all, then turn around and declare him clever and astute. Publisher of the Year."

"I wish now I'd just told him to fuck off."

"Olympia's a good paper."

"I know, right?" Stafford smiled. "How about you, Pat? At some point, you know as well as I do, you're going to wear this place out."

"Maybe. But for the moment I'm still in the war."

"Yeah. Keep in it. It's hard. But that makes it worth it, I know. Also, you're the editor up here, so it's your show."

"Yeah, if I was only reporting, I'd be gone, too."

"Don't give up, but you know...," Stafford gave Feeney a frank look.

Feeney understood. "I know. We'll see. And what about Tom?"

Stafford looked miserably down at his drink. "Ah, yeah..."

"What? Tom's a good writer... I'm sure he'll find..."

"He's found a job. But..." Stafford shook his head. "He's sort of thrown in the towel. He didn't even bother to call around the papers. He answered an ad down in Seattle for a PR slot."

Public Relations.

Feeney didn't have anything against that work. He just couldn't see himself spewing out puff pieces day in and day out about some company's prospects and successes.

But, to be fair, he could almost understand how people might end up liking the job... learning the intimate workings of a company to the point they would become the actual voice of the thing.

"Plenty of stuff down there..."

"That's what I thought, too. I figured it might be something with the regulars, maybe the big ones. The Port. Boeing. Peterbilt. But it's not. Just one of those new ones. You know... those technical things, with computer guys. Some place called Microsomething."

"Oh, yeah. I've heard about them. Sort of hand-calculator companies. The whiz kids."

"Tom says it's gobbledygook, and in the interview even told them he didn't know shit about what they were doing. But they just looked at his clippings and said that since he could write well, he was exactly what they wanted: someone who could write for the people they were aiming to sell things to. People who don't understand jack shit about this computer stuff. They even gave him a semi-managerial position."

"Who the hell would want to buy...? Who are their clients?"

"Tom said the company wants their clients to be literally everyone."

"Everyone?" Feeney smiled. "Right. Just what I need: a computer. And what else: a rocket ship and an electron microscope?"

"Anyway, Tom says these guys aren't even in their thirties... just sort of hippie nerds programming computers. Software. You know what software is? I thought he was talking about lingerie."

"And he's going to write about that?"

"I don't know. He's paid more than Dean was giving. And I guess he'll get some regular stock options whenever they go public."

Feeney laughed. "For whatever that would be worth. I'm sure he was impressed."

"You can imagine. Anyway, we'll stay in touch."

"You in Olympia?" Feeney smiled. "You can believe it."

He barely got in the door at his place when the phone rang. Parker must have been ringing every ten minutes.

"It's after seven, Dean..." Feeney began.

"Half an hour."

Chapter 17

Feeney Gets a Compliment

FEENEY lived only a ten-minute walk from downtown Monroe and the newspaper office. When he turned the corner, he saw the lights were still on in the front lobby and Marlene was there.

"What, are we all going to start working overtime now?" he said.

Marlene wasn't amused. She had two young children at the house that her husband was going to be making dinner for and putting to bed, and she wasn't sure which worried her more: an all-staff meeting called by Parker, or her husband's skills in the kitchen.

She flicked the intercom and leaned over it: "He's here."

She then got up from the desk and headed to the back shop. Feeney followed. He thought he was going to get laid off too.

He was almost hoping.

They were all sitting around the conference table in Dean's office. It wasn't often that Feeney saw the whole staff together.

The three ad "girls," Cindy, Anne, and Christelle—one in her twenties, the others in their forties—sat next to each other. Mrs. Hagy and Roberta Nelson, the typesetters, were there. Jimmy, two unknown student reporters, and two of Dean's stringer reporters whose names Feeney couldn't place, then Dean, Marlene, and Dean's advertising consultant, his accountant, and his lawyer. The last three being dour-looking men who would have preferred being at home, or at their local Masons meeting, or down at the yacht club in Everett. And then Feeney. Missing, of course, were Tom and Greg.

Dean sat at the head of the table, and when everyone was settled, said: "Glad to see you all here."

Feeney held up his hand, but the look on Parker's face stopped him.

"Just let me get on with this, Pat. I know what you were going to ask. No, Tom and Greg aren't here. And there's a reason. That's what we're here about tonight…"

Feeney hadn't been about to ask about that, knowing all about that already. But he pretended to have no idea, which was another professional habit. You always learn more about things when people think you've got no idea. Feeney even took that to such extremes that people often considered him so far out of the loop as to be practically ignorant. Even stupid.

Feeney sat. They all sat, with varying degrees of shock, surprise, or sadness, through Dean's Doleful Disclosure.

Marlene kept looking at Feeney surreptitiously. He could see she was trying to figure out why he looked like he was listening to the weather report. Impassive, maybe even bored. He finally looked back at her and gave her a wan smile. She frowned. He felt secretly gleeful.

Dean saw them looking at each other and paused for a second in his long list of explanations, recommendations, and directions. Feeney looked back at his boss with a look of sincere interest, and Dean continued.

The thing was, Feeney reflected as his boss's voice droned on, there wasn't much to be done that they hadn't already been doing. But there was no way to explain that to Dean, who thought he was the only one who could solve everything.

There was nothing to solve.

They were just in a situation, with the Star War going.

The Star War.

Feeney had taken to calling it that, what with two Star Wars films already out, and rumors of a third one supposedly coming that summer.

The meeting itself was hopeless. Dean was in that appalling state of mind bosses get into when they have no idea what to do, and so do the only thing they really know how to do: talk a very great deal, and in great detail, about anything they could think of. Or fire people.

It wasn't until after the meeting was over that Feeney was finally at the real meeting.

Feeney had nearly made it out the front door before he felt a touch on his arm. He turned to see Marlene, her face squinched up with bad news.

"Oh, no," Feeney said. He looked at the clock there in the lobby. It was nearly eleven-thirty.

"Don't complain. I've had him all day."

Feeney walked back to the back shop and into Parker's office.

"I swear to God, Dean," Feeney said, coming in the door, "I'm dead."

Parker waved his hand toward a chair. "A few more minutes, Pat. Just needed to get this guidelined for you."

"Guidelined?"

"Yeah, the… parameters. You know."

"No, I don't. You mean, what I didn't hear during the last three hours?"

"Don't be obtuse." Obtuse was a favorite word of Parker's, as he'd learned that calling people idiots, morons, or stupid, wasn't particularly productive. "There have to be some adjustments."

"Adjustments…"

"With Tom and Greg gone, it means filling down valley as well as up valley."

"You want me down valley, as well?" Feeney's voice rose.

"No, no! Let me finish, will you please?"

Feeney shrugged. "Please."

"What we need to do…" Parker went on, "and I've given this a lot of thought. A lot. Is that we have to not just multiply our efforts, but multiply them intelligently."

"Intelligently?"

"What are you, an echo? Listen, Patrick, I'm not saying you're not doing fine up there. You are. You are. Everyone can see that. We've been taking and running nearly every feature article you've been writing up there and a lot of your other articles. People seem to like them. I've even got a couple of the association people saying we should, you know, enter them in this year's contest. But that's not enough. We have to… this is… we have to get inside this thing."

Feeney opened his mouth—

"No!" Parker held up his hand. "I know what you're going to say…"

Feeney's eyebrows went up. "Oh?"

"That you're neck deep as it is."

That was almost exactly what Feeney was going to say. "I certainly wasn't going to say that."

Parker ignored him. "But that's not what I mean. What we need, what you need, is to make a personal connection up there. I think even after a year and a half people still see you as an outsider, an outside man. Not… connected. They don't know you. Who you are, or anything."

"What do you want me to do, go to church up there? Join the clubs?"

"Don't be funny. But… maybe start writing editorials."

"You told me not to on the point of fucking death, Dean."

"That was because of Seager's problems. But that time has passed. It's died down."

"Oh…. I don't know about that, Dean. They've got that new bunch in Sultan systematically going after Peace. Systematically. And I don't even want to talk about Gold Bar or Index."

"Then, just be fair about it. Show all sides."

"Huh. I would have never thought of that."

"I get calls, Pat. I hear things. You know, the usual. That the paper's one-sided."

"Oh, for god's sake. There's no sides up there. There's the town, and there's this totally bullshit, populist, torches-and-pitchforks side. There's a former councilman up there…"

"Branson. Yes, he's the one who calls."

"Brahnler. Dick Brahnler. He's one of those guys everyone loves exactly because he's so dumb you never have the slightest problem understanding what he says. If that fucker was mayor for

105

one week, the town would have twenty lawsuits. But some people don't care, because he speaks their language."

"And you don't."

"You want me to buddy up with him?"

"No. I want you to find ways to talk about things. Don't get too fancy. Write about things in such a way you connect with everyone. And, I don't know… put down some roots."

Feeney's face fell open. "Roots? Like what? Buy a house? Sure, give me a fucking raise. I'll start bungalow hunting tomorrow."

"Don't get sarcastic," Parker growled. "I mean… look… I mean, can I ask you…" He went into a long non-Parkeresque pause.

Feeney raised his eyebrows. "A personal question, Dean?" He sighed. "Why the hell not? Why the fucking hell not? That's all that's missing at this point."

"Do you even like it here?" Parker said. "Just out of curiosity."

Feeney smiled. "Oh, you mean *those* roots. You mean the shy schoolmarm, followed by the picket fence and planting daisies? Is that it? Do I have a social life? Um… Really?"

Parker wasn't saying anything now, and Feeney went on: "If you wanted roots, then I have a simple question for you. If you wanted roots, why didn't you keep either Tom or Greg on, two good married men with roots galore?"

Parker, who'd in truth been casting about with Feeney, unable to say what he wanted, now knew exactly what it was.

"Because you're the only person we have who can really write, I mean with imagination and original insights, and who has any chance at all of writing us out of this mess."

When he came out of the office, Marlene was waiting in the hallway and they walked out front. She had obviously been standing in the hallway just out of Dean's sight, to hear it all.

"I don't know how you get away with it," she said, shutting off the lights. "Talking to him like that." She picked up her purse off her desk.

"I talk to him the way he talks to me."

"People don't talk to Dean like that."

"Maybe they should."

Marlene began unlocking the door.

"So, you heard all that?"

"What do you think my job is around here?"

Feeney smiled. "I know exactly what it is. And if he didn't have you, Hon, the place would fall apart."

"Seems he feels that way about you, too."

Feeney grimaced. "Oh…"

Marlene shook her head. "It sounded like a compliment to me, Patrick. I don't hear him do that very often."

Feeney looked at Marlene for a moment. "Maybe it did. And maybe," he smiled, "he even thought it was one. But let me tell you one thing," he nodded at her, "whatever you thought you heard… the last thing it was was a compliment."

Marlene gave him a long look, and then said, "You already knew about Tom and Greg before you got down here, didn't you."

Feeney nodded.

She tilted her head and sighed. "God, you guys."

"Guys?"

"Reporters."

Part 2

Not Their Finest Hour

More apologies to W.C.

Chapter 18

Being One with the Community

SHE finally left. Feeney sat there as silence fought its way back into his office, and then let himself drift away with it... ominous thoughts...

It was just a sort of gloom that she had brought with her and left behind. And there he was with that.

He stared out at the parking lot.

The weather certainly didn't help. It had been raining more than normal. All day. And with the long afternoon drawing on it was getting darker out there.

It was more than just a storm. The storm had turned into weather.

That was remarkable because up there in the Cascade foothills at certain times of year it can rain every day and nobody would notice. But that rain would come and go across a long gray day in a series of drizzles and wind-whipped drenchings. It didn't drop like this in buckets and barrels for hours on end.

Which meant the hills were now soaked, the high lakes full, and even the highest-altitude rivulets, up deep in the forests near the timberline, were gushing downward in riotous torrents. And now, minute by minute, the rivers were rising up their banks almost tide-like, with heavy intent. Feeney, calling down to the weather bureau, had the news that there was no break in the large system that had moved in over the peninsula from the Pacific. Even if the rain had stopped dead in its tracks, the river would have kept rising for hours to come.

But near as it was to flood stage, there was no letup expected.

He looked out at the parking lot where gusts blew with white sprays across the standing water. And he was wondering how it would go this time.

His office had been flooded more than once, the river riding over its bank and then the highway spreading and spilling across the relative flatness of the parking lot where it pooled as the river rose. The last time it had happened the building had filled with more than two feet of dirty river water which destroyed several hundred back issues. Unfortunately, because of carelessness, many of those issues had been those surviving from the days when the newspaper had occupied a building over in town on Main Street.

Feeney wished he were in that building, which sat at least a dozen more feet in elevation than where he was. In fact, he often tried to convince Parker to let him move back over there. It now held an accounting and tax service, and a real estate office, both on the upper floor, but the main floor was like a revolving door of ever-failing enterprises: a jewelry bead shop, a pottery barn, a musical instrument repair shop, a cobbler.

Back in the days of George Shire, the long-gone and semi-legendary owner and editor of the paper, the rear of the main floor held the presses, with the reception up front, and the upper floor had a variety of offices for the different office staff. It was hard to believe that at one time the paper had more than two dozen employees. Anyone Feeney met in town who was over forty, or better over fifty, and who spoke for any length of time about the Skykomish Register, eventually mentioned Old Man Gig, or Ol' Gig, or just Gig.

Feeney had no idea how George Shire had come to be called Gig. He did know from pictures and stories that Shire had been a short, thickset, gruff, cigar-and-whiskey man who—at least in terms of providing information to the public—had ruled over this part of the county for a period including the two wars. It was also clear that most of the town's sense of having a serious, full-service paper with local, national and international news had dried up long before Feeney had come there. High-water mark, indeed.

Well, he knew that.

He didn't resent it. It was true. One look at the paper from those days made that clear.

But Feeney did resent the insinuations that he, himself, was party to the decline. He knew he could no more change the course of that paper than change the course of the river, now raging on the other side of the highway. Western boom towns, and their papers, had shown themselves to have a built-in life expectancy when it came to sustaining all the services and choices of larger towns.

At one time, the main street in Sultan had every shop and service anyone could want. Clothing and shoe shops, a department store, a home furnishings store, a hardware store, several cafes, lunch counters and restaurants, a milliner, other shops with business machines, musical instruments, a soda fountain, and even a movie house. Now, it was surprising there was anything there at all.

Feeney didn't really have anything to do. So, he made a pot of coffee, went over to the business side of the office and looked through the ad receipts while the coffee brewed, got himself a cup, went back over to the subscription renewals.

Then he gave up.

He decided to go for a drive. Who knew?

He had no meetings to attend, no leads to follow up. But today the story was simply dropping out of the sky. He grabbed his camera and a roll of film out of his drawer and ran out to his car.

As he drove, and despite the rain, and the flood stage of the river, and his general peevishness about life, Feeney began thinking about the interview he had finished earlier.

With Mrs. Richard Brahnler.

What could have been a better combination? A flood, and Dick Brahnler's wife. Who had succeeded in getting under his skin.

Not that she had said anything in particular. Because she made him feel his integrity was inadequate. Or else a royal liar. A hypocrite, pretending to be friendly and interested when he was anything but.

Ostensibly, she'd come down to drop off a classified ad looking to sell a riding lawnmower. The essential part of the visit had started when she'd finally rounded to her not-so-delicate point of where the main problems in the town were to be found: with outsiders.

Like, clearly, him.

"... the sort of people," Peggy Brahnler was going on, "you know, who get to thinking they have some sort of power, and they try to lord it over you. We've seen a lot of people come and go around here who were like that."

Feeney nodded amiably and looked down at his desk. Piled with crap, as usual. Press releases. None of which seemed useful. He slightly pushed one aside. Why would anyone think he in Sultan would be interested how several north Idaho local governments had passed resolutions to secede from southern Idaho and form a new state?

"We aren't against Bill Spencer, like some people think. We're just protesting against the undemocratic way he was hired. Peace is wrong. And we're just questioning, you know."

Feeney looked up at her. It seemed he had been dissimulating his disinterest well enough to convince her she had driven home her point.

"You understand. Nothing is personal. We're sure he's a fine chief of police."

Despite his efforts, his eyebrows rose a little in amazement, but he diluted the effect by nodding his head.

Total.

Whatever.

"Oh boy," he said, a bit involuntarily, "well, that's good. Good to hear."

"My husband is a good man, Mr. Fff..., er, Patrick," she struggled with him insisting on using first names, "but is the victim of certain new and... nasty... elements in the town. All Dick and I have ever wanted was for everything to go toward the betterment of Sultan. We want to make it a wonderful community to live in not only for our family and for our neighbors' children, but also for anyone else who decided to come live in the town."

"Sure," Feeney said. "Of course, you know whenever you get involved with community activities, you can open yourself up to talk."

114

"We sure do," she said, somewhat pinched.

"It's normal. It's important, of course, to take part and try to contribute, criticize when need be, and so forth…"

"Dick doesn't just criticize…"

Feeney thought back, and honestly couldn't remember when Dick Brahnler had done anything else. "Oh, of course not. But still, there can be impressions."

Peggy's mouth twitched, and not with humor. "Right. Depends on what they get told."

Feeney just so wanted to launch on her. Every single council meeting for more than a year had consisted of her husband delivering his endless point-of-order reproofs, comments, opinions, commentaries, judgments, objections, quibbles, blasts, swipes, or outright faultfinding denunciations, which sometimes only barely avoided slander. And sometimes did not.

There was nothing left but to be contrite.

So he said contritely, "Well, we all do what we can. The town needs help. I do what I can, too. You know about the Logger Show, and how the Merchants want to do this street fair thing…"

"Yes, I heard," Peggy said. "Judy says you've already asked if she wanted to advertise her restaurant."

Feeney could see he wasn't going to be able to divert her, and things were going to devolve into tit for tat.

He stared at her, his face expressionless.

All that time, even as she'd delivered all of what was a well-prepared series of remarks, she'd held herself as immobile in that swivel chair on the other side of his desk as a short little jade Buddha. Now though, suddenly satisfied she'd said what was needed, she brought her hands forward together in a clap and stood up.

Feeney blinked, and then realizing she was leaving, gathered himself to his feet. "Ah, yes, yes, well, these are things which it's good to discuss, of course. Uh… so glad you came in."

She turned slightly, but looked back at him. "Me too."

He waved his hand vaguely, thinking maybe they were going to shake hands or something. "So important I get a chance to talk to people. Get to know them." He forced out what sounded like a self-conscious laugh. "People treat me like a doctor, you know. Always the professional thing. A rare thing for people to take the time to come down here and tell me what's going on. Thank you, Peggy."

She'd left, with Feeney staring out at the rain.

Feeney's fingers tightened on the steering wheel. A headline began forming, the hook of the lead paragraph: Richard Brahnler as the innocent victim of evil machinations... the untold story revealed over ensuing weeks...

Dick Brahnler, Civic Consciousness Personified. Dick, the faithful provider, now threatened in his own home town by malicious new outside elements; by a man, hired undemocratically, who was obviously not right for his job. And by a newspaper, written by a total stranger who was as ignorant as he was unfair.

Feeney could add his own, more accurate observations about why Peggy Brahnler had come by.

She and her husband were digging themselves out from under the wreckage of a lawsuit which had followed on the heels of an infamous night, in a bar downtown, that Brahnler had made statements in front of a number of people, and which had got him directly sued for slander. The topic of that slander? Bill Spencer, of course.

Feeney had heard about all that and had been gathering his notes, and then had been given direct instructions by Parker to leave it alone.

That had been hard. Brahnler had carried that lawsuit around like a shield of glory for weeks, and Feeney had just been itching to go for it. Told to stay away from it, he had nevertheless told a reporter he knew down in Everett about it, who had found out from a bailiff that in the back chambers of the circuit court down there, the unamused judge had handed Brahnler his own head. About a week after that, in another one of those parking lot conversations where Feeney often learned more than he ever got officially, Brahnler's own attorney—a man who disliked his client with a fervor only matched by the anger at having gotten gulled into the case in the first place—was happy to confirm that Brahnler had got

116

his "ass kicked, and for good reason."

Brahnler was now settling with Spencer discreetly out of court. Hence, Peggy Brahnler's social call.

Feeney wanted to rip the whole thing down. The curtains, the décor, the lights… the whole crazily theatrical show being put on by Brahnler and his friends. But all this had fallen neatly within Parker's principle of keeping the waters calm.

It was impossible. On one hand, he wanted Feeney to become "one" with the town, but on the other hand, sweep the dirt under the rug.

And he had been trying.

Evidently, from Peggy Brahnler's visit, it still wasn't enough. For the past month, ever since Parker's compliment, Feeney had tried to minimize Brahnler's town-meeting outbursts to what appeared as only questions or pointed observations, managing—to Feeney's eyes—to make Brahnler come off as actually sober and sane.

But even this backfired in other ways. Peggy Brahnler didn't think it was enough. That was clear. But on the other hand, by making Brahnler look so contained and relevant, Frank Peace had complained that his attempts to counter all that could almost be seen as harassment.

A particularly vicious deluge hit his car, blinding him for all of five seconds on the highway, and he realized he had better pay more attention to his driving.

He'd gotten into the car to drive, hoping it would result in inspiration. For an hour he'd driven, first up toward the pass, then back down. But he had nothing. And he knew there was no point in going back to the office, and as he passed through Sultan he just continued on toward Monroe.

And then he saw, far to the west, a yellow sky.

The storm was past.

And he was at loose ends.

What to do?

It was Friday. He thought about that.

Considering his social life, that didn't mean much. In fact,

Friday nights had become very nearly the one night he was guaranteed some peace and quiet if he wanted it. Beebee, knowing she could never drag him out into bars—which were in fact her favorite Friday-night activity; he could never get her to go with him down to Everett just to see a movie—mostly left him alone.

But he didn't feel like going home. Suddenly, some inner rebellion had its way with him, and he headed for the one place he never went on a Friday night.

He'd just have to cross his fingers she wouldn't be there.

Chapter 19

Where Feeney Should Have Gone Home

THE way you get hired has a lot to do with the way you quit. Feeney was turning over that idea. It had struck him as interesting the first time it had occurred to him, but now he was trying to figure out if there was any truth to it. The problem was, he couldn't quite remember anything actually being said. He'd wandered in, and next thing he was up covering a story.

Feeney was sitting with his scotch at the spot where the bar curved back behind the door leading out to the restaurant. From there he could stay out of the way of the Friday-night crowd that would start arriving in little more than an hour.

Marsha walked over and deposited a small plate of olives in front of him, but didn't stay, and only gave him a smile.

He watched her walk away, and realized she was one of the only people he knew up there with whom he had no professional business, outside of the fact that she served him drinks. And it was a minimal thing, but she seemed to like him. Nearly from the start she had seemed already to know that he was one of Dean Parker's guys, and the only one who patronized her bar, and after a while had learned enough about him, and developed enough confidence in knowing he wasn't too bothered by the rumor mill, to share with him one night that Beebee had told her that a girl could do worse than to know him, even if she wasn't the girl.

Feeney liked Marsha for having said that because she did it in a way that made it seem as though it fell in with her own appreciation of him. And also because she knew—knowing Beebee as well as she did, and him, to a certain extent—that nobody was going to get messed up. Marsha, like most bartenders, had a stock of irony concerning the social lives of single people frequenting her bar. But, like many bartenders as well, she also carried a small, unquenchable human hope that these people, some of whom she knew nearly as friends, would somehow survive whatever was happening to them, more or less unscathed. And after she had confided that to him, from then on he classed her as a foxhole partner.

There were, of course, other reasons she liked him. Not the least of which being that he had never once shown a sign, unlike some of her regulars, of becoming infatuated with the illusion he might pick up the bartender.

For Feeney, this hadn't been a question of lack of interest. It had simply been the acceptance of reality. He never ignored realities. He wasn't her type. He didn't know why, in particular, he wasn't. He wasn't unfit, he kept himself tidy, he was polite, could in fact make her laugh uproariously and inspire actual, sincere sympathy. But he just wasn't her type.

Which was a minor tragedy because Marsha, he liked to think—being a bachelor and prone to speculation—might have very easily been Feeney's type. She was that unpretentious, girl-next-door type, a quick smile and a wink, and possessed that sort of pert and perky self-confidence which was more flattering for some men to have around, than simple good looks.

Feeney picked up an olive absent-mindedly, popping it in his mouth, and got back to the issue at hand. It wasn't so much the question of quitting. It was a question of whether he could right there and then. He did, after all, have a sense of professional responsibility.

Damn. Olympia. Damn.

As he sat there, mulling away like that, some local band—guys wearing satin shirts, with man-perms and sideburns—began their sound check. Donna Summer. That was enough for him.

He drank off his scotch and turned to go when—with shocking suddenness—the Honorable Judge Jim Dodd loomed hugely out of nowhere and dropped his massive hulk onto the empty seat next to Feeney, cutting Feeney off from the rest of the bar. Or the world, for that matter.

It was not a casual encounter and Feeney knew things were about to get complicated.

Dodd was nominally Marsha's boyfriend. Feeney had never been able to figure that one out. If Feeney wasn't Marsha's type for some vague reason, Dodd made no sense at all. Marsha was small, tight, and neat. Dodd was a monster. A giant who might have been fat but wasn't, with a giant's beard and giant's haircut, the way you saw them in fairy tales, with a medieval fringe across the heavy brow and a heavy mass of rough hair coming down over the ears. Supposedly, he was more sensitive than he seemed.

Dodd signaled Marsha and then turned his beefy face in Feeney's direction, peering at him suspiciously with his small eyes. Feeney peered back. Whatever Marsha might have seen in him, Feeney thought Dodd was a posturing, overgrown opportunist, and maybe not all that perceptive regardless of the fact that he was the district judge and not dumb. Feeney didn't feel guilty about harboring such thoughts because the dislike was reciprocated. Dodd thought of him as an over-educated, liberal smart-aleck.

A sort of trade-off of mutual professional disrespect.

Feeney, though, felt he had the moral edge. Dodd disliked him for perceived politics and the requirement of his job to question everything. Whereas Feeney just disliked him as a person, unclouded by personal beliefs, dogma, opinion, viewpoints, persuasions, or attitudes. Or by the fact that he had Marsha as a girlfriend.

Marsha came over and deposited a glass with three fingers of something in front of the judge, but didn't stay. The bar was filling.

Feeney looked straight back at Dodd's glower. At least, he thought, the ogre hadn't stalked into the place once again in his duck-hunting waders and shooting vest. Most of the time the judge went around looking like a blimp-oidal poster boy for Sports Afield... although to Feeney's mind he looked more like something that should have been in the sights of, rather than sighting down, a gun's barrel.

"You still banging away on that rag?" Dodd said, emphasizing his disdain for Feeney, The Skykomish Register, Dean Parker, and journalism in general, in one typical, crude, all-encompassing epithet.

Feeney came close to, but managed to suppress, his immediate comeback, which would have consisted of repeating back Dodd's remark, word for word.

He wouldn't have meant it, of course. He really did like Marsha. But the glib perfection of it almost made it happen, even though the clever tit-for-tat that would have almost certainly got him punched halfway to Pluto.

Too bad, though. It would have been nice to have come back with something to show this steroid version of Perry Mason that a few other people could be as foully rude as he felt at liberty to be.

Not being able to come up with anything else, Feeney did have another card up his sleeve. And, in fact, it was even more unpleasant. Just the day before he'd heard about it and he hadn't yet got around to thinking how to handle it.

"I hear Charley Hirsch is going to keep the Dorin thing up here."

Dodd frowned, which was no small thing. His forehead shifted down toward his nose like a rockslide. With brows like his, Dodd's face was either only threatening, or blood-curdling. More than one young, driving offender had come close to wetting his pants beneath the sight of Dodd's face glaring down upon him from the high bench.

"That goddamn palm-greasing Yid would."

Feeney kept his face neutral but wondered of which he was the more: disgusted or insulted. The judge had always shown Feeney that he felt himself above every man, woman, child, dog, or social regulation that might exist. Racial slurs, slander and innuendo straight to the local newspaper editor's face showed the depths of his contempt. But Feeney felt an inwardly contented glow. Whatever else Dodd might say or do, just the mere mention of the Dorin case would cast a foul wet blanket over his evening.

Dorin was an up-valley dimwit who also owned a pit bull. The pit bull, named Babe, who had never been treated like a dog but more like a lawn ornament—tied to a tree in the front yard and deprived of any sort of human contact which would have curbed any aggression—had become the first home-grown, nationally reported lawsuit concerning a savage, unprovoked attack-dog assault.

Babe's owners were fighting now for Babe's life, and concurrently against the responsibility of two million dollars, some for medical and psychological bills but mostly for punitive damages. Babe, Todd Dorin had told the papers, was a gentle, child-loving dog. A member of the family who had never, ever shown the slightest aggressiveness. It was unfair to make out Babe as a criminal, technically or otherwise, and incidentally to make out Dorin himself that way too, when, after all, Babe was just a dog.

The fact that Babe had come close to mangling a seven-year-old girl named Melanie—luckily, they'd got the dog off her before he'd really got latched on—was just an unfortunate freak event which had nothing to do with either an owner's responsibility or liability.

What was even more unfortunate, at least for Dodd, was that the prosecuting attorney, who shared Feeney's dislike for the judge—for personal reasons, they having grown up together—was determined to keep the case in Dodd's jurisdiction.

Dodd had been maneuvering against this from the start. Not that he didn't like publicity, with his local-boy sense of grassroots opinion, he often sought it out. But this case was just too nasty. Above all, it was national. It was incredibly rare that a district judge would go national, and it was something they tended to avoid like poison ivy.

One might have thought this would be the opposite, especially for a man who counted on getting elected every few years. But logic had nothing to do with the psychological politics of small towns. Small being the key word.

Small meant small stores, small streets... and small ambitions.

Going national would make it difficult for Dodd to remain the regular guy, the local judge. Despite everything he could do, he'd be considered too big for his already extra-large-sized pants.

The upshot could mean that if he wanted to stay a judge, he'd probably have to look to run for the circuit court. And this, exactly, was what had him on the spot. Feeney had seen it on several occasions. Dodd was perfectly happy there in Sticksville with the speeding cases and domestic lawsuits. And any time something came up from County, he avoided it.

And then, there was what Charley Hirsch had said.

Dodd, if he ever got down-county, either as a judge or a practicing attorney, would be skinned alive. Dodd, Hirsch had told Feeney, had barely got through that small-beer law school on the other side of the Cascades and only had his job because the judicial business was a family thing in Monroe. His old man had been a judge there for so long people probably thought they were still voting for him, rather than the son.

"You think the County might take it?" Feeney said easily. He knew quite well the County's refusal, despite Dodd's behind-the-scenes insistence that Dorin could get no fair trial in Monroe—in effect overstepping his authority and actually pleading the defense's expected opening gambit for them.

"That's all confidential," Dodd said slowly, mouthing the words as though he was some sort of punch-drunk boxer.

Feeney raised his eyes sympathetically. "Good grief, Jim, haven't you heard the news?" He let a long pause develop, watching a quick look of fear pass over Dodd's heavy face.

"Heard what?"

"Dorin's injunction?" He let it drag out further just to watch this human version of Big Foot slowly twist in the vague vapors of fate.

"What injunction? And what goddamn news?" Dodd was now practically off his stool, his beard twitching, his eyes now only slits.

"The one," Feeney intoned, "that Dorin's lawyer is going to slap on Bill Spencer concerning the recorded details of the aid-car response."

Dodd settled back slowly, like a sinking freighter, onto his bar stool.

Feeney could see the realization sink in. No matter what, a local injunction meant it would be in his courtroom.

No matter what.

"Sorry, Jim," Feeney said. "A lot of court time coming your way, eh? And... bad business all the way around. That's for sure. Sort of like dog shit, isn't it? No such thing as only stepping a little bit in it." And it was true enough, he thought. Dodd could start wearing his duck waders to work as well. But he had no sympathy. It was Dodd's responsibility, period.

The judge, now sincerely glum, grabbed his glass and drained it, then pushed it across the bar and nodded at his girlfriend as though she was a total stranger. "Please," he growled.

Marsha came over and gave him a jolly look. "What's the matter, Dingo? You look like your favorite dog got run over."

A plausible muscle spasm caused Feeney to stretch slowly, turning a bit away from both of them. And he had to cough.

Dodd's voice came low and threatening. "Just give me a goddamn fucking seven, and shut the goddamn fucking-to-hell up."

So much for Mr. Sensitive.

The spasm gone, Feeney brought himself back around to Bar Center to find Marsha, with a pained look on her face, shakily pouring some Seven Crown into Dodd's glass. When she was done, she looked up at Feeney but he remained oblivious and she went away. For quite a long pause, Feeney and Dodd sat side by side, not talking. Dodd was busy observing his situation and Feeney observing the judge. Finally, Dodd reached out, grabbed his drink and downed it and shifted off the stool.

"See you later, Jim," Feeney said cordially. "I'll be down next week to talk to you about Sternman vs. the Sanitation Department."

The judge managed a dim nod and left. Feeney turned back to the bar and found Marsha standing there staring at him.

"OK, Pat. What the hell was that all about?"

Feeney considered. Although he had no regrets concerning Dodd, he felt bad for Marsha. But it wasn't something to be discussed across a bar. He pursed his lips.

"Patrick, please."

The way she said it, worried and even nervous, now made him

feel even worse. Where he had been gloating with triumph, he now felt shabby and petty.

"I'm sorry, Marsha. I can't really say much," Feeney felt truly ashamed. "But I can say that it doesn't have anything to do with you. If that's what you're worried about. This… this just isn't the place to discuss it."

For a second, he thought that she felt relieved, but then the look in her eyes showed something else. "Seems that for about the last ten minutes, it was."

Feeney winced. "It just came up. It's…," Feeney felt frustrated. He now began to feel angry, himself. Dodd's bad manners had provoked his own bad manners. And, if truth be known, the case was just a professional issue that the judge should be fully prepared to handle, and not be trying to avoid.

"What?" Marsha said.

He looked back up at her. "I said you're right."

Marsha gave him a long look. "I didn't say anything."

Feeney gave her a long, honest look. "Yes, you did. Anyway, it's just about a case, Marsha."

There was something about the way he was looking at her that made her now look back at him in a way he hadn't seen before, as though there was something about him she hadn't noticed. And she nodded, still looking at him, and then did a surprising thing.

"Finally, I can see you now, Pat. I usually figure out people pretty quick in here. You took longer. You're not what I thought you were. Not even close."

Feeney laughed, but couldn't help himself. "How so?"

"You're not as easy-going as you look. I thought you just sat there, watching everything. You don't. You get in there."

Feeney took that in, a bit startled, but had nothing he could say to any of that. Even if he had found something, she wouldn't have given him time to say it, just going on: "In case you're forgetting, things are going to start getting lively around here pretty soon. Friday night and all."

He nodded. Where he wasn't sure what she'd been talking about before, he knew exactly what she was getting at now. "Yeah."

He turned off his stool and started putting on his jacket.

She nodded back at him. "You know, Pat," she said, making him pause to turn, "there's better out there."

He felt the smile come up. Once again he resisted the temptation, but this time for more noble reasons. "If you say so. I haven't found that to be the case, though."

She shrugged. "I didn't say around here."

Chapter 20

The Stalker Springs Forth

IT was becoming regular: a hundred and fifty more non-renewals, classified advertising down twenty percent...

"Hi."

The rain had stopped that morning, and the morning air was cold and wet. Despite that, the Stalker was dressed as though it was already ninety in the shade. Just tennis shoes at the ends of smooth, bare legs, a pair of short, tight jean cutoffs, and a wide-strapped tank-top shirt, all of which didn't cover much of anything.

Wandering down the street with a cup of coffee, it took Feeney a full three seconds to climb out of the trenches of his early-morning thoughts.

Carey Williams, the adolescent girl who lived next door, wasn't an overly pretty girl, "pretty" being the only attribute Feeney could apply to teenage girls. She might someday be something else, but it wasn't easy to say for the moment. She did have good cheekbones and attractive, inquisitive eyes, but most of all she made sure everyone could see as much of what figure she had, which wasn't really that much, as was legally possible. Feeney, who wasn't particularly self-conscious in any damaging way, had been caught off guard and had accidentally given her the automatic, male, head-to-toe appraisal she sought to provoke. Which he regretted. He hated falling into automatic anythings.

He didn't call her the Stalker for nothing. Feeney's front yard was long, with his house nearly at the back. The Williams house next door sat more toward the front of their lot, which meant that any time he came in from the street, he walked very nearly under her bedroom window. And had noticed that he was being watched repeatedly.

He'd gotten used to her. But these occasions when she popped up out of nowhere were dismaying. Not for any reason of personal discomfort, but because as with all those other things he tried to maintain a pretense of serenity about—a list consisting of, among other things as immediate and minor as the nearest deadline, unpaid bills, the unfair expectations of Dean Parker, the condition of his car, or whatever contentious meeting or event he was supposed to show up at, or even the larger and vaguer things such as his nonexistent love life, his career in the sense of whether he actually had one or not, and lately the state of the newspaper war—they were at least part of the normal.

Carey's interest, manifested through a barely concealed surveillance, didn't fit into the usual existential categories of catastrophe, disappointment or frustration, whether major or minor.

What she represented in terms of existential catastrophe went on to a completely different level. Feeney could have given any number of obvious reasons why he avoided her.

When he had first come to town, his thoughts were preoccupied with the work and he hadn't thought much about the increasing presence of the girl next door. But after a while he became aware of how she always seemed there when he got home. Out cutting grass, watering flowers, playing with the dog. And then he noticed when she wasn't out there on her folks' lawn, there was the movement of that upstairs curtain. That was when she became The Stalker.

He had little contact with his neighbors, other than rather grim exchanges of hello with, mostly, her father. But through his profession and the natural curiosity on which it was based, he'd learned things about them, and her, despite himself. None of it was particularly flattering, especially not for Carey.

She didn't seem to have much going for her. On the one or two times he'd actually exchanged a word with her—Carey taking those opportunities to talk as much and as fast as possible about herself as she could possibly manage—he'd gleaned that she was doing rather badly in school. Didn't get along with teachers and didn't have much in the way of friends. It seemed her only interest was to go with a few fellow rebels up to the Jackson Dam during the school day and "party." Feeney could imagine her and her friends. Going up to the dammed-up lake: smoking, drinking beer they weren't old enough to buy, and getting high enough to forget about whatever it was that life was lacking.

Carey, probably for some disciplinary reason, didn't go to school in Monroe, but was enrolled at Sultan High School where, she had said with a desultory shrug, she could hardly wait to graduate.

More than anything else, it was that listless indifference to anything that made him leery, if not actually alarmed, about her covert and sometimes not-so-covert interest in him. His worst fear was that her initial curiosity might evolve into a sort of inarticulate, wistful form of dumb, animal infatuation.

A teenager.

He could no longer even sit out on his porch and have a beer in the night air.

Sweet home.

"Hi, Carey," he said. His eyes flicked automatically down the street toward her house.

"You're a real morning person, aren't you..."

Feeney nodded. "A person might observe that, I guess. But they might say that about you, too."

She reddened. "Yeah, I am. I'm a morning person. Everybody knows that about me."

Which meant, Feeney knew, that nobody knew that at all. "Well, I always like to be out before the town's up. Take a stroll. Makes me feel like I have an advantage. Although it's a bit cold this morning."

"Yeah, it's making my goosebumps stand up."

That wasn't all that was standing up. Feeney took a sip of coffee, philosophically, and then blew out a breath of vapor into the air. "Uh, yeah," he said, "OK, I'd better get going."

"But you haven't just been walking, have you?" She shifted

130

from one foot to the other and in essence blocked the sidewalk. Feeney wondered if she was aware of herself doing that.

"No. That's true," he said. "I've been out looking at porches to see if the Star is still being delivered."

Carey's mouth turned down slightly. "Star?"

Feeney nodded. "And that's that."

Carey stood there, evidently unable to find anything else to say, and Feeney wasn't about to help her. He took another sip of coffee and waited. He could see she had no idea what he was talking about.

After a bit she shrugged, obviously confused by cryptic conversations with older people. "Right," she said, turning, "see you around."

"Yeah," Feeney said, letting her get far enough away so they weren't walking side by side. As he headed toward his house, a cold rush of wind came down the street bringing a hard-flung blast of rain. Two more steps and he saw what looked like a wall of water coming straight for him. He jettisoned what was left of his coffee and ran for it.

Chapter 21

One Last Bad Day, Sort of

IT was raining so hard that morning that it felt almost like imprisonment to be sitting in his office. Black, and increasingly somber, out there. With his office lights on, it seemed like night outside. The sky just emptying itself.

He'd gone through the week's ton of mail. Sorted out the bills and mailed-in ads. Culled the news releases from all the state agencies and private organizations, looking for anything of local interest. Or simply what he thought might be pertinent. Anything at all. Blood bank notices, fishing regulations, meetings. Most of it looked an awful lot like junk and then turned out to be just that, which made it time-consuming. Then came the letters. The usual: complaints about neighbors, suggestions for how to run local, state and federal governments, anti-tax letters, anti-highway letters, anti-business letters, anti-everything letters, and then the sugary little self-congratulatory notes from local clubs and organizations. His energy level long gone, he was using more and more of this stuff to fill the paper. He knew only too well—and it was a dangerous thing—that if he didn't want to, there was little he had to write to produce a newspaper. Plenty of struggling small-town newspapers did just that to save on paying reporters.

Lately, along with this barely relevant reading material, he'd even taken to letting photos get larger. Three weeks earlier, he'd gone so far as to do a Picture Page, stuffing it with photos of townsfolk down at Sultan Park. Although it wasn't a bad idea, it was without doubt completely cynical, using the knowledge that people wanted to see themselves in it. There must have been twenty individual families captured in those photos. He made sure everything was in focus.

Predictably, the paper had jumped off newsstands up and down the valley.

He knew he could do better, but he was just running out of ideas. He'd written his way through his entire list, and that had barely made a dent in the renewal hemorrhaging and diminishing ad sales.

Feeney checked his watch again: 9:45.

The day was already dead.

A sudden blast of wind threw a sheet of rain hard against his big windows, and even caused his door to bounce in its frame. He got up and, for the next half hour, walked in circles on the administrative side of the office, down to the front window and then back to Mrs. Hagy's desk. Down and back, down and back. At one point he even watered Mrs. Hagy's plants.

And then gave up. Nothing.

No inspiration.

He sat back down at his desk, stared glumly at his telephone for a full minute. Yes? No?

...OK...

He picked up the phone and dialed a number ringing a phone in a bank down in Monroe.

"It's Pat."

"Hi." Beebee's voice was always surprisingly sweet.

"What's up?"

"Really busy."

"What're you doing tonight?"

"It's Wednesday, Pat."

Which meant, home taking care of her kids. It was only on weekends she was free, her ex-husband taking over parental duties.

"I know what day it is."

"Did you leave a message on my windshield?"

"No." Feeney looked at his watch again. "What? When?"

"It melted off."

"You want to go to the movies?"

It meant driving all the way down to Everett, but Feeney felt he had to up the ante.

"It's Wednesday."

"I know, but come the weekend…"

There was a pause, then Beebee's voice lowered as though shielding itself even though Feeney knew she had her own office. "Is that a complaint?"

For half a second, Feeney came insanely close to just asking her if she wanted to get some lunch. "Maybe I did leave you a note. When was it?"

"Don't lie."

"Do you want to get some lunch?"

A pause. "I could call Tony, but I don't know. He said his starter conked out yesterday. I don't know if it's fixed."

Feeney never, under any circumstances, responded in any way to any mention of her ex.

"Hey," she said, her voice changing. "You still going to do the Duffs?"

Left field. It took a moment, and then Feeney remembered.

Larry and Marge Duff were a prehistoric couple Beebee sometimes asked to watch her kids when her ex couldn't. There was nothing interesting about them except for their being about as old as the trees towering on the mountainsides over the valley.

Beebee, on occasion seeming to like how she was dating, or something, the local newspaper editor, often threw story ideas at him if only because she also liked the idea of seeing her suggestions hit the paper. This story, though, he hadn't followed up because he'd already done something like it twice. Old People. Beebee had a lot of respect for them and thought that just the fact they were still alive made them interesting. Feeney did not feel the same. They all did indeed have a story to tell, and it took an entire afternoon to tell it.

"Um…" Feeney frowned, and then thought of something. "Is Gary going to be around there this afternoon?" Gary was the bank manager.

"Why?" Beebee's voice had a worried sound.

"Nothing. But you know how things are going. There was

something Joel Myer said the other day that got me thinking about Gary."

"The bank's advertising is safe, Pat."

"Yeah, but I saw it ran an ad down with Jansen."

"Gary said it was free."

"Yep. Like anything is, right?"

"You going to say to him what you said to Joel?"

"What did I say to Joel?"

"Everybody knows, Pat."

"Oh, for God's sake…"

"Yeah, he'll be around. Want me to tell him you're coming?"

"Nope."

"Warn me when you walk in?"

"Yep."

"I think I'll go run some errands around three."

"You don't have to leave. I'm not going to start a fight."

Beebee audibly drew a breath. "I'll give Tony a call. But no promises. I'll call you back. What do you want to see?"

"Escape from New York?"

A slight delay, then: "There's also Endless Love."

Several hours later, the phone still not having rung, he got up to go over to the Egg to get something to eat.

As he went out the door he checked the drop box by habit—he'd already checked that morning—and found that he'd overlooked an envelope. He pulled it, tore it open, and read the jagged scrawl:

I've got something interesting for you—Bill.

Again.

Feeney stuck the note into his pocket and struck off, sprinting off across the parking lot toward the Egg, cursing for the millionth time the megalomaniac size of the lot… the developers insanely envisaging a shopping mall or something.

Asphalt, fucking, dreams.

Halfway across, at full, centerfielder run and breakneck speed, he slipped in an oily puddle and nearly went down in a wild, flailing sprawl, barely catching himself in time. Somewhere up by the supermarket someone gasped.

135

Feeney had onion rings for lunch.

Bill Spencer wanted an article about illegal parking.

Tony's starter got fixed.

Gary assured him the bank wasn't planning on buying ads with the Star, and said so with so much honesty that Feeney knew Gary was planning on buying ads with the Star.

Endless Love was awful.

Chapter 22

Aimlessness, and then Something

FEENEY'S thoughts the next day, sitting again at his desk in the morning and watching the rain still coming down, were neither about the ominous advertising sales figures, nor about his lurking next-door neighbor down in Monroe, nor Beebee—certainly not about Beebee—or much of anything else, but rather about his general usefulness in life. And, incidentally, the weather.

In terms of the latter, on any particularly rainy day, he could gauge the strength and duration of the precipitation by the condition of a far corner of his office ceiling. Normal rain caused a perspiration-like sheen. A downpour caused spreading stains. Flood season congealed into drips.

Parker had promised to have the roof resealed.

The corner over there was now sheened over, the stain well-developed, and drips were pattering down into a bucket.

He watched the steady drip, and knew what he was looking at was going to become newsworthy, and he knew that, at any second, his phone was going to ring.

And Feeney just waited and contemplated in the relative quiet of a cinder-block building being buffeted beneath an enormous deluge emptying itself onto a region spanning from the deep end of Puget Sound down around the Nisqually delta all the way up to Bellingham. It was almost peaceful, and he let things drift back in his mind as far as they wanted to go.

Which was pretty far.

Feeney defined the progress of civilization as the movement

of humanity out from the fearful, conflict-ridden darkness of the cave toward the light of general peace and tolerance... as measured against the slow march of time. In some places, it had been relatively smooth... in others in fits and starts... and in some places so superficial that at times it actually fell backwards, disintegrating into chaos and madness where before there had supposedly been enlightenment. It was the superficial ones that needed to be watched most carefully because they also tended to be the loudest in proclaiming their advanced ideals and high attainments.

Given all that, and as chronicler of what passed for civilization there in Sultan, Feeney could only say that what may have been progress at one time had come to a stop. In the early days of the then sparsely populated country there had been an idealism of self-improvement. But all that, at present, had now given way to a civilization—if you wanted to call it that—consisting of complacent self-satisfaction and the laziness created by unlimited convenience.

Feeney knew all that, having looked through the copies of the early years of the Register, where articles proclaimed the pride of growth and advancement and the attainments of the town and its citizens. And it was plain, from the way the paper was written, that there was also a pride in being curious about the world, and in achieving higher levels of understanding.

People informed themselves about real things, thoughtfulness was admired, and almost everyone was involved in more than one community organization or effort. And the Register was as much a part of that evolution, with the paper growing, becoming more richly written and interesting, nearly from one year to the next.

In a way it was startling, all that energy. To see how people had made such a concerted effort in those days to lift the town toward ever higher goals.

But it was also very revealing about where things had come to. Feeney could look back at those issues, and then mentally think back over the hundred or so issues he'd been responsible for.

It was as though everything had ground to a halt.

Feeney couldn't help wondering what would happen, what things would be like in another twenty, thirty, forty years, when some future editor of the paper would open one of Feeney's papers—if there was still a paper for an editor to work on—and what they would see.

Would they think: Man, what sad doldrums those days were in. Or... worse... would they think these were vibrant days?

He spread his hands across his desk, pulling together his notes for the next issue. The dead weight of writing what had already been written a hundred times before sat on him like a mountain.

He was a chronicler of entropy.

He simply had nothing.

He looked at the notes. Mainly information from various town and county organizations about meetings and initiatives. Not even any cop-shop tidbits.

Feeney pushed it all away across the desk in a sudden rebellion. If it came down to it, the articles could be typed out in thirty minutes flat and he could leave it all sitting right up to the Monday deadline, when Mrs. Hagy came in at eight in the morning to typeset. He could start at seven-thirty and pound out some of them even as she was working.

He took one last look at his telephone as though daring it to ring, and then stood up, reached for his coat, and ran out of the office to his car.

Peering through the slowly enlarging defogged spot in his windshield, on the lookout for the rain-whooshing furies of logging trucks, he noticed how the Skykomish River was beginning to spill over the levees in a few places.

Big, grey, and fast-moving, the heavy menace of it was all too obvious, but for the moment it was just water. It was only when the river started dragging bend-clogging, bridge-choking hillside matter down out of the hills that things turned nasty. Still, its presence, huge, murky, and relentless over there, the opaque surface reflecting only the ashy obscurity of an impenetrable sky, was a cold, reptilian sluice, uncaring and looming, with its violence more for the moment in how inevitable it was, than in what it was yet to do.

Feeney felt grim.

The valley had always been subject to flooding, and frequently, despite attempts to tame the rivers—killing off steelhead and salmon runs in the process—with dams. And as Feeney knew well, this was also the only major story produced in the valley on a regular basis. With raging waters carrying off cows and chickens, and unauthorized trailer houses, the governor and county commissioners and news teams from Seattle would chopper in to survey the mess—almost always after the river had done its worst—and there gaze upon the spectacle of people paddling plastic dinghies around main streets and getting mud-filled basements shoveled out.

Feeney drove up the highway, looking at the state of the river and seeing how people in the towns going up were preparing themselves, sandbagging doors and moving whatever they could to higher ground. He knew what he'd be doing, soon enough.

Of all the possible events that got Dean Parker energized, few matched the onslaught of a major flood. Feeney remembered the first time he'd witnessed it, down at the Monroe office, with Dean bounding around like an ecstatic, somewhat overweight mountain goat, calling the fire and police departments, the hospital, the Land Management people and the rest of what would someday be known as first responders. And once he'd gotten a feel for how disastrous things were he then sent his reporters off to valiantly chronicle all that in the most responsible and spectacular way they could.

Parker, during a flood, was literally shameless.

And it was for that that he'd run away from the imminent phone call down at the office.

Miles back, as he had crossed over the bridge before Sultan, he had looked down into the sullen waters of the town's little tributary, the Sultan River. Normally a black, quiet run of water there, it had become an agitated and boiling race, running out to join with the roiling Skykomish. It hadn't been hard to see that the tributary would flood Sultan with its waters long before the Sky joined in from the other side of the highway.

Feeney, now well up the valley toward the mountain pass, barely watched the landscape go by as he drove higher and higher. Up there, the river was lost from sight in deep gullies and canyons, shrouded by the thick forest. When he got all the way up to Skykomish, he didn't turn around as he usually did, but kept going. Toward the pass, and the ski area, the gateway up there to Eastern Washington and, if it came to that, the entire rest of the continental United States.

He almost never went all the way to the top. Although there was a certain measure of economic interaction and impact between the towns down below, there was next to no trickle impact from the ski area into even the closest mountain town, despite persistent attempts by local business to lure skiers in.

As he reminded himself for the hundredth time, the area up there among those alpine peaks was almost like one of those miniature European bank states, existing within its own fiscal definitions and social mores. A lot of people were up there spending a lot of money at certain times of the year, but for Feeney it was worthless. As far as his news coverage went, that area represented the least news or advertising.

At one time, Feeney thought he might chronicle how many broken legs were generated up there per week but finally decided against it, not so much out of any respect for good taste, but because it would have taken up too much time.

As well, he had no contacts up there. Most of the employees were seasonal, often just ski-bums, and as for the chalets, hotels and ski-lift operations, they didn't see any reason to advertise in papers down valley because they knew—better than anyone—that the local residents of those logging towns gave a flying rip about non-motorized winter sports.

In the eyes of Sky Valley natives, skiing was indeed just for the rich, smartass Seattle crowd. The locals preferred the time-honored sports of deer blasting, salmon snagging, and drinking beer. To put on a fluorescent pink and green snowsuit with matching gloves, and a pair of high-tech ski boots making you look like you've just stepped in a pile of robot shit... and then go falling all over a shaved mountainside strapped to a pair of hundred-dollar fiber-carbon-resin slats... was for snobs and morons.

Of course, at Parker's insistence, Feeney had tried to get some advertising out of all that breathtaking, dollar-generating glitz up there. Inventing countless angles—even to the point of discussing possible distribution of the paper up there. As if weekend skiers gave a good goddamn about what was happening, news-wise, in the area they were recreating in.

All that effort, predictably, failed. The ski area remained a journalistic black hole.

No-man's land.

Which, oddly enough, was almost literally true, because it also represented the limit of the papers on the other side of the pass, coming up from down on that side, over in Eastern Washington. There, the coverage of the Wenatchee paper's area also ended. And they didn't make any money up there either.

Before long, the road winding ever higher up through the dense rainclouds toward the tree line, towering Douglas fir, western hemlock, and spruce gave way to short-branched alpine species, and Feeney finally entered it, the apex of Stevens Pass at a little over four thousand feet.

The skies were clear and blue and nearly cloudless, and it was for the moment as though he was weightless and floating in space.

Nothing, literally no thing, could be stranger for a newsman than to be in a place where news does not exist. It amounted to a paradox, as though Einstein might have predicted it along with those of optical bending or time perception at light speed.

Up there at the summit Feeney existed and yet did not. He was...

Almost free.

At the top, Feeney drove into the center of a huge, dead, ski resort parking area, got out and stood in the cold, exhilarating air. Bare and massive hillsides ran upwards toward the high crags towering even higher up into the freezing, sun-drenched air.

That was no miracle. Stevens Pass rarely showed anything but a brilliant, clear blue sky, no matter what filth was falling down on the west side of the Cascades where all the rainclouds blotted themselves against the mountains and emptied themselves. It was no wonder Eastern Washington was as dry as an old barn.

Feeney looked around. The ski season was over. While snow still lay up on the slopes, rough-graded parking lots were clear of anything except thin sheets of snowmelt and mud.

Carnival-like in winter, nothing could be as cheerfully soiled-looking as a ski area in the off-season. The naked slopes little resembled mountain hillsides, the chairlifts seeming to pin in place what was left of the ski runs against the struggling growths of high mountain heather and lichen. Chalets, boarded up and empty, stood around the edges of soggy parking lots like semi-toxic toadstools popping up with the withdrawal of the snow.

He stared at all that for a while, and then got back in his car and headed back, descending once again into the grey mist. As he dropped farther, the rain began and he went into it as if into a tunnel.

Halfway down, at Index, not far from where the swollen north and south forks of the Skykomish converged, he remembered he still had no main story for that week and took the branch road toward the town.

When he came out, just short of the bridge, it took him a full five breaths to absorb and realize that the town was under an onslaught.

Being the first of the valley towns to have any parts of the Skykomish hit flood stage, it was going under. Pandemonium had arrived at nearly the same time as he had.

And it was newsworthy.

Chapter 23

Serendipity

HE surveyed the scene, taking it in. Flood rescue teams were gingerly crossing over to Index on the old iron bridge where the road came down from the highway. All other traffic was forbidden. The north fork of the Skykomish was raging just inches beneath the threatened bridge.

Moving a large PRESS card onto his dashboard, he nosed his car past the fire trucks and sheriff's cars and pickups to the road beyond the access to the bridge and there saw people at other cars getting into raincoats and ponchos. He knew them on sight: down-county newsmen and photographers. Evidently the long-awaited calls had come in and there they were: Index, in flood season, was always the first to go.

Feeney was happy to find himself there. Pure serendipity. While he'd been far up the highway, his phone down in the office must have been ringing off the hook.

He got out of the car, but didn't hunt around for his poncho. Despite the rain, there wasn't much wind, and the town was even getting filmed from the air by helicopters from the three network affiliates in Seattle. Feeney watched them for a while. They seemed to have a system, one moving slowly down over the town while the other two hovered above it at safe distances, and once it had made its run, it made a large swing out toward Mount Index, letting another one come down. For all he knew they could be live, especially given how a fairly decent spectacle seemed to be in the making with someone's house, just below the bridge, on the verge of toppling into the grasping waves roiling over and ripping away at the soil along the top of the bank.

Feeney, closer to the bridge than the others, snagged a ride on the running board of a tow truck going over the bridge, jumped off on the other side, ran up and down the short main street and just over by the tipping house, and in less than five minutes managed to get good photos of Index Awash before he got kicked out by the emergency crews.

He made his way on foot back across the rain-pounded bridge, snapping more photos up and down the river, and then headed over to talk to one of the Sheriff's deputies who also let him get some information from the county dispatcher. Everyone expected things to get worse. Feeney stood there for a few minutes, wondering if he should stick around. It looked like half a dozen houses were threatened, and maybe even the bridge. But then he decided he had enough and walked back to his car, waving at the black looks of the reporters, all of whom had been reduced to using telephoto lenses.

Because of the looks, he hadn't gone over to talk to anyone, but he did notice that none of Jansen's people were up there. Feeney, feeling a rare sense of professional smugness, climbed back into his car and left. This would be easy. He wasn't going to have to hit deadline like a lot of the other guys. His paper wouldn't come out for several days. He could glean any usable information he didn't have from the other papers and juice it all up with his "scoop" photos.

Feeney swept down the highway toward Sultan feeling, he imagined, what a proud hunter must feel, dragging home some mangled piece of ex-wildlife for his admiring brood.

But as he drove, his elation providing other ideas, he had another thought. Besides the regular story, he would build an even bigger one covering the human dimension. It wouldn't be hard, and he certainly had the time to do it, and it would give him that rare thing: a larger story built on what was hard, breaking news.

God knew where it had come from. God knew where it ever comes from. One minute, bored and entertaining thoughts of quitting, and the next minute... he was a reporter. As long as the

145

Index bridge didn't wash out that night, he'd go back up and get the larger story of a tiny town no one covered except on disaster day.

It almost wasn't fair but he knew: serendipity was what you made of it.

Even before he got fully through the door into the office he could hear the phone ringing. When he came through the door, it stopped, and he took his jacket off and went into the washroom. When he came back out the phone rang again.

"Yeah?" Feeney said, looking at some notices someone had left on his desk, bracing himself for an indignant blast from Parker.

"Patrick Feeney?" The voice was indignant but it turned out to belong to Ted Barnwell, the school superintendent.

"Hi, Ted."

"I've been trying to call for the last hour. I even called Dean."

"Hmmm." Feeney looked at the envelopes on his desk and cut one open. The high school was holding a fundraiser.

"Is this about the fundraiser?"

There was a pause. Then, "Faith took a few days off."

Feeney stopped rummaging around and looked out the window at a renewal of the torrential downpour descending on the parking lot, his thoughts touching briefly on how those helicopters up in Index might have to be grounded, before leaping irresistibly to visions of Barnwell's secretary, The Ever-Lovely Faith Rockford. Feeney barely dared to think of her most of the time... out of self-preservation. Something to do with the concept of impossible. For which, as a concept, Feeney had a lot of respect.

"You're calling to tell me your secretary is on vacation?"

"Oh, no. No," Barnwell said. "I mean, I've had to do this myself. Don't you guys have some sort of central communications system?"

"Communications... system?"

"You know, for information."

Feeney looked down at the envelopes on his desk and picked another one up. It was from the Fish and Game Department. "Well, I've got a big manila envelope taped on the front door... people drop stuff off in that."

"What?"

Feeney sat down. "What's up, Ted?"

"Well, what it is… is I've got something important to talk to you about. And not just after the regular meetings, but here in my office."

"That so?" Feeney slit open the F&G envelope, pulled out a press release about efforts to clean up salmon spawning grounds, and threw it into Mrs. Hagy's inbox.

"Yes. You'll find it… very… interesting." There was a slightly conspiratorial note of humor in his voice.

Feeney picked up another envelope and ripped it open. "What's it about, Ted?"

"Oh, I can't talk about it here. It would get too involved."

"Hmmm…." Feeney picked up a pencil. "Go ahead. When?"

Feeney noted the meeting down, hung up, and then pushed all the envelopes aside and pulled his typewriter into place in front of him, contemplating his opening line for the flood story… Had to get those ideas down. Clean it up later. He started typing.

Two hours, seven hundred words, and three calls from Parker later, Feeney went into Bedossa's and, with the help of a double scotch, let the day drain out of himself.

He'd written a damn good start to that flood story.

"If I say so myself," he said, taking a drink.

Nobody was going to write anything with the depth of that story, backed up with on-the-spot photos.

It was good.

Very good.

And he felt happy.

Of course, there was always the nagging thing. The thing that just dragged everything down, day after day.

Dean, despite his hysteria at the prospect of another flood edition, hadn't let Feeney forget about it. Ads weren't falling, but the ad department said there was a client coolness these days that didn't feel good, and they were having trouble picking up new, over-the-transom ads.

Feeney didn't want to think about it. Hadn't thought about it.

He'd been writing, writing, writing. The ad sales weren't his problem, per se. And Dean hadn't been riding him too much. Even Dean could see Feeney was keeping up his end, smoothing over relations with the fractious town elements, going around the town administrations schmoozing with mayors and council members, going to meetings.

But still, that supplement was still there, week after week.

But... damn it. He was onto one hell of an article.

He looked at his glass, and caught Marsha's eye. He might as well celebrate while he could.

Later, when he got home, he climbed into bed with a tired sense of doom. Unfinished writing efforts had that effect on him.

But he still felt good.

At least he had something. It wasn't the thing, but it beat whatever else he'd been doing.

He closed his eyes with a sigh and went immediately to sleep.

And somewhere beyond him, beyond all of it, things were already in motion.

Because the best good news was always the worst bad news.

Chapter 24

How it Began with Ted

HARD to believe it could still be raining so hard the next day. It had been non-stop. Flooding was all over the place, and he could have spent the entire morning going around and looking at it, but he didn't care. Sleep had supplied a raft of inspiration and he was in a rush to get it all down on paper.

He added, cut, spliced, reworked, and then reread it all. It would take another go, but it was close. After an hour of that, to take a break, he opened his notebook to find something else to write about, leaving the feature article to stew. He flipped past a few pages and then came upon the notes about Chief Spencer's articles. Here was one about drunk driving. He figured he might as well get that one out of the way, and began typing, almost mindlessly.

He was down to a part about accumulated DWI arrests and the fine-and-penalty scales, when the phone rang and Ted Barnwell's secretary, The Ever-Lovely Faith Rockford, was on the other end.

"Hi," Feeney said. "Have a good vacation?"

A slight pause, then: "Sorry?"

Feeney winced.

The fact was, Faith—and her thick, golden, wavy-haired ever-loveliness, her green gaze—always disconcerted him. Which she seemed to know. But was kind enough not to do anything deliberately to make him feel like the awkward dolt he made himself feel like.

It wasn't her fault... she was just so impossibly beautiful. He mumbled something.

Another pause, somewhat longer, then crisply: "You know you have a meeting with Ted this afternoon?"

"Yes, I do."

"He just wanted me to make sure you didn't forget."

"It's on my calendar and everything." Feeney didn't have a calendar.

"That's good."

"Um..." Feeney began doodling on a random piece of paper. Although he knew better, he had a bad habit of always attempting to prolong conversations with Faith. Create... something. In this case, some sort of conspiratorial... something. "Anything else? I mean, anything in particular you could tell me about what's going on?"

Whatever he thought he was doing didn't work.

"No," she said.

Feeney dropped his pen. "Okay."

The connection clicked dead, leaving Feeney listening to the dial tone. He hung up. He looked down and after a second realized with irritation he'd just doodled a woman's lower leg wearing a high-heeled shoe on a letter Dean Parker wanted him to deliver to the Sultan mayor's office.

He slid the envelope into a drawer and rubbed his face. Something, indeed, was up with Ted. Normally, whenever he would see the School District Superintendent at the quickly dispatched School Board meetings, he could barely get the time of day out of the man. Now, suddenly, two consecutive calls.

He liked the superintendent. Feeney had met enough public officials and had seen everything from narcissistic self-importance, obsequiousness, pettiness, and bad tempers to a whole gamut of other major and minor failings. But Ted Barnwell, no.

Barnwell, at some time, had been a teacher, but then as a young man quickly moved into administration, becoming a junior high, then high school principal in other state districts—the normal ladder of ascension. His job at Sultan was his first superintendency and, to all appearances, he took it very seriously. Almost too much... which accounted, Feeney thought, for his pattern of avoiding conversations with the local newspaper editor. Feeney had often wondered if something had happened somewhere, to make him like that, but he had never gotten around to making any inquiries.

In any case, it wasn't a difficult school district. Small, it comprised two elementary schools—there and in Gold Bar—a junior high, and the Sultan High School. The elementary schools were doing all right, well-provided with enough colored paper, scissors, crayons, and pots of white glue to get them through Halloween, Christmas, Valentine's Day and Easter. And the junior high school served its purpose of confining incipient pubescent adolescence to a virtual prison/day-care center for three, heavily patrolled years. But the high school was another thing.

It was that bond rumor. It had to be what Ted wanted to talk about, and this could only be the announcement of it... or... Feeney had another thought. Maybe Ted was quitting. It was also a pretty good possibility. Small-town superintendents didn't stick around much anymore.

One or the other.

In terms of a story, it would be better if it was the school and a construction bond. Upgrade the building. Bond stories almost never went anywhere.

He knew the school's history—an old, three-story brick construction erected by construction gangs of returning soldiers in 1919. After that, a series of hastily conceived expansions.

The first, from the late thirties, with an attempt to mimic the other WPA public buildings of the time replete with bas-relief sculptures of sturdy working men and women carrying out those tasks upon which the society of the New Deal demanded of them, now looked like something the Soviets would have put up during the Heroic Era. The next addition, tacked on in the late fifties to handle a growing population of students, was a long, unsightly length of concrete block and window glass in the minimalist—meaning cheap—style of the time. Le Corbusier may have ushered in modernism, but he also gave everyone the excuse to throw any sense of style out the spec-catalogue window. Form followed function, school rooms defined by demographic projection and storage space. Utilitarian. And anyway, there was no use in building anything of permanence or beauty when it might be nuked out of existence any day now by the Russians. And then finally, in the sixties, some temporary portable classrooms built of plywood and painted bomber-belly gray—an outcome of a festering national pessimism exacerbated by the Kennedy assassination, the buildup in Vietnam, hippies, freedom marches, and the collapse of the concept of the single-paycheck family—had been deposited in an unobtrusive section of the parking lot and had since then fulfilled their destiny of becoming permanent fixtures.

Nothing was more permanent in modern America than the temporary.

Because of all those additions, everything inside the school had a dismal, jury-rigged feeling to it as one went up and down connecting ramps and staircases, going from one hallway of worn, nondescript linoleum to another where time-darkened wood floors creaked beneath each step.

If it was an upgrade bond, Feeney could easily begin to think of the outlines of the story...

He'd have to be careful, of course. School building stories were often like dry tinder because no matter how small the town, school taxes were a big-ticket item. Local government provided a little under half of the funding and more than eighty percent of that money came straight out of property taxes. Which no one wanted to see rise. Which then sent districts scrambling to find other financing solutions such as bonds. Which no one wanted to pay for either.

Which made a newspaper editor's position ticklish, because of the very unpopularity of the issue, no matter how needed.

But that building. The only thing that came close to blending things together were the ubiquitous coats of paint in the traditional school colors—froggy pastel greens, grayish pinks, and chalky yellows. Mercifully, the prison-block shades of grays or blues were kept down in the boiler room.

Aesthetics had been long extinct—whether in surroundings or as a subject—in the education of American children. All the knowledge of proportion, the concepts of human interaction, the language of architecture and style built up over centuries of urban life had been tossed out in the post-war expediency of building suburbs and malls. Public life was degraded into boxlike dullness where there was no sense of the street and neighborhood, but just neon-lit maintenance sheds surrounded by acres of parking lots like moats of asphalt.

Probably, he thought, the high school building could get along for another thirty years with only periodic maintenance—touch-ups of paint, re-tarring the roof, and re-grading the faculty parking lot. But something else seemed in store.

Feeney, drifting away into his contemplation of the architectural ruin of America by way of strip malls and suburban sprawl, suddenly came back to himself. He glanced down at the Crime Stopper's Notebook article, and pushed it away.

He could do that in his sleep.

He had, this day, bigger things to think about. The interview with Barnwell was just a couple of hours away and that meant...

The Ever-Lovely Faith Rockford.

Which meant he had something else very pressing to do.

Chapter 25

Laurilaure's

NORMALLY he was still weeks away from the point when what was happening above his ears would finally cross some strange Rubicon of disarray, to the point he had to get a haircut. But an impending encounter with Faith Rockford suddenly made it seem worth attempting.

Not, of course, because he thought it might boost his attractiveness to her. She, even more so than Marsha, was in no way like any of the women who had ever been attracted to him, or even like any woman he might have wished to find him attractive. Feeney's soul had been blasted by previous disasters into that unshakable pragmatism men like him develop, where even the thought of dreams became barely humorous anecdote. And memories brought no warmth, but only thousand-mile stares directed toward the nearest wall. But that didn't mean he was dead, either.

It was interesting to Feeney that, when thinking either of Marsha or Faith, he could find himself seeing both of them as attractive, and yet in most ways they had little in common. Marsha was an earthy animal. Faith... good god.

It turned out she'd worked in public relations before she came to Sultan. A random phone call one afternoon to Weyerhaeuser to ask about their New Urbanism project in DuPont got an off-the-record question from George Petrakis, a PR officer in their real estate division.

"So, you're the editor at the Register? You have someone

working for the school district named Faith Rockford?"

"She's the school district's assistant to the director. She worked down there?"

"Five years. Then just bagged it, telling us she'd gotten an offer up there."

"That'd be a big cut in pay and opportunity."

"Yeah," George said. "Huh, how about that…? So, it's true. Yeah, we could never… Well, anyway, I guess it depends on what you want. Say hello some time for me."

Faith wore fashionable outfits, with her golden hair falling softly around her face—a thicker, longer, wavier echo of a Dorothy Hamill cut, looking smooth and glamorous, and… ever lovely. Almost like the woman that buffoon prince of England had married, Diana. Wrapped up in the mystery of why an attractive single woman would give up a good career to move to a backwater foothills town like Sultan, compounded by her aloofness, she could project just about any desirable female quality—or at least those that seemed desirable to him. In Feeney's experience, unknown, attractive people almost always seemed more interesting than they turned out to be. But he wasn't rigidly stubborn about this and was willing to take chances. And where unknown, attractive women were concerned… And such a sweet smile.

She made him conscious of his hair.

His hair.

From time to time, he considered just having it shorn off. It was hopeless. Even short it never combed or brushed the same way. Mornings for Feeney entailed a never-ending plight of re-recognition as his hair overnight transformed itself into original and ever more revolutionary forms. When he'd been in junior high, he'd tried sleeping with a ski hat on. But it made no difference. And the longer it grew the worse it got, with the climate helping none. If there was a lot of humidity, his head simply gave up and became a Sargasso Sea of slowly drifting tangles of wrack and flotsam, a Medusa nightmare in Irish orange.

He had been considered cute as a child.

But that was then, and he was generally immune now. Except

on those occasions when he came up against true, physical beauty. And there it was. He was going to see Ted Barnwell, but Faith Rockford would be there and...

Haircut.

He dashed through the sheets of rain between his office and his car, there cursing as he struggled to find his keys in his overcoat pocket. There are certain Northwesterners who—gleaning this information from God only knew what source—like to maintain that it rained no more, and in some cases less, than several other large, well-known cities which had no reputation at all for inclement weather.

Feeney had no illusions about the weather on that side of the Cascades. If you had the misfortune of living deep in the folds of the western foothills of those mountains, you might as well go off to work wearing a wetsuit and air tanks.

As he went into town, he checked the flood conditions. The Jackson was ever more threatening, sandbags now being laid at the near end of Main Street at the place where the old Sultan River bridge had stood. Thank God he had that story, he thought. Otherwise he would have been forced to be out there in all that all afternoon.

At the far, still dry end of Main Street, he pulled in front of Laurilaure's Styling Salon. He could have gone to Buck's white-sidewalls barbershop on Main Street, but having been to both, he preferred the roaring of Laurilaure's row of battle-sized hairdryers drowning out the conversations of the women underneath them to the babbling of the good ol' boys dropping by Buck's. And as well Feeney had come to think his hair needed more precision than what Buck, an ex-logger with half his fingers missing, could provide.

Laurilaure gave him a quick shampoo and got him settled into the big chair. Normally, in those circumstances, he allowed himself to forget nearly everything. But he had regretfully picked up a copy of the Star supplement that had been on one of the waiting-area tables and found himself looking through the ads, and seeing that Jansen was now claiming that the print run was 18,000 copies.

Given that Parker's papers had lost another hundred renewals, five more Main Street advertisers, and that two down-county towns had published their official notices in Jansen's classified section, this was just salt in the wounds. He tossed the supplement onto the next chair over.

Thirty minutes later, he strolled out of Laurilaure's salon with his hair swept back, up and over, with an expertly sculpted pompadour.

Feeney had been all admiration, watching her manage to brush, blow and whack his hair into something resembling a well-trimmed juniper bush. What was even more admirable was how he could barely recognize himself. He thought he actually looked good, with his hair flowing effortlessly back over his head like the slipstream Ferrari profile of a movie star. He felt so normal he was convinced he could have stood in the middle of any crowd, and no one would have noticed him at all—hair-wise, he right there owned the perfection of style which guaranteed anonymity.

Which was gone in the thirty seconds it took for him to swim to his car.

Chapter 26

First Manassas, that was to say, First Ted Barnwell

FAITH glanced up at him. For a millisecond, her amused green eyes flicked up, and then she waved him into the superintendent's office.

Feeney reached up and defiantly pushed the damp ruins of Laurilaure's efforts away from his forehead, and went through the door.

"Patrick," said Ted Barnwell, getting up from his desk and coming around it. He was a massive man, had probably played football as a linebacker, with the square jaw and thick neck to go with it. He also had gorilla-sized hands. He put one of them out, and Feeney only slightly hesitated before taking it. "Good to see you," he pointed to a chair in front of his desk.

Feeney took off his coat, hung it on the coat-rack to drip dry, got out his notebook and a small cassette tape recorder, and sat down.

"All right," he said to Ted with a smile. "Where do you want to start?"

An hour later, having already flipped out two cassettes, Feeney was staring blankly at the superintendent.

"... so," Ted Barnwell said, "that brings us to the other side of the coin. We are forced to take action, but which one?"

Feeney fought a desire to heave a huge, long sigh.

For something like the twentieth time the superintendent had managed to navigate through a series of digressions, developments, re-digressions and commentary, finally getting into the neighborhood of whatever question Feeney had asked. He no longer regretted never having had many words with the superintendent.

Luckily, Feeney had the recorder running.

A whispering memory: an image, half-remembered, half-dreamed, a remote corner desk warmed by springtime sun coming through the high windowpanes, a teacher's voice fading quietly behind the muffled fidgets and scuffles of schoolmates, a slightly opened window letting in the sounds of a bird chirping from somewhere in the trees lining the playground, the smell of sweat, chalk, and glue... and the hot, perfumed scent of Judy Williams, sitting right in front of him.

A cramped message of pain began shooting through Feeney's left buttock from being crushed on the oak chair. He nodded at Barnwell, checked to see the tape recorder was still turning, and shifted his weight.

Amazingly, Barnwell, who had almost managed to approach a response to the original question, had suddenly found the need to make another circle of explanations, qualifications and supporting arguments, before once again getting back to the starting spot. As though he had arrived somewhere.

Or perhaps, Feeney thought, the man was just getting tired.

"We therefore have a sort of spectrum of responses," Barnwell was saying. "The problem with the choice within that spectrum is what it means in the short run, and then the long run, for the community. May I be completely honest with you for a moment?"

Feeney nodded. "If not me, who else, Ted?"

"It's complex. I am, of course, a professional educator, and my view of the world places a fundamental emphasis on the importance of school. But as a pragmatic administrator, which I must be, I realize that education in this country, based as it is on local input—whether in how it is carried out or to what extent it is funded, is sometimes a carrot-and-stick affair. More often than not, it is the carrot which has to be offered." Barnwell gave Feeney a keen look. "This is strictly off the record, you understand?"

"Absolutely, Ted," Feeney said. "You can have total confidence that none of this will be in the paper."

Barnwell nodded contentedly. "Just man to man, now," he went on, "I should tell you that I know that, in Sultan, for example, the driving forces behind student, hence parental, interest, are sports for the boys and social activities for the girls. You can go blue in the face talking about the very real dangers looming for these kids if certain curricula or materials are not made available to them, unless you sweeten the pot. In almost every issue that has come up in my tenure here, not one important issue, whether it is a matter of procuring computer equipment or having new toilets installed, gets passed if there isn't a sports or social proviso tacked on or exploited. With all that in mind, to just propose the idea that students would receive a good education for generations to come, would be a failure."

Feeney tried to look surprised. "That's surprising."

"Yes. I know. Amazing, isn't it? No rational argument, in my view, will work, no matter how true. Not the one that good facilities attract good teachers. Not the one that good facilities enhance community growth. Not the one that good facilities attract state and federal funds for special programs. Not the one that good facilities are an end in themselves which create a true snowball effect in just about every imaginable way. Schools, for me, are the heart of the community. And in a community like Sultan, a school could very easily become the focal point for a renaissance."

Feeney's eyebrows rose, this time for real.

"Renaissance?"

"But... and the stinger is this," Barnwell held up a prophetic finger, "none of this will happen unless... unless..."

Feeney waited patiently, but could see Ted was stuck, and so decided to help out. "... unless it also means that all the boys become football heroes and the girls prom queens."

Barnwell nodded helplessly.

And at that, Feeney gave up. For a while, even with the recorder running, he had tried to note the times when he might have actually had something to report on, but there was no way he could make anything out of this stream-of-consciousness anxiety.

When he had told Barnwell not to worry about any of this

getting in the paper, he'd been telling the truth. Because none of it was worth a single line.

Did Ted Barnwell actually expect him to write some exegesis on the complexities of running a school district? Or how it was the heart of the community? It would mean coming over here nearly once a week. A quick image of Faith Rockford returning, he nearly sighed but then, quickly and luckily, caught himself. Barnwell, who in this strange outpouring of explanations, supporting arguments and asides bordering on outright self-pity, would have interpreted it as a tired reproof. Which, in truth, it could easily have been, as well.

"... and so that means that it will be necessary for the town, and not just parents," Barnwell was going, "to provide a clear, well-explained understanding of what the issues are all about... to help the town know... what the issues are..."

Barnwell came to an embarrassed stop, his eyes bulging a bit in his heavy face as he searched for what he wanted to say. But luckily for him Feeney's attention hadn't been that far afield, and into the lengthening pause Feeney said with an unavoidable flat cynicism: "You mean explain everything in the way you want them to think, before they know what the issues are all about and can figure things in different ways."

The moment he said it, he regretted it, but a moment later could see he had nothing to worry about. Barnwell was so frightened of public opinion he wasn't offended at Feeney's obvious complaint. In fact, the superintendent fully accepted it. Because, in fact, that's exactly what he had meant to say.

"No! I didn't mean that..."

"I'm kidding, Ted."

"Yes, but people might think that! People might think they are being manipulated..."

"Aren't they?"

"... before they've even had a chance to make up their minds."

And that was it for Feeney. He had been there for well over an hour. He had allowed the superintendent to empty his sack. And he could now see that whatever the hell they thought they wanted to do, no decisions had been made. Yet.

161

There was still no news.

He decided to end it right there and held up his hands.

"Listen, Ted. I can see now that you've spent a lot of time thinking about this... there really is a lot of good stuff here. But I think we should, for the moment, stop here. Good foundation, you know. But sort of stop to get some bearings. Because... you know... um... Well, for one thing, I'm not sure I really know where all this is coming from and I've got to organize the approach. Otherwise, I really don't have much here and I might as well just write something about the Homecoming Dance. Which I'll probably have to write anyway, oh boy, oh boy. Bleeding to death, Ted. Bleeding to fucking death, Ted. The Homecoming King and Queen. But... I mean... can you answer me one simple question?"

Barnwell, having recovered from Feeney's crassness, looked at him with what seemed apprehension, but then nodded.

"OK," Feeney said. "What's going on?"

Barnwell stared at Feeney for a full five seconds, licked his lips slowly, then stared at him for another five seconds and then finally looked down, reached into his desk and pulled out an envelope. Even from across the desk, Feeney could recognize who it was from. Barnwell pulled the folded one-sheet letter from the envelope and handed it over to Feeney.

Feeney unfolded it and glanced down through the text. Finally, he thought, here it was. All of it. He looked back up at Barnwell. "Jesus, Ted. I'm sorry."

"Off the record," Barnwell said.

Feeney set the letter back on the desk. "Off the record, Ted? This is already on the record if anyone wants to look. Which for the moment, they don't. Or don't know how. Can I have a copy?"

Barnwell nodded, and reached to punch the button on his intercom. And Feeney clicked the off button on his recorder.

Chapter 27

Bits and Pieces

IT was from the Washington State Department of Education. More specifically, from the office dealing with health and safety. He could see why Ted Barnwell was rattled. This was the last thing he'd been looking for in Sultan.

Feeney could sympathize.

Barnwell, ambitious in his first posting, was trying to figure out how this sudden calamity would affect district education politics, and incidentally, his own career for years to come. Feeney wasn't about to criticize the system where wider public good often came on the heels of narrow self-interest. As long as the good was done.

The letter was both clear and unclear. State inspections had recently been done. That would account for the town rumors. The results said that the actions—though not in the letter—were imperative.

From the way Barnwell had gone on, coupled with what Peace had said concerning the bond issue, it meant something was seriously wrong. But he still didn't know. For some reason neither Barnwell nor Peace had wanted to say exactly what the issue was.

But people seemed to know things.

Leaks were evidently beginning to get out, and things Feeney had barely paid any attention to were beginning to make sense. Just the other day in his cross-county wanderings he'd heard—where was it? Yes, up in Skykomish—as he'd been dropping off advertising brochures at the so-called hotel, he'd heard the owner, who was also a volunteer fireman, mention that they were nervous about their own school up there "because of that shit down in Sultan."

And then there was that incident in Gold Bar. He'd gone up there to take pictures of some third-grade students and posters they had made, but before he could do that, he had to help the teacher put the posters back up. And while they were doing that, she groused that the inspectors from the State Fire Marshal's office had taken them down so they could inspect the wall. And why? Because they'd decided after Sultan to check all the schools.

Feeney hadn't thought much of it. It seemed normal enough that state inspectors would go around.

But now he wondered, and he made a note to ask if it was a routine check.

Back at his office, Feeney began to make the calls. Up and down the valley, down to Everett, and down to Olympia.

Nobody wanted to confirm or deny that anything was happening—or not happening.

When he called the health and safety office at the DoE, he was told by a low-level administrator that there was no information to be had. And he was told the same thing by the administrator's immediate supervisor. And then the same thing again by the supervisor's deputy chief.

Feeney wasn't surprised. While most public offices had quite a bit of transparency, nothing was more difficult to determine than the safety and inspection records of public buildings.

The sum of all the information he had amassed from all those phone calls was exactly zero. He had nothing. No leads, not the slightest confirmation of the slightest rumor.

And Feeney felt he was in the presence of salvation.

Because it wasn't that there was nothing there—it was in the way he was being told that there was nothing there.

It had to be this.

He was sure. The high school had recently had an inspection that had Barnwell and Peace scrambling.

This was it.

But... how could he make it his, and his alone, without Jansen getting onto it?

Feeney's mind ran with it: how big was it? The worst, of course, was that the school was in such bad condition that it would be closed down.

If the Fire Marshal was involved, that would mean... Feeney's mind played with the words with near delectation... a Red Tag order.

A shutdown.

With literally only two options for resolution: either immediate rehabilitation of the school, or its destruction and replacement—a political disaster with far more impact on the local economy than even the worst flood.

This could be the salvation of Dean's newspaper business.

If it was handled right.

Feeney felt a bit shell-shocked. Red Tags. It was nearly too good to be true, and it was like he'd just walked through a door and been instantly transported to a different universe. Almost never does an editor know beforehand he's sitting on a winning public issue—one that would be covered for months on end... providing a backdrop for ringing, patriotic prose which would bring the crowning laurels of success to his thoughtful, civic-minded brows.

Feeney felt a wave of relief wash over him. This was even better than the flood story

And it wasn't just a cynical happiness at having a profession-saving story to run on. He honestly did have a soft spot for education and felt the world could indeed be a better place if someone made a serious attempt to make something real of children and not just provide a cursory lip-service program. It was nice, once in a while, when it could all come together.

And it was proof you could be an idealist and also hedge your bets.

Chapter 28

Errare humanum est

PARKER could barely get it out, he was breathing so hard. "So where's the... THE... the goddamn... where's the goddamn fucking RIVER?"

Feeney could almost feel sympathy for his boss and had plenty of explanations at the ready. But he held back. Shadings of meaning were minor when one had walked straight into a carpet bombing.

"Good. Fucking. God..." Parker, nearly out of breath, stared at Feeney.

The door to the office was open and now that Parker was no longer ranting, Feeney could hear the absolute quiet out in the back shop. It didn't take much to guess that Dean had let the entire building know what was on his mind well before Feeney had got called in.

He wriggled, trying to find a more relaxed, neutral, and inconspicuous way to sit in the chair. Parker was angry enough without being provoked by suggestions of indifference, apathy, or inattention.

He glanced down at the guilty issue of the Skykomish Register, condemned explicitly with red exclamation points and question marks made with a blunt-tipped marking pen. It looked like a dripping bloodbath. In fact, the paper was so gored with Parker's fury that Feeney held it instinctively at the tips of his fingers.

He looked up. Parker was still giving him a frozen look of furious disbelief, as if sitting in front of him was the Son of Blob.

Feeney tried a wan smile. "I know it was… an unusual approach…" As he spoke, he tried to move the red-stained remains of the newspaper toward the floor. "For example, the crushed geranium in the mud puddle…"

Parker's eyes didn't waver.

Feeney brought the paper back up and pointed to a rather dark image of something looking like a pale dumpling floating in a grey cloud—or at least, that was what it would have looked like, if not savagely crossed, smeared over, and lashed with vicious hacks of red ink. Actually, the picture was quite out of focus. With all the running around among the emergency vehicles, trying to get shots before he got kicked out of there, a lot of his pictures ended up blurry. But it had seemed to look all right in the dark room, and Feeney had thought that might give readers a sense of tragedy and urgency that had been there at the scene.

"Or…" Feeney went on, "you've got to admit that the shot of the reflection of the garbage cans in the Index House window was pretty good."

Feeney picked out one of the few photos left almost untouched, only a big, wild "X" crossing the image.

Parker looked at the paper, and then with his voice going up a full octave, wheezed out, "That… ISN'T… the photo that goes with the sanitation story?"

Feeney turned slightly as though to reach back and swing the door to Parker's office shut.

"You leave that fucking door open!" Parker was now red-faced. He took a breath. "Would you tell me," he said at last, "as near as you can, just what it is you think the purpose of a newspaper is… MY newspaper?"

Feeney, knowing with every word he was digging his own grave, threw out his standard answer about how the purpose of the paper was to inform the public of those things the public didn't have time to find out for itself… they were stand-in representatives… that democracy was built on the education and awareness of the common man, and also that they were there to provide opinion, entertainment, and amusement.

Parker waited, using that time to catch his breath, and then when Feeney was finished waited some more, like waiting for some bad smell to drift away. Then finally, he spoke:

"If you think you can convince me that you and I are a couple of nincompoops, you're even more out of your mind than you just might possibly be." Feeney opened his mouth but Parker cut him off. "I don't know what you think but... and this is it... the purpose of my paper is to make me money. And enough so that I will continue wanting to do this, and incidentally keep you and everyone else on the fucking payroll. News, for your information, is a goddamn commodity like shoes and if people want it they're going to pay me to get it for them. But if they pay, they'll at least be guaranteed to get something that resembles the news... not," Parker pointed at the crushed-flower-in-mud photo, "something that looks like somebody's dog got sick on the front page."

Feeney did not say anything, which seemed appropriately abject, so Parker went on. "Honestly, what were you thinking? I mean, did you actually have any idea what you were doing?"

At this point Feeney figured he had nothing left to lose. "OK, you know what was up there. You know Everett and Seattle were all there snapping away, and that... that night, and the next day, there were going to be hundreds of photos of Index Under Water so I figured that since we weren't going to get out for six days afterwards and everyone would have seen all the normal stuff, so maybe it would be better to go for something more soulful."

"Soulful?" Parker's voice was calm. "Fuck soulful. I want, exactly, the normal stuff. I don't want anything but the goddamn normal bullshit that everyone else, Everett, Seattle, Jansen—did you see Jansen's?—puts on their fucking normal front page."

Feeney let out a sigh. In truth, the whole thing had come about because of a weak moment of rebellion in the darkroom. Feeney himself had joined in with developing the pictures and as they were hung up to dry, he found himself with a complete collection. Water racing below windows. Cars washed into trees. Trees into houses. People up side streets with wheelbarrows full of clothes, clutching their VCRs.

168

Luckily nobody had been drowned. And as the photos appeared in the dim red light of the darkroom, the sickly-sweet smell of developing fluid around him, he'd begun to feel ill. It was the crying mothers, frightened children, distressed and hollow-eyed men, exhausted rescue workers. It was the side of the news he'd never been comfortable with. Pictures of disaster up close, of stunned, frightened eyes.

Feeney had shelved all that and then thrown a handful of more or less unrecognizable photos across the page. Let his text tell the story. Those pictures were now there on Parker's desk, in a manila folder.

"You did see what Jansen ran?"

"Yeah."

"He creamed us. Some of his guy's pictures even got picked up on the wire."

"I know."

"Pictures the guy took the next day!"

"I know."

Parker's hand slapped down on the folder. "There are pictures in here nobody else got."

"I know it."

"Fuck, Patrick," Parker said. "And I mean fuck. But... never mind. This is what we're doing: in the next issues of both the Post-Ledger and the Register, we're going to run a special photo section, a sort of collector's edition, with all those pictures of the flood you didn't run. I'm doing the layout myself and will pick the ones I want, and you'll be in here early to have them cropped."

"All right."

Feeney waited to see if there was anything else. But Parker seemed to be done. Which was surprising. Usually, at this point, once Parker felt he had someone beaten to a pulp, he usually came in with one last zinger. The estacada.

But, nothing, not even something like whether he'd seen the latest sales figures.

Feeney stood up and walked through the back office and down the corridor to the reception, receiving here and there faint smiles of encouragement. He passed Marlene without looking at her.

"I liked the article," she said. There was just the slightest bubble of a chuckle.

He turned and looked at her. "Swell. You, too?"

Marlene laughed outright. "Seriously though, the article is really good."

"Thanks."

"Now… don't be that way."

"Any ideas for what way I should be?"

"You know… he's really almost out of ideas."

"He's not the only one."

"I was sort of hoping to never hear you say that."

Feeney looked at her for a moment. "Pretend I didn't, then."

Feeney trudged out the door onto the sidewalk of Monroe's main street and looked up and down it.

No matter what, the flood story wouldn't have made a difference.

But those Red Tags…

There was hope.

Chapter 29

Rumors of rumors

"WE all know," Brahnler said, "that there's a rumor going around which is making this town's government a joke or worse."

"What rumor is that, Dick?" Newton Powell's voice was theatrically weary, his eyes rolling upward, fixed on a distant point, maybe in the ceiling, maybe beyond that.

"Well," Brahnler said with a half-smile, "maybe I shouldn't have said rumor..."

Powell brought his eyes down and looked straight at him. "No, Dick, you shouldn't have used that term."

"... It's not that. I'm not saying anything about anyone in particular..."

"... we're sure you're not, for your sake..."

"... but let's just say that, just to be honest, confidence is the main thing a town official has to have to operate..."

"... which you lost in the last election..."

Powell smiled at the room. He had decided to use a new approach with Brahnler, punctuating everything the former councilman said with a comment or correction. From this point forward, it was like a tennis match, with Brahnler and Powell trading swings.

"... and how can we expect this town to operate, and trust the people doing the job, when there might be a double standard going on?..."

"... There is. One for you, and one for everybody else..."

"... You know, for example, if I wanted to burn leaves on

171

Saturday, I couldn't go around telling people they couldn't. That would make me a hypocrite, wouldn't it?"

"… What an idea…"

"… Well, how would my neighbors feel if they knew it wasn't allowed to do something, and found out that I was doing it? And worse, that I could keep them from doing it?"

"Get to the point, Dick," said Charles Peace, who from the look on his face seemed as irritated with Powell as with Brahnler.

"I'm just saying that, for example, if I have to go to work like everyone else and I want a pay raise or something, my boss sure isn't going to like me taking time off work to take classes so he has to give me a pay raise. And worse, make him pay for my time off, and for the classes as well. I mean, my boss would be an idiot to go along with that."

Feeney looked over at Brahnler sourly. It always seemed that Brahnler had access to the sort of dirt Feeney should have had. But bad as that all was, it was galling that it was exactly the sort of dirt Feeney would have to write about. Which meant, worst of all, that he was constantly being publicly manipulated like this, and there was nothing he could do about it.

"All right, Dick, we get your point," Powell said. "But the real point is, there are procedures and, yes, privileges which town officials may take. By law. One of those is the ability to attend any or all training courses, classes or special instruction which can help them do their job better. If I remember, there was one councilman who took a class in land and property deeds, real estate sales, and roll-over tax filing laws that cost the town sixteen hundred dollars. And nobody said boo to it."

"Yes," Brahnler nodded, "as chairman of the town revenue commission it was my duty to make sure I had all the latest knowledge. But for the record," he looked around the room, with just a bit of a pause in Feeney's direction, "I also took that course on my own time…"

"… And the town council, or the fire department, didn't see one benefit from it either, did it? It's on the record. There has not been one single amendment to the local revenue regulations in the last thirty-four years. Not one single proposition came out of your one-man commission. And..." he nodded at Brahnler's frown, "... you bet I noticed. As I also noted that all that information must have come in damned handy six months later when it came to the sale of your father-in-law's dairy farm down there in Duvall."

"There's nothing wrong with the fact that I could use what I learned in my private life."

"Oh no, of course not," Powell said with an amused equanimity, "just as there's nothing wrong with Chief Spencer taking a fingerprint course and attending a management seminar, either. Two things, by the way, I doubt he would be able to apply to his private life, unless he wants to go around fingerprinting his family and placing his household budget under the aegis of the town's financial operations. Would you, Richard Brahnler, like to go on record right now as being in opposition to our police force keeping up on the latest techniques for running a budget? Would you? Bill Spencer made the case that this was part of his duty, and we felt he was right to go."

"Lucky him." Brahnler gazed around with a grin. "Too bad my tax course hadn't been held in San Diego, too."

"Just for the record, Dick," said Peace, "we paid him the legal per diem and transportation was based on bus fare, legally received in cash. He paid the balance on his plane ticket himself."

"Yeah, right," Brahnler laughed at Peace. "So Spencer takes a semi-paid vacation to San Diego. Takes his wife and kids down there. Goes to one, two-hour course every day for a week, and then goes to the zoo or the beach for the rest of the day."

"He paid for his family's tickets, and for all costs above per diem, which we had based on a motel room for one person. And, as for his free time, what would you expect him to do?" Powell said, a laugh rasping scornfully in the back of his throat. "Sit in a motel watching Dialing-for-Dollars?"

"And the taxpayers of the town pick up not only the tab for his paid vacation, but for the course, and will now have to foot the bill for his pay raise next year? What does he have now? Sixty-eight credits?"

Feeney ignored the crack about paid vacation; that was an exaggeration. And he could be cynical about how well Brahnler knew the ins and outs of how the system could be taken advantage of, if only because he did it so well himself. But he had to admit that Brahnler had made a point. The town had a merit system which allowed officials to win pay raises and bonuses based on, among other things, self-improvement classes they took. And, while most everyone from time to time might have taken a class here or there, the town clerk taking a brush-up accounting course, for example, Bill Spencer was by far the most consistent applicant. An All-American medal winner. Going for the Gold.

Feeney would have bet good money the police chief had been a Boy Scout, and not just a member of one of the Booze Patrols for whom a trip to the woods meant packs stuffed with whatever forms of alcohol, tobacco or drugs teenage boys could get their hands on, and the usual girly magazines. No, he would have diligently and proudly earned every merit badge under the sun. Glowing then in the praise heaped upon him. No quietly humble, modest, helpful epitome of perfection, he.

But scout or not, the result was that Spencer spent just about as much time profiting from town regulations concerning time off and self-improvement, which translated to higher pay and even more time off, as he spent time on the job. All perfectly legal. There could be no more precise description of the truly bureaucratic mind.

Sixty-eight credits. Not bad, Feeney thought. It took ninety for the next pay increase. In two years' time, Spencer had managed to move himself up through three steps in this manner, a process that normally took five years.

He had also managed something else which Feeney knew about, but which Powell had advised him not to report on unless it had to do with a legal filing. Spencer had also achieved a step in rank.

This sort of thing was invisible to the town, since he was already police chief and couldn't go higher. But it did move him up on the state's law-enforcement rating system. It wasn't the sort of thing that generated a raise in pay, but it did represent something which would be of value if Spencer ever looked for a job elsewhere.

A bigger town or city, for example. Feeney wasn't sure even Brahnler was aware of it, the record of it being in Spencer's personal file, which a private citizen could only access by filling out a FOIA request. He looked up from his notes.

"At the end of his course," Peace was explaining, "he'll have eighty-six."

"Four to go, huh?" Brahnler mocked. "In the amount of money you guys have spent helping him take classes for his next pay raise, and then adding in his pay raises, you could have bought a new squad car last year like you promised."

"We're getting our money's worth," one of the council said.

"Someone is." Brahnler, getting a laugh from the crowd, looked over at Feeney.

And Feeney nodded back. Yes, Dick, he thought. Well done. You've managed to toss another metaphysical grenade into the council meeting and sidetrack everyone away from the humdrum business on the agenda. Diversion and distraction. And victory was his. And even the newspaper editor was hog-tied.

Feeney looked at his notes:

- Spencer. Merit system. Powell quotes.
- Need quick interviews: Peace, Powell, Spencer.
- Brahnler?
- Fuck Brahnler.
- No, get him to respond to something.
- No, fuck Brahnler.

There had been so many times his meeting notes looked like this he might as well just create a fillable form. But, for the first time, he wasn't as bothered as he usually was.

Because he had bigger fish to fry.

Anyone looking at Feeney during the meeting would have believed he was assiduously taking down everything he heard, evidently set to write a major article about all that. But if they had looked closer, they would have seen that the council-meeting notes were all made in a narrow, ruled-off space. The rest of the page was given over to an outline development of the school bond issue.

He had lists of names of people he needed to talk to. He

needed official confirmations, and access to papers. And he would have to push people like Peace beyond even the material he'd given at the coffee shop. It had been informative, in a general way. But it didn't have the hard figures. The impact. Or the most important thing of all: the cost.

That was what would blow it all wide open.

Feeney knew Peace and all the other members of the council wanted to control the flow of information, waiting for the right moment. Prepare the town opinion. But that wasn't Feeney's problem.

Looming larger than any other consideration, town opinion, town welfare, town reaction, was simply the need to get this all out, correctly and completely, before Donald Jansen did.

The first paper out of the chute would be the one everyone turned to.

Feeney figured that, what with Peace's hesitation and Barnwell's inability to create a public narrative, it would take another week to get that first story lined up.

Or so he thought.

Because at just that moment, with Feeney thinking the meeting was done, Brahnler dropped much more than just a grenade, and it was probably the thing he'd waited the entire meeting to say.

"But that's not the only thing," Brahnler said, still standing. "Other things are going on that are known but not known. Things the taxpayers are going to find out about soon enough which even the town, or the so-called newspaper, can't hide anymore."

Brahnler looked over at Feeney again.

Feeney lifted his chin. He didn't want to raise his hand, and suddenly become a permanent part of the town's record, but it was an obvious invitation for Brahnler to be less cryptic.

"What?" Brahnler said. "It's no secret. There's a bond issue being prepared. But it isn't just your usual, once-every-five-years public squeeze. This time, there's a big difference." He made a knowledgeable smile. "A big difference."

Feeney's eyes narrowed.

Brahnler nodded back. "That's right," he said. "You know the expression: Where there's smoke…"

He gave another look at Feeney and then sat down.

Feeney looked over at the council table, and didn't see much happiness. Peace and Powell were looking at each other as though having a silent exchange. The council members looked back and forth from each other and then to Brahnler.

And all of them, as well as Peace and Powell, at one point or another came to look at Feeney.

Feeney looked back at all of them, stood up, held his notebook in front of him, pointed at it, and then pointed toward the door.

They all knew where he was going, and where he would be waiting.

Chapter 30

The Scoop

IT wasn't for nothing the paper always came out the day after the council meetings up and down the valley. Outside of advertising considerations, that is. It ensured that Parker's papers always had the first run at any main story.

Generally, Feeney would have his notes and could type everything up while Mrs. Hagy was going through the regular stories. But this one meant an all-nighter.

After the meeting, Feeney had gotten everyone into Peace's office, told them what he was going to write, and got them to confirm everything he was saying on record. He also got Peace to turn over a letter confirming the rumor.

The school risked getting red-tagged. Officially. A fire hazard which, if not addressed within six months, would end in closure.

Pure and simple.

He even got all the papers with the Fire Marshal's recommendations concerning safety features, entailing extensive remodeling of the existing structures.

It cited razing as a particularly efficient solution.

Right from Peace's office, Feeney called the town's volunteer fire chief, Dale Hilsop. "Were you there for the inspections, Dale?" Feeney asked, looking at Peace and the others as he spoke.

"Yeah, I was. I had to take off half a day."

"Have you seen the report?"

"No, just the recommendations for the department."

"Which are?"

"It's five sheets long, Pat."

"About what?"

"About how, if we had to go in, what our main priorities would be depending on where the fire started."

"Do you have a copy?"

"Peace does."

Feeney smiled. "Perfect, Dale. Have a good evening."

He hung up the phone, and then looked at Peace and Powell.

He wrote until nearly four in the morning, the material consisting of paragraphs cut, rearranged, and taped together, so that some sheets were fifteen or twenty inches long. Mrs. Hagy would just have to type her way through all that.

It was immense for a first article. Easily two thousand words, about seventy column inches, which would have to be bounced across several pages. Which would also mean digging out some stock photos for each page. But he had to do it, to make sure he had the entire scoop and left Jansen nothing to better. He wrote about all the details. The cost, the regulations, the inspections, the condition of the school. And then he wrote about the impact on people. As he was writing that he knew he was suddenly writing the most important part, and out came the scissors and tape. And once he was done, he moved all that up to his lead. If the school failed, the high school kids would be bused down to Monroe for a while.

On a secondary note, which became a second lead, it wasn't certain that if the high school disappeared, the district wouldn't just be absorbed by the bigger one down valley.

It was maybe a more subtle point, but it meant not only would the kids have to get bused down the highway, but decisions concerning the school district would end up as much in the hands of voters in Monroe as in Sultan.

Even Feeney cringed as he wrote that.

There were a lot of things he couldn't write about. One was how Barnwell had confided, with a remarkable openness, that if the district disappeared, his career would pretty much be over.

School districts don't hire superintendents who manage to lose school districts.

179

His ass was on the line.

And he couldn't write about how Peace hated having this sort of bond issue to prepare, where it wasn't just a question of yes or no, but literally a matter of changing the fate of the town. Taxes were always better off left in the realm of personal choice. This one was a gun to the head.

Feeney, as he was writing, came to see things a bit differently. He came to think both Barnwell and Peace were in better shape than their fears suggested.

For most public figures, an unimpeachable position of being on the right side of an issue was rare, newspaper editors included. But this issue was clear. The school was unsafe for the students. And if it wasn't fixed, the town risked losing its educational independence.

He brought that out, and backed it up with all the details, and made sure everything was verified and confirmed with quotations from documents. He wanted nothing left open to innuendo bordering on opinion.

It was a lot of writing, but it was also good writing. As good, or better, Feeney thought, than the flood story.

It showed the impact, and it would have an impact of its own. A clear and obvious impact.

There was no way Jansen could come anywhere near this.

Chapter 31

No Taxation... Period

THE paper came out a day later and disappeared from distribution points so fast they had to run another printing. Parker was delighted. Feeney was relieved. But it wasn't until two days later that the real impact hit.

The man stood in front of Feeney's desk, watching him. Feeney stared at the ads he had before him on the desk. Just the size of the ready-made ads was enough to give him pause. But taken together—size and number—they left Feeney speechless.

He looked up at Bob Hawthorn, a rangy man who'd retired from state work and had moved up there from Olympia. Up to that moment, Feeney had only known him as a man who had bought a small farm and came in once in a while to place a small classified ad for help, or tools, or a tractor, and joke lightly about how buying a farm, that common retiree decision, was as bad as buying a boat. It guaranteed virtual enslavement.

Feeney had liked Hawthorn from the start. He was a self-contained, self-reliant sort of man and Feeney had always thought that if he could get him to sit down and have a cup of coffee they could end up being friends. But here, Feeney was getting no chance.

All he'd got that morning from Hawthorn was a dry hello and a manila envelope thrust across his desk.

The ads, evidently created in a print shop somewhere and sporting the usual cheap stock images of patriotic America, full of flags and mothers and fathers with their children gazing proudly off toward some heart-stirring horizon, were large-font paid rebuttals of everything Feeney had written about the school bond.

Not only were they big, but they were also wordy, like mini-articles. Unlike the usual run of negative political ads that took one idea and made it as invincible as possible, these were discursive. Each had several negative points followed by a written paragraph. None of it, however, discussed the school situation. They were all about taxes.

From a strictly professional point of view, the ads weren't very good in either concept or visual impact. But impact wasn't what Hawthorn, as president of a little committee he'd set up, saw as the need. He obviously felt the paper couldn't provide what he considered fair coverage of the issue. So he was going to do that. In effect, he was buying himself onto the paper as a stringer reporter.

Feeney had seen things like this before, people buying the space to launch personal rants. But this… they were just so damn big.

A third of a page.

Multiplied by five.

Five huge declarations that the school bond was not only unneeded, but unconstitutional and undemocratic. He didn't actually use the words communism or socialism but it wasn't far. Taxes.

Feeney set the ads down on the desk and looked up at Hawthorn.

"It might be cheaper, Bob, for you guys to just start up your own paper. Either that, or maybe just heave a bomb through the front window." He got no laugh.

"Don't tell me you're going to refuse to run them."

Hawthorn's aggressive behavior—he'd obviously got himself all steamed up just driving down there that morning—didn't have any effect on Feeney. He'd tried to be polite, even show humor, but now he decided to match Hawthorn's unwarranted sourness with detached indifference. He set the ads down and looked up at Hawthorn coldly. "Just for your information, I can refuse anything I want. I won't, but I can."

"No, you cannot," Hawthorn said. "I know my rights."

"Do you now?"

"You can't deny equal time to a political issue."

Feeney got up and went over to the coffee maker where he began loading scoops of coffee into the drip dispenser. Hawthorn had been waiting for him even before he got up there to open the office. He slapped the coffee maker closed, punched the button and spun around to face Hawthorn. "That applies to political parties. Which political party is this, Bob? Are you registered? And which political party do you think you're debating with? I'm not one. The town or the school district isn't one."

"I don't know what you're talking about."

"No doubt, but it doesn't matter." Feeney shrugged. "We'll run these ads, no problem."

Hawthorn frowned. "I'd love to see you try not to run them."

"Why do you keep saying that? I keep telling you we'll run them. What the hell's wrong with your hearing?"

Something about Bob's face told Feeney he'd scored a point. If Hawthorn was just down there spoiling for a fight and nothing else, Feeney wasn't going to play. He went on, calmly. "Listen, we could get into a big discussion about advertising and all, but... just a question: Seems to me this is a bit on the overkill side."

"Not from our point of view. We saw the slant."

"Slant?" Feeney laughed. "I haven't had time to work up my jingoistic, yellow slant, Bob. That'll come later. If you actually read this week's paper, all it consists of is setting out what happened. The inspection, the state recommendations, the administrative actions the town and school district are required to take at this point. I didn't write an editorial. We will eventually. But for the moment, it's just news. Just facts. Which isn't slant."

"Is it ever."

Feeney nodded. "I can see how you'd think that, Bob. The situation over there is so bad it doesn't give many options. And no options looks like railroading. But you guys aren't doing much better at the slant." Feeney pointed at the ads. "I don't see you proposing any alternatives. You're all so dead set against the bond you don't even address the question of the school—just totally blocking out what's written there. And refusing to see the article as my trying to provide some information and balance."

"There's nothing balanced there, Feeney. Everybody can see only one alternative. The school board's."

Feeney gave up. "I don't see any alternatives here either, Hawthorn. All I see is a bunch of well-off property owners who only give a damn about taxes."

"I guess you don't pay any," Hawthorn sneered. "So you don't have any sympathy for people who have to pay for some hyped-up... super school."

Feeney nodded. "I've got sympathy. You want to come up here and buy your thirty acres of land, that's your right. But you haven't bought an island, you know. Your land is within the school district, and you're part of the community. You can't buy fiscal isolation. You want to do that, move to Switzerland. But you'll have to pay property taxes there as well. It's called civil responsibility. For me, the question isn't taxes, but what sort of proposals the town and school district are going to make."

Hawthorn had calmed down, but wasn't open to any of it. "I pay my taxes. Probably more than nine-tenths of the people up here. We worked goddamn hard, both me and my wife, to be able to have what we've got today. We didn't take anything out of anyone's hands to get it. I'm not going to stand here and have anyone try to take it away from me."

"Nobody's looking to take your land. This is just a problem the school district has, that the town has to solve. Why don't you guys go down and get involved in the conversations about what needs to be done. I mean... to be honest... look what you're doing. Here you come through the door spending, what? Seven hundred dollars on one week's worth of ads? That looks pretty rich for people who can't afford a property-tax hike."

"You said you're going to run our ads, which you have to do anyway. So, all I hear is you trying to convince us not to."

"No, I'm not. I just..." Feeney blew out a sigh. "Fine. But for what it's worth, if all you're going to run are these anti-tax ads, you'll make it so I do have to balance things... against your arguments. Not only do I have to write about developments, but you and your group become a news item. Who you are, and why you're doing what you're doing."

Hawthorn stared at Feeney for a second. "That's against the law, like you not running these ads."

A total disaster. Personal, professional, diplomatic, political. Every level except financial. Dean Parker was going to love it. "Do you have any idea how much money you're going to spend?"

"We've got a pool. We've figured it out. We can run until next June if we have to, and will still come out in the long run."

Feeney laughed. "Christ, you guys are willing to pay thousands of dollars to avoid paying hundreds. But we'll be running them, don't you worry."

"You'd better, or you'll be seeing our lawyers."

That was the last straw. Feeney walked over to his desk and picked up the envelope and held it up. "See this? This is advertising. It isn't a political response to a political party. But even then, you know what? I don't have to run a fucking bit of it. This is a private enterprise, this paper, for one thing. And we're also covered by the First Amendment. That means we can refuse to run any story, or any advertisement, we feel like. You go call up any goddamn lawyer you want, and find out how fast they'll all turn you down."

Hawthorn was breathing heavily again. "Just send me the bill."

Feeney shook his head. "Before, maybe," he said. "But now that I know this is all about money, and considering how nearly two full pages of my paper are being taken over, you'll pay up front."

"You can't do…" Hawthorn began.

Feeney cut him off. "You sure aren't listening this morning. You want the ads run, you get me the money, in advance. And if you bring a check, it'll have to clear the bank."

Hawthorn looked at him for a long moment, then just nodded and walked out the door.

Feeney poured a cup of coffee and took it to his desk. He could understand Hawthorn's point of view. The school board and the newspaper were, in fact, going to be ramming this school-bond thing down everybody's throats.

He could understand, but he didn't have any sympathy. He and his friends didn't want to participate or find out anything. They weren't looking to show up at board meetings to find out what was going on and eventually offer suggestions. Give Barnwell some realities to work with. Instead, it was just going to be a giant detonation of extreme partisanship where no matter what happened people would feel cheated rather than that they'd managed to find some compromise.

Feeney took a sip of coffee, reflecting on how nobody seemed to like the concept of compromise anymore. And then he reached toward the pile of mail.

Regardless of everything else, those ads from Hawthorn's group were a windfall. Pure gold.

He wasn't ever going to say another word to Hawthorn about them.

Chapter 32

Down in Everett with the Boys

HE'D had only a few minutes to feel any happiness about the advertising before the phone rang.

Dean Parker.

Had Feeney seen the new figures on the Star supplement? No? They were eye-watering. Print run 23,000. But get this, the worst... Joel Myer had called to announce Safeway was cutting back to once a month. Parker hung up before Feeney could mention the Hawthorn ads. He hung around in the office a bit longer, finishing the mail, and then went out to his car and drove down to Everett.

By early afternoon, most of the Herald's older reporters were scattered around nearby bars taking the edge off the day. Younger and more ambitious men would either still be up in the newsroom working on feature articles for the Sunday edition, or else out doing research or tracking down leads. Young reporters down in Everett were always looking to move on. The older ones just dreamed of fly-fishing trips to Montana.

The long-time reporters always reminded Feeney of used rubber erasers with their dumpy forms wrapped in sports jackets and crumpled overcoats. Whatever elegance they once might have had had dissolved into little more than a movable coterie of human flotsam disciplined and conditioned by mid-morning deadlines.

Feeney parked in the Herald's lot and strolled back toward the Three Sheets Tavern around the corner. The place was a dive and terribly named, but it had the singular advantage of being the closest bar to the news building. When Feeney was looking for dirt in

Everett he never went into the newspaper, especially not anywhere before deadline. He would just go into the Sheets and wait.

Here it was well after deadline, and Feeney found the bar well populated with older reporters hunched over their drinks. He looked them over, then went and squeezed in between two thickset lumps of flesh known professionally as Charles Springer and Peter J. Feldstein.

Springer was the distinguished economics reporter, and Feldstein handled county politics unless Olympia was in session, which it obviously wasn't or else he would have been doing his drinking in a bar just as dingy as this one, down there.

Springer, noticing the activity at his shoulder, turned slightly. "Patrick Feeney..." he said. "Whose Irish parents simply had zero imagination." This was him being nominally polite.

Feldstein, catching the name, turned and nodded at Feeney.

Feeney nodded back. He looked at the mostly empty glasses of his bookends and made a circular sign to the bartender, who brought back a glass and poured the whiskey.

"Good article on Index," Springer said.

Feeney thanked him outwardly for the compliment and inwardly for not mentioning the pictures. Feldstein made up for that.

"Must have been rough up there," he said. "What happened? You drop your camera in the river?" He coughed a phlegmy chuckle. "Trying to recreate those shit-ya-pants shots of D-Day?"

Feeney smiled. He liked Feldstein. But they didn't call him Peter the Prick for nothing.

"It was a goddamn good article, Weiner," Springer said. Springer called him Weiner, or Willy, or Dink, or Pud, or anything of the like... just to throw some variety into a joke that was going on twenty-five years.

"Yeah, sure," Feldstein said.

Feeney took a drink. "I had time, you know." The reporters both nodded at that. "But I've got to admit, sometimes it'd be nice not to have to write up four-day-old news."

"You always say that," Springer said. "How many times has Oldermeyer offered you a job?"

Edward Oldermeyer was the Herald's managing editor.

Feeney examined his glass.

Feldstein shrugged. "You don't really give a shit about late-breaking news. You always get to be the reference those assholes," he jerked his head vaguely in the direction of the Herald building, "have to follow."

"It's never breaking."

"At least you don't treat it like that," Springer said. "That's to your credit. Not like that... you know that jerk up in Mount Vernon? You know the one, Dink? The shithead who makes everything sound like it's coming off the wire, even a week later."

Feldstein grunted. "To your credit. But don't say you don't get breaking. That school-bond story caught everyone flat-footed. You know, I'm supposed to go up and see Peace and... and that sup..."

"Ted Barnwell."

"... yeah, Barnwell. Tomorrow."

"Good luck with that. If he goes on for more than ten minutes, pull a gun on him."

"Hey..." Springer suddenly cackled. "Did you see Harrison's thing on the dog?"

Warren Harrison.

Feeney knew only too well this new addition to the ranks of the Herald's wonder-boy rookie squad. He had a degree from the UW, where he'd been an actual something on the Daily, and his articles had quickly caught Feeney's eye because, no matter what the subject—anything from a new fire truck to a train derailment—he wrote like it was a possible entry for a Pulitzer... or a job application to the papers in Seattle. And he wrote with The Style. It was called New Journalism, as in exciting, cynical and tough. Feeney didn't think of it as new at all, and called it Old Journalism. As in Yellow. With a lot of verve, all right. And occasional but clever plagiarism.

Very clever.

"You think I wouldn't?"

"What it looks like," Feldstein said, "is that he didn't think you would."

"Looks more like he didn't give a shit."

Feldstein tapped an imperative finger on the bar. "Why the hell don't you ring Eddie up and give him shit?"

Feeney, who accepted that journalism was both a public service and a scavenger economy, had been angered to see, after his own long piece came out about the pit bull case, a virtual duplication appear, with the improvement two weeks could make, in the Sunday "Issues" section of the Everett paper. Feeney knew that Springer and Feldstein would have loved nothing better than to have Oldermeyer discomfited, and Harrison discredited, by a charge of plagiarism.

"Anybody else notice?" Feeney said.

"We all noticed." Springer nodded.

"Then Ed must have noticed."

"That's not how it works," Feldstein said. "Hell, Thomasson did it to me all the fucking time. Every time I ran something on the prison scandal, I saw the same fucking thing, inside information and all and without accreditation, spilling out all over his columns."

"What did you do?"

"I screamed bloody goddamn murder, is what I did." Feldstein poked his finger defiantly at Feeney. "And that bastard hasn't had the guts to show up in Olympia in nine months."

"He was posted to Washington, Pud," Springer said.

"The point is, he's not on my turf anymore."

Springer shrugged. "Yeah, well. You know what. I'm going to go see him. I've got some other things to straighten out and this is just another thing Eddie has to understand. Anyway, it won't be any shock. He already hates Harrison that much."

"Why?"

"Why?" Feldstein laughed and he and Springer exchanged looks.

Feeney could hear the animosity but suddenly realized he felt the way they felt. With that stunt with the dog story, he now saw the Everett reporter as nothing more than an unethical climber whose ego outreached even his demi-talent in the demi-monde of reporting.

But Feeney could understand. Such were the results of a

190

business where, if you were ambitious, you could get to feel as though at any moment a hard-charging horde of younger reporters would plow you right under.

He could understand. He could understand all of them Barnwell. Peace. Brahnler. Hawthorn. Even Jansen. And even Harrison. They all had their rows to hoe. Just like Feeney had his.

But in terms of Harrison, it was personal.

And regardless of how he turned it over, he suddenly couldn't help half hoping that Springer would carry through his threat.

And bring down a load of bricks on the mercenary little bastard.

Chapter 33

Dirt

FEENEY was on automatic. Five weeks of school-bond coverage had yielded more than three dozen articles, with each issue carrying a major story and one or two related stories. Hawthorn's ads had kept pace, sometimes taking up more than two full pages of space. Counter sales had nearly doubled and classified ads had returned to their original numbers. And what was best, as far as Feeney was concerned, was how much of the PR churn had been reduced. Everything had improved. He even dug in places where he'd rarely spent much time. Finding, sometimes, surprising dirt.

That entire morning, he had spent up at the elementary school talking to those teachers about how the high school issue would affect them. He actually didn't need to go there; the story could be written without the visit, but he needed to collect appropriate remarks from the appropriate people if the story was to have any authenticity.

He left the school with the usual mixed bag. Most people did not make for good, pithy remarks or well-honed opinions. Suddenly faced with a reporter recording their words, most began aping other people's opinions. Feeney got around all that with the usual method of fabricating quotes, blatantly suggesting a few very large and glittering avenues of thought, or literally offering up a fitting expression which they would agree or disagree with, which he would then write in a way that made it sound like they'd said it. People were often amazed and proud at how intelligent they sounded in the newspaper.

After the elementary school he headed over to the high school to get some pictures. There, he wandered through the corridors aiming his camera, looking for something both grimy and identifiable. Especially identifiable. The flood pictures still hung over his head like a cloud, with Parker now having an irritating habit of looking at all the layout pictures in the Register before it got sent up to the printer. After a while, he stopped in at the head office, sharing a little gossip and job-related complaining with the two secretaries there, Flo and Edie. Flo had a huge mane of frizzy hair, Edie a sleek bob, and both shared two qualities: the first was that professional good humor and thick-skinned patience which had come from working with students for twenty or more years. The other was they were both chain smokers and so they had to spell each other throughout the day as one or the other went for a walk off school grounds to grill a cigarette. As Feeney loitered there, students came and went, some sent on missions from teachers, others with special needs such as a nosebleed or a headache; there were even a few sullen disciplinary cases sitting on hard chairs outside the vice-principal's office.

But that morning, a rare thing, both Flo and Edie went out of the office. And both of them had palmed their cigarette packs. It must have been a semi-declared time-out. He looked up at the clock, but that gave him no clue why this might be happening, and then he just looked around the office.

It was a classic public-school main office of little interest, with a room-length counter and those pictures of Washington and Lincoln, but it did have one thing Feeney—his inner snoopy reporter nudging at him—always stared at longingly: the immense, tank-like roll-a-file squatting next to the counter. Held inside its green enameled steel shell was all the confidential data collected on every kid since the day the school had opened.

In the past, when he'd talked to Flo and Edie, he would often idly turn the brass crank which spun a series of well-greased gears which in turn smoothly and easily rolled the big file hangers, each packed with hundreds of files. He would have loved to have been able to spend an afternoon looking through it... but with no particular aim. Just a professional deformation where curiosity had become second nature, looking through those files in the same way he did when he would pick up a crumbling, yellow copy of the Skykomish Register from his own back office. And certainly not with any malicious intent. He had no particular interest, for instance, in seeing Dick Brahnler's school record. In any case, he could pretty much guess.

And Feeney was again turning the brass crank, absently rolling the drum, when he suddenly saw a file that piqued his interest more than any other name would have. There, typed and tagged on the file, was the name Carey Williams.

It seemed a bit thicker than the rest, even that of Boyd Harrel, the join-everything, do-everything class president.

He stared at that file, and then professional shame came over Feeney. Moral shame. Legal shame.

But... such a thick folder.

He couldn't help himself.

He couldn't just lift it out, of course...

Between the desks of Flo and Edie sat a table covered with a variety of documents and files, including student files which needed to be put back into the roll-a-file. It could be easy enough to slip a file back in among the others. Before he even finished the thought, Carey's file was under his notebook and he was going for a walk.

There are few quieter public places than the corridor of a school when classes are in session. Standing at the far end of one of the hallways out of sight from the main office, Feeney opened Carey's file.

Everything in the file was highly confidential, and what he was doing was not only unethical, but illegal. He took his time.

The top sheets covered recent years and were bland. Personal information, medical information. Grades were middling at best, although she occasionally made a better showing in English. Nothing, at first, seemed to justify the size of the file.

And then, a first sign.

About three years earlier when she had been fourteen and before she had been kicked out of the Monroe school district, a

194

counselor had tried to put her into a special, advanced-level English class.

Feeney frowned. That must have been a complete mistake... unless the counselor had thought she was some sort of idiot savant.

At Sultan, though, she had shown no aptitude at all except page after page of bleak disciplinary records, many consisting of the usual stark and bitter remarks from teachers and other staff. Some of the remarks, Feeney noted, seemed a bit more bitter than he thought necessary.

Then came the section on learning aptitude and evaluation, and it was there that Feeney's mouth fell open.

Carey's IQ, last tested when she was fourteen, went right through the rafters.

The kid was stratospheric.

Somewhere a door banged and heels clicked sharply, but Feeney just stared.

Her results were astonishing.

English... he had expected that from the earlier note. But now, for History. For Math. For Science.

For everything.

Flat out, she had the highest scholastic aptitude rating of any kid in the entire school district—in truth the highest ever, going back across the several decades they'd tested for such things.

Suddenly, the bitterness of teachers' comments made sense, complaining how Carey never did her assignments, never read the textbooks, barely paid attention in class, but then came in and passed final tests with remarkably high scores.

Carey was a frustrating and horribly brilliant example of failure. What was worse, despite their best efforts, teachers could not reach her anymore. Whatever interest she might have shown in school was long dead.

Feeney saw a few counselors' notes, but all of that was speculation. And letters from her parents showed they were aware, but preferred she just be left alone.

There were also some police records, for a variety of things. And Feeney now knew she'd been kicked out of Monroe for having got caught, one night, breaking the windows of her English class.

And that was all.

It was true he now had a different way of looking at her. He knew a kid could be as much a victim of being at the high end of the bell curve as at the low end, depending on the circumstances.

He shut the folder, reflecting ruefully for a second about his own school career—where he'd been more concentrated on baseball and girls than grades—and made his way down to the office. Edie was alone, Flo most likely down some side street still inhaling a Lucky Strike.

He hung around just a bit until Edie turned her head for a second.

Chapter 34

The Beginning of a Fine Friendship

TARI Baron, the new PTA president, stood on the sidewalk outside his office. He parked the car, checked his clothes for bread crumbs, and got out.

"They told me you had just left the school," she said.

He pulled the door open and waved her in.

"You don't lock?"

"When I remember," Feeney said, flicking on the lights. He checked the coffee. Still hot. He pointed at it and lifted his eyebrows at her.

Tari laughed. "Oh… uh, no."

He took a cup and poured. Jet black and smelling like burnt rubber. "Nothing better than four-hour-old coffee."

"You should be careful leaving that on."

Feeney nodded toward the wall. "My neighbor keeps an eye on me. Anyway, so you found me. I don't remember telling them I was coming back."

"No… I…" She actually seemed flustered. "It was about lunchtime."

He grinned and went around his desk, motioning her to sit in one of the chairs. For half a second he hesitated, very nearly going back into the restroom to see what his hair looked like, but he resisted and sat down. She was that attractive. As she sat, he gazed at her a little absentmindedly.

Tari Baron was not a fashion-plate beauty. Just a good-looking brunette with a figure that was the obvious result of exercise and self-discipline, topped off with a brilliant, wide, generous smile beneath intelligent and playful blue eyes.

Feeney was well aware of having fallen for her like a sucker.

Whatever she had been before, Tari was now devoting her time and energy to raising her three children, managing a real-estate listing business she ran out of the family house while her husband, Frank, was off at his Seattle office, and, lately, very much to the affairs of the PTA.

Looking at her, Feeney decided her real beauty was in her confidence and general air of generosity toward people.

"So, how can I help you?"

"Depends," she said, pushing a bunch of papers toward him. He glanced at them. Another series of articles she had written about PTA-sponsored projects.

"You know," he said, "you don't need to talk me into running these. They're a legitimate part of what the paper prints. You can just drop them in the box."

"I know… that's not why I came down here. I really wanted to just have a talk. I don't think we ever really had one, and I wanted that."

For a full second his mind froze, but then he took a sip of his coffee, which not only smelled like but tasted like burnt rubber.

"I just wanted to see where things were. If the PTA needed to do something. I mean, these articles in the Register, they're so great. They really are, Patrick. All of us think they're just fantastic and make those horrible ads of Bob Hawthorn's look just stingy and mean."

Feeney nodded happily. "Well, if you're going to talk like that," he said, "I should tell you everyone I've talked to says you're doing great work with the PTA."

Suddenly, a small cloud of something serious went across her eyes, a momentary doubt, and Feeney realized that despite her seemingly bottomless self-confidence she didn't take things for granted. And as she looked at him, with that more serious, thoughtful expression, he suddenly realized she was one of the most

198

handsome women he'd ever seen. And he realized that, in fact, he'd just fallen into some sort of love. Not that it was that sort of love, like the impossibly heartbreaking one he had once known. But those days, anything was better than nothing. Faith, now Tari, and even Beebee in a way. All impossible, each in their own way, with Faith way up on top. But they were all he had, and he took whatever shades of romance he could get.

"Thank you," she said, somewhat quietly. And then, more brightly: "So is there anything?"

"I really don't know. I don't know to what extent the PTA could get involved. You can see for yourself not everyone feels the same way. I'm guessing there are some parents whose sympathies are more toward Bob's committee's point of view."

"A few," she agreed. "But my position is that we represent the teachers and school district as much as the parents, and our goal is to promote good education. And, as you've written, if we lose the school, it can't be good for education in the district, can it?"

"I'd think not."

"So, what are you going to write about for next week? Maybe if I knew in advance, I could coordinate what the PTA does."

Feeney, despite her attractiveness and a sudden bashfulness, couldn't help laughing. "Oh, sure. Coordination, interaction. Those are always right up there with my favorite topics."

She also laughed. "OK. I guess that was vague."

"Look," Feeney sighed. "As far as what I'm working on, to be honest I'm not really sure. I've got another meeting with Ted this afternoon and I'm... well, I never know with Ted."

"Oh?" she said. "I don't really know Ted. I haven't had much of a chance to talk to him. Just mostly the teachers. Ted's sort of out of our league over at the PTA."

"Ted isn't out of anyone's league, believe me."

He paused for a moment. He would have loved to launch into describing for Tari, a relative newcomer to the town, the way things worked. The personalities. The political undercurrents. Or even about the Register, Dean Parker, and all the rest.

Would have loved to...

"Anyway," he said, "there are plenty of ways this school bond issue is going to go over the next few months, depending on the information that still needs to come in. The final inspection and Fire Marshal's report, and decisions by the town and the school board, and tentative estimates. It's going to be fluid. The main thing is that nothing can be taken for granted... and because of that make sure people know the facts, and not just rumors and hearsay like it was in the beginning. And, at some point, I'll have to wade into it."

Tari looked surprised. "You seem pretty well... waded."

Feeney shook his head emphatically. "Oh no. All those articles, that's not wading in. That's just been reporting. What we haven't done yet is go on to the opinion page."

Tari stared at him for a moment, and then it visibly came to her. "Oh! True! I hadn't noticed. I guess just because the articles seemed to say everything that needed to be done, they seemed like they were boosting the idea."

"That's what Bob Hawthorn thinks, too," Feeney nodded. "It's a common illusion people have with the facts. When the facts support what people want to believe, they're true. When not, they're false, or wrong."

"I suppose. But that means at some point you're going to do it? Openly support the bond issue? I think that would be so... sort of obvious. And of course, helpful."

Feeney looked down at his desk ruefully. There was an awful lot that Tari didn't seem to know about the town and how, taking things into account, the local paper had a business model based on political neutrality. He decided to let her in on it a bit.

"These are decisions. My boss and I have talked a lot about all this. And we've come to an agreement that at the right moment the paper will come out for the bond issue. My boss... well, you know... he's a businessman. But he's also a member of the community, and takes education seriously, and he considers it the right thing to do. That the newspaper isn't just an advertiser, but contributes to the betterment of the towns. And that's the way I feel. But," he nodded at her, "this is a double-edged sword. I'll be glad, of course, when it comes time to take a stand. In some ways it will make things a bit easier. But in some ways, it's going to be a hell of a lot more difficult. You understand: I have to make sure this doesn't get too out of control. Make sure the paper doesn't just turn into drum-beating. The last thing I want is to have people think the paper's become unfair or untruthful."

All the time he'd been speaking, Tari had watched him quietly, sometimes nodding. Her eyes were now looking at him in a knowing, more collegial way, appraising and evidently agreeing with him. But also, there was something else. Something like admiration. She shook her head. "I can see now. It's more complicated than I thought."

"It can get to be a sack of knots, it's true," he sighed. "But usually, just by taking things a step at a time and not getting too dragged off base, we manage. So that's it. And I'd like your help, but I need a little time to get my thoughts more organized about it all. When I do, we can sit down and talk about it. How's that sound?"

He was being completely sincere about his request, and his mind was even beginning to move toward some ideas, so it came with complete surprise what she did next.

Standing to lean over his desk, she cried out something like, "You great guy," clamped her hands on each side of his head, and planted a kiss in the middle of his forehead.

A bit later, as he stared out at the parking lot, he suddenly realized—and not that it mattered—that he had no idea how long he'd been staring out at the parking lot.

Chapter 35

Ted Redux—Faith Excisus

"JUST to talk about this sometimes turns it into a Chinese puzzle," Barnwell admitted. "You want to answer one question, and you immediately think of three debate points of disagreement to counter with. That means you have to go to a more fundamental level with the question, explain that there, before you come back to the first level. But at the second level you also encounter disagreement, and are forced to go deeper, and so on. It is maddening, I can tell you." Barnwell smiled at Feeney. "Or maybe I don't need to. But allow me to finish my thoughts, show you what we're up against here... In each spectrum, you have various facets, each one spinning within its own sphere of influence, reflecting upon all the others and, in turn, being reflected upon. Any given choice has a counter-choice which may, in fact, lead to the same conclusion. We are thus placed in the position of having to decide between the lesser of two evils, which is unfortunate since we could just as easily be choosing between the greater of two goods. But the problem isn't there alone, but also in the fact that in the long run, no one will remember the short-term considerations, while the short-term considerations are, for the time being, going to take precedence, if not all, over the long-term. Some small considerations may seem small—football uniforms, for example—but then you take a larger consideration such as... such as..."

A loud click stopped him.

Feeney, picking up his tape recorder, went into a rapid manipulation of it, punching buttons, juggling the cassette, punching buttons again. He never went to any of these meetings anymore without several cassettes. With the cassette turning again, he looked back at Barnwell and raised his eyebrows as though with intense interest. He'd already been there for an hour of this. The superintendent, thrown off track, gave Feeney an accusatory look. "The larger considerations," he went on, "... considerations of..."

"Money?" Feeney said helpfully.

It was like throwing a hammer into madly spinning gears. Barnwell came to an abrupt stop. He eyed Feeney for a moment, feeling, strangely, both insulted and relieved. Feeney, he thought, wasn't wrong with that casual cynicism, but he evidently didn't understand how deeply complicated all this really was.

"Yes," he said. "It's going to cost a lot of money. You see...," he paused, taking a breath.

Feeney knew better and jumped in. "Let me guess. Either there's the quick-and-dirty fix, getting the building up to code any which way, like installing sprinklers everywhere, or you go for glory, bulldoze the place flat, and build a gleaming new school on the hill. And you don't like the first choice but know how the second will go over with the town. Your problem then is to push for the best school you can without pushing the taxpayers over into a No vote. A one-hundred-percent Yes means paint and sprinklers, and another bond issue in less than five years. So you need to find a better solution, but one that would still get you at least a sixty percent Yes vote. Basically, you have to figure out how far you can go before you lose more than forty percent of the vote."

Barnwell was staring at his desk pad. "I'm going to really walk the plank on this one."

That was putting it mildly, Feeney thought. He gave Barnwell a sympathetic shrug. "Don't worry, Ted. First of all, you really do have the kids in mind. You're an education guy, at bottom. So, no matter what happens, you'll always be the good guy. You are the good guy, Ted. You certainly are, as far as I'm concerned. As time goes along, you'll have plenty of opportunity to gauge public reaction. My advice would be then to keep your options open, open this thing up to a public debate. Find out where that sixty percent is. And let people let off steam and feel involved."

Barnwell looked up with horror, and gave a hard laugh. Feeney, who seemed to have a certain well of humanity, although with a touch of cynicism, Barnwell thought, was also obviously as naïve as they came about this sort of thing. "Oh, no... no, no, no... I'd have this whole thing come down around my ears. I'd just be telling everyone I was incapable of doing my job. Balancing options, making decisions."

Basically, he was telling Feeney he'd be a laughingstock. Feeney didn't think that was true at all. But there was no way he was going to enter into a discussion of the man's insecurities.

Feeney nodded, and then suddenly realized if he didn't ask or say anything else, he could get out of there. "So," he said, "I'll be seeing you again soon to see how it's going."

With relief he saw Barnwell nod and agree.

But then, something bad.

When Feeney picked up the tape recorder and started putting it away, Barnwell pointed at it. "Oh, hey," he said. "You know I think these meetings are very important. Extremely important. Maybe even historical, if you see what I mean? I'd very much like to see a full transcript of our meetings. Given how much of what we've talked about—ideas and avenues I haven't yet fully organized—I'd like to read in print what I've said out loud so I can have a good basis to proceed."

Feeney's heart sank. Transcribing even the shortest interview from cassette was like getting your ass kicked. In hell. Here, he had more than an hour's worth.

Bad as that was, what was astonishing was that Barnwell might actually think Feeney had the time, or intention, to set down everything that had been said and sift through it as though every word he'd spoken was golden.

"A full transcript?"

"Yes, I would very much appreciate it. Of this, and our previous conversation."

Feeney pursed his lips, squinted at the superintendent for a moment, and then made a suggestion. It was a simple suggestion, but it also carried an important implication: from that moment on, it could become an ongoing condition of their interactions. Barnwell, after a few moments of puzzled agitation, finally nodded his head. Seemed like a reasonable request to him.

He pushed a button on his intercom, and Faith walked in, and he explained that Feeney would give her the tape to transcribe and provide them both with a copy.

While this was being explained, Feeney carefully avoided looking at Faith. When Barnwell was done, he looked up at her and held out the tape.

She gave him a cool look.

You think you're not pleased now, Feeney thought as she took the tape. Wait until you find out what's on there.

"Thanks," Feeney said to Barnwell as he stood up.

"That's what it's all about on this one. We'll all pitch in," Barnwell chirped. "Together, I think we can steamroll this one right over the top of the usual doubts."

Feeney paused. "Uh, Ted, I don't think steamroll is the best term we could use."

A tiny glimmer of worry came into the superintendent's eyes. "Oh! Of course not. I mean, but... what I mean, is that we'll have a good organization on this. A good machine, of sorts. You know what I mean?"

"Sure. Sure, Ted." He turned to go, and then remembered another thing and turned back. "One last thing, and this has to do with the newspaper. We're always trying to find ways to make a better connection to the community. After all, although we may not be the most profitable businesses here, we're one of the oldest, almost an institution. And what I want to do is set something up, with the school. I want to create a junior journalism internship program. Give any kids from the school who might be interested a chance to get some experience learning how to write stories."

Feeney stopped there. He could see Barnwell liked the idea.

"So, let me know," he said. And left. Following the old salesman's dictum: once you've got an agreement, get the hell out the door.

Faith had listened to all this with what actually seemed like interest. But the moment Feeney really looked up at her, she just glanced at the tape, and back at him, and walked out to her desk. She barely looked at him as he walked past. He saw she had put his cassette into her in-box, which meant she had no idea, yet, of what was on there. As always, he couldn't help glancing at her features, that long, fine nose, the wide, well-modeled mouth… the…

And realizing what he'd just done, his heart sank.

Whatever he might ever have let himself imagine—trying to start a conversation, see if there was anything at all, ask her to dinner—he could forget about all that forever.

He knew perfectly well what was in that in-box. Even if she had absolutely nothing else to do it would take her all of one day and most of another to type up that dour mess.

He smiled grimly as he headed for his car, wondering how long it would take before she would get over being infuriated with him.

Give her four or five days to cool off? Another four or five if he wasn't around there again?

Barnwell now wanted weekly meetings.

Feeney now formally put an X across certain ideas and conjectures.

Faith Rockford, in terms of any social speculation, was no more.

Chapter 36

Some Damn Thing

PARKER, following everything else, was now expounding on how Feeney was going to have to go confront Joel Myer. Feeney shifted the phone to his other ear, listening.

"So, we're losing the account?"

"No, no! Of course not!" Parker practically yelled. "This is about the planned highway development and the mini-mall."

Feeney made a face. "I know you're not kidding, Dean. But c'mon, you've got to be kidding. Jansen's now getting Joel to pay something for those ads, so we're not dealing with freebies anymore. And now you want us to give him freebies? You're talking about county projects that are ten years off, at best. We don't even know if there will still be a Safeway up there by then. So this is just spoiling Joel, giving him a spotlight for nothing. He's going to end up thinking his ad is the paper."

"It is the paper, goddamn it."

"No, it isn't."

"The hell. That ad represents our reputation."

Feeney couldn't argue with that. "I'm only saying that as long as our subscriptions are more or less stable—and they are, suddenly, with this bond issue story..."

"Stable up there maybe. Down here we're barely hanging on, with just under seven thousand a month now."

"But enough. As long as we can show that to Joel, he can't ignore it. I don't care how many copies Jansen is running. Ours are still paid."

There was a pause on the other end of the line, and Feeney waited, hoping. To no avail.

"I told him you'd be down there before closing, Pat. So I'll expect to see the copy by tomorrow afternoon. With pictures."

"Of what?"

The phone went dead.

The next morning, with his mind given over to a near stream of consciousness, he knocked out the article—complete with Joel Myer's smug quotes about Safeway's commitment to the growth of the community—in less than half an hour, his electric typewriter in a nonstop clacking flow, broken only by the need to change sheets of paper.

When he was done, he looked it over quickly and then threw it in his out tray. It was well written and it was a bad story, barely connected to any real interest readers might have. Which made it the same as most of the PR churn coming through the door. If it wasn't for the local angle and Parker's political needs, he wouldn't have put his byline on it.

He stared at the tray. He had everything there. All the notices, the regular town news, even Spencer's cop-shop churn, ready for typesetting. And all the ads in, including the half dozen or so from Hawthorn. All he needed was the main article.

He looked up at the wall clock. He had a five-hour deadline, but no idea how long it would take.

He took his phone off the hook and reached for a fresh sheet of paper.

Three hours later he sat back from his desk with a pencil, adding the typesetting markings.

Thirty-five inches, maybe not quite long enough, but if he needed to he could fill out the page with pictures. In any case it was good. And what was particularly good was that it was about an aspect of the school bond issue—some of the building problems—that none of Jansen's part-time stringers could have thought of.

It was becoming obvious Sultan needed a new school. This wasn't a question of if, but when. And the Register was moving closer and closer to the point the story would have to bleed over onto the opinion page. And Feeney knew, at some point, he too would become part of the story.

In a sense, it had been part of what he'd thought the job might mean. Being someone making a contribution to society. Helping, as the newspaper editor, to help the town achieve things.

And here, he was trying to help the town's children get a solid education.

It was the others, of course, who had the responsibilities and the knowledge, the administrative know-how to handle cost estimations, bids, project management, timelines, state matching-funds regulations, voter regulations, insurance packages...

But Feeney had the words.

Feeney stared out his office door for a moment, contemplating the softness of the grey clouds drifting slowly up the valley from the Sound. It was good, he thought. But not quite enough. He needed a bit more punch.

And then it came to him.

It was time.

Feeney flipped his Rolodex around to a number, then tapped his phone, resetting the dial tone that had gone dead several hours before, and began spinning the dial with his pencil.

It took him a while to wade through a maze of channels down in the Marshal's office at the state capital. Nobody could help him, though he knew almost every one of them could. But this was how it always was in dealing with Olympia, sand sifting in the Sahara.

He'd seen bits and pieces of the Fire Marshal's report, or more precisely, correspondence alluding to it. The time was coming when it would all go public.

The last thing he wanted was to be caught off base, and the best thing would be to have an idea of what was in there so that he could prepare the ground. Lay enough groundwork so that when it hit, nobody would be surprised.

If anybody asked, he had his arguments. This wasn't a political hot potato for the Marshal's office, this time around. Nobody's career was at stake. No elections were imminent.

Within ten minutes of call transfers, Feeney was in contact with a guy he actually knew: an assistant district supervisor named Kevin Short. Five minutes later, after Short had finished reading the key paragraphs over the phone, Feeney gave a low whistle.

"You said it's completely disinterested? Sounds more like screaming hysteria."

Short chuckled. "That's probably the best way to tell the report isn't lying."

"Jesus. I don't know. Your boss got a grudge against someone up there?"

"Nah.... He don't even know the Mayor, let alone the Sup. What this is, is what we call down here an antacid job. I mean, in a good way. You know... what with all the shit we sometimes put up with... some district over here is going to hand the governor seventeen thousand votes... a company over there is going to hire three hundred people... that sort of thing... reports get watered down until they wouldn't nourish crabgrass. Enough to give everyone heartburn. Get it? Then, once in a while, along comes something like this."

"Nice to hear our miseries helped you guys feel better."

"Well, for that, we actually think it'll help you up there."

"You'll have to explain that to me. This is scorched earth. The Fire Marshal is going to sign this one off with Zero Option. I've got the district Sup moaning, the town council's up to its political ears in shit, and rumor has it that a good part of the local businesses thinks the only way this town can be saved is to turn it into Disneyland. This is a favor? I see the stick, but I don't see the carrot."

"Nah...," Short disagreed again. "Fact is, that pile of unholy shit up there you call a high school would be a public danger even if only one person stood in it. With two hundred kids and teachers, you've got something nobody even likes to think about. Shit, just think of a few of the little assholes smoking in the boy's room... I mean, I hope not. Really."

Feeney picked up his letter opener and began tapping a shuffle beat. "Are any of these papers up here?"

"Sure, hold on..." there was a sound of paper shuffling and

then Short came back on. "And I'll tell you something else. This was a no-brainer. Even if that building is crawling with every stinking political disaster you could name, we would have slapped a red-tag on it anyway. It blows every code violation in the book and nearly invents three new ones. How's that for a lead angle? But I've got something even better. We've got a draft proposal for man-hour allotment to work on a new code structure, and it's been called the SCA. For Sultan Code Amendment. In other words, your town is going to make bureaucratic history. Got your pencil ready?"

Feeney spent the next five minutes meticulously copying down the three new situational code violations the Marshal's office staff was outlining.

"I can quote all this?"

"Sure, all you need to do is ask to see the actual papers up there. And there's no reason they can say it's confidential at this point."

"OK," Feeney said, and he hesitated, but then just got it out. "Listen, Kevin, can I ask you a favor?"

He heard a small chuckle. "Don't bother," Short said. "I'm for sure the only person you would have gotten this out of, and the only reason you did was because of that thing you wrote about the refinery. It made me look good and I appreciate it still."

Feeney nodded and looked up at his clock again. Plenty of time. He could get this written up as a side bar to the story he'd written. They fit together well enough. But only as a preliminary piece. In a sense, a teaser. So he could prepare the way for it to run as a full story the week after. Regardless of the teaser, he knew Jansen's people—not even the boys down at the Herald—would be able to get ahead of him. So all he needed was to find out where he had to go to get the report. He'd do that first, then come back and write.

"Good man," he said. "So where is it?"

More papers. "Where is it, where is it…," came Short's voice as he looked through files. "Oh yeah, here it is. Let's see. Item one, item two. Yeah, it's all there. We sent it up there. Easy for you. No politics. Addressed to Faith Rockford, administrative assistant to the District Superintendent."

Chapter 37

Caught Again

WHAT did she do, Feeney thought? Set her alarm clock for this? She stood in front of him on the sidewalk as though being out there at six in the morning was a completely natural thing to do.

"What are you doing?" she said.

"I could ask the same thing. But me, I've been going up and down the street checking to see if this is still on everybody else's porch." He waved the Star at her.

"Oh, that. Still?"

"Yes, still." He handed her the supplement he'd been carrying with him.

She opened it and looked through it quickly, then did something that surprised him. What caught her eye was the Safeway ad, which she lingered over for a long moment. He could see it. She knew what that ad meant.

"You're worried this is going to be permanent?"

"That's what they want."

Carey looked up. "It's not fair."

"Fair isn't always the definition of business. In the beginning, everyone has their place, but after a while… things grow."

"But you still have this Safeway ad."

Evidently, she read their papers. "Yes. But we don't know what this arrangement means. The main thing is, if this thing takes off and they start getting serious paid-subscription numbers, Safeway will be looking at a choice."

Carey looked again at the supplement, and then up the street at all the other houses. "But they're still dropping these papers off for free. So how can they get subscribers? I mean, I can't see my dad would change papers until, you know, his subscription with the Monroe paper was almost up. And someone would have to come around and get his subscription right from him."

"They're doing market testing now. They'll distribute free in some places and not in others, to see if people... having gotten used to them... call for a subscription."

"It must be awful expensive to print up all these papers."

"Not as much as you think," he said. "All it's costing the Trib's publisher is the salary of a special reporter, or the time of one of his regular reporters—which isn't that much if you're just covering the main things up here—and the cost of the layout, which probably means one other person who also might be regular staff. As for the printing cost, the money is in setting up the press. To get all these papers, all they do is let the press run for another twenty minutes with a few more offsets engaged for the supplement. The idea is to give this away as long as it takes to get people hooked."

Feeney was looking around the neighborhood, waving his hands as he talked, and then looked back at her. And at that he suddenly stopped. Carey was staring at him in open, adolescent admiration. And he realized, with a sudden shock, he was flattered

But her admiration was also the last thing he wanted.

Two things at once, and both brought on by what he had read in her file. Here was this girl who was leaps and bounds ahead of her peers and who had trouble in school most probably for that reason. She was shockingly smart and also shockingly off the rails. And somewhere, he'd wanted to give her an opportunity to be treated like an intelligent adult. She was certainly intelligent. But she was also very young. And that was the problem. He felt this absurd, white-knight desire to help her, but at the same time she was way too young. And very capable of girlish attractions for an older man she respected. Someone who treated her as an adult. Someone she felt she could trust.

It wouldn't take much for all that to go badly wrong. Not for him. But—and he could feel it as the most obvious thing in the world—it could end up being something impossible to explain.

"Never mind," he said. And he was about to just stop everything there but suddenly a quixotic thought came to him which overrode his misgivings. Maybe a pretty stupid idea. But on the other hand, the sort of thing Feeney was looking for. Some sort of redemption. For something. "Say. Do you like to read?"

Carey shrugged.

Feeney nodded. "I mean, if you're interested in how the business works, I've got some books I can lend you. Explains it."

"Oh, yeah?" Carey's face brightened.

"Sure," he said. "Come take a look."

He didn't expect her to come into his house with him, but when he stepped inside she was right behind him. For a second he almost told her to go back and wait outside, but went over to his bookshelves instead. He didn't have much left on journalism. A few books on editing, copywriting, and layout. One on reporting and writing techniques. Another on press law. And the autobiography of one of the famous muckrakers, Lincoln Steffens.

Four books. "Maybe too much?" he said.

But Carey not only took them, she looked at the rest of his books. "You sure have a lot."

"Not really. But they do pile up."

"And..." she paused and then frowned.

"What?" he smiled.

"Sorry," she said. "I was going to ask if you've actually read all of them."

She looked at the books again, scanning the titles, and she got another frown, but of a different sort. "You were reading these sorts of books when you were young, too?"

"Yeah, I'd begun to. But it really got going in college."

"Which ones are your favorites?"

Feeney smiled. "All of them. For different reasons."

"OK, what did you like when you were in high school?"

"Do you want to read a few?"

She nodded.

"OK, help yourself."

214

He looked them over and then took down a few. Maybe not the ones he had liked the best, but the ones that had stayed with him the longest since then. He didn't give her any from that one author that everyone thought was the best, but who really wasn't if you spent any time at all thinking about what, exactly, he wrote about. Which was himself. Or at least the impeccably faultless version of himself. She took the ones he gave her and practically ran out of the house, evidently with a desire to go straight to reading them. And Feeney, feeling absurdly knightly again, went to make his morning coffee and with his mind setting aside the mess he might have made, turned to another he had already made, knowing he would have to go... there... and dreading what he might run into up there.

Chapter 38

Good things

HE had figured it probably wouldn't be as bad as he expected. But it wasn't even that. The day before, Faith had just listened to his request, gone over to the filing cabinets, and taken out a folder. "Do you want photocopies?" she said, handing him the Fire Marshal's correspondence. She even smiled.

He'd just stared at her. "Uh, uh, no," he'd said.

"OK. Just bring them back when you're done with them. The town has the other set."

"No," Feeney said, still grappling with why she hadn't hit him with a chair or a telephone. "I don't need that. I just have to verify what I wrote has already been submitted to the town."

"Have a seat. Would you like some coffee?"

Feeney shook his head, sitting down there in the reception. It took him a full minute to pull his mind from his surprise at the Suddenly Friendly Lovely Faith, to read the file. But when he did, it confirmed everything, and more.

One thing was clear. If there was any political gain to be made, he could see the Fire Marshal wouldn't be going empty-handed into any committees in Olympia this year as far as administrative code reform was concerned. He looked through those reforms. They were technical, but he could make them understandable. And so they were newsworthy. He went into absolute concentration, taking notes and flipping pages, and had a minor shock, when he finished, to look up and find Faith watching him in quiet contemplation.

He stood up and took the files back to Faith.

"Thank you," he said. "That's all I needed for right now. But I can also see there are other things I can use. I don't want to take them with me. I'd prefer they stay here. Safer."

Faith took them and gave him another smile. That glorious smile. Feeney almost sighed like a schoolboy.

"As you wish," she said. "So... I guess we'll see you next week."

"That's right." He turned to leave, but then couldn't help himself, and turned back to her. "Listen, um... I'm sorry about that cassette. I mean, I know what that's like, to do that, and..."

"It's OK. It's OK," Faith said.

"I figured you'd never speak to me again."

Faith laughed, a much huskier laugh than he would have expected from her elegant frame. "I did hate you, pretty much," she said. "But..." She made a sort of quizzical look.

"What?"

"But as I was transcribing it, and listening to the conversation And... OK. I know, and you know, what Ted can be like."

"Oh, yeah. Well, as to that..." Feeney grinned.

"But what was nice, though, was listening to how you spoke to him. I don't know if you're like that with everyone. But you're really nice to him, despite all that. Helpful. And sometimes really funny, even though I don't think he knows when you're being like that. I think that remark you made about... you know, the Homecoming Dance...?" The memory of whatever he'd said caused her to laugh again.

Feeney couldn't remember what he'd said, but smiled.

"Anyway," she went on, still amused. "A few of my friends, some teachers... it's gotten around. I couldn't help it."

Feeney's eyebrows went up. "You know, that's..."

She shook her head. "Don't worry, Patrick. My friends aren't gossips."

He got back to his office like he was floating, feeling his heart go pitter-pat. Pitter-patter Pat.

He'd gotten all his articles finished and ready when Tari Baron came in to drop off the school breakfast program information.

"Hi, Pat," she said to him. "I know it's getting late and I thought

I'd better run this in here before you skulked off somewhere again."

"Thanks," he said, feeling appreciated for the second time that day. Wasn't life just swell, he thought. As he opened the first brochure, she plopped herself down on the wood chair and swiveled in creaky playfulness there as he began to scan the information. The brochures were all government-issue material, National Education Association, or NPTA, on elementary school breakfast programs.

"It all says pretty much the same thing," she said as he flipped open another. "Kids who don't get something to eat in the morning hit a brick wall somewhere between ten-thirty and eleven o'clock. If they don't actually go to sleep, they might as well. Inability to concentrate, slowed retention rate, loss of abstract thinking... all on a small scale, but proven. And just because the blood sugar nosedives."

He saw that, but what now caught his eye were the sheets of paper she had provided. On each sheet, separated by wide spaces, were brief paragraphs in sometimes incomplete sentences, outlining the problems and solutions which the Breakfast Program was to address. They were astute and complete, and the way she had done it arrested him.

Tari knew exactly what she wanted to have printed. He could see she was fully capable of sitting down and writing the articles herself. He looked up at her.

"You don't need to be diplomatic with me," he said. "These are great and, no, I wouldn't be offended if you just wrote them out yourself. Frankly, it would save me time. And I appreciate it. I have to churn through all sorts of press releases. I get all the government agencies, corporations, businesses. And I get a lot of weirdo stuff. Sometimes it's just feisty seniors' groups but sometimes outright neo-fascist white supremacists... and then, flashy, camera-ready advertisements with no check enclosed. And a surprising amount of local stuff, much of it depressingly illiterate and needing to be rewritten. Which is just time, burning up."

"I can guess."

"But this is good. And I can see you've spent so much time making it so clear that there's no way I can screw it up. I suggest you just do the right thing and write it yourself."

She had started smiling, then chuckling as he went along, and by the time he got to the end she let out a full burst of a laugh.

"I'd even give you a byline, but I'm assuming you'd prefer this all seem to have come through the newspaper."

"OK," she said. "I'll do that next time."

He put the material into his in-tray and gave her a look. "I gave you the impression my ego needed that much stroking?"

"I figured you could give it the professional sheen it needs."

"Yeah, right." Feeney pretended to sarcasm, but he felt wonderful. For the second time in a single day he was being flattered... by a woman who seemed to not only like but respect what he was doing. And it didn't hurt that they were both wonderfully attractive. It made him feel there was something like hope.

He suddenly wondered... could she tell? Could either of them tell? They say women have a sixth sense for knowing whether a man is attracted even if he's working not to seem that way.

And he was working, or had been working, where Tari was concerned. Out of a pure sense of self-preservation... and for all the obvious reasons.

Tari had stopped laughing and had taken to looking at him, and then suddenly reached across his desk and touched his arm. "Oh, Patrick. Just accept a compliment, for once."

Her hand lingered on his arm long enough for his mind to lift free of his body. No, he wasn't drawn to Tari in any simple way. But it was remarkable, at least to him, that any attractive woman would find him worth noting. It helped.

She didn't stay much longer.

Feeney stared out the windows of his office at the parking lot. The evening had come on. He walked over and went out the door, stepping onto the sidewalk to get some air. And as if on cue, just over the top of the Douglas-firs beyond the Delicate Egg, a star appeared. His star. He decided it was his star... rising into a pale, tentative dusk.

He stood there gazing at it, paying no attention to Claudine staring at him from inside the open door of her knick-knack shop. And then he spread his arms wide and embraced the faint but steadily twinkling light of the stellar omen. Two, in fact. Kindness and interest. In one day…

"Star bright, star light…" he said.

For a moment, he stood like that, then dropped his arms and turned back to his office. He glanced at Claudine and winked at her. "You never know," he said, pulling his door open.

Claudine screwed up one side of her mouth. "About you, you mean."

Chapter 39

Something

DEAN Parker showed Feeney his palms. "See any holes here?"

"It wouldn't be that bad."

"Try again."

"Here I am trying to do exactly what you asked, and this is what I get. What do you expect?"

"What I don't expect is all this pissing and moaning."

"I'm just asking you to show up. Rumor has it you're a business owner up there as well as here."

"Sarcasm."

"It's true. But OK, consider it a favor."

"I don't need to do you favors. I hired you."

"What's that got to do with it?" Feeney rolled his head. "I'm just talking about a bit of backup once in a while. Solidarity, Dean. I think it's a legitimate request considering how, any day now, you're going to have me putting my head in the noose on the bond issue."

"The merchants' meetings," Parker lifted his finger, "are your responsibility. Anything the paper needs to do to contribute to the Merchants Association is your call. It's your baby, Pat. You've got the blank check."

"Yeah, right. I'd like to see how that would work."

"Still smarting about Index, eh?" Parker now grabbed several letters off his desk, letting Feeney know it was to be a short meeting.

Feeney glared at Parker. "So, you won't do it?"

"No."

"Man, Dean. You go on and on about how we have to keep

our ties with the movers and shakers."

Parker set the letters down. "These aren't really movers and shakers."

"It's just one meeting next week, and then I've got the others up to the bond issue. It's a question of setting the right tone."

Parker laughed. "And what? You want me to stand up and tell them they're a bunch of boneheads?"

"No. Well, yes. The bond issue is going to go off like a bomb, and all they're doing is fiddling around with this town-image crap."

"Nothing's changed then."

"How would you know?"

"Last time I went up there, with Kirby—and I might add that he, too, thought it was a good idea—all I did was sit there listening to all their crackpot schemes. Everybody taking their own sides. Like that bar owner..."

"Tom Carlton."

"Asshole. Moron," Parker nodded. "And then all the others. With those people, Pat, the paper isn't a business. It isn't even a newspaper. It's just a bulletin board."

"It's different now. People are going to get warmed up. You've seen the ads, and the letters to the editor. The moment the town and school board announce the plan and set the bond issue, it's going to get really hot up there. I just think the paper has to be seen as more than just what you call it, a bulletin board. It needs to be seen as a presence, and you're the presence that makes my job take on substance, that makes me more legitimate, if you see what I mean."

Parker laughed.

"You afraid of getting lynched?"

"If the only voice, when those opinions start to run, is seen to be just me, I don't know what impact they'll have. They need to know the opinions are of the paper. People just need to be reminded who you are."

"Oh, no you don't. Don't start that shit. They know who I am. I don't have to go up and plant my butt in one of those Sultan Merchants jack-off sessions."

"That's not what I'm saying."

"So you're saying you don't weigh enough up there? Whose fault is that?"

"Oh, stop. There's a difference between the guy who owns the business and the guy who gets paid to run it."

"Goddamn manipulative," Parker said, shaking his head, "all you goddamn journalists. Just forget it, Pat. I'm not going to be coerced into going up there."

Feeney stared at him. "I'm beginning to see why Kirby told me he sometimes felt alone up there."

"And you can do the same as I told Kirby. Get a dog."

Feeney walked out through the back office to the front. There, he sat down in one of the waiting-area chairs and morosely watched cars creeping along toward Monroe's one and only downtown stoplight, making, right there, the exact sort of bad company Marlene wouldn't put up with. For long.

She did try to ignore him, but he finally got to her nerves. "So," she sighed out, "how'd it go?"

"Ah, shit."

"I told you not to bother."

"Sometimes I wonder why the hell he's even in the business."

"He's not that bad at it."

"He just sits in there adding up his balance sheet and writing his overblown letters to all his favorite customers."

"He's a pillar of the community."

Feeney raised his hands and his eyebrows. "That's exactly what I was trying to—"

The buzzer on Marlene's intercom cut him off, and he heard Parker's voice. "Is he still out there?"

Feeney looked at Marlene beseechingly.

"Yes," she said.

"Well, tell him to quit bitching and come back here again."

Feeney wandered back to Parker's office and stuck his head in the door. "I wasn't bitching. What do you want?"

"That merchants shit distracted me," Parker said. "You really know how to distract me. What I wanted to tell you this morning was that I don't like the way you're lining up the response to Jansen."

"Oh, OK. I thought it was something serious." Feeney weighed diplomacy, then dumped it. "You've got to be goddamn fucking kidding."

Parker looked up at him. "I'm not going to go around again on things like we've been doing this morning, so let me lay it out for you. I want deeper coverage out into the new developments. I mean, I would have thought these ads from that Hawthorn guy would have been a wake-up call. You've got all those new people out there on the Upper Monroe Road, and we don't have a hell of a lot of subscriptions out there."

"When you consider I've got to go to town meetings, cover this school bond, do the occasionally appreciated feature article, you're saying the two thousand I brought in, or brought back in over the last three months, is not a hell of a lot?"

"We should have four thousand."

Feeney laughed. "So now you're just going to pick numbers out of the air. Why not six, why not seven? Who the fuck knows, but hey, we should be doing way better."

"Whatever, but I'm not talking about drives. I'm talking about coverage."

"You want what, articles for suburban immigrants who think their front lawns have to look like fucking putting greens?"

"For instance."

Feeney gave his boss a menacing look. "Dean..."

Parker picked up the rival's paper. "I see here a pretty good article on the best type of ornamental trees to plant in this area. Pretty informative."

"House and Garden."

"It's interesting."

"You don't even have a garden."

"My neighbors do."

"You call crabgrass, dandelions, and hacked-at shrubs... gardens?"

"It doesn't matter what they have. Homeowners like that shit. And homeowners subscribe." Parker looked at the supplement. "But I don't know, maybe it is too much, what with all the rest. So much in town, outside town, and now all this political stuff. No real time. Jansen can do it because he isn't doing all these monster articles on the school and the bond like you've been doing…"

"And yet, Dean, he will, sooner or later. Last couple of school board meetings, he's had a freelancer show up."

Parker wasn't listening. "That's what the thing is. We can't give up any territory to him at this point. Got to cover all the bases."

Feeney stared at him. "Dean?"

Parker looked up. "Well, okay, Pat. Thanks."

"Thanks?"

"Yeah. I'll talk to you later." Parker reached for a black-bound contacts book and picked up his telephone.

Feeney stood there looking at him, frowning, but Parker just started dialing. When it began ringing out somewhere, he looked up, nodded at Feeney, and waved his hand.

Feeney made his way back up front again. Marlene gave him a warm, even inquisitive smile, but this time he didn't sit down.

The sun was now well up and bright as he walked down toward his car parked in the bank's lot. He'd originally thought that, once his meeting with Parker was done, he'd go in and say hello to Beebee, actually see if she wanted lunch or something. But now he just got in his car and drove away.

Paranoid? No, of course not.

And absolutely.

Chapter 40

Paranoia

"THE council has the same problem as the school board," Dick Brahnler said, standing up in the back of the meeting room with his forearms crossed like a couple of hams across his chest. "You people think you don't have to answer to anyone."

"You're forgetting," Tom Scragg replied from the council table, "that we got elected by some people from hereabouts. You might not actually know anybody who didn't vote for us but... weird, huh... somehow there was a majority that voted you out. And guess who we're answering to."

Brahnler wasn't easily deflated.

"That's not the sort of thing I hear when I talk to folks around town."

"Since when," Peace said, "do you let anyone get their opinion in about anything?"

He said it with a smile, and there might have been a laugh or two, but it had been a long time since town council meetings had anything light about them.

An old, bearded man sitting at the back raised his hand. "You know, Dick, the school board is also an elected body. Those people also have their backers."

Brahnler wasn't impressed. "I never hear anything good about them, either."

"Then where the hell do you spend your time?" Newton Powell said.

"You guys just can't accept criticism, can you?"

"And you can't stand to lose," John Porter, another councilman, said.

"I'm making comment as a private citizen concerning town business. If you or the school board, or anyone else, doesn't like it—and tries to keep me or anybody else out—you're going to have trouble."

"Nobody's trying to keep you out, Dick," Peace said.

"No," Brahnler said, looking around the room, taking in Peace, Powell, the council, and Feeney. "But I'll tell you this. Lately, it seems, it's pretty damn hard for anyone who has a different opinion in this town to get heard. Sure, I got voted out. But I'll tell you this... nobody has ever said they couldn't get a fair hearing from me."

Feeney knew that wasn't true. Brahnler and a few other council members got voted out not only for mismanagement but for ever-increasing levels of high-handedness.

"What the deal is," Brahnler said, "is how it's getting to be that just a few people think they've got the right to make all the big decisions for everyone else and not listen to anyone's opinion."

"Like yours, for instance," Powell said.

Brahnler nodded at them. "I can tell you all right now, you're going to pay. Same way the school board's going to pay."

"You mean, you aren't for a new school?" Scragg said. "Your oldest girl's the same age as my boy. You don't care if she's got a school to go to or not?"

"Not the one the school board and a few other people," Brahnler glanced over at Feeney, "think we've got to have."

"Since when do you know anything about school construction codes?" Helen Steinman said, practically quoting from Feeney's last article.

"I know what a school needs to be, like a lot of other people know, without having to be some architect from Seattle or Spokane."

Feeney was stunned. The bidding finalists were supposed to be confidential and yet here was Brahnler publicly revealing them. And even more astonishing, it was now being discussed openly.

"The Bothell plan meant moving the site," Scragg said. "And

the Longview plan didn't take into account a recreation field or that we wanted twenty-four- and not thirty-six-tier bleachers."

Feeney stared in amazement. It was all now completely in the public. He looked at Powell, who looked back. Feeney shook his head and frowned but Powell just lifted his shoulders.

"You're going to want thirty-six someday," Brahnler said. "And they have it so that it fit right over the cafeteria wing."

Details. Common knowledge. People had just been blabbing.

"The point is," said the bearded man, "we all went to school, Dick. But what sort of education do you or any of us know about that's going to help our kids now?"

Here again, Feeney was hearing a version of one of the arguments he had been running in the paper.

"Oh, c'mon," Brahnler said to the old man, but as he spoke he turned to look straight at Feeney again. "What needs to be so different? What's this modular concept they're talking about, that's all so damn important?"

Feeney had worked hard on that article. He would have loved to respond directly. But he couldn't, of course. Regardless of what he wrote, whether an article or the soon-to-be-launched opinions, he had to be a completely neutral presence at the meetings.

"That's something new," Peace said to Brahnler. "The interactive flexibility is something we never saw. The studies they've done show that no one domain is separate from another, and that the learning curve is better when there are natural... uh... connections to the place. In the modular way, you can transform the environment from single to multiple to open-room participation. We're talking about integral education with affiliations."

Feeney had used the word alliances, but it didn't matter. No matter how carefully he tried to write about it... make the concepts clear... when spoken aloud, they quickly became a garbled mess. This was a problem he hadn't anticipated, and now he was worried. Was the school board's position, professionally and meticulously well-intentioned, also incomprehensible to most of the town? If so, the all-too-clear message of Hawthorn's group—no new taxes—would carry the day.

The issue, Feeney saw, could end up simplified into a sinister symmetry. On one side, the professorial school superintendent, lost in layers of meaning, stubbornly struggling to untie the Gordian Knot. On the other, Bob Hawthorn, standing rocklike upon the most American of public positions as a property owner.

After all that, the council somehow managed to get back to its agenda. With relief, when it was finally over, Feeney made his way to the door. Deep in thought, as he came out, he ran directly into Bill Spencer in the bright corridor.

"Ah, Patrick, glad I caught you," he said loudly, with the rest of the council meeting's audience shifting to get around them.

"Hi, Chief."

Feeney caught how people were looking at him and Spencer, and saw how some of them exchanged what looked like knowing looks with each other. There was no doubt that, as Brahnler had insinuated, some people believed the town was being run by a sort of unholy triumvirate consisting of the town council, the school board, and the police force, all backed up by the newspaper.

Feeney knew that thoughts like that could make people feel paranoid. Make them feel that other people were wrecking their chances of having a life the way they wanted it to be.

And it wasn't just on one side.

For educated people, even if it was impolite to admit it, there was the distrust of the unenlightened. The unknown was less feared by this group than considered a challenge. But nevertheless, they could be made afraid, even paranoid, by just spending a few minutes imagining their future ending up in the hands of... what else could you call them... simplistic louts? It was the old truth: dummies wreck anything they don't understand.

Feeney knew his job was not to fall into that way of thinking. His was to provide information and understanding. If not, there was no hope at all. Walls, long erected, would stay that way forever.

But it would never be easy. The distrust went deep, and seemed every year to get deeper. Feeney had noticed how politicians were beginning to take advantage of that divide, working on the fears of one part of the population looking at the other, who always seemed to be talking in ways nobody could understand, doing things in ways no one could comprehend, making things nobody needed, going places nobody had any business going, and thinking things that didn't have any practical value, but ended up grabbing all the important jobs and getting all the respect.

With the result that regular folk got screwed.

Feeney knew they felt that way, and could see it in their faces as they passed by him and the police chief.

It wasn't just paranoia. And it wasn't completely strange that for a brief moment Feeney felt as though he was staring anxiously off into the dark night from the top of an ancient parapet, seeing out across the distant fields the gathering flicker of homemade torches.

"Yes," Spencer was saying with a voice one would use to hail ship-to-ship. "I just wanted to tell you how much I've appreciated your articles about the new school."

Feeney nodded. Great, he thought, just great. And he would have just smiled and left, but Spencer, as always, had plenty more to say.

"Of course, you know the police force has taken every measure necessary. Even though red-tag implementation is imminent, you can be sure the town's aid-related forces, ourselves and the fire department, will ensure the safety of the students."

"Thanks, Bill. Just... thanks."

"I'm so glad the school board finally got around to this problem," Spencer went on, some people now beginning to stop and listen. "We, naturally, have been concerned about the safety conditions at the school for a long time. I've noticed there's some opposition to the school. The usual grumbling. I'm convinced, though, that the intelligent people of this district will make sure this doesn't become a second-class town by refusing its very children a school system. I know this town, and its people, and I want to assure you, because I know how hard you've been working yourself to help pass this bond issue, that the sort of ignorance and mean-heartedness needed to defeat this issue simply doesn't exist here."

Feeney could see out of the corner of his eye that even

Brahnler had stopped to look at them.

Later, he couldn't remember how he'd gotten himself out of there.

It wasn't late when he got home, but it was exceptionally late to have Parker call him.

"Dean?"

"Listen...."

There wasn't much to it. Some bad news first, about how Joe Myer had said he was going to "hopscotch"—that was the term he'd used—his ads between the supplement and Parker's papers. And the second was simply that he wanted Feeney to come by the office in the morning. Again.

"This is getting to be a habit, Dean."

Parker hung up.

Feeney listened to the dial tone, said fine, and set the receiver back down.

Part 3

The Grand Alliance

More apologies to W.C.

Chapter 41

First Thing

As he came in the door, Marlene gave him an inscrutable smile. Really inscrutable. He smiled back, but inwardly was alarmed. Marlene was many things, but never inscrutable.

"Someone getting shot this morning?"

"Prepare yourself." She turned back to her mail.

"What..." Feeney started, but she shook her head and pointed at the hallway.

Feeney, to prepare himself, made several obscene gestures as he walked down the corridor toward the back offices, sending them on ahead like a telepathic message.

"Knock, knock," Feeney announced himself.

Parker sat behind his desk like a sated Buddha, fingers interlaced across his belly and not even pretending to work.

"We've really hit the jackpot, Pat."

"Have we now..." Feeney hesitated, and then just took a seat. Uninvited.

"Sometimes we get lucky." Parker glanced up at the clock, then down at his wristwatch. "Should be here soon. Eddie told me he was a very punctual guy." His eyes flicked towards the wall clock again.

"Eddie?"

"Oldermeyer."

"You've hired a reporter..."

"You could say that. A real corker."

Feeney grimaced.

"Who'd you get, Dean? The secret clone of Edward R. Murrow?"

"Practically."

"A guy could almost feel insulted."

"That's not what I meant. You're doing a great job. Just great."

"I'm getting reamed."

A look of exasperation came over Parker's face. "You know your problem? You need to open up your mind. This is going to be a good thing, Pat. You'll see. What you'll be especially happy about is that I'm going to give him the full range. You'll both share the news load... forty inches of feature each week, up there or down here, and a fifty-incher with sidebar every two weeks. You get the calls on the items, but with time, when he's got his feet on the ground, he'll submit ideas to you. You'll always have the final decision on anything from Sultan on up."

The guy was punctual, all right. And overdressed. Gray pinstripes. He looked more like talking-head material than a print reporter, except for the stylishly overlong hair. On TV, everyone wore The Helmet. A professional smile. And a decisive way of nodding his handsome head and squinting his eyes to convey seriousness and intelligence. All that, and he was only twenty-seven. Warren Harrison, Wunderkind. A hand stuck out. "I'm really looking forward to working up here."

"No kidding?" Feeney stared at the hand, then finally took it. Who the hell, he thought, wore pinstripes? He spoke to Harrison, all the while looking at Parker. "I would have thought a guy your age would prefer the pace and size of a daily."

Harrison laughed like a baritone from Rigoletto. "Not at all, Pat. The weeklies are really hot these days."

"They are?" Feeney looked over at Parker again.

"Everybody's getting into it. It'll really be a pleasure to work with and learn from someone like yourself."

Feeney looked over at Parker. Again. Parker grinned back happily. "Isn't this great?" he said. "We can now easily say we have the most high-powered news team in the valley."

Harrison squinted and nodded. "I only hope I can be of help

up here. You know, Dean, I was thinking about what we talked about last night. I think I have some ideas that will really help you get out in front of the Star over the next few weeks."

"Great," Parker said. "Well, I know you've got some things to get done down in Everett, but try to be back later this afternoon so Pat can get you up to speed on the main issues up valley. For one, the school thing. That's going to be a big, big story and we've got to make sure Jansen won't find a crack to get through. We need to get it all, but also build up a heavy load of regular things. A lot of area to cover. Very different communities, and each one with its own way of doing things."

"Sure, boss," Harrison said.

Parker laughed. "Just don't get us hauled into court."

They all laughed, long and loud at that, Feeney the longest.. *har, har, har*...

Parker picked up a couple of pieces of paper off his desk and handed them to Feeney.

"Here," he said. "Just write up the appropriate announcement for Warren being hired. You know... create some excitement. You know how."

Feeney took the sheets. It was Harrison's résumé. He nodded.

"Sure, *boss.*"

Chapter 42

Second Thing

FEENEY, even without the Harrison surprise, had expected a yin-and-yang kind of day. The yin was that Ted Barnwell wanted an impromptu meeting.

Him, too.

But the yang, of course, was another opportunity to say hello to Faith. The last two times he'd gone, he'd found himself getting into conversations with her, easy, almost natural, and he was beginning to wonder how he might slide in some sort of out-of-office meeting. He had a couple of ideas. She knew he needed help in wading through some town documentation, and if he could get her to go down to city hall... there was the coffee shop across the street... and...

Unfortunately, she was out for the day, and all there was, was Ted.

That evening, he made himself spaghetti for dinner. He rarely cooked, although this wasn't really cooking—boiled pasta and a jar of Bolognese sauce. But he needed something to accompany the bottle of red wine he'd bought on his way down the valley.

He ate in his living room, in the growing dark, contemplating the different ways people coped with the day-to-day necessities of life. Vacations seemed to be the main thing. The idea of getting away from it all, as they said.

When people said that, Feeney thought, what they really meant was that they wanted to get away from each other. As far away as possible.

Either that, or they threw themselves into some hyperkinetic swirl of activities, drowning themselves in such a sensorial overload that they forgot everything.

The yin of vacations, the dark side. He'd known guys whose dream vacation consisted of staring at the big plastic titties of Las Vegas showgirls, throwing all their money away at craps tables, eating monumental platefuls of American Face Chow, and drinking like suicidal sailors.

And then there were others, drawn back to nature. Back to the land. As though for some brief moment living in the existence of primal earth. Yang.

Feeney picked up his wine glass, drank it off, and then poured it full again. And the spaghetti could have been worse.

Feeney thought about it. Maybe, probably, he was more drawn to the pastoral life. Not that he was fundamentally anti-social. But it just seemed so peaceful.

And maybe that was the thing.

Live in a world where every day you'd just have whatever it was you had to do, to do. And not the sort of day where, by the end of it, you wouldn't find yourself drinking a bottle of red wine and eating a plate of fucking spaghetti, feeling utterly betrayed.

Harrison. That had been one thing.

But then Ted.

Yin and yang. But here, the contrast was that where Parker fully knew Feeney was going to feel betrayed and angry, Barnwell had actually thought he'd be thrilled.

And why not?

Bring in a political consultant to map out the town's, the school board's, and incidentally the paper's way of presenting the informational campaign for the bond issue.

Ted Barnwell, maybe not as Buddha-like as Parker had been, had nevertheless given off the aura of self-satisfied contentment and serenity.

He'd cut the Gordian Knot.

Technically, Feeney could not blame Barnwell for anything. The superintendent was just doing everything he could to get the bond issue passed, which included somewhere recognizing he wasn't fully up to the task.

Feeney felt a disappointment with himself. He knew he was being unreasonable in his reaction to the hiring of a political consultant.

But why, oh why, did it have to be Tickler Steele?

Chapter 43

Sympathy

"HAR, har, har...!"

Feldstein laughed with a hell of a lot more sincerity than Feeney had in Parker's office.

Feeney stared off toward a corner of the ceiling.

"Both of them!" Feldstein wheezed out over the telephone. "So Parker's is where Harrison landed. I thought for sure the kid would've had to go out of state, the way everyone felt about him. And there he is, ba-da-boom... out there in East County."

"Why didn't Eddie just fire him?"

"Oldermeyer's too kind-hearted for that."

The irony oozing from Feeney's earpiece made him grimace. "Yeah, right."

"C'mon, Pat. You can get it. A kid like that is worth his weight in machine-gun bullets."

"Eddie's got that much of a grudge against Dean?"

"Don't be a sap. Oldermeyer's got a grudge with anyone you want."

"So it wasn't a setup?"

"Nah. Harrison did get a general ref out of Oldermeyer. But you can imagine it was a doozy. A real work of art. Oldermeyer was one hell of a writer in his day. Beautiful, just fucking beautiful. When he felt like it. I'll bet he set aside a whole afternoon to write that letter of recommendation for that little bastard."

"I don't need to imagine. Parker made a point of having me read it."

"Oh, har, har, har!"

"You think this is funny, Peter? So now we've got that little bastard up here."

"Hey, look on the bright side," Feldstein said. "At least he won't be plagiarizing your shit up there, right under your nose."

"Maybe I'll turn him loose on county politics."

A slight pause on the other end. "Now, Pat. I didn't do this to you. And, anyway... Parker would notice."

"Yeah. Just like Oldermeyer noticed."

"Okay, okay. Never mind. I feel for you, Pat." Feldstein's sympathy was real, at least. "And on top of that, Tickler Steele. He'll jolly things up for you. Got anything I can use?"

Feeney didn't mind Feldstein having gotten the shovel out, even though it still rankled that the Herald's reporter found Harrison's presence up there at Parker's funnier than anything else.

"The opposition's already in high gear."

"Yeah," Feldstein said. "Interesting how that always organizes faster than the serious side does. Keep your eye on how fast people are flocking to the no side. It's something you can use."

"To be honest, I don't know how they're going to get this bond through."

"Oh, that's looking practically impossible, given Ted." Feldstein had met Ted. "Actually, it's sort of strange Steele's stepped onto this one. Usually, he only goes in when there's half a chance. A school bond, I mean, usually only goes through when you've got a lot of new people. But out there, not much has changed, I don't think, for... what... about twenty years now. Is the school full?"

"To cracking. And the elementary, too."

"Oh, well, maybe there's a chance. It doesn't stand out much to me."

"You know, I thought Steele just did it for the money."

"Yeah, but he's got to keep his win column up, too. I'm going to take a look around. Maybe there's another reason. What are they paying him?"

"Rate. Or that's what the superintendent says."

Feldstein laughed. "If it's anywhere near two thousand a

month, that's more than twice what anyone else would get."

"Shit."

"Well, I don't know. He can always claim it was as near a dead loss as you can get—show how dead it was and how close he got it anyway. Something like that."

Feeney blew out a sigh. "Talk about the end justifying the means."

"If I were you, I'd attach Harrison to him like a limpet mine. They'll fall in love."

"No doubt. But would I want that?"

"C'mon, Pat, where's your sense of fun?"

Chapter 44

Mona Lisa

AROUND a dozen applied for the four spots. Feeney selected three of the least bad to accompany the shoo-in.

Of the three, one was a dairy farmer's youngest boy, dreaming there could be something more to life than endless udders, yet resolutely writing about nothing except the 4-H and FFA clubs. Another evidently wanted to be a sports writer and indeed, with the casual mangling he gave the English language, he showed the distinct talents needed to succeed in that category of writing. He also had a knack for taking indistinct action photos of contorted bodies. The third one was a Sultan High cheerleader who was also the president of the French Club, an elected member of the Student Body, chaired the Fundraising Committee, was on the volleyball and tennis teams, took part in the Junior Chamber of Commerce, sold beauty products for Mary Kay, and made Feeney feel organizationally inadequate, socially unimaginative, and tired. She redeemed herself as a human being, though, by not being able to write three words in a row without inserting either an exclamation or an exaggeration. His hiring of her had nothing to do with her full civic dance card, but mostly because he knew he could count on her to produce the articles he assigned. Nevertheless, he couldn't help a twinge of resentment at how one of his internships had been picked up with the same expectation of getting it as she would have had applying to the Glee Club. And the fourth intern was Carey.

The idea was that the four would bring their articles to Feeney, who reviewed, corrected, suggested, and encouraged with as light a touch as he could find. As the first papers came in, he was not surprised to find that Carey's work showed some creativity. But she also revealed some skills in the bullshit department. Evidently, she had a well-developed set of tools for her fool-the-school-system act.

"You can do that with a history exercise," he told her. "Throwing out opinions nobody can really oppose, but you can't fake information any more than you can fake clarity. Just because you say it's clear doesn't mean it is."

This was her third piece, a short history of Sultan's first separate high school. Her face was tight as she concentrated on her marked-up paper. She nodded, and he could see neither resentment nor disappointment in hearing criticism.

"Do I need to do it all over again?"

"No. You just need to go through and put a frame of structure around some of these sentences. The conversational approach is becoming a convention, but you can't do it endlessly. You have to anchor it on the theme to give the reader somewhere to stand."

He pointed at the penciled connections. "The other thing is to try to keep your development more closely attached to the overall scheme I gave you, and keep the parts balanced. Don't stretch out any one section too far or you'll end up making the reader feel they've suddenly wandered into an entirely different article."

"Even when it's interesting?"

"If it's that interesting, it should be a separate piece. But another way is to weave your main idea back into the secondary material to keep that thread in the reader's mind."

Carey stared at her paper, nodding. Feeney hadn't guessed the extent to which she would become attached to the internship.

It had been quixotic, yes. White-knightish. But he might have guessed this sudden passion for something might happen. In truth, she had just been a kind of buried intellectual eagerness, finally ready for something to latch onto. And she was primed.

Several dozen novels, histories, or biographies had made the journey back and forth from his living room to her bedroom, the place she devoured literature. At first, the initial shock of entering the world of books had been rough going, having to develop the ability to dive into another world rather than being entertained by the frantic bombardment of electrons against a glowing plasma eye. As for the rest, Feeney was sure that with time a true interest would replace her crush… reality overcoming fantasy.

To give her material for a follow-up article, Feeney went back in the storage room and dug down through first paleolithic, then neolithic layers of old issues dating back to the time when Sultan's school consisted of a whitewashed clapboard building with, he'd been told, a tuneless bell, twelve stuck windows, a dusty blackboard, and fifteen splintery pine desks.

At first he was shoving things around alone back there, and then he suddenly was aware that she was now there too, watching him. He felt himself beginning to sweat. It was warm work, shoving around moldering piles of topical ephemera.

"Big flood," he shifted some more bundles, "wiped out a lot of the stuff between the early thirties and the mid-sixties."

"Completely gone?"

"Now only on microfilm and the bound copies at the library."

"So, not really a big loss."

"If you ask me, the real shame was that it didn't wipe the whole place out." Feeney could no longer count how many times he had been forced to crawl around in this yellowed mountain of moldy pulp, just to find a paper—for an embarrassingly high price—that possibly mentioned someone's long-dead great-aunt.

"I don't know…" Carey picked up a gray-ochre relic from the twenties and peeled open the first page.

Feeney knew what she was seeing. The Sultan paper, being the only form of news anyone up there could really get at the time, printed not just local, but state, national, and international news as well. Which had given a young Gig Shire the perfect right to blast away on every topic ranging from the surfacing of a local roadway to the bungling of the China Issue.

He stood up, there in the depths of the storage room, and looked back at her. Backlit by the light from the office, she could almost have seemed a much older woman… that light creating around her an aura, making her tight shorts and shirt nearly disappear into a haze. Female, but ageless, almost formless in the light—primordial. A Cro-Magnon Eve sending faint beacons of remembrance from the very dawn of a human civilization which, to Feeney's way of thinking, had not begun with the invention of writing, agriculture, or even fire, but with woman as the creative, nurturing primal—both bloom and fruit of consciousness.

For the males of the species, at least.

Feeney knew Carey still had that infatuation for him, even though she could now be distracted into this new interest. But the original seeds were there, and he knew they could flower at will if encouraged.

He was in no way going to encourage anything like that, but suddenly, in that darkened storeroom, overly warm now, he felt like he was falling into a chasm of nearly forgotten memories of youth. Of those early lovesick yearnings, which to his surprise could still be summoned up. Time had removed them to a different place, like a home-like country once visited to which he believed he would never return.

Some men, he was thinking, maybe even a majority of men, liked returning to that country, as though it were an opportunity to travel back in time and erase the mistakes made because of youthful shyness, lack of understanding, or simply misunderstanding or being misunderstood with erroneous assumptions, awkwardness, peer pressure, or worst of all, the pride of youth. The sorts of mistakes that let true love, or at least the earliest apparition of it, the purest, deepest form of it, if not recognized in time, slip by.

Feeney, though, just stared at all that as though looking at exhibits in a museum, stored away behind glass like toys, tools, and weapons from a bygone era. Simply, and weirdly perhaps, his ego wasn't much flattered by being the object of that tearing, tragic, first love born aloft upon emotions not yet tried. Unfired, untampered, and lacking the mettle that experience brought. And far from the real, burning, awful, unmanageable purity of first love.

Into which fountain of youth could Feeney dip, in search of something similar? As he looked at her, standing there, interested in the old newspaper but also emanating that aura, that ancient pull of attraction of which he wasn't convinced she was yet fully aware... he knew how easily he could let that backlit figure, surrounded by a corona of shimmering illusion as though an obscuring, concealing curtain, turn into that of a woman.

When in broad daylight she was a kid.

He had no desire for Carey, but she was setting off within him that lingering pain of a lost love, something he had buried deeply but imperfectly within himself in an attempt at deliberate amnesia... and hopefully for the rest of his life.

With an irritated shove, Feeney slammed a bale of ancient newsprint back into its dusty hole, and stood up, grasping several copies from a time before anyone knew or cared where the Maginot Line stood.

"This ought to do you," he said, handing them to her.

Warm, despite no exertion, Carey reached for the papers, her damp shirt clinging to her... to everything.

Feeney, of course, wasn't noticing that. Or, to be more precise, was doing everything possible not to notice it. And Carey, of course, was noticing that he wasn't very, very much not noticing. Which caused him to frown. And caused that small smile to come to her lips, that understanding, sympathetic, all-knowing, terrible smile.

The smile, the one any man who looks upon the Mona Lisa knows. Of Eve. Of Woman. Of Hope and Destruction.

He'd tried to believe, for a desperate second, she hadn't seen, but then saw she had. Of course.

Feeney got back out to the office, got a cup of coffee, sat down, cursed himself, and proceeded to have what he could only describe as a five-second out-of-body experience.

As though he was standing there watching himself just barely step out of the way of a landslide.

This white knight stuff, he was thinking... once Carey had finally come out, gathered all her things, and said cheerfully goodbye... wasn't as simple as he'd thought.

Chapter 45

Frank Baron

TARI'S husband, Frank Baron, could easily have been a great guy—on the strength of her choosing him alone. Feeney put a lot of stock in the concept of worthiness.

There was no doubt the guy had plenty of things going for him. A stock market consultant, analyst, or something or other—no one called these guys stock brokers anymore—he was a big, well-paid piece of beef of the Washington Athletic Club variety, padding well-exercised shoulders into tailored shirts and fashionable suspenders. And he had all the things, including, incredibly, a phone in his car.

And it was a nice car. Undeniably. If you were into Pontiac Trans Ams... which Feeney wasn't. Muscle cars, for him, were there in his personal dustbin of outdated bad taste, right next to Disco. But Feeney just couldn't stop looking at the phone. Some Motorola thing that cost God-only-knew-what, and was literally the first-ever phone available like that, it seemed. He was fascinated, and just stared at it, almost in a trance as he tried to imagine what he could do with such a thing, as the three of them stood next to the car in front of the Baron house in Sultan.

Feeney, shocked by the presence of such a monstrous idea of a telephone that could go anywhere, was actually embarrassed. As though asking questions about such a thing bordered on vulgar curiosity.

But Baron, seeing Feeney's fascination, was all too happy to fill in the sumptuously delicious details anyway.

"Just to keep from getting ripped off, I had to spend three K on the alarm to protect five K's worth of electronics," he complained with pride.

Feeney felt like an idiot. "I thought you guys just ran on pagers."

Baron smiled. "Pagers are for doctors. I need my office with me."

Tari laughed. "You should have seen what his Rolodex looked like."

"Actually," Baron said, laughing, "I still keep one around."

"Me too," Feeney said hopefully.

"Dinosaur Land, yeah? For the pocket protector guys. But, to be honest, only a fool would go whole-hog with electronics. I mean if it crashes, I can still call my secretary and she can get me back on line, pronto. Remember Bill Weber?" He looked at his wife, sharing with her a condescending look for whoever Bill Weber was. "Crash and burn, baby. The poor dumbshit couldn't find his dick in the dark without his Rolo."

Feeney felt Tari glance at him, but by the time he looked back, she was looking away.

"Different strokes," she said.

Baron sneered and gave Feeney a half wink. "Yeah, whatever. I just think a guy needs to be organized. I mean, in terms of worst case. I think you have to keep a backup system. For everything. Contingencies. Sure, you need the technology to keep up. Things move too damn fast otherwise."

Feeney was suddenly thinking about this increasingly insistent techno-world. Parker had salesmen coming at him all the time trying to get him to test out equipment. Desktop stuff. Everyone had heard about papers around the country trying out some sort of computerized method not only to write, but to make layouts. Some paper back in Philadelphia had been one of the first. But Feeney ignored it. Rich-paper gizmos right out of Buck Rogers.

"But you just got to make sure...," Baron was saying, "you never get caught with your pants down. I'm sure you know all about that, huh, Patrick?"

Feeney looked at Baron and all that frat-boy-corporate

complacency. "Pants down…," he said, "yeah… no… that's the best idea, of course."

Baron gave him a look and then a disdainful curl of the lip. "Oh, yes," he grinned. "The best idea." He had just decided Feeney knew, basically, nothing.

Feeney found Baron's ego something worth watching but also knew he needed to steer things towards the things they all had in common. That was the reason he was over there talking with the Barons in the first place. "We were talking about the school bond…"

Baron nodded. "Got to get moving on this thing. They're sort of getting out ahead of us. Too bad they already got the name, Citizens Committee, sewn up. Citizens is about the last thing those creeps are. And no response."

Feeney could have felt—no, he was—insulted by the open insinuation his articles hadn't been a match for the advertising, but he let it pass. "At least they didn't use the term taxpayers."

Another thing, though, bothered him more than Baron's insinuations. Feeney didn't agree with Hawthorn and as for his group's name he couldn't care less. But they didn't deserve to get called names. Creeps. He didn't want to get dragged into an approach based on insults that sounded like class warfare. And a strange one at that, considering that Baron was normally someone you'd expect on the side of the tax revolters.

Baron looked thoughtful. "Not a bad idea, actually. It could be really interesting to look at the tax rolls. What do you think?"

Feeney sort of laughed. "Oh, digging around in the county records doesn't get you that much. I mean, I've spent hours on end hunting down records trying to find where the bones are buried and, in the end, you don't end up with much."

"This could be really serious, though."

"So is what happens when you start digging around in the tax records of private citizens, Frank."

"You're a pro, aren't you?"

"That doesn't mean criminal. It looks to be an expensive enough campaign, without adding lawsuits," Feeney said mildly. "As a newspaper, we'll have an opinion about it, and we'll cover the issue fairly enough that everybody will understand what's at stake and can form an informed opinion."

"People don't know shit, and you and I both know that."

"Well, there are certainly days that…," Feeney, having almost got pulled into that, almost sighed. "But anyway, I'm not going to go slagging off people just because they run counter to this issue. I don't want to set people off against each other."

"That's what this is all about."

"All right, let me put this another way. I'm not going to do just whatever, no matter what anyone thinks about it. For the moment, this is a local resistance to a local school bond. But if you go up and down the Sound talking to people, what they don't want is for things like this to evolve into a general revolt against everything, like Proposition 13 in California did."

"That, actually… I sort of liked it."

"Oh, really? The dust still hasn't settled from that, but what did get whacked hardest was K-12 funding. Just whacked. I don't know how they'll make up for it. And also what got whacked was local government. Down there, the state had to take over everything, and that nuked infrastructure funding. Nuked it."

"Well, I don't know about all that," Baron said. As they were talking, Feeney more and more noticed shades of either embarrassment or irritation crossing Tari's face. Whatever else this couple consisted of, the pure shadings of unconditional respect weren't in it.

That's pretty obvious, Feeney thought. "You know, just a suggestion, but if you're going to fight Hawthorn, I wouldn't bring up Proposition 13… and especially not that you sort of like it."

"Oh," Baron shook his head in agreement. "Of course not. But we do have to hit hard. Ted says we have to give it all it's got."

"That sounds pretty decisive for Ted."

"He's a good man."

"We just need to watch the limits. I'm pretty sure no matter how hard we go after the Citizens Committee, Ted wouldn't want the School Board to get hit with a lawsuit."

"Ted's got a solution for that."

Feeney looked at Tari.

"A solution? From Ted? Last time I talked to him, I still can't make heads or tails out of what I wrote down. It looks like crib notes on the Critique of Pure Reason."

"He's got someone coming in to help with the campaign," Tari said. "A professional who does this sort of thing."

"This I heard. I'd like to know how he came up with this glorious idea. He take a magic potion? Or managed to get a good night's sleep?"

Tari laughed. "It wasn't actually him. The School Board got a letter from this man and invited him up. He came up and had a meeting with them, and everybody's really excited."

"Surprise, surprise. A professional campaign manager came up here and convinced the local school board he needed to be hired."

A slight frown creased Tari's brow. "We're not a bunch of hicks," she said.

Feeney was instantly sorry. But at the same time he was a little ashamed for her, for all of them.

"I'm not saying that. I know there's been frustration with..." Feeney wanted to say Ted but knew it would make him look just that much more judgmental. "I just wish people up here had talked about this more. Maybe checked a few things out."

"You'll meet him," Baron said. "And you'll see. We've got the big guns on our side now."

Tari nodded at Feeney with a look of you'll-see encouragement. Feeney looked back at her husband, who gave him a nod more along the lines of believe it.

"I can hardly wait," Feeney said.

"It's just so important, Patrick," Tari said with sudden earnestness, her eyes suddenly full of a surprising emotion. And at that Frank Baron did something surprisingly cynical, and actually rolled his eyes. And Feeney finally understood.

Normally, everything about Baron would have made anyone figure he would have been on the side of the Citizens Committee. But this team thing... rah rah, sis boom bah... was an act. Plain as day. And Feeney, both noticing and doing his best to pretend he hadn't noticed, had seen a glimmer in Tari's eyes, showing she was aware.

He really wished, he thought as he walked to his car, he could figure out how an incredibly beautiful, intelligent woman could end up with a man like Frank Baron.

Worthiness be damned.

Chapter 46

Tickler

IN all of history, there have always been snake-oil salesmen. Of course, Feeney thought, you could no longer sell snake-oil to anybody.

Oh, no.

But you could sell just about anything else, starting with the so-called necessities: time-saving kitchen appliances, a credit line, televised religion, new fashions, new cars, lifestyle equipment... and on and on... until everything was a consumer good to be either bought or bought into, including fad diets, the six-o'clock news, professional sports, free enterprise, the dangers of socialism, family values, lottery tickets, patriotism, celebrities, redemption from moral turpitude, mutually assured destruction... basically any form of instant gratification... even certain types of newspapers. But best of all, campaign promises. Which had their own specialized salesmen: campaign managers.

His attention returned to the animated, charismatic figure occupying the other chair in front of Ted Barnwell's desk.

Tickler Steele, handsome, impeccably dressed, with shiny, wavy black hair whitened dramatically at the temples, was gesticulating enthusiastically, waving his hands at Feeney and Barnwell in an assured, point-making manner as though he were about to show them how twenty white doves would pop out of his sleeves.

"It's not what they're thinking that matters," Steele was saying in a rich baritone, "but what they aren't thinking. We, of course, don't want to wake them up to that, but get them down below even that, to the place where they aren't even aware of what they're thinking. Oldest trick in the book, but I guarantee it works." Steele smiled with a brilliant, wolfish flash of teeth.

Feeney, keeping his face blank, looked at Steele. To have said a thing like that, and actually seem to mean it, took a lot of chutzpah, and Feeney began to see what Steele's success was really based on.

"Oh!" Barnwell cried, almost as though he was being delivered from sin. "Of course, of course!" He looked over at Feeney with delight.

Feeney scratched his neck. "I suppose," he said. "Although I'd say it's pretty obvious that what the people are thinking, where they might not have thought it before, is that the high school is falling down and something has to be done about it." Feeney gave Barnwell a steady look. "Which is what we've been telling them. As for what might be below all that..."

"Yes," Steele agreed with a beaming smile, "and we think you've been doing a bang-up job. Ted and I are grateful you've been drawn to our side of the public debate and have given it so much coverage."

"I'm glad you and Ted are grateful," Feeney said dryly. "I... uh... it's not so much that I was drawn to the cause. If memory serves me, I was part of the effort to define and explain the problem from the outset. The paper was never neutral. And the school board's decision to launch a bond proposal came well after the decision by Dean Parker and me to support any proposal aimed at the improvement of the present facilities. To our way of thinking, based on our experience in public information, the decision was that the paper would not come out with a recommendation until we felt the issues were fully understood. Opinions without the facts have no impact. You, Mr. Steele, I'm sure you know that."

Steele began waving his hands, but Feeney would not be interrupted.

"I'm just a little worried. These are mighty large billboards you want to put up all over this town. Way bigger than anything ever seen in a town of this size. They're going to up the tension, that's for sure. But are they going to change minds, or entrench them?"

Steele's friendly signs of protestation now took on a more guarded look.

Feeney ignored him. "I don't mean to say that your campaign is overselling the issue. It's only that I have a feeling we might give people the wrong impression. After all, people do have their pride. And this looks like they're being lectured. Talked down to. I mean, for chrissakes, these things are 400 square feet in size. And that one down on the highway, what? 500?"

"650."

"Jesus. That's all you see for the last mile before you get to town."

"That's the idea," Steele grinned. "I understand your concerns. But let me assure you, because as much as you are committed to this project, for which Ted and I are sincerely grateful, I also realize you haven't seen an actual bond-proposal campaign in action. There are some things one must do to assure victory even though one might think one could dispense with them. I am, as you are, a professional, Patrick. The last campaign I handled, down in Steihelacum, brought in over eight million dollars in property-owner matching funds. That was one of the largest bond issues passed in state history. For which I was the campaign director, hired by the Steihelacum school board. That campaign was little different from this one. It's a matter of politics. You need to understand how politics work."

Feeney felt the irritation at his neck spread behind his ears and into his scalp. "I don't know much about political campaigning, it's true. I'm just raising concerns. For my own interests as much as the town's. And I'm sure that more than one person is going to ask a few questions like this."

"Absolutely! We realize you and the paper have a lot to contribute. I said that. I did. And as far as the general community sentiments go, believe me, we understand them very, very well and are prepared to work upon those understandings. And if there are any questions, we'll answer them should they arise."

"It's not a question of whether people might ask questions. They will."

"Yes. Yes. But you've seen for yourself how the people who

come to the board meetings are firmly in favor of the success of the bond issue?"

Feeney felt trapped, coming off as negative and argumentative, but even that statement he could counter. Everyone knew those few people who regularly showed up at school-board meetings, the do-gooders, community-minded and so forth, were generally on the board's side of everything. And that would change. He decided, though, he'd said enough. "OK, we'll see what happens after your new billboards go up and next week's paper comes out."

Against Feeney's advice, Steele had bought the bottom third of every page and a full two-page spread in the center. Feeney had shuddered when he was first handed all the ad copy, calling Parker to discuss it. Parker said it was in pretty bad taste, pretty top-heavy for this early on, but it all would look the same sitting in the bank.

Steele shrugged. "Steihelacum looked like a fire sale for two months, and nobody minded."

Feeney felt his temper give way. "Listen, Mr. Steele..."

"Tickler, Patrick, we're all friends here..."

"...Tickler. Listen. Steihelacum is not Sultan. You know as well as I do the demographics are completely different. Down there, everybody is either commuting down to Olympia, or Evergreen College. They're all upper-middle-class professionals. It's got one of the most popular lake resorts in the state right in the middle of their landscaped neighborhoods. When it came time to put up the money for a new school all that wall-to-wall upward mobility just rolled over for it. Those parents are that close, anyway, to putting their kids in private prep schools. If they can get away with providing prep-school education, at a third of the price—just by hiking up their property taxes a couple of hundred dollars a year on a bond—they'll jump at it. Those people understand economics. You know it. I know it. Sultan... what can I say? In some parts of town that rat-hole of a high school would be a palace compared to the homes. The population? Unemployed loggers and lumberyard workers aren't necessarily going to put the school board's double-paned glass, indirect lighting, and AstroTurf high on their list of educational priorities. If they have any. Right?"

Steele was staring at Feeney, and Feeney could see exactly what he was thinking. But he didn't care. He knew Steele had Barnwell in his pocket, and the school board's money, probably town money as well. But he'd be damned if Steele was going to think he'd had the newspaper in thrall as well. He could pay for all the ads he wanted. Fill the paper, as far as Feeney cared. But it stopped there.

After the meet-and-greet session had finished, smiles all around, and Steele had left, Feeney was just turning to leave, himself, when Barnwell stopped him. "I just wanted," he said, "for all of us to meet like this, so that we'd all be on the same page. That you would feel as good about Steele as I do."

"Sure, Ted. I'm sure he'll be a great help."

"I know he will," Barnwell said, his enthusiasm coming back. "I can't tell you how relieved I feel having a real professional here now to take things in hand."

"Oh, no fears on that. He's a real professional."

But Feeney was no longer thinking about Steele, Barnwell, or the bond issue. When he had first come into the office, saying hello to Faith, an idea had begun to take form in his mind. And all through the meeting, he'd felt it coming over him in small waves, as Barnwell and Steele had been talking. It was almost a distraction, and had contributed to the irritation at his neck almost as much as Steele. Or, perhaps, had been the reason for it entirely.

When he walked out, Faith had already gone to lunch.

Chapter 47

Warren

THEY were standing on the sidewalk squinting idiotically in the bright sunshine like a couple of turtles high on swamp gas when the bright red Porsche convertible came burbling up to the curb. Feeney guessed it was a 911 Carrera. After a well-practiced half-minute of insouciant idling filling the air with testosterone-laden rumblings, Warren Harrison cut the motor, leaving only the powerful whine of the turbo to die away in the air.

As Feeney's ears accustomed themselves to the empty sound of the natural world once again, he heard Chief Spencer say under his breath: "Good night."

Feeney nodded.

"I hope he's got the thing paid up."

"Hi," Harrison said as he climbed up out of the car. He flashed a grin at Feeney, and then nodded at Spencer's uniform.

"Warren," Feeney said, "this is Bill Spencer. He's the police chief around here."

Harrison stuck out his hand. "A pleasure, sir."

Spencer gave the hand a quick shake, putting on a suddenly dazzling smile to match Harrison's. "Pleasure's mine."

Feeney looked at Spencer's gleaming teeth. God, he thought, any deferential crap in the wind...

Harrison looked around, as though there were some official reason the police chief and the newspaper editor should be out gazing over the parking lot, then back at them. "Nice day, huh?"

"It's all of that," Feeney said.

"Especially nice day to be wheeling around in the manner you've got there," Spencer said.

It was only the polite thing to say. Someone pulls up and all but shoves fine European engineering in your face, you'd be ungracious not to at least acknowledge it. After all, that was half the reason anyone would go out and buy the goddamn thing in the first place.

"True enough," Harrison's handsome face was complacent. "No worry, though. No tickets. At least..." he grinned, "not around here!"

"Hope not," Spencer said after a pause, with sudden tightness in his voice.

Seeing the luster had just as quickly left Spencer's smile, Feeney couldn't resist. "Not that the coffers couldn't use a little help."

"Yeah," Harrison chuckled sarcastically. "But with the highway running right through the town, that shouldn't be much of a problem, right, Chief?"

Feeney's glee began to bubble up toward his lips but he managed to keep a straight face. Spencer flicked a glance his way. Feeney noticed the glance, but he was mainly interested in looking at Harrison. Of all the things he'd expected, this clueless lack of self-awareness hadn't been among them.

"You know, Chief?" Harrison went on. "Dean Parker told me there would be quite a few good articles generated from your department. That you've been instituting a lot of modernization up here."

"I've been trying to do that," Spencer said, giving Feeney a quick, guarded look. "And we've been trying to improve our public presence and give the community a clearer idea of what we're doing."

"Not always easy, though," Feeney said, seeing that Spencer was looking for backup. "Towns like Sultan don't have the depth of trouble... vice, crime, mayhem... you saw in Everett. You get some of that, sometimes. But mostly, what stands out up here is the domestic, or between-neighbor, level of things. And when Bill and the boys have to wade into those squabbles, they can't help getting caught up in it. That's how just about everything works up here."

"Controversy is everywhere," Harrison said.

Spencer shook his head. "Not really controversy," he said, with a touch of a frown. "It's usually more a matter of personalities."

"Human interest."

Feeney looked at Harrison with curiosity. "Um... no," he said. "Not really that, either."

Harrison gave Feeney a sudden, semi-conspiratorial grin. "Don't worry. Dean already gave me the speech about being non-controversial."

Feeney resisted looking to see what Spencer was doing. "Controversy," Feeney said, "is sometimes the air we breathe. It's not really something that can be delegated elsewhere. People don't really know it, but what they want isn't the details—it's to find what's fair. That's what the chief is up against, and us, I guess."

Harrison nodded. "This ought to be interesting," he said, and it was clear he was saying it more to himself than to them.

Feeney nodded. "Oh, I'm... uh," he looked over at Spencer and couldn't help grin, "I'm sure it's going to be interesting."

Spencer looked at him sideways.

"Well," Harrison said, "I might as well get set up. Dean said you already had a couple of things to work on, and I'd like to see if I can get them out of the way before the weekend."

"Uh... sure." Feeney, in fact, had nothing for him. It was just like Dean, he thought, to go and say something like that.

Harrison stuck out his hand to Spencer again and gave him another smile. "It'll be good to work with you, Chief. See you soon."

"Right."

Harrison went into the office, Feeney's office, as though he'd already been there a hundred times before, leaving Feeney and Spencer standing out alone again on the sidewalk. For a second neither spoke, then Spencer finally sighed. "You're not thinking of leaving us, are you?"

"Not that I know of."

Spencer nodded, and then after a long pause, sighed again. "Boy. Sunny day after all that rain. Makes you sort of tired."

"Days seem longer, that's for sure," Feeney said sort of

automatically, but then he looked over at the police chief and realized they were both thinking the same things. And that did it. "You know, Bill," he said. "I meant what I said about the fairness thing."

"And you're right."

"Then you know, too, there's going to be no such thing as win or lose for you as far as Brahnler goes."

"Christ," Spencer puffed out. "There's just no way you can know where it's all coming from. Or even where it begins."

"It's pretty tangled up," Feeney nodded. "But when it comes right down to it, these guys couldn't live without each other. Dick would get lonely if he didn't have Charlie to head-butt every Tuesday night."

"Or me."

"But with the difference, you can't butt back."

Spencer pursed his lips for a moment, and then took a breath. "Yep," he said without enthusiasm.

"But you know something?" Feeney nodded at him with sincerity. "And just remember this, whenever it starts to seem like it matters..." He paused for a moment, as though looking at his life suddenly spreading out across the parking lot like a dull sheen.

"What?" Spencer said.

"Oh." Feeney found his train of thought again. "Just remember, you're not alone. We're both in that same boat."

Spencer looked at him, and for a second a smile came to his lips. And then he just hitched up his utility belt and strode off towards his cruiser.

"Well, he's kind of a prig, ain't he?" Harrison said when Feeney got behind his desk.

Feeney was rustling around in the drawers, looking for a few odds and ends of office material to hand to Harrison. "We've all got our quirks."

On the other side of the office, Harrison was leaning back in his chair, one foot up on the edge of his desk, a new desk Dean had sent up, gazing around at the little space. "Don't get me wrong. I don't have a problem with cops or authority or anything."

Feeney pulled some notepads from the bottom drawer, and then began trying out a few old pens. "Good thing," he said. "That'll bring some balance in here."

Harrison put his hands behind his head. "So what were you saying it was to be called? Anything but Crime Stopper's Notebook?"

"Let's make it really catchy, huh?" Feeney kept doodling away. "How about You and the Law." Feeney gave Harrison a droll look, expecting a giant guffaw.

Harrison didn't laugh. "You and the Law?" He made a thoughtful sound. "You and the Law. Not bad. Sort of thing that would really catch the eye, right? Make someone go, hey, yeah, me and the law."

Feeney threw a couple of pens into the trash. "I don't think we've got that big a well-spring of paranoia up here."

"No," Harrison was rocking now, making a slow squeaking noise, "but people do wonder, you know, where they stand. People don't think about it, but every once in a while, it happens. And there they are, somehow not on the right side of some code or law, or something, and it's always a bit of a surprise."

"That was the chief's idea."

"So, you want just a short thing, huh?"

"Oh, God, yes. Just run something about three or four paragraphs on top of the cop shop. Unless it's something really complicated or controversial. If it's important, and it's something people really don't know jack shit about, we can do a whole thing."

"Like drunk driving?"

"Come the weekend, that's the number one participatory sport up here."

Harrison cranked his head around at Feeney. "How is the nightlife?"

Feeney saw Harrison eyeing him. He didn't even want to begin to think what he was thinking. "You're kidding."

"Doesn't matter," Harrison said with a shrug. "I don't like the bar scene, anyway."

Feeney made a polite sound.

"Parties are the only thing."

"Yeah, well, that takes getting to know people."

"You can't do that up here?" Harrison was looking at him again. "Wow. That bad? Anyway, yeah, I guess that's more a college thing you can drop into, or else when the company is big enough. You guys don't have parties, do you? No? Right... I guess not. Too bad, though. You'd think the newspaper people would know people all over town."

"It also helps to have a yard or something," Feeney said.

Harrison sighed. "I'm really out in suburbia now, aren't I?"

"Not even. You're in the fucking sticks," Feeney said. And then actually tried to be helpful. "There are the regular sorts of social things."

"Which you don't attend, either."

Feeney conceded. "True enough, there's not much action up here."

"I didn't expect any, anyway."

"No girlfriend?"

"Well, down in Everett... but nothing steady," Harrison said, and then stretched. "I don't feel like, you know, settling down. Not for a while. Maybe someday things will get all organized and rational First, find the right place to live. And that ain't here," a grin, "then, get the career set up. Or the other way around. And then, and only then, have some babe fall in love, get married, and hunker down into a long string of weekend barbecues and beach outings. Babies. Or whatever. But only when, you know, you're... done."

Feeney didn't know whether to feel wistfully nostalgic or jealous. There had been a time when he, too, had thought of things somewhere along those lines, but never in terms of just having the sporting life first. He'd always been looking for someone, the one. Harrison though, flashy and unconcerned one way or the other, probably had a hell of a lot better chance of doing just exactly whatever he wanted. Just falling into it.

Under other circumstances, Feeney might have felt he was suddenly dealing with a social competitor, as well as a professional competitor, but since he didn't have any real social life to speak of, and no prospects—not really—he could shrug it all off.

"Well, I can't give you any hot tips," Feeney said.

"S'all right. Don't matter. I'll be having too much work here for a while, anyway. You can't give a shit about something that doesn't exist, right?"

Feeney nodded, as if that was something just to agree with. But there was the proof, he thought, of how different he and Harrison were. All he seemed to be doing lately was worrying about things that did not exist.

Like peace of mind.

He looked back at his desk.

One good thing: Bill Spencer at least would now have someone who felt enthusiastic about helping him with his public relations.

Fairness, sometimes, was whatever you could make of it.

Chapter 48

Tripping the Light Fantastic

SHE had come in alone and sat down beside him. She showed him pictures of her horse, and of herself and her horse standing in front of a horse trailer and a grey pickup truck.

Her name was Abby—short for Abigail—and Feeney guessed she was in her mid-thirties. She had long, jet-black hair so thick it was almost like a hood, was a little stocky, eager in a simple, dignified way, but also shy and, as shy people often do, talked mostly about herself. Her last name, she said, was Badb, which nobody could say right, but inevitably led to the joke of calling her Bad Abby. And that, she further expanded upon, could lead to people getting ideas. She gave him a look, but Feeney—who hadn't come into Bedossa's with something like this in mind—left it hanging. She wasn't put off by that. At that moment, the band for the night finally got going and she smiled at him.

"Want to dance?"

"I never dance..." Feeney lied. He stopped himself, having nearly compounded it by saying he didn't like to dance. The truth was, he loved to dance, going all the way back to his first year in junior high and the Friday-night dances where he copied the moves of the older guys and dared himself to dance with every girl in his class. Those dances were every Friday across the winter quarter and although it took most of that time to do it, he won his dare.

Before Abby could respond, Marsha came down with a couple of fresh drinks, but instead of leaving she planted herself in front of them, her hands braced against the bar.

"So," she said, looking at Abby with a grin, "who have we got tonight, Good Abby or Bad Abby?"

Abby looked at Marsha with a friendly smile that Feeney didn't think was all that friendly.

"We don't know yet," she said.

"We?" Marsha looked over at Feeney, who looked back. Drily.

"Yeah. Me and us, the two Abbys."

"Ah, I see. I misinterpreted that." Marsha squinted at Feeney, who squinted back, and she looked back at Abby and gave her a smile.

"It happens often enough," Abby said, giving her black hair a shake, then making a short cawing laugh. "But maybe Bad Abby for a change... why not?"

Marsha looked at Feeney again, who looked back again. But this time tiredly. "I haven't seen you around much lately, Pat," she said to him. Then to Abby: "He never came around much, even when he used to come around."

"I didn't know I was missed," Feeney said.

"You don't even come down weekdays anymore so how would you know if your buddies missed you or not?"

"What buddies?"

Marsha winked at Abby. "He makes friends easily."

"Could have fooled me."

Feeney raised his eyebrows at Marsha. "What buddies?"

Marsha gave him a look that went on just a bit too long. "Oh, you know...," she said.

He knew exactly who Marsha was referring to and, his eyes narrowing, gave a slight shake of the head that wasn't meant to signal any confusion. "I know?"

Marsha saw she wasn't being funny and made the adjustment. "Sure...," she said. "Jim, for instance."

Feeney was actually startled for half a second. It had been just too much of a transition. Then he nearly laughed. "I doubt Jim misses me much down here, considering he's seen me at just about every court session for that mutt for the past half year. And he doesn't ever seem all that happy to see me when he does."

"He's just feeling harassed."

"By me?"

"Oh, no. But he doesn't like having all these Seattle lawyers coming in and clogging up the entire docket."

"Yeah, I know. He'd rather just be doing his drunk-driver lectures to the high-school idiots."

Feeney had no illusions about Jim Dodd's election-winning methods. His theatrical beratings of teen offenders was something everyone in the town knew about and whenever some kid they knew was up for a hearing they would show up just for the fun of watching youth getting officially scolded and reprimanded.

"He doesn't mind your articles."

"What he probably doesn't mind is how they've gotten pushed off the front page lately."

Out of the corner of his eye, Feeney could see someone down the bar trying to get Marsha's attention. She noticed as well but didn't move. She was definitely on a mission. He began having an ominous feeling.

"He likes you, Pat," she said. "He says you're fairer than Dean Parker ever was."

"Dean...," Feeney smiled. "I can't even... Anyway, it's not really a question of fairness."

"Maybe not. But he feels that way."

Abby, who'd been looking back and forward, had begun to notice things. She didn't know what, of course. But there were definitely things. "This is nice," she said. "I didn't know you two were such close friends."

"Oh, this is nothing," Marsha said. "You should see us on a good night." She looked back at Feeney. "Right? You being the town's party boy, social director, most eligible bachelor, and all."

"Uh...," Feeney started off by nodding his head slowly, "sure..." Wherever this craziness was coming from, he decided he'd just match it. "So, when are we all getting together for our next barbecue?"

Feeney saw a small flash in Marsha's eyes.

"I thought maybe this time you could throw it," she said.

269

Feeney and Marsha did not really know each other all that well, and this by-play, just to get around the Beebee thing—or whatever it was—with someone else present, had drawn them into an oddly intimate situation. As though they really were friends. They looked at each other and it was obvious neither wanted to say anything.

"Um," Abby said. "I need to make a little trip. Be back in a sec, OK?" When Feeney didn't say anything, she inclined herself slightly in his direction. "OK?"

Feeney nodded and then watched her make her way through the tables towards the women's in the back. When she disappeared, he looked back at Marsha. "What's the deal?"

Marsha made a pleading look. "Sorry. I was just trying to find a way to tell you that if you've got something going, you better get it going..."

Feeney hesitated, and then said, "I see. And, no, I don't have anything going. Why would I want *more* of that? I was just sitting here." Feeney shrugged. "And as for the other thing... just so you know, I don't care. But... since when do *you* care?"

"I don't, Pat. I just go with what comes through the doors. And it seemed to me that, at some point, this was something I was seeing."

He smiled. "That's decent of you."

"Don't be a cynic."

"I'm not," he said. "I'm just not used to the feeling of having people seem to know things about me. Or, more, caring one way or the other..."

Marsha laughed. "You've been here long enough. And you should know better."

"Maybe so," he admitted. "But I try hard not to."

"Yes, that's also something that's noticeable. But you know... just saying... with your car out in the lot, and everything..."

"Ah, yeah. I hadn't considered that."

"Obviously. That's why I thought I'd just, sort of..."

Feeney looked back towards the women's. Nothing. Then back at Marsha. "All right, since you're now my friendly neighborhood DEW line..."

270

"Dew?"

"Distant early warning..."

"Yeah... you know... the odds are..."

"Okay, more than odds," Marsha said. "I got a call earlier. I'm sort of friends with Beebee... you know. And she said she does like you pretty much. But..."

"But... if she saw my car in the lot, she'd come in or not based on what's happening."

Marsha looked cagey. "If it was just her decision, yeah. But you know how she can be."

Feeney felt fed up. "Yeah. Fucking desperate. Which I'm beginning to feel, myself, right now. It's nothing more than that, Marsha." He pointed down the counter. "Your bar's going dry."

Feeney had nearly made up his mind. He was feeling different levels of anger, pride, and annoyance... and was suddenly ready to let those demons run. Just... to hell with it all.

When Abby got back, he turned to smile at her, and then the exact thing Marsha had warned him about happened.

Beebee walked into the lounge. Although this time with a girlfriend.

Marsha, down serving at that end of the bar, looked back at Feeney, giving him an I-told-you-so. Feeney nodded and watched Beebee looking around the room until, finally, she spotted him.

This was no coincidence. Beebee always knew exactly who was where before she walked into anywhere. He had learned that right from the very start.

On the first time they'd decided to have a drink together, Beebee doing the driving, by the time they had passed through the third bar's parking lot on their way down the highway to Everett, he began to think she was eliminating places in terms of parked vehicles. Later, he knew she did that. And that defined pretty much everything else. Feeney, in Beebee's life, existed mainly when everything else was empty, including the lot where his car was parked. Wherever she'd been to that evening, it hadn't been to look for him. Until now. She came quickly down the bar, ignoring a few of the heads turning to greet her.

"Hiya," she said to him, and then gave Abby a quick look-over, slightly pursing her lips.

"Hiya," he said.

"Mind if...?" Beebee smiled at him vaguely and sat down on a stool on the other side of Feeney, her friend sliding onto the other beyond. "You're up late."

"Well...," he looked at her, then at Abby, then back at her, "I figured the cows could just wait for once..."

Nobody laughed.

"Haven't seen you in a while, Patrick," Beebee's friend said to Feeney. She was a heavily-bespectacled young woman with a pinched appearance. Feeney recognized her, but couldn't remember her name. She was one of the supporting cast of thousands in Beebee's Eternal Quest.

"He's a busy boy," Beebee said, and turned to him. "You want to dance?"

Abby elbowed him lightly and he turned to see her smiling at him. "You forgot to tell me your girlfriend was coming," she said.

"No. I, uh..."

She picked up her jacket and slid off the barstool.

As he watched her walk away, he heard Beebee sigh behind him. "Oops," she said. "Fucked that up, didn't I? And making a waste of your time."

Feeney didn't turn immediately back around but looked off across the tables full of partiers as though he might find some sort of inspiration out there. He supposed he should at least have felt bad for wasting Bad Abby's time there in Bedossa's. "Story of my life," he said, mostly to himself.

"Sorry?" Beebee said behind him.

"I said," Feeney turned around, "not much different from us."

And it was true. Beebee was also a sheer waste of time, with only a slight distinction being that there was a slim bit of history now attached to it, and something resembling friendship, of the shared-foxhole sort.

"Flattering," she said. "If I'm understanding whatever it is you're talking about."

272

"Hey... want a laugh?" he said. "Marsha decided to let me join the club tonight."

Beebee looked down the bar. "Ah. That explains the way she squinted at me."

"You wanted to dance?"

"Not at all," she said.

Feeney saw the other woman looking at both of them with curiosity.

"Um... Joan?"

"Close," she said. "Jane."

He nodded. The softball team. "Aren't you from Marysville?"

"Beebee thought it might be fun for me to come down here."

"How's that panning out?"

Jane looked at Beebee who was looking at Feeney. "A few places. Sort of all right. I think we passed by here a few times and I thought it looked interesting and Beebee finally agreed we should come in. So here we are."

"Should?" Feeney gave Beebee a smile. "Things are a should?"

"Nothing's ever a should," she said.

Jane stared at both of them, and then thought she was supposed to laugh. "You two have really been doing this for two years?"

"Doing?" Feeney said.

Jane decided to laugh again. "Now I get why I was doing all that driving."

"Why's that?"

"Because..." Jane began, and then realized she didn't really know, or at least not in any way she could say out loud without making herself look like a sap. "Well, it seemed like a plan."

Feeney smiled. "Always good to have a plan..."

"Some people do..." Beebee said.

Jane got up. "I think I'll go introduce myself to those guys."

Beebee and Feeney watched her head over to a table where four men were talking. Feeney had never seen any woman, anywhere, do something like that. Beebee shook her head.

"I guess I might as well admit that being out with Jane puts a whole new spin on the evening." She looked back at the table. "She doesn't give a shit anymore."

"What does that say about you, Bee?" Feeney shortened her name any time they actually talked for real.

"It doesn't say anything good, Pat," she looked back at him. "I'm just kind of out of ideas." She looked back at the table. "I would never have introduced her to any of them, but she'll figure them out soon enough." One of the men stood up and he took Jane out onto the dance floor. "Howie...," she said. "Naturally, he'd be the first."

Feeney looked at the other three.

"Tony, Gene and Bobby," Beebee informed him. "Me, personally, that whole table would be a no. But Jane can have a soft spot for trash when she's in the mood."

Feeney smiled. "Is there some sort of compliment in there?"

"You going to offer me a drink, at least?"

Feeney signaled to Marsha. Then he picked up his glass and took a drink. "Well," he said. "I'm glad I'm at least not a question of mood."

"You never were, Pat. Never. Anyway, we really haven't seen each other in a while."

"You know where I've been."

"Phones work both ways."

"No," he said. "They don't."

Marsha brought Beebee's drink. "And for your friend?"

"Wait to see where she sits."

Marsha looked at Beebee and Feeney for a moment, and then just clicked her tongue. "Okey dokey...," and went away.

"Marsha told you I was out and around, eh?" Beebee smiled.

"She wouldn't need to tell me that."

"But she did anyway. I can tell. She must have thought it was important."

"It wasn't."

"Now who's not nice? And, anyway, I wasn't really out and about. And I hadn't made up my mind."

"Even worse. Much worse. It's really, really not nice to not make up your mind, and come in anyway." Feeney looked at Beebee for a moment, thought of a wisecrack he could add, but then something came over him. "You know?" he said. "You're right. It isn't nice. And you know what else?"

"You're sorry..."

"No. I'm not talking about any of that."

"OK...," she said, her face becoming guarded.

Feeney nearly smiled, but didn't because that would be another thing that wasn't nice to do. "Never mind," he said. "Just, never mind, Bee."

Beebee took a sip of her drink. "So, anyway, now you have Marsha looking out for you. That's a new one, Pat. I guess she finally decided to believe me."

"Believe you?"

"That you're one of the really good guys."

"Not obvious enough, as it is?" Feeney looked up the bar at Marsha, and suddenly had a vision of whatever it was Marsha's world was like. Working at one of the only decent bars in the area, where just about everyone who might go to a bar eventually did go, sooner or later. Making her practically an expert on the local singles scene. Who was with who, or was no longer with who, or who was trying to be with someone, or who was trying not to be with someone... sort of a social seismic meter.

"Not in a cocktail lounge, Pat. Nothing's obvious in a place like this."

"Oh...," he smiled. "Some things are. Bad Abby certainly was."

"I'm not talking about that, Pat," she smiled. "And don't be creepy."

"I was creepy?"

"No, but it is creepy."

"Fair enough." He sighed.

Beebee looked at the dancefloor, and then sighed herself. "Shit," she said.

"What?"

"Jane drove," she said. "I didn't think this through."

He looked over and saw that Jane was now dancing with Tony.

Or Gene or Bobby. He nodded and looked back at Beebee.

"I'm not saying anything," he said. "I'm not that kind of not nice."

"You never could be."

"But I should."

Beebee smiled. "Yes," she said. "You should."

"But I'm not. When she gets done dancing over there, go have a word with her, and I'll take you home."

She looked back at him, and an actual look of tenderness came over her face. Almost the misty-eyed sort. And then she sighed again. "God," she said. "What a damn shame. I'm not kidding, Pat. You are one of the sweet, real ones."

Feeney took that in, and then even though he didn't believe a word of it, he smiled. Because why not.

Beebee shook her head. "Oh man, I went and spoiled everything, didn't I?"

"No, you haven't. I already did that a long time ago. And I mean, a long time ago."

Beebee frowned for a moment, and then squinched her eyes. "You know, I do love you, Pat."

"Yeah," Feeney said. "Me neither, Bee."

She laughed.

"Good thing we really aren't in love."

"C'mon, let's go."

As they left and moved down the bar, Feeney looked at Marsha as he passed and saw her point her long, long-nailed index finger at him, and shake her head. For what it was worth, he thought as he went out the door with Beebee, he could see he'd made a new friend. And with Beebee, he was true to his word. He did take her home. But when he drove into her driveway, he left the motor running and leaned over and gave her a kiss. A tender one. And then smiled at her.

Beebee glanced at the ignition key, and realized what was happening.

"Oh, Pat. You are a lovely man, a real man."

"And you're a real woman, Beebee."

Beebee nodded. "So we don't have to worry about each other anymore."

Feeney nodded back.

"Thank you, Pat," she smiled. "You know, this could just as easily have been me."

"Tonight, it just happened to be me."

She looked at him for a long moment, and her eyes even got a bit misty. "Good night, my good love," she said. She gave him a peck on the cheek, and got out of his car.

Forever.

And as he drove away, he felt exactly three things. Free... yeah, that... tired, but more of a general, life thing... and empty. Once again... that. But not disappointed. That, at least, was something.

Chapter 49

PTA

IT was a remarkably large audience. With the school bond issue beginning to come into focus—explained now by Tickler Steele's district-wide letters, signed by Ted Barnwell, and two lengthy articles in the town's paper—the Sultan Parent-Teacher Association felt it needed to add a few supplementary meetings.

Feeney, along with his superhero sidekick, Warren Harrison, had gone to the meeting with high expectations, but was dumbfounded by two things at once. The first was discovering that neither Barnwell, Steele, nor any of the board had bothered to attend. And the second was that he realized he was suddenly one of the only persons in the room who actually knew anything, the other being Faith Rockford, who had come to take notes for her absent boss. She looked so lovely over there. He wanted desperately to go sit by Faith, but the seats beside her were already taken. And, he was stuck with Warren, anyway.

Being the only one who knew anything. That was never a good thing, he thought as he and Warren found seats.

In fact, a pretty bad thing.

With Frank Baron sitting near the front nodding encouragement, Tari got the meeting under way and, as president, did her best to outline some of the main ideas, the audience listening politely.

Feeney looked around the room as she spoke, noticing the men gazing at her thoughtfully, obviously enchanted by her attractive charisma, while the women seemed to respond to her earnest but modest demeanor. She didn't do too badly, even though her points were mainly superficial and it was only occasionally that Feeney found himself strangling the urge to clarify and correct misstatements.

At first the room seemed to be settling into agreement. The teachers unsurprisingly all supported the idea of the new school, and for several minutes there seemed to be no controversy. But then a small crack appeared when someone wondered whether such a large budget for the high school wouldn't end up impoverishing the middle and elementary school budgets.

"It all looks good on paper," said Joe Dixon, a bearded fourth-grade teacher who Feeney knew to have two unrequited ambitions, one to be promoted to the high school where he wanted to teach history, and the other an alarmingly obvious infatuation with Faith Rockford who he kept glancing at even as he spoke to Tari, "but I remember the year they re-grassed the football field and we couldn't get the multimedia material, let alone start it, and had to scrap that reading method for the year."

Tari looked at Feeney, who half-closed his eyes and gave a slight shake of his head. Dixon was as well-meaning as he was completely off the track. The football field reconditioning had actually come out of a county-wide, five-year budget set up years before by a county school commission which saw that it was not only unfair that certain school districts could afford better athletic facilities than others, but in some cases actually dangerous to leave the status quo in place. Some spindly-necked sophomore could lose his footing on a torn-up potato patch of a field somewhere in the county and get clobbered, and after the lawsuits died down the county commission's insurance rates would be orbiting the moon.

Feeney would have loved to stand up and explain all that, and also explain to Dixon that the loss of federal funding was the real reason the reading method Dixon spoke about had suffered. Conservatives in Washington had a pragmatic view of education, figuring that nearly half the country could get along just fine with being functionally illiterate. A dumb electorate being every politician's dream. At least, for those politicians who had the most to gain from getting elected.

After the general hubbub about Dixon's remarks died down, a large woman in an even larger, one-piece pink dress stood up. "On the new football field, will they put in those big lights like down in Monroe?" She got some verbal support for that and sat happily back down.

And just like that, the meeting began to drift.

Tari spent the next several minutes trying to answer that question, which had nothing to do with the school bond, and when she was finished she had another question about the lights by another woman, and another man, and another woman.

Feeney tried to write down notes. Warren was doing the same, and not knowing names Feeney would try to identify people in case he wanted to get a quote. Thin woman, black jeans, Indian shirt. Dumpy guy, sweatpants, John Deere cap. All, evidently parents, although he couldn't always tell what school their kids attended.

This went on so long that Feeney finally realized he was taking notes about nothing he would actually write about. The main show, he knew, hadn't yet begun.

He turned to Harrison. "If you find anything worth writing about with this light stuff, go on ahead. For that matter, if you find anything interesting that's not on the bond topic, it's all yours."

Harrison looked back dubiously, but nodded, and went back to his notebook.

Relieved of that chore, Feeney now just doodled to pass the time.

"We live across the street from the field," a woman said, "and the lights are already so bright right now we have to close the drapes to watch TV." Feeney scribbled: "Just give up and go to the game, lady."

Another: "Are they going to keep the same school colors and the Fighting Eagles name?" Feeney wrote: "Sultan Sasquatches? Sky Steelheads? Vicious Chipmunks?" That last wasn't as flippant as it sounded, Feeney having run into many an aggressive chipmunk in the parking lot in front of his office.

"Why don't they buy Hec Edward's farm up there on the

Williams-Cooperston Road and build the high school up there? I was thinking that's a great spot for a school." Feeney wrote: "Hec might suggest another great spot could be your backyard."

"I hope they pass a school law about those cars." Feeney wrote: "Cars?"

"I think they shouldn't build it all on one level, like they did with the Elementary school, but in three or four stories. That way the school building will leave more room for other things. Right now, they have to park their cars all over the place." Feeney wrote: "Cars. Aha!"

"So, is the bond issue going to be deductible?" Feeney wrote: "Why, yes, you deduct that, and your income tax, and the state sales tax, and the tax on all the liquor you use to pickle your brain."

"Is the public going to be able to supervise the ongoing process during the construction phase, considering the considerable input of local funds involved despite state matching funds transferred here for the purposes of the school district's high school building program?" Feeney wrote: "Can we watch?"

"Will the diploma be different?"

"Will students take more classes?"

"Will they still need Homerooms?"

"Are they going to have to cut down the maples in front of the old school?"

"Does this mean there are going to be more students at the school... or that there will be the possibility of more students at the school? If it's the former, where will they be, as in where will they be at? And if it's the latter rather than the former, when do you think that possibility will take place?"

"Why don't they get rid of the old utility shop?"

There were a few statements as well, some offering rebuttal or correction in an effort to get things back into some semblance of forward motion. But after a while, Feeney's hand went dead in his lap. It wasn't fun any more.

Tari now had a patient but frustrated look on her face. Faith, over on the other side of the room, just looked frustrated. At one point, she glanced over at Feeney, with a puzzled look, and he just shrugged and shook his head. She sort of smiled. Feeney smiled back but Harrison was suddenly leaning over to Feeney, saying, "I don't think I've got enough gloss in my entire body to cover this up."

Feeney looked away from Faith, and stared at Tari, who was now staring back at him with something that looked like desperation. "Then don't," he said. Feeney glanced at Faith again, but she was now back to concentrating on Tari.

"We don't want them looking like idiots, do we?"

Feeney felt his heart sinking, for several reasons. But managed to say to Harrison, "they're not idiots. They're just supremely uninformed."

"You'd think they hadn't read the paper."

Feeney shrugged. "I wonder where the fuck Ted is?"

Harrison shook his head. "He made the right decision. That would have made it political."

"It is political. Can't you hear how out of it these people are? What more could you ask of a political issue?"

"A school is a community issue."

"You don't think public education is a political issue?" Feeney looked over at him. "You don't think a property tax fits the definition of a political issue."

"Ted is not an elected official."

"The school board is. And they should goddamn well be down here defending, or at least explaining, what the fuck they've decided to do."

Feeney's voice had carried a bit toward the end and a couple of nearby heads turned, one even nodding approval.

Harrison shook his head. "Nah, I think that would make them look defensive and weak. They propose, and then it's up to citizens' groups, like Frank's, to carry the ball."

Feeney turned his attention back to the meeting, and the struggling participants. It was true that they'd gotten badly off track. He could see the parents were overwhelmed, with one worry following and digressing from the last one. But the main thing was, they all could see there was a foreseen school closure at hand and that the school board was now talking about the need for a new school.

People, Feeney had discovered, when faced with a big issue and the need to think and talk about it, often spent most of their time thinking and talking about everything under the sun except the big issue. As though solving all the little problems that didn't matter somehow took care of the whole thing. But he knew this couldn't last.

And it didn't, and it was with some relief to Feeney's ears, when a tall, thin, stoop-shouldered old man stood up in the back of the meeting and said with a quiet voice: "Well, I don't know too much about all this. I don't see there are very many details here yet. I just wanted to say that the way everybody is talking about this thing right here, I don't think the issue is going to pass."

The room went dead silent. The man looked around the room, especially at the teachers, and then went on: "You folks want this new high school built. I think it's right. But you better figure out what's going on better than this. Or explain it better."

Feeney didn't know the old man's name and looked back to make sure the fellow wasn't leaving yet. When he turned back around he found Tari looking at him again. For a moment, they held each other's eyes as a general murmur of assent and dissent swept around the room. Feeney looked at Frank Baron, but Frank was just having an argument with a neighbor—he could tell it was an argument by the way they had their chins out—and he looked back at her and shrugged. Tari gave him a faint smile then tapped her gavel.

"I think Mr. Owens made the main point," she said when people finally quieted. "We don't really have the details. We don't have the plans. We don't have the building schedule. We don't have a contingency plan for students while the building program is taking place. We certainly don't have any hard figures as far as the actual bond issue, yet." There were signs in the room that people wanted to ask a barrage of new questions or make statements, but Tari went on.

"Within the next few weeks, the school board is going to be

making decisions about the scope of the program to be proposed. It is going to be complicated, as everyone here can see. The school board has to look at all the factors. The present student load, projected loads, construction costs, placement. They have to decide all that before they can ask for bids and get some preliminary designs, even. So, you can see, it has all got quite a ways to go before anything's anywhere near final."

She paused a moment as though letting all that sink in, looking around the room calmly. Feeney was impressed at this show of authority. She glanced at her husband, but Frank sort of shook his head, so she looked back at the room. "I think what we need to do," she went on, "is write down all our concerns and get them into the hands of the school board. What we can do is this... either you write directly to one of the board members, we have their names printed out here, or else you can bring suggestions to me at the next meeting and I'll pass them along. Also, the PTA leaders and I have decided to send out a questionnaire to all the households in the district, to gather some basic responses and concerns about the issue. And that way the board will be able to respond directly."

She had done it neatly, Feeney thought. He looked around. People seemed satisfied with that and some even seemed to be preparing to leave. Fifteen minutes more, he thought, they'd be out of there.

"Well," he said to Harrison. "That's that. We can split this up. We need to get our notes synchronized, and also make sure it aligns with the PTA and the school board. That means we need to check with both Tari and Faith over there, who's been taking notes for Ted."

Harrison grinned. "Sure," he said. "I'll leave Tari with you."

Feeney turned to look at Harrison, but then saw something else out of the corner of his eye. "Oh shit."

"What?" Harrison said, and then turned to look where Feeney was looking.

Bob Hawthorn was on his feet.

Feeney could tell from the way he rose that the real meeting was only now beginning.

284

"Just a question, Tari. Following up on Phil Owens' question a little. Don't you think it's a little strange that the school board will go ahead and make choices about the school project, without having first held an open, public debate?"

A murmur of assent rose from the crowd, but then Frank Baron, with a look of exasperated impatience, stood up and half turned toward Hawthorn. "What do you think we're doing here?"

"Looks to me like an information meeting. And only that."

"Looks to you," Frank smiled. "That's the point. The only sort of meeting that would have any meaning for you would be one you were running."

"I suppose I could say the same sort of thing, and say the only sort of meeting that you would prefer, is one where you don't hear any serious questions."

"You haven't heard any serious questions tonight?"

"I haven't heard anything that gives me the impression people have any real idea what's going on, or are being given the full right, by way of input and real information, to discuss all the pieces of the project."

"Well, maybe you're just not listening, Bob."

"I'm listening fine, Frank."

"Is that right? You call listening coming down here with your group, just to throw a monkey wrench, any old somehow, into the whole idea."

"We came down here to make sure we know what's going on. And we're not feeling as though anyone's making much of an effort to help. Or that anyone is willing to talk about any point of view except the one that's going to ramrod a school bond down everyone's throat."

Frank looked around the room with an air of triumph. "You see how open they are? Right there, you get the whole thing. Ramrod. That's how they picture it. Like this is a dictatorship."

Harrison leaned toward Feeney and whispered, "Frank's a champ, eh? Putting that fuckwad in his place."

"Some people have different concerns," Hawthorn said.

"We know what your concerns are. They don't include the

education or safety of the town's schoolchildren."

Hawthorn's face went stiff. "That's a lie."

"Disprove it, then. Deny that every time you people put an ad in the paper, all you talk about is the money. The property tax. Taxation without representation."

"That's because, for the moment, that's all we can talk about. The school board is being so hush-hush about the plans, won't let anyone else in to discuss them."

"Bullshit, Bob. You don't want to discuss plans, you want to derail them."

"Come by one of our meetings, sometime."

Frank laughed. "Yeah, right."

Harrison leaned toward Feeney again, chuckling and whispering, "yeah right."

"You were the one mentioning dictators." Hawthorn turned to the audience. "They can't stand it when someone might disagree with them."

"You should know all about that."

"So... explain to me," Hawthorn turned to look at Frank, and then more pointedly at Tari, "why nobody from the school board is down here, or Ted Barnwell, or any of the council members or Charles Peace?"

It was a good question, and everyone in the room, including Frank Baron, knew it. Feeney looked up at Tari and raised his eyebrows, and she nodded. But even if she couldn't help agreeing that it would have been helpful for them to be there, she couldn't let what was left of the meeting go that way. He also looked over at Faith to try to catch her eye, but she was concentrated on the debate.

"This wasn't a regularly scheduled meeting, Bob," Tari said gamely. And then, with what Feeney had to admit was impressive creativity, she went on: "as you can see, we are here in fact to do just what you're talking about. Getting input. We don't have all that yet."

Hawthorn wasn't to be distracted. "I didn't ask that. I asked why it is that we aren't able to debate actual proposals. The details."

"You don't want a debate," Frank said. "What you want is to monopolize the entire issue with your point of view."

"Well, at least someone is offering a differing point of view."

"Yeah," Frank got the sneer on his face Feeney knew quite well. "Too bad that point of view is based only on ignorance and self-interest."

"Who do you think you are, to talk to me like that?"

Feeney could see that most of the people in the audience were uncomfortable with the exchange. But at the same time, he couldn't help feeling that most of the people sympathized with Hawthorn. At the very least, they seemed more comfortable with the calm way he pushed aside Frank Baron's aggression.

Feeney looked at Tari and drew a finger discreetly across his throat.

"All right, all right," she said loudly. "I think we can agree from what we have heard this evening, that this is a complicated issue. And we must also be aware that questions of all sorts will need to be answered before too long. But I hope that you'll also agree that we have made some steps towards doing that, tonight. And the next time around, we will all have a better picture of what's happening... how's that sound?"

Feeney looked back around at Hawthorn. It was obvious that it really was his call whether to keep this going.

Hawthorn, surprisingly, just nodded. Although, catching sight of Feeney, he gave him a look and then wiggled his finger back and forth to signal you and me. Feeney nodded, but just held up his hand like a telephone.

After the meeting, Feeney and Harrison went around finishing off their notes. Feeney, unable to catch Faith before she left, was speaking with Tari when Harrison finally came up and said that he and Frank Baron were going down to the highway restaurant to talk about the bond issue.

Feeney gave a quiet, steady look at Harrison. "Oh, sure," he said, "the bond issue."

"Yeah," Harrison said brightly. "Get some information about, you know, the point of view of people involved with the school district, doing things..."

"Yeah, uh... just a second, Tari, I've got some more questions.

Warren, let me give you my notepad, just in case." He pointed at his chair, where his jacket and another notebook sat.

They both walked toward his chair and when they'd got out of earshot, Feeney said calmly to Harrison. "What the fuck is this about?"

"What do you mean? He's got a great tone. We need to have his point of view, get these people's point of view."

"So, you're proposing to do an interview with Frank Baron?"

"Why not?"

"Why not? His wife is the PTA president. Not him. What do you think readers of that article are going to think? About the article? About us?"

"What about us?"

"It's going to look like we're only promoting a point of view coming out of the school board, talking to people who agree with it..."

"Wow," Harrison laughed. "You make it sound like you're more worried about the paper's image than the town's needs."

"Um...," Feeney rocked his head as though thinking. "How do I answer that? Oh, I know... yeah, for example. Although normally the idea is to do both."

"But his point of view is legitimate, and he's more articulate about it than his wife."

"You mean more belligerent."

"Belligerent sells."

So, Feeney thought, did other things. "You realize you're forcing me to have to actually do a balance article with Bob Hawthorn."

"Great."

"I should make you do it."

Harrison's face, which had been smiling, fell a bit. "You'd do that?"

Feeney stared at him. "Damn straight I would. Depends what you write."

So, later, as they walked down the sidewalk from the school, Feeney said to Tari: "That questionnaire mailing idea was genius.

You made it sound as though you'd had the idea the whole time of the meeting."

Tari laughed. "What a mess. But I'm glad I thought of it. This is proof that we need to get way more informed."

"It's not your fault. I can't believe Ted left you hanging."

"You know," Tari looked over at him. "Bob Hawthorn had a point tonight. Now that the PTA has stepped in, how are we going to be able to maintain such an innocent, open-to-all-sides position, the moment we take in hand the task of informing people?"

"Welcome to my world," Feeney smiled. "I can hardly wait to see the questionnaire. The questions are going to be like, what? Uh... do you feel your child deserves a better education? Do you care if the school district dies? Does it worry you that the school is a fire hazard? Would a new school help the town's image... that is, if the town has an image in the first place?"

Tari laughed. "You're not giving me much credit."

"Maybe not. But I defy you not to write: do you think it will have a serious impact on your already scrimpy and threatened household budget to know you will have to shell out anywhere from tens to hundreds of dollars more to build a school that will be used by maybe a little over twenty-five percent of the town's families?"

"That's awful."

She laughed again.

"Most true things are. And, what's more, given that there are a hell of a lot of retired folk in the district, we're also telling them that they're probably being asked to pay for something that only other people's kids are going to benefit from. Their own kids long since gone."

"Demographics show...," Tari laughed, holding up her hands.

"And Hawthorn's thing," Feeney went on, "half of them moved to this district to avoid paying exactly those property taxes other areas of the state are hit with to pay for their big school systems. And now here they are being asked to do it here."

Tari gave him a look of consternation. "Whose side are you on?"

"I'm just saying what they'll say."

They fell silent, each in their own thoughts, and for a while just walked quietly along the sidewalk beneath the dark trees.

He took a breath and looked at the houses along that particular street. Most of them had been built in the late twenties. Built after the decline of Sultan had already begun, but before anyone had noticed. Solid homes. Nothing imposing. Yet big, comfortable homes for big, comfortable families that still had plenty to do there in the valley. Big, comfortable porches where a young man, the kids off to bed, stepping out in the evening to take the night air and look at the fine street of new homes fronted by young maples and chestnuts along the new sidewalk, might feel secure. Those days, a man could still hold a big, comfortable optimism about the future.

Eighty years later, Feeney thought, a young family man could step out on the same porch and wonder: how the hell can I keep the mortgage payments up on this damn old barn? And stare at the uneven sidewalks heaved up by the roots of those heavy maples and chestnuts. And look at the sorry, rundown condition of other houses down the street. And if he thought about it at all, he might think how it could still be a fine enough neighborhood if only the town had enough money for the upkeep of the street, and the people living in the other houses had enough money to keep their houses at least painted and their yards tidy.

Big, comfortable houses, Feeney thought, full of big, uncomfortable problems.

The night was pleasant, leaves on trees still heavy with summer. A canopy of black overhead to shield Tari and himself from the occasional glaring pools of streetlights as they made their way down the silent street.

"Oh, God, Pat," Tari said suddenly. "Do you think we've got any chance at all?"

There, walking in her company down the street and forgetting the town's problems, Feeney's mind had drifted miles from the bond issue. He struggled to return to it.

"It's going to be very hard," he said. "Only with a lot of work, and with the right sort."

"The right sort?"

290

"Yeah. I'll be honest. I'm a little worried about a few things that have happened lately."

Tari gave him a look. "I see," she said. "You know, Ted called me and said the PTA should have a meeting with Tickler so that our efforts could be coordinated. He thinks the faster we get organized, the better chance we have."

"Great."

Tari gave him another look, and then smiled. "I didn't think you were a jealous sort of guy."

Feeney looked up into the trees, chuckling, and then he looked back at her. "There's some of that, OK. But look, Steele's occupation is, by definition, direct competition with the editorial side of any town's newspaper he comes into contact with. But he's here, and that's the way it is. But I was just saying to Ted that it would have been better if Steele had spent more time getting the lay of the land before all the publicity started."

"I hate his name."

"You're being diplomatic."

"No, seriously. Who would want to be called Tickler?"

"Yeah," Feeney sighed.

"You know, Pat, I've always thought that if things are meant to be, for good or bad, they eventually happen one way or another."

"I'd like to think so."

"And I think the new school is meant to be."

"It probably will be," he said. "But also, it probably won't be what you expect."

They had come to the end of their walk and were now standing there, looking at each other. Feeney smiled at her and then, just for an instant, he almost could have thought something passed through her eyes as she looked at him.

"What do you think we expect, you and I?" she said.

Feeney's mind went completely blank, and then he became extremely self-conscious and realized, among other things, why he had stopped walking with her right there. Having descended the length of that tree-guarded street, they had ended up nearly all the way down at Main Street, but stopping there before the glare of the streetlights was upon them. The sign of Tom Carlton's bar blazed a few blocks away.

Seeing the sign, it just came out: "You want to come have a beer?"

"Oh," she said. "That would be, uh..."

"Oh," Feeney said quickly. "Yeah... no... I just..." And he kicked himself. Then kicked himself again. He knew what it was, and knew it was just that goddamn kneejerk loneliness bashing away at him like some junior-high bully, and letting himself get wistful about spending more time with a woman, an attractive one at that, who seemed to find him interesting. And he also knew, it wasn't really Tari that had caused that.

She reached out, with a smile. "That's okay. Flattered, actually, but you know..."

Feeney hadn't really meant anything. It had just come out. But it would be worse to admit even to that. "Right, right," he said aimlessly.

She smiled. "I have to go down to the restaurant and rescue Warren."

"You mean, Frank."

"No," she laughed. "Warren. He has no idea what he's got himself into."

Feeney nodded, thinking, he's not the only one. The only difference being that Feeney knew he could recognize that in time.

His only saving grace.

Chapter 50

Pillar of the Community

A LOOK of pain crossed Feeney's face and he switched the phone to his other ear. When Parker was unhappy, phone calls became protracted affairs, his voice climbing uncomfortably into the higher registers.

"... and they want me to give a speech. A speech! Can you imagine? Jesus H. Christ. It's bad enough I have to spend both goddamn days down there in that swirling pool of muck, but now I've got to say something in front of those boneheads."

The swirling pool of muck he was referring to was the Washington Journalist Association's annual meeting, a two-day event of hobnobbing, speeches, roundtables, job seminars for journalism school graduates, and whatever else two hundred off-duty newspaper people could get up to in forty-eight hours, all topped off with the annual WJA Media Awards ceremony.

"It's your turn this year," Feeney said, looking out into the parking lot.

"And you know what every one of those ingrown bastards will be thinking? They'll be going, there he is, that's what's become of Gig God Almighty Shire's papers...," Parker paused to get a breath. "Shit! There are times I really hate all this, you know?"

Feeney nodded toward the office as though it were full of people listening to the call. "I don't know, Dean, I mean, it's sort of part of being a pillar of the profession?" He was going to say more, but that was as far as he got.

"And what's your part, Patrick?" Dean snarled. "Oh, never

mind. You know when it went downhill? It was when they let those con-man advertising swindlers descend on the place like flies."

For the next ten minutes Feeney sat back in his chair looking at the ceiling, contemplating the pattern of tiny holes in the acoustical tiles. From time to time, he nodded and said "yeah" or "sure." The rest of the time he stared at his desk, the ceiling, his fingernails.

Up to a certain point, Feeney had felt alarmed by Parker's call. From the way Parker had started grousing about it, Feeney had felt a chill come over him, sure he was going to be sent as a replacement. For a full five minutes he'd been horrified.

Up to that point, he'd always managed to avoid the Convention, where he could only envision himself following Parker around like a trained monkey while the publisher accosted people with an endless series, Feeney had no doubt, of particularly out-of-place tales of woe, indiscretions and bad jokes. But then, from the level of complaining, he realized Parker's real annoyance came from there being no way he could turn down the WJA commissioners. Because of the speech. Once Feeney realized he was off that particular hook, he just juggled the phone from one tired ear to the other and from time to time interjected sounds meant to convey sympathy and shared outrage or disapproval.

As for Parker's grumbling about the speech, Feeney barely listened. It was indeed Parker's turn to be among the speakers, and as much as he might hate the idea of giving one, he would never trust anyone to write it for him.

Parker was now droning on about how cheap the commission was, and Feeney smiled. It seemed the meeting was being held this year in... God... where? Way out on the coast somewhere. Grays Harbor? Aberdeen? Feeney's olfactory memories recreated a whiff of oil-soaked, low-tide seaweed and dead oysters. Or... worse, maybe somewhere even farther on down. Long Beach.

Feeney's mind went out to those towns, all the way the hell and gone out on the Pacific side of the Olympic Peninsula. The Puget Sound was generally considered by most people in the state to be the Rainy Side. Out there on the coast, it was the Monsoon.

Why way out there? Because for about five years' running the conventions had been held in Wenatchee or Yakima which, true enough, were more centrally located. But they were also the biggest community papers in the state and tended to sweep up all the awards. Complaints, therefore, forced the Convention Committee to go for some far-flung place. And because they'd been in Eastern Washington for so long, they'd decided far-flung would mean some town out on the Pacific Rim.

Feeney wondered.

Grays Harbor? It was an old mill town. No one went there except a few lost tourists looking for an ocean beach. Salient local points of interest were heaps of cedar and fir bark, disintegrating shake mills, oily estuaries, rusting sea docks, and constant rain drizzling down through a thick and ever-present ocean-born fog.

Aberdeen? Much the same, minus the charm. Thank God, he thought, he never had to go to these awful things.

"Well," Feeney said, "at least they're picking up most of the tab this year."

The Convention was held in late October. Supposedly, the Committee was shelling out for the accommodations to offset travel costs for papers from the other side of the state. But in reality, they were doing it because if they hadn't, half the state would never show up.

"Shit," said Parker, "they'd better goddamn well pick up the fucking tab. We're all going to die of pneumonia." It was true. After September, that part of Washington consisted of being cold most of the time and wet all of the time. "Ilwaco…," he went on, "my ass."

Feeney almost laughed out loud. So, it was Ilwaco. Even farther down than Long Beach, on that last rocky extension of land sticking out toward the Pacific, on the north side of the mouth of the Columbia River. In fact, you couldn't go any further south and west than that unless you took a boat from Ilwaco's harbor.

"You never know, Dean. It might be nice."

There was a long pause, and then Parker said: "You think it might be nice, eh?"

"Maybe not nice…" Feeney felt himself cringing. Parker's voice had radically changed with that question. It had almost sounded normal, and no longer angry or bitter, and maybe even cheerful... considering how utterly laden with sarcasm it was. That tone never meant anything good.

"Yeah..." Parker drawled. "Maybe not. But you know something? You know what I think?"

Feeney knew his employer's changeable moods by heart, often first noticing them in the changing tones in his voice. This particular tone, of sudden cheerfulness, often accompanied discussions he had with Feeney where he knew he was asking him to do something he wouldn't want to do. But which got Parker out of spots he didn't want to be in.

Feeney was now holding his breath.

"You there?"

Parker's voice had now risen a bit.

"So, here's what I think... You there?"

Feeney looked up at the ceiling, his heart sinking. "Yeah."

"Okay, so listen," Parker said sweetly. "Here in the next week or so, I'd be grateful if you'd draft up a few ideas for my speech. This year's theme is 'Making a Difference.' See what you can come up with."

Parker paused, evidently expecting Feeney to begin offering excuses or pleas for mercy, but Feeney said nothing, so he went on, sounding almost disappointed:

"And also, no jokes. I hate that bullshit. It should be funny, though. You know, from time to time, really funny. But no jokes. I'm not going to try to pretend to be like some fucking stand-up comedian... like some of those guys do. But also, I want some tough... true... touching... honest and real stuff. Ten minutes, max. Oh... maybe fifteen. I can always cut it down. But whatever... just make it so they understand our presence. And no shit about Old Gig Shire. I'm not going to do that shit anymore. Got all that?"

"Fifteen minutes? Fifteen? That's fifteen hundred words, Dean."

"I asked, did you get all that?"

"Yeah, I got all that, Dean."

"How long do you think it'll take?"

Feeney thought quickly. He had nothing to do that afternoon, and figured he could write something in about two hours. He looked up at the clock. It was only one o'clock.

"Sometime next week okay with you?"

"That long?"

"Well, you know, it'll need some reflection."

Then there was another pause. And Feeney thought, with some relief, that Parker was finally done.

But he was wrong.

"Oh, and Patrick?"

"Hmmm?"

"This year, you'll be joining me."

The phone went dead in Feeney's ear.

He set the phone back in its cradle, thought for about thirty seconds, and reached for a sheet of paper.

All told, it took forty-five minutes. Six double-spaced pages. He felt neither spite nor resentment, but it truly was a Machiavellian work of art. Sincerely earnest, homey and honest, generous and considerate... it was one of the easiest things Feeney had ever written.

Dean Parker, he knew, would read it once, scowl, and then decide it was exactly what he had meant all along.

All he had to do was imagine how Dean Parker thought, and write exactly the opposite.

Chapter 51

Brother in Arms

THE hour of our mornings, unwatched. As in the hour of our birth. As in the hour of our—

At three in the morning, not knowing any other way to feel, Feeney let philosophy run its course.

A different sort of day loomed as Feeney rolled north on the empty predawn highway. Even so, faced with the semi-adventure of a changed routine, his mind caught for a moment on the usual banalities.

Parker had been adamant. Under no circumstances was the paper to start writing a balanced report of the school bond issue, pro versus con, when ten thousand dollars and two hundred new subscriptions per month were now pouring across the transom.

The attitude was petty. Mean. It was purely commercial and showed utter bad faith. And despite his misgivings, Feeney went along with it because it was making mincemeat out of Jansen's efforts to gain a foothold in the valley.

Everywhere, Parker's papers were mopping up the valley on the strength of the bond issue. The paper had expanded by another dozen pages to hold all the ads, stories, letters to the editor, discussion columns, interviews and "man in the street" comments. Feeney had finally convinced Parker it was no longer necessary to fawn over Joel Myers. Nobody, not even the Safeway manager, would be moronic enough to ignore the paper's swelling circulation.

Thus, a mind could relax its focus. Muse. And Feeney let it go as the empty miles passed.

Alone.

Taillights far ahead, dim twinklings in his rearview mirror. Fellow travelers on his highway, but distant on this morning born of biological necessity.

One of Parker's "ad-girls," a normally statuesque but lately very pregnant redhead named Connie Brockton, had rung Feeney awake at a quarter to two to let him know her waters had broken and that she therefore could not take the paper up to the printers. Feeney had agreed instantly, and it was only about five minutes later, as he incurred the pain of actually waking up, that he wondered whether he should feel flattered or insulted at having been considered the only staff member she could call at that hour.

He went over to the Post, collected the layouts, drove out to the highway, got some gas, some coffee, and a couple of glazed doughnuts, and headed in toward Everett and the interstate.

There was no doubt, Feeney was thinking by the time he got to the freeway interchange and took the on-ramp north, watching the increasing density of suburban development, that the planet was going to end up an anthill. But then, who knew? Maybe when things really began to go bad, another big mess would take place, with all the usual high ideas, low brutality, tragic misdirection, reprisals and manipulation, and wipe it all back to the Middle Ages.

Feeney yawned at the highway, then smiled. It was 3:30. By now, Connie was down at the hospital, going through the business of squeezing their third child out into the wide, wonderful world, a boy this time, supposedly.

He would be named James. Forever after, Jim. A solid, no-nonsense name: Jim Brockton. The sort of name that fell into place, as no doubt Jimmy Brockton would, like a well-mortared brick.

Feeney looked out across the Snohomish flood plain to the east, where, beneath the first glimmers of rising light, the long black line of the Cascades, still featureless in its gloom, stood like a ragged wall. Down on the plain, in a vast dark grayness across salt marshes and alder woods, dairy farms tucked like puzzle pieces into the foothills, with the occasional light from equipment sheds or bars to mark their locations. Even as he drove, a faint rose-and-yellow dawn increased over the silhouetted mountains, creating an ever-eerier luminescence in the patches of fog and mist drifting low across dry fields and over the winding creeks and riverbeds.

A world still and quiet. Still quiet.

Feeney ate his doughnut and drank his coffee. Wouldn't it be nice, he thought, if all his mornings began like this.

Kent Poole was press foreman at Marysville. Like Feeney, he was hovering around thirty. He was strongly built and had thick, straight blond hair that often went a long way between haircuts, and so tended to give his square-jawed face the look of a yeoman farmer's. He smoked cigars and wore, at least every time Feeney had seen him, the same old grey coveralls.

Because of Kent's confidence and talent at running the big, thirty-roll offset, and the laconic good humor with which he did so, Feeney always felt a little self-conscious in his presence. After all, a scribbler like himself, compared with a sturdy workman such as Poole, who rarely said anything that wasn't of direct concern, could seem inconsequential. What was news, after all, but a kind of gossip?

Of course, the other reason Feeney always felt self-conscious when he showed up in Marysville with the page proofs was because Poole and the rest of the pressmen would have expected the ad-girl. They liked Feeney well enough, but were always disappointed it wasn't Connie, and he didn't blame them a bit.

He stood in the chill of the pressroom, watching Poole prepare the proofs. The big door out onto the loading dock was open, and from beneath the hard brilliance of the lights in the shop, the lightening sky outside returned to seeming black as midnight.

He warmed his hands on a coffee cup. Poole brewed an even more hair-raising version of coffee than Feeney did, but Feeney contentedly sipped it while Poole and his crew burned in the plates—watching with admiration the somewhat obscure work being done professionally, expertly, and easily.

Young as Poole was, he had already worked at the press for more than twelve years, since before he had finished high school. He knew everything there was to know about running a press. For that matter, he knew pretty much all there was to know about running a newspaper, and held, not surprisingly, well-advised views on a lot of the papers up and down the Puget Sound, many of which he printed. And he knew plenty about most of the newspaper people, whether owners, editors, reporters, or shop people.

It was an extensive, eclectic backstage knowledge that made Feeney both envious and curious, and he always made an effort to pry some of it loose. Poole, though, was not the easiest person to get to talking as he backed and filled around that big press, adjusting rollers, pressure heads and plate alignments. But, being single-minded about it, Feeney usually managed to get the pressman to spill some of his store.

Some of it was only office gossip. Always interesting, all of it, if supremely worthless. But other observations were indeed highly valuable to Feeney, especially one day when Poole came to analyzing the differences between Parker and his predecessors. When Poole had first started working at the press, Arnie Bradshaw, although long retired, had still been writing the occasional article and still, on occasion, paying a visit to the press to see some of the older pressmen he'd known for decades.

Poole told Feeney that Arnie had been George Shire's right-hand man for so long that, when he finally took over, few people noticed much difference at first. Eventually, though, they sure did.

Poole wanted Feeney to understand that he did not mind Parker too much. Maybe the guy had a few quirks, but he was less boneheaded than some others. Arnie Bradshaw, however, had been something else. From what Poole had gathered, people ended up respecting Bradshaw more, in some ways, than they had Gig Shire.

Gig had represented the heroic era of the paper, chronicling the efforts of those little towns to hack their way up out of the rough pioneer, logging and mining settlement beginnings. Arnie Bradshaw had taken all that and then transformed it, modernized it, managing to make people feel that culture and civilization were just around the corner. Two different tempers, two different styles. Although Poole had conceded, in response to a remark from Feeney, that it could have simply been a question of two different times.

Where Gig's youth had found him panning for gold in the

Klondike, Bradshaw's had been back East getting an education. Where Gig, chomping on a cigar, loved nothing better than wandering into the smoke-filled antechambers of the capital building in Olympia, completely at home there amongst the waist-coated dealmakers, Arnie spent most of his glory years chairing any number of committee meetings concerned with community affairs.

Despite those differences, Poole said, the underlying principle remained the same. Old Gig and Old Arnie had been rock-hard, states-rights men who made up their minds about an issue and would as soon have got run over as hesitate to speak out about something they felt was right or wrong.

Both had managed the paper like a personal mission, and in the end knew that county, and the state for that matter, right down to the last blade of grass.

The upshot of all that, Poole said, was that whether Parker won the newspaper war with Jansen or not, Jansen would never, ever have tried it at all with Arnie Bradshaw still up there at the helm. Maybe not even with that Conroy fellow, the first of several mediocre publishers between Arnie and Parker.

"Why not?"

They were standing by the big press. Poole was up on the catwalk between two presses, a spatula in hand, cutting out hunks of printer's ink from a bucket and then smearing it into the trough at the top. "Arnie wasn't the sort of guy you messed with."

"He had a lot of pull?"

"Ah, no. Nothing like that. That was how Gig Shire ran the papers. Although Arnie had plenty, too, by the time he took over. Every time Scoop came back from D.C., he'd go straight out to see Old Man Arnie, because it had been the Old Man who got Henry Jackson elected way back when... at state level. But not because the Old Man pulled strings. But because he was the Old Man. That was all there was to it. You could like the guy, or you could hate his guts. One way or the other didn't matter much to him, as long as he figured you were being honest with him the way he'd be with you. But either way, I never met anyone who didn't respect him—either as a newspaperman, or as a man."

"Jansen wouldn't have tried anything?"

"Jansen wouldn't have done shit."

"Well," Feeney sighed, "now, he is."

"Thirty-six pages this morning." Poole eyed the presses. "You guys seem to be doing all right."

"Jansen can't touch Parker for the moment." Feeney nodded.

"Dean's lucky with that school bond rolling behind him with all that weight. And your articles are good."

Poole had seen all the political ads in the paper, and knew as well as Feeney how Parker had managed to pump up the circulation and advertising on the heels of all that. As well, his remark showed that he didn't see any reason to do any ethical hand-wringing about Feeney's reporting. Poole was a newspaperman before anything else and knew that when you were in the trenches, it was the wrong time to be delicately balancing the various philosophic approaches to battle strategy. Let alone the ethics of your own position. They shot at you; you shot back. Whoever had the biggest bullets, or the most, would win.

Jansen, of course, was just being a businessman. But none of the newspaper people in the county liked him for it, if only for the reason that he'd been, up to then, one of them. If he had been an outsider, someone coming up from California or from back East, it would have been another thing.

"Yeah, Dean's lucky," Feeney said. "But for me, sitting up there in the middle of it..."

Poole nodded. "Yeah. See? That's the difference between the two of them, right there. Although it never would have happened. . and if it had, I'm saying... the Old Man would have waded into it right up to the neck." He was still troweling the ink along the inking gutter, but then stopped, this being one of those rare instances when his conversation with Feeney became more important than the work at hand.

"That's the big difference between a guy like Old Man Bradshaw and a lot of these other guys..." He waved the spatula in a little circle to indicate other small and medium-sized publishers in the neighboring towns. "Things haven't changed all that much from the Old Man's time to now, except that now, nobody's willing to really speak out anymore. Some of them, you know, are just pussies, but the rest of them seem to act as though they're trying to publish the Wall Street Journal. They don't talk about half the things going on in their towns because it seems too far beneath them anymore. You know what I mean?"

Feeney did.

"I don't know," Poole went on, giving a shrug. "Maybe that doesn't matter at first, these guys making their towns sound like nothing weird ever goes on. But in the long run, it makes the publishers seem like they're reporting from a thousand miles away. And nobody can do that and still seem like a part of things the way the Old Man was. Or how Gig Shire was. I don't know if it's good for anyone at all."

Ready as ever to be as philosophical as the next man, Feeney decided not to join in, if only because Poole's reflections were just too close to his own endless thoughts on the subject. He shrugged, though, in agreement.

"The weirdos get plenty of press. Believe me."

It was Poole's turn to shrug. "I guess it could get tiring, reporting on that sort of stuff. End up feeling like you got no job at all. Not even important. More like running a barbershop or a feed store, the only difference being that the paper actually prints the talk. But you know something? That's what we're all about. Otherwise, everything just ends up the same. One person talking sounds like anyone else, one town like another, one paper like another. A lot of those guys, you know, grew up in these towns. Even Dean Parker. But it's strange how they don't look at things the way their parents did. Some of them, like Dean, are mercenaries. Or some of them went off somewhere and came back and now it's all too small. Whatever. Or else it's the reporters they hire. Right out of school. First job. Who want to write everything like it's meant for the wire services. The papers end up more important than the towns. You say the weirdos get written about, but I'm not so sure. I see less and less eccentricity." He gave a last smoothing to an ink tray, set his trowel down, took a big pull on his cigar, and blew out a cloud of smoke into the cold air of the pressroom. "Less and less, Pat. If you guys don't write about the kooks, sooner or later the kooks are going to get away with anything."

Poole picked up his trowel and headed down the catwalk to the ladder, nodding at one of the press boys, who walked up to the side of the press row and hit a big, red ink-stained knob. A bell rang, a horn blasted, and the presses began to roll, slowly at first, and then gradually spun up to an ear-deafening running speed. There was no way for Feeney to talk with the presses turning. He turned and walked down to the press outflow belt.

Feeney loved to watch the press run, the paper streaming up from big rolls into the presses and then running down into the folding and cutting machine where the paper was spat out onto a conveyor belt like a lava flow.

Standing by where two press boys were throwing bundled papers onto a pallet, Feeney stripped out random papers from the outflow to check the ink. But he also read the articles, giving them the critical eye one could only give one's own words when they were actually in print form, ready for the public's eyes. Too late to change.

Not that he felt any anxiety about his professional capabilities. He knew the words and structure of the articles were above reproach. But Poole's comments rang in his ears.

On the surface, the paper was fine. The front page was harmonious. Large, medium, and small photos balanced down the page. Headlines overlapped, wrapped, and balanced one another, descending in a gradient of size as they dropped down the page, giving the reader a quick overview in headline and first paragraph, if not from the photos themselves, of the major stories of interest from the last week.

Every article was written and presented so that it could be read in three or four ways: either fully read, half-read, skimmed, or even skipped, in which case the headline did the work. Each one of Feeney's stories was a silent attestation to his skills at reporting.

The lead-off article—avoiding giving absolute prominence to the school bond issue—concerned a new child-abuse center being set up at the same Monroe hospital where Connie Brockton and her husband were at this moment undergoing a rather intense episode in the joys of parenting.

The next story concerned the town council in Sultan. Dry stuff, but also informative, especially about some sewer work which would begin in a few weeks and would disrupt traffic. After that came the school stories. His and Harrison's. The particular bent of the one he'd written concerned the way the world was now imposing new demands on students, how they were expected to develop an intuitive feel for the new work tools coming their way.

The story following was a Merchants' Association wrap-up. The merchants were moving into high gear now for the logging show. Try as he had, it had been difficult for Feeney to maintain a straight reportorial face when writing how some of them had lit into each other about the desirability of inviting carnival people.

Then came shorts covering community charity and volunteer events.

Most of the big stories on the front page, and even some of the smaller ones, spilled inside the paper, using the time-honored technique of bringing the reader inside to finish an article, only to be confronted by a similar article or the opinion page. Making sure the reader got hit, at the same time, with as much of the advertising as possible.

The school story now almost always spilled into a page leading into some related piece, if not directly across from the Op-Ed page where Feeney had been given the liberty to take a free swing at the issue.

Following that, and running past the ads out to the end of the paper, were the rest: the news releases and what Feeney called "Show and Tell" stories, where he would go out and capture a few locals doing whatever it was they did, and ensure that the town really knew it was being written about. Something that Jansen had yet to be able to duplicate.

But in the whole paper, from the flag right through the last ad in the last right-hand bottom corner of the last page, there was not one single moment of eccentricity, not one wayward thought, no flight of the imagination upon higher planes, no treading through the lower. All white meat, and tastefully so.

Sure, there was the implicit controversy brewing over the school ads. But ads were ads. And letters to the editor were just letters to the editor. That column was a complete dog's dinner of not only thankfulness, intelligence and thoughtfulness, but disgruntlement, idiocy, and mean-spiritedness.

Feeney saw that Poole was right. Readers learned everything about the town except all those things, for good or bad, that made it different from other towns.

Feeney looked at the roaring presses. He did not have to stay and watch. The proofs were now back in their binders and set alongside the door for the delivery truck, which would be there at any minute. But he remained, watching the streams of newsprint flying up across the big machines, watching the pressmen as they adjusted pressure rollers and springs to ensure that the paper printed evenly and that all the pages were lined up going into the cutting machine.

Poole and his boys were the lucky ones, Feeney thought suddenly. The production side of the paper was the best. Just a mechanical flow to be nudged here and jiggled there. And stripping papers from the outflow, their concern was simply that the ink was smooth and the edges were straight. But they read as well. Quickly. Each and every article. Once again to ensure smooth inking.

God only knew, Feeney thought, what the effect was of reading upwards of forty different newspapers every week. It would make for a very special sort of newspaper reader. Strangely enough, given the way things worked in Marysville, it could almost seem as though Kent Poole and his boys represented both ends of the process. And standing there in the press room, a reporter could feel he was just getting in the way. The paper flowed, the ink drums rolled, and out the other end shot a product giving no indication, in itself, of any of the efforts made to produce it. As far as the pressmen were concerned, whatever made its way into the paper came by pure natural selection. A no-brainer.

It could make the same reporter wonder why he bothered to go through all the intellectual, moral, and ethical gymnastics about what got written—if he did, that was—when none of that showed through. At all.

Feeney stared out at the daylight now shining in from the loading dock, then went over and picked up the layouts. The regular day had begun, and he had regular things to do, although, if the morning rush-hour traffic down the highway wasn't too bad, he had time to stop by the hospital to see how the suddenly increased Brockton family was getting along.

Chapter 52

Shots in the Dark

FEENEY was doing something deliberately idiotic... wandering around Main Street early in the morning in hopes of bumping into... anybody halfway friendly. Maybe Tari, who he knew liked having breakfast downtown. Or... better, much better... Faith. Although he had no idea what she did, or didn't do, in the mornings. Idiotic.

He shivered in the cold air and wished he'd worn a sweater. It didn't matter what season it was; the morning mountain air was always chilly in the early hours, especially when it came with gusts of wind. After half an hour of freezing idiocy, Feeney finally dove into the coffee shop, and there directly into the presence of Tickler Steele.

Unpleasant as that was, it was no surprise. Steele was omnipresent those days as the bond issue campaign unfolded. Feeney managed to avoid him most of the time, letting Harrison deal with him. But they crossed paths often enough anyway.

"I'm just on my way over to see Ted," Steele said. "I got another idea this morning. You'll find it interesting."

Feeney looked at the lady at the counter and spread his hands to indicate the biggest cup possible, and then sat down opposite Steele.

"We were thinking," Steele went on, "that what we need to do is have some sort of rally. You know, a town meeting where we can get people together and show them the project."

This was something new. Up to then, Feeney had thought the whole idea of the campaign was to present the bond in the most hygienically sterilized manner possible. Now Steele was suggesting an actual open forum. The long-avoided town meeting Feeney had thought, after the first PTA meeting, would be organized, but hadn't been.

"Really?" he said. "I thought you and Ted had decided against that. Why change tactics now?"

"Change tactics?"

Feeney's coffee came, and he took a sip, which made him pause. The difference between this coffee and what he made at the office... or at home, for that matter... was startling. He frowned, getting his concentration back.

"Yes. Taking the issue into the open."

"It's been in the open from the start."

Feeney smiled. "So open we've got a citizen's group willing to pay almost sixty thousand dollars in advertising fees just for the laugh of it."

"That's politics, Pat. And you know what else? I'll bet you anything Hawthorn's got something else on his mind besides this school bond. You just watch. A man like that... you know... could get pretty bored after a while playing Old McDonald."

"I don't know about that, Tickler. He's pretty devoted to his place up there."

"He works a lot, period. He's the sort of guy who works because he doesn't know how to rest. Sooner or later, that restlessness turns to something else. You just watch and see. The bond issue is just the start."

"Maybe so. But anyway, why are you changing your methods?"

"I told you, nobody's changing tactics or methods."

"But you just said you wanted to host a big meeting."

"That's right." Steele made his voice sound patient.

"Okay, okay," Feeney said. "That's not the point. You know I agree with the idea. I always have. But you know as well as I do it will be messy. Meetings have been promised time and again." Feeney had a bitter moment thinking how Tari, under pressure from Barnwell, Steele, and her own husband, had never followed through on a second PTA meeting. "And if only for that, you're going to have the opposition standing on chairs and yelling at you." Feeney shrugged. "But if you can handle the immediate criticism and then get to the issue, maybe we'll have a chance to get people thinking the public is indeed being let into the process. Me, you know, I think that's what's been missing."

A puzzled look came and went on Steele's face, and he shook his head.

"No, no. You've got it all wrong. I see what you were thinking. You think we're planning one of these bullshit town-hall things that are so popular. So-called debate and all. God help us if we did that. No worry about that. I said a rally. Get as many of our people together, and those we can get committed between now and then, and have a big pep talk so we can send them out with a sort of mission. A get-out-the-vote sort of thing."

Steele suddenly frowned and reached out a finger to tap Feeney's arm.

"What's this, though, about the issue needing something else? What did you mean by that?"

Feeney ignored the look on Steele's face.

"I was just thinking," he said, "that maybe this whole thing is getting so canned that the people who haven't decided may just stay that way. They might figure it's already locked up, so no matter what—maybe not even if you hold a rally every week until the end of February—they're not going to vote. They won't think they need to."

"That's not the way to do it. Maybe someone like you needs to hear five hours of jawboring before you can make up your mind. But most people just need a little pat on the back to get moving."

"Or a shove."

Steele's face changed. "Or a kick in the ass."

Feeney smiled. "You know, Tickler," he said, "I don't need anyone to take a kick at me to help me figure out what side I'm on. And I'm pretty sure there are a few other people in town who would tell you the same thing if they heard the way you talk. And... if we're going to be frank with each other... even though the paper is fully square on this issue, at some point it's going to backfire, the way

311

we're being used to lambaste this town. If we haven't yet actually maligned the opposition with libel, we've done just about everything we can to discredit them. Our position is such that anyone reading the paper who doesn't agree is bound to feel a little abused by now."

Steele narrowed his eyes, his head beginning to shake, but Feeney held him off.

"I don't know," he went on, "Dean thinks it won't matter. Or he hopes that. But he's got other considerations, you know? For me, though... my opinion, which I can now see doesn't really matter but I'll say it anyway... is that I'm wondering how good a rally of the sort you're talking about will be. And I'm not just talking about the bond issue, but about the town's paper. Or the town. Because, and here's the deal, long after this is over, long after you're gone, Tickler, the town and the paper will have to find themselves again and heal what's becoming a pretty serious division."

Steele stared at him for a long moment, then spoke with obvious anger.

"I didn't think I'd be hearing this," he said. "Not at all. We've got enough to deal with without you going soft on us. You just stop for a moment and think about all the time and work a lot of damn good people have put into this. People who really care. People who have kids, or people who are on the side of the district's kids one way or another."

Feeney's eyebrows rose and he smiled. "If I didn't know better," he said, "I'd almost believe you lived here."

Steele's eyes narrowed. "And I'd almost believe you didn't. What is this, Patrick? You have some idea that undecided voters need to be treated with kid gloves?"

"No, but just with a bit more respect than throwing rallies which would make them feel excluded, or browbeaten."

"You're willing to throw a lot of hard work away. You've got a lot of nerve. I'll say that."

"Nerve. Or... ethics?"

It wasn't long, just a bit more than a slow blink, but it was something... a certain shading in Steele's eyes... that caused Feeney to realize he was no longer dealing with someone who considered him a partner. And in the next instant, he could even think there was something worse.

"I don't think a guy like you has any lessons to teach anyone about ethics." The soft, slightly unfocused stare was still in Steele's eyes, but the mouth was now hard. "As a matter of fact, just because of you, we've had to change the way we do a few things around here."

Feeney, as a newspaperman, was used to hostile interviewees changing the subject, so he didn't put much weight into what Steele was saying, other than to ask: "What's that mean?"

A smile came onto Steele's face. "Like I have to tell you."

"Like... yeah. Maybe."

Steele shrugged. "Fine. I wouldn't... I wouldn't, you know, turn my back on a bit of that either. But the point is, as far as the school bond issue goes, there are places now where we can't have certain people together. You know? So, like I said, one, you haven't made my job or anyone else's easier. And I'm not going into it... but don't give me any lectures about ethics. Just... do me a favor... do us all a favor... don't go fucking up this thing for everyone else, regardless of whatever you do, or all the rest."

"Me fuck it up?" Feeney stared.

Steele sat back in his chair. "Maybe it wasn't right to do it," he said, half to himself. "We just figured it would work like it usually does. If the newspaper commits itself, that's usually all there is to it. But now I can see we have to deal with the editor as something different from the paper. Ted talked me into it. Said you were on the team. If we had known, we could have run the campaign in a different way, based on a noncommitted newspaper. Or a compromised editor. That's a whole different method."

"What the hell are you talking about? The paper's been committed from the start. And, what the serious fuck? Compromised..."

Steele nodded, though in a way that showed he wasn't all that interested. "Yeah, so you say. But committed in your way. Not the way needed to get the bond issue through in the best way. Now I can see it was a mistake."

313

"I don't see that it was any mistake."

"You wouldn't," said Steele with equanimity.

"In terms of the first thing, you think I don't know newspapers? You guys are always wrapped up in thinking people actually read your papers. All we wanted from you was one solid response for the community to note, once a week. One solid response, one way or the other, which we could work off. What do we get? We get a goddamn fucking public confab."

"That's what people expect."

"No, they don't," Steele laughed. "They want to be told what to think. That's all they want. You say you're on our side. Well, to be honest, whatever. I deal with politics. And what I do is the lowest, simplest form of politics. There are very simple rules to follow in getting a bond issue passed. You make it so there's no choice, and make the opposition sound like crackpots. Period. The point is to win the fucking vote and not worry about whether everyone feels personally enabled or whatever. You get it?" Steele held his hands up. "Hell, even Ted understands. Or sort of. At least he understands that politics is not a game of guesswork and chance and floaty ideas being batted back and forth. You, however, treat the whole thing as though you somehow know better. What I don't understand is whether you really want the bond issue passed or not. You act as though I don't know what I'm doing, and you do. And you act as if the only thing that matters to you is the newspaper. Or maybe not even that. Maybe what matters is your place as editor. To which I can only say: I don't really give a fuck about you and your role as editor."

Feeney was amazed. "You actually think I'm afraid that if I take a stand on the bond issue I'll fuck up my job?"

"Yes, I do."

"Oh, that's rich. Now who's externalizing?"

Steele and Feeney stared at each other for a long moment, then Steele picked up his cup and drank off the rest of his coffee.

"Never mind," he said. "Now that I think about it, not even you could fuck this one up."

"Thanks."

"I don't give a damn about your feelings." Steele took out his wallet, pulling Feeney's bill over and adding it to his own. "No, this is on me. Write what you want. It won't make any difference. From here on out, I'm going to modify things as though the paper is noncommitted. Or against us. All those fucking ads from Hawthorn's bunch. Jesus Christ."

"He's paying for them, and if you think Dean would refuse them, you're sadly mistaken."

"I know all about your little problem with your competitor."

"It isn't a little problem, Tickler."

"You seem to be doing all right."

"For the moment. But that's mostly because of this bond issue and Hawthorn's ads."

"I get it. And that's why you don't want to take sides. Playing one side off the other just to rake in the money."

"We're not playing one side against the other, as you say. We were, and are, fully in favor of the bond issue."

"Whatever. Do as you need, and we'll do as we need."

"It doesn't matter," Feeney frowned. "You talk about me. But for you, this is just another notch in your belt, and you won't convince me otherwise. You might actually believe you're on the side of the righteous. You do have a track record of helping school districts. But... on the other hand... with these things, school districts are always the ones who can pay your fees. Right? So, for all I know, this is just mercenary."

"Son of a bitch. Fair enough. But do me a favor?"

Feeney waited.

"Just one thing. If you actually are on our side, at least... if you can... clean up your act."

"My act?"

Steele stared at Feeney for a long moment, and then stood up.

"Question of... ethics," he said with a slight sneer. "And... it's a small fucking town, you know?"

Chapter 53

More Red Tags

ALL of it... from Mrs. Hagy's typesetting juggernaut, to the entombed mass of mouldy back issues, to the battleship-grey metal desks, to the typewriters, to the creaky oak chairs, to the chaos of the filing cabinets, to the washed-out posters and morbid potted plants, to the peeling insignia on the front window, to the stained ceiling tiles and dusty linoleum floor, to the pencil stubs, paperclips and odd assortment of ink pens on Feeney's desk, and right down, if it came to it, to the soap, paper towels, and toilet paper in the cramped washroom, everything there in Feeney's office was the official property, bought and damn-well paid for, of Dean R. Parker. It was no wonder, then, that whenever the publisher stuck his nose in the place on one of his rare forays up valley, Feeney could feel more like a visitor than the host.

Warren Harrison was out of the office and Parker was now planted comfortably in front of his desk, settled in as though sending down roots and eyeing Feeney with an air of insincere benevolence. At least he hadn't taken Feeney's chair.

No doubt, thought Feeney. This was trouble.

"Nice day," Parker said, staring at the cabinets.

Actually, it was a nice day. Outside. One of Feeney's eyebrows twitched. "Irony will get you nowhere."

"I thought Warren might be around. Since we need, especially, to talk about this school bond thing."

Harrison, Feeney knew, was over at the park playing tennis with Frank Baron. "He's digging up some background."

"Too bad." Parker pursed his lips. "Would have been good to have him here while we batted a few ideas around."

Feeney hunched over his desk and let his hands roam over the accumulated detritus in search of something to fiddle with, settling on an old eraser and then, feeling like a vaudeville straight man, cast a glance at Parker, and smiled. "Such as?"

Parker eyed Feeney. "You going to get touchy even before we get started?"

"It saves time that way."

"Goddamn it, Patrick Why is it every time we have one of these discussions, you have to get sore? Why the hell is that? Every time, you take everything as a criticism."

"Because every time, it is a criticism."

"I do not."

"Yes," Feeney nodded, "you do. But never mind."

"Christ." Parker made like a suffering soul. "We haven't even got started and you're already pissed off at nothing."

"Well then start, so I can have something real to get pissed off about."

"Don't pull that impatient... flustered shit. And that's the thing, see? That's what I've been talking about. The pressure and everything. Going off the rails. Upset at me. Upset at the town." Parker spread his hands. "But, hell, we all get that way from time to time. We get our faces shoved into it so much, you know. Know what I mean?"

"No, I don't. What do you want, Dean? You think I need a vacation, or something?"

"Let's not say things we might regret, huh?" Parker said.

"Oh no. Let's not."

Parker stretched his neck over his collar, looking up and frowning at the tea-colored stains on the ceiling tiles. "So you know who felt he had to come down and see me this morning?"

Feeney puckered out his lips and made a rude sound meaning he had no idea. "Let me check my list."

"Tickler Steele," Parker said.

This time Feeney stuck out his tongue as if he were retching.

317

Parker held up a finger. "He says you're fucking things up with the bond issue."

"What the hell? We're running our support for the bond right down the center of Main Street. Warren's all over the story like a shit fly. We've got ads, counter-ads, meetings, interviews, features, news items. And now we're even going to promote these rally things he wants to do. The only thing we haven't gotten around to yet is actually buying votes."

"Steele says you're not on the team."

A smile worked its way slowly onto Feeney's face. "Team."

"That you're not a player."

"I'm the editor of this goddamn newspaper..."

"He says you're just jealous that he and Ted Barnwell... and that Baron guy... are stealing your thunder. Running the show."

Feeney lifted his hands. "Well, there you go. There's the whole ball of wax, right there."

"OK," Parker shrugged, "maybe Steele's full of shit on that one."

"Maybe."

"The thing is, Pat, I don't care. None of that matters. But what I do care about is how it runs out."

"What's Steele think I'm going to do, scram out on the bond issue?"

"He's got that impression."

"And you believe him."

"I'm not on Steele's side. The paper is on the side of the bond issue."

"Yeah? Have you seen it lately or over the past three months?"

"Like it or not, Steele is the political expert. He's the one who should know if the campaign is running right or not. He's the one with the feel for it, no matter what you might say. Don't get me wrong. I'm not saying you're doing things wrong on your end. I think the paper is presenting what needs to be presented. What I'm saying is that the political expert on these sorts of things isn't getting a good feeling about where you stand."

"He means I'm not running things the way he would. So...

what's the deal? You going to make Steele editor for the interim?"

"I was thinking more of Warren."

Feeney smiled. "Warren would get this office firebombed within three weeks flat."

Dean's eyebrows went up, and his eyes flicked around the office as though actually imagining it. "In reality?"

"In reality, in effigy, what's the difference?"

"I'm not saying he would run the paper, just that he would take over the editorial and liaison side of the bond story."

"I know what you meant."

"Well, that's pretty much what Steele was talking about." Parker, at this point, got another frown on his face and scratched his neck pensively. "Okay, well, there's all that to think about. Just think about it a bit. Might make things easier for you, me, and everybody. Just think about it."

Feeney sat back in his chair. "Right, Dean. As if."

Parker realized he had gone too far. "Sorry, Pat."

"You're sorry? You get one goddamn complaint from that guy, and it's Katie bar the door. Me, I've had to see this guy every week, twice a week, three times a week, for months now."

Parker started waving his hands as though shooing away bugs "Let's not get all that started up again. Let's just figure how to keep all this shit on the rails, okay? He just makes one damn remark. I said I'm sorry. Just forget I said anything."

Feeney stared out the window, and then mumbled to himself: "I wish I knew how to play tennis."

"Huh?" Parker put his hands on Harrison's desk and stood up. "Just take care of it."

"Sure, sure," Feeney said.

Parker came around the office divider and stood for a second looking at the potted plant on the top of the file cabinet next to the coffee maker. He stuck out a finger and touched a leaf. "How is Mrs. Hagy doing?"

"She got a new dog."

Parker turned. "That so?" He grunted. "I thought Duke would live forever."

"She thought so, too."

Parker looked back at the plant, nodding his head, and then straightened his shoulders and took a breath. "Boy," he said. "Some days, huh?"

"Yeah. Some days, Dean."

Parker nodded his head again, and then glanced over at Feeney. "Just another thing, Pat. Steele also wanted to insinuate a few other things, uh, concerning you."

Feeney looked up. "Insinuations? You mean insinuations? Did you let him?"

"Of course not."

"Yeah." Feeney stared back. Steele's innuendo had made him think—who wouldn't? At first he thought it would be about Tari. But that was impossible. There was nothing to see. So it had to be about Beebee. But what the hell—there were all sorts of loose and iffy relationships up and down the valley. And nobody could have cared a stick about him and Beebee anyway. He didn't know Beebee's ex-husband, Carl, at all, and didn't think he would have cared one way or another. And as for anything else, it was all completely interior. Whether it was the Tari infatuations, or the imaginings about Faith Rockford—who could know that? "I don't know. Small towns, Dean."

"Tell me about it." Parker smiled. "Actually, I thought at first he was talking about Warren."

Feeney gave Parker a slow blink. "How flattering is that?"

Parker grinned. "Well, he is our local movie star."

Feeney looked down at his desk. "Oh, great."

At that, Parker turned and headed over to the door and pushed it open but then stopped and looked back again. "Just to let you know, Pat," he said. "I told him he was full of shit."

Feeney watched his boss as he crossed over to his car. Watched him get it started and then slowly drive away. And then sat there quietly, staring off into space, the eraser he'd picked up turning softly in his hand as though time had stopped. Then, with a flick, he sent it flying over Warren's chair.

Chapter 54

Testimony

"SHIT." Harrison threw his tennis racket into the corner and flopped himself down in his chair. "The guy's a goddamn bull. It's like trying to hit a cruise missile."

Feeney threw some junk mail into the bin. "Parker was up here complaining that Steele and company don't get the feeling the newspaper editor is on the team concerning the bond issue." He turned to give Harrison a steady look.

Harrison didn't bat an eye. "Yeah, Ted sort of gets worried about that."

"Ted does not 'sort of' get worried. He comes unglued."

Harrison pulled his head back. "He doesn't come unglued."

"Maybe not to you. But then, you're on the team."

"I thought we were all on the team."

"No," Feeney said. "I mean the team team. You know, the one where everybody gives the stiff-arm salute."

Harrison laughed. "Lucky thing people don't hear the way you talk."

"The way I talk? You expect me to sit here at my own desk, sounding like one of my rah-rah editorials?"

Harrison squinted. "Wow… a bit hypocritical, no?"

"No. It's a bit real."

"Frank doesn't believe you."

A sudden vision of Harrison and Frank Baron's tennis game flashed through Feeney's mind. "Frank can believe what he wants." Feeney said. "I believe me, and that's all that counts."

"What he means is that you don't sound convincing."

For just a second, Feeney wondered if Harrison had something to do with Parker's visit. No way to tell, of course. But he wouldn't have put it past Harrison.

"Other people think I'm convincing," Feeney said. "Including Frank's wife, for example."

Harrison nodded slowly. "Yeah, funny, huh? They're really different, those two."

"You think?"

"You know, Frank's a real dynamic guy. Ambitious. Hard-working. Got his heart in the right place, and all. But he doesn't really know how lucky he is. You know what I mean?"

Feeney knew exactly what he meant. But he didn't trust Harrison enough to get into any conversation of this type. "I don't... uh...."

Harrison leaned back in his chair. "Not many guys do, you know."

"Know they're lucky? Oh, I think so."

"No, know anything at all." He looked over at Feeney and grinned. And Feeney grinned back, wondering how much of this was the Porsche, the flashy smile, the clothes, the hair, or whatever was doing the talking.

"Is that right?"

"Just a matter of knowing what they want. Once you know that, all the rest is easy."

"Ah, the big secret. Give, then."

"It's no secret, man," Harrison lifted his eyebrows dramatically.

"Okay, Warren, the whole entire planet Earth is waiting. What is it that women want?"

"Women want," Harrison held out his hands, "everything... and nothing."

Feeney stared at him, and then a smile started up.

"It's the truth!" Harrison nodded.

Feeney nodded back. "And a very helpful one, at that."

"I'm serious. Look, it's complicated. What you've got to do is not let yourself get complicated to match it. And be mysterious."

"You just try to give them everything... and nothing," Feeney said. "Got it. And be inscrutable."

Harrison held up his thumb. "That's the key, right there. You don't choose. You see, there's no way in hell you can give them everything. Right? But what you can give them is nothing."

"Women must just adore you."

"I'm not saying nothing as in nothing. I'm saying you have to recognize the way, and the time, she doesn't want anything. And you just go along with that."

Feeney gazed at Harrison. It would have been contemptible not to admit, he thought, that most women would have found Warren Harrison attractive. And Harrison knew it. Feeney accepted that and wasn't jealous about it, although he could also admit that he might hope that perhaps once the initial contact had passed, at least for some women, Harrison's allure might dim. But Feeney, who, though by no means an unhandsome man, really had no way of knowing. Some people, like Warren Harrison or Faith Rockford, were born to turn heads, and some were not.

"I don't know. You make it sound like for women it's just all about pragmatism. I know a lot of guys who'd like to believe that." The bitter ones, Feeney thought. He smiled at Harrison. "Maybe you should write a book."

"You like it, huh?"

"One theory's as good as another, I suppose."

"Not a theory," Harrison shook his head. "It's a testimony."

It indeed was, Feeney thought. And very much Harrison's kind.

Several hours later, Feeney was alone in the office when the phone rang and Frank Baron was on the other end.

"Is Warren there?"

"No."

"Damn," Baron sighed. "We didn't get the details worked out for the rally."

"There's time, Frank. Deadline's not until next week."

"Yeah, I know. But we want to get it right."

"Yes. We do."

"Will he be back?"

"Don't know. You want to stop down? I'll be here for a few more hours."

Feeney listened to a pause. Then Baron said, "That's all right. I guess I'll try him at home this evening."

Feeney replaced the receiver with a lazy drop of his hand. Well, he thought, to hell with you, too.

He'd been thinking about it. And thinking about it. And this call had finally gotten him over the line.

He would tell Harrison tomorrow, and then everyone would be happy. Dean, Tickler, Ted, Frank... and maybe others. But at the very least, he wouldn't have to put up with any more of this.

He looked back at his typewriter, typed "fuck you" a half a dozen times, then backed over it with x's several times and kept on typing.

That'll be something, he thought, for Mrs. Hagy to see.

He doubted, though, that it would be much of a mystery to her.

Chapter 55

A Social Call

SHE worked out of her house, having converted the attached garage into an office. A door on the side gave onto the garden, and as Feeney approached it he could see it was open. Without looking inside, he knocked on the jamb.

"Hello?" he said.

There was some movement inside, and then Tari came into view. She gave him that usual brilliant smile of hers.

"Hi, Pat! What a surprise! Come on in," she said, pointing inside.

He found himself in a large room no one would ever have guessed had once been a two-car garage. A desk, office shelves, and equipment took up one corner of the space, and the rest was given over to a couple of overstuffed chairs, a large sofa loaded with pillows, a coffee table with actual coffee-table books, a television, a large woodstove, and a big glowing fish tank full of very small fish. There were no bookshelves, but some watercolor landscapes, vases full of flowers, candles, and a few hanging ornaments made the room a cozy, very homelike, feminine space.

"I didn't know you knew where we lived," she went on.

"Sure, I did," he said. "I remember you saying you worked here during the day, and I was just sort of roaming around..."

"Roaming around."

"Yeah... not even really a reason."

Tari laughed. "So just a social call."

"Pretty much," he said. "You'd be surprised how much of my

work is based on just roaming around and social calls."

"Well, I'm glad you roamed around over this way."

"Hmmm..." he nodded. "This works," he said, looking around.

"It was originally going to be for both of us, but since Frank is so rarely around, I just ended up making it mine." She looked toward the office and shrugged. "I know it just sort of looks thrown together, but I like it."

"This is thrown together? Well, that settles that."

"Settles what?"

"There wasn't much chance of it, but I can now guarantee you will never, under any circumstances, see what my place looks like."

Tari laughed. "I can imagine."

"Oh no, you can't."

"Sure," she said, twisting her mouth with irony. "You think I've never seen a bachelor pad?"

"Oh... well, as for that..." Feeney said.

And then he stopped, an embarrassed grin starting to form.

Tari raised her eyebrows. "As for that...?"

The grin froze. "Um..."

Of all the things he had ever imagined talking to Tari about, none of them would have been the particulars of her social life as a beautiful young woman before she got married. And he wasn't even curious; that desire was something he reserved for things he didn't know or couldn't guess.

"Yeah..." Seeing he could go neither forward nor back, he let himself slide into his oft-used talent for prevarication. "No... no... just some things are better left to the imagination."

"Some things..." she said. "You know... that's the sort of thing that could make a lady wonder..."

It was so small he might have missed the flick upwards of one of her eyebrows, but he never could have missed how her eyes took on that soft gaze—sometimes untroubled, sometimes not. Every man knew when a woman was looking at him and suddenly really seeing him, and thinking about him.

This time it was untroubled, and for once in this circumstance, where normally he would have had something to hold him back, he said exactly what came into his mind at the moment it arrived.

"It shouldn't," he said.

Feeney didn't know how she did it, but her expression barely changed before she suddenly laughed.

"Oh, no! I suppose not!" She laughed. "I suppose not! Me, being married and all..." Her voice trilled away into a long, delighted laugh that Feeney could only watch and admire and, in a way, could almost feel jealous about. For himself, never liking the feeling of being an open book, he could admire how easy and open she was about things that touched on the personal.

He watched her laugh helplessly.

And he realized she saw right through him.

It was terrible, he thought, how devastating a woman could be once she decided it was safe to tease a man she knew was attracted to her. And there was no doubt here she knew he found her attractive. Well, she was a good-looking woman, and very likeable. Why should he deny that, even if she was married?

The only question was whether she had always known, or whether she had just discovered it.

Probably, Feeney thought, she had known all along, and his only hope now was that he hadn't been too oafish about it. Although he also knew it didn't matter. Because if there was one other thing there was no doubt about, it was that she was used to such things.

"I'm being awkward, aren't I?" He smiled, with that relief and salvation that only these sorts of confessions offered. He hadn't expected he'd ever do this with Tari, but he had long known that nothing cleared the air better than simply admitting to a woman she was attractive. At the very least, it gave you somewhere to put your weight back down on.

"From the start," she said.

"From the..." He frowned, and wanting to know, pointed his finger downward as though to mean that moment.

"No, from the first time we ever met."

"Ah, that bad, huh?" He smiled.

"Not bad. Sweet, in fact. I mean," she slightly rolled her eyes, "if circumstances were..."

And she stopped, giving him a different look now.

It was the sort of look that could be interpreted either way. Regret. Or a suggestion that there just needed to be some persuasion.

If everything else in the last few minutes had seemed like going downhill without any brakes, this was like going over a cliff.

He had no idea where things were going. He didn't mind her knowing he found her attractive, but regardless of what she was doing with the if and the circumstances, he was suddenly aware his confessions to her had to stop there.

Pure self-preservation. And a tidal wave of paranoia.

"...like," she went on, walking over to pretend to straighten things on her desk, "back in college, when... you know... it was just so much more..."

She kept pausing, and he knew now where things were going. Those pauses were like blanks left for him to fill in, one way or the other. The next confession was just standing there, waiting to be evoked.

All this, he knew, was his fault. He had been lazy, and let himself find it pleasing she might like him in some way. Much as he could have wished Faith Rockford might like him, but with a giant difference.

Tari smiled, turning to look at him. "You think you're an enigma...?"

"I try," he said, and then suddenly realized what he wanted more than anything else was an exit to all this. "It's a professional reflex."

Tari laughed again. "Maybe. Or maybe it's just a way to look for an exit."

It was a shock to hear that exact word. Feeney's eyes widened, but he managed to get out, "That obvious, huh?"

She watched him for a moment.

"How about a cup of coffee, Pat? Since you were just roaming around."

"Coffee?"

She smiled. "It's just in the kitchen."

She didn't even wait for his answer but walked past him and through a door leading into the main house. He stood there for a moment, not actually hesitating, and then followed her.

He found himself standing in the kitchen.

"You know," he said to her as she brought down a couple of mugs from the cupboard, "I actually did want to talk to you about the bond issue and all. These rallies and all."

Tari glanced sideways at him, a mocking look in her eyes. "I'm sure you did, and all."

As she poured some coffee and handed him a mug, he looked around the kitchen. It was like something right out of Sunset Magazine, with cool ivory-colored cabinets, gleaming copper pans and kettles hanging all over the place, marble countertops, and gleaming silver and brass fixtures.

Feeney ran his hand over the marble, feeling its glass-smooth coldness.

He ignored her tease.

"I wanted to say that... I think... well, here it is: Frank should expect that Bob Hawthorn is going to show up at these rallies. I don't care what Tickler Steele says, you can't keep away people who don't feel the same way, and you can't expect them to remain silent. That argument out in the parking lot after the last rally—that wasn't necessary, but I saw how upset you were. You've got to expect these things, Tari. And Frank does too."

She nodded. "I know."

Feeney, glad to be moving away from everything that had gone before, nodded. "So that's all. Just don't worry about Frank and Bob. That sort of thing just blows away after a while."

"Frank gets so mad sometimes..."

Feeney didn't want to start criticizing her husband. And partly that was because he didn't want to open up another avenue back into personal topics—even though he really didn't care much for the man himself—but because, in truth, he could understand the frustration Frank felt.

Hawthorn simply held the high ground with a set of emotionally convincing and articulate arguments. More battles down through history, Feeney knew, had been won on those two things alone than on any amount of strategy, tactics, or armament.

And Frank, who had become increasingly involved alongside Tickler Steele in mounting a fierce public battle—aggressive and even arrogant—at these school bond rallies, was also becoming ever more agitated.

"I can understand," he said. "There are days it gets to me, too. You know, people get passionate about the things they believe. Hawthorn's the same way."

"Yeah, but it's more than that. People like Bob Hawthorn. And... well... Frank doesn't have the same thing."

"You think people don't like him?"

"They don't know him."

Feeney smiled. "I don't think that situation is going to last."

"I don't know," Tari said. "You know how it is in this town. To be from somewhere else. I mean, we're sort of one foot in and one foot out—Frank being all the time down in Seattle—even though I'm almost up to my neck in things."

"I have to admit," Feeney said, "I was surprised Frank would even notice, let alone care, about what happens around here."

"You don't like..." Tari paused, and then went on, "you like Bob Hawthorn too, don't you?" It wasn't a question.

"Few people are really unlikable."

"Frank hates him."

"I've noticed."

"But then, Frank hates a lot of people."

"I hope I'm not on his list."

"Well... he hasn't made up his mind."

Feeney looked over at her. That would normally have been a joke, but he could see it was not.

"I hope I've had some sort of defense."

"You did. I mean, I try. I understood what you meant the other day. But that still doesn't convince Frank. He thinks you're being soft."

Feeney looked down at his cup, wondering if there would ever be a time he could like Frank Baron.

330

"It's too bad he thinks that way."

"It's always worth burying hatchets."

"I don't have any hatchets out, Tari," he said. "But you know something funny? That, for some people, is almost the same thing."

"They call it passive aggressive."

"That's only the way I am when I wake up in the morning. The rest of the day I'm actively aggressive."

She laughed with a sudden complete release. What he'd said had not been particularly funny, but somehow it had either fit perfectly with her thoughts about something, or it had been the way he'd said it, and she was nearly in tears.

Feeney then joined in.

And it was when they stopped laughing, and Feeney had trusted himself to take a sip of coffee, that he felt her hand move against his where his hand had been gripping the countertop, her finger touching his.

It was surely accidental. Surely, she would withdraw it.

But it remained.

And he was suddenly damned if he was going to move his hand and reveal something.

"I don't think I've ever been so passionately involved in something as this," she said.

"It's not bad to be that way sometimes in life."

"Maybe, but Frank thinks I spend a bit too much time on it. Working here, and then over with the PTA, and with Ted and Tickler, and then down there at your office all the time."

"I hope he isn't jealous."

"Of working on the bond issue, how could that be?" Tari smiled.

"A guy can be jealous of time as much as of anything else, I suppose."

Tari had a quiet look come over her face. "He was never like this before," she said suddenly. "I'm beginning to wonder if it isn't this town."

"You mean small towns."

"Yeah. I guess."

"Small towns can create big jealousies fast," he said. "I've also had to learn things like that."

"So that explains that."

"What?"

"You're trying to be an enigma. The Invisible Man."

Feeney smiled. "Nobody's invisible."

Suddenly he remembered how easily he could forget himself looking at and thinking about her attractiveness, and how she had on occasion noticed that and then actually given him back looks that...

He realized now that she had indeed noticed how...

Tari broke into his thoughts.

"Can I ask you a personal question, Pat?" Her voice sounded casual, but he could now hear a husky undertone of deeper breathing.

"Sure."

"How is it that you aren't married yet?"

He took another sip of coffee. "Who in her right mind would see me as a husband?"

"So," Tari smiled, "you've been afraid to ask. Why is that? Afraid of getting turned down? Or letting someone know your feelings?"

Feeney smiled. "Oh, I've been turned down plenty of times. I'm used to that."

Tari laughed. "So… you've never asked anyone."

Feeney looked at her laughing, at how attractive she was when she did that. "When you say personal, Tari, you really meant it. But… yeah. I haven't felt to do that yet."

"You said it was okay."

"I did."

"So... why?"

"So..." He took a breath and then looked over at her. She still hadn't moved her hand. "I guess I just haven't met anyone I could trust with my life."

"Would you have trusted me?"

Feeney nodded. "I think so. I honestly do."

But that wouldn't have been enough, he thought. What it really would have taken was someone as kind and generous and giving as her, who would also have found him worthy of her love.

And he couldn't imagine anyone seeing as worthy a guy who drove around in a rusting, eight-year-old Vega, making two hundred dollars a week, and who didn't know from one day to the next whether he would still be doing the same thing a year from then.

"That's a flattering thing to know, Pat."

He moved his hand—but not away from hers. Instead he placed it gently on top of it and then lifted and dropped again, in an indifferent pat.

He had been damned if he was going to show himself recoiling from her, but he was also damned if he would be outshone in the sweet-friendship department.

Hers had been subtle.

His was overkill.

And it worked perfectly.

It killed everything.

"I'm flattered too."

And as he looked into her eyes, he could see she understood. And for just a second there was a look. Something shadowed.

Then she brightened to her smile again, slipped her hand out from under his, gave his a quick pat, and picked up her coffee.

And that, Feeney thought with relief, was that.

Chapter 56

Innocents Abroad

IN Everett, he went straight to the Three Sheets. Edward Oldermeyer and Charlie Springer were at the bar, eating sandwiches. Feeney took a seat next to them, put his elbow on the bar, his cheek on his fist, and stared at them. Especially, he stared at the managing editor.

"Guys."

Oldermeyer, although a little older, could have been a copy of Charlie Springer, except that there was something a bit less ragged about him. Authority and a desk job had better powers of preservation, despite the pressures of also having had to develop the enormous patience needed to fend off the inanities coming at him from the press floor up and the accounting office down.

"Hi, Pat," Springer said between chews.

Feeney kept staring.

Oldermeyer looked at Feeney. "A little glum today, I see." The editor glanced at Springer. "I wonder what it could be. Business, or life in general? But then... what's the difference, eh?"

"Well, we sort of get paid for the one," Springer said.

"Actually," Oldermeyer said, turning to Feeney, "we were just thinking about you."

"How nice, Eddie. Especially with my birthday only six months off." Feeney took his head off his fist and waved the barman over towards one of the draft beer pulls.

"Actually, you know what? I've been thinking a lot about you lately, too."

"Ah, c'mon. Don't get sore." Oldermeyer shook his head. "How'd I know Harrison was going to parachute in on you up there?"

"Why the hell didn't you just fire that fuck?"

"I didn't have any cause."

Feeney's beer came and he nearly flung his money at the bartender, turning to give Oldermeyer another look.

Oldermeyer shrugged. "Okay, so what if I maybe did have cause?"

"So what?" Feeney paused, and then went on, "Oh fuck this. You let him resign and save face, or maybe he's not even aware yet that he had any face to save, and he just goes sailing off to wherever."

"Not really wherever," Springer said.

Feeney looked at both men, and then his eyes narrowed. "You telling me you fucking aimed him out towards Dean?"

Oldermeyer's eyes widened. "Oh no, Pat! No no! We wouldn't have done that."

"How do I know?"

"Jansen could have picked him up, too, you know."

Feeney smiled. "You think Warren didn't try there?"

"We don't know," Springer said. "But we didn't set anything up so he stayed in the county."

"But you obviously didn't set anything up so he couldn't." Feeney watched Oldermeyer cock his head in that professorial way he had. Feeney stopped him. "Don't, Eddie. Don't you dare use the words ethics and Harrison in the same breath. But... let me guess. . You guys shut down Seattle and Olympia for him, didn't you? You didn't want any eventual Seattle or Olympia blowback from your cronies down there. Or even Tacoma, for that matter. Gad."

"We really didn't figure he'd stick around."

"Oh... bullshit. I could have bet good money. What did you tell him it was, a cutback or some damn thing?"

"Some damn thing."

Feeney drained his glass. "Okay. Never mind. He's up there now. And *Dean*... fuck you, Eddie... *loves* him."

Springer laughed.

"Really?" Oldermeyer said with what looked like sincere interest.

"God, you guys are hopeless."

"So use him. He can write when he gets a notion, and..." Oldermeyer shot another glance at Springer, "he can't plagiarize you sitting right there under your nose."

Feeney opened his mouth. "Ha ha ha."

"And," Oldermeyer went on, "Harrison has something to prove."

"It's true. Dean's got him combing the upscale housing up there, digging up whatever the Japanese stone garden set is into."

"I saw that piece on commuting. That wasn't so bad," Springer motioned towards the barman, whirling his finger.

"Dean's got the idea to do a whole series like that. You know, the changing face of the valley and all. But we're trying not to scare the old-timers at the same time. Dean's paranoid."

Oldermeyer looked over at Springer. "Not a bad idea, huh, Chuck?"

"Don't look at me."

"I wasn't talking about you doing it."

Springer turned and gave Feeney a smile. "But you guys are beginning to clean Jansen's clock."

"For the moment. But this bond issue isn't going to be forever. And I can guarantee the dynamic duo of Feeney & Harrison isn't going to be forever, either."

"You're wrong there about the first thing," Oldermeyer said. "There's only so far Donald Jansen can get, and either he breaks through, or he runs out of gas. And I'm not sure, but I don't see he's done anything lately that shows he's expanding."

"The distribution is..."

"That's just paper. He could just haul all that out into the middle of the ship channel and dump it to the bottom."

"But the advertisers still think it's real."

"Until it isn't, and that's the point. Prepare yourselves, then," Oldermeyer said. "This is where he's going to get dangerous. If he goes for one last push, you've got to meet him."

"You really don't like him."

"Normally, it's true, I wouldn't care too much. But I'll be honest: I wouldn't want to see him get his foot up on the county, and end up being the only one out there."

"And what if it was Dean?"

"Not the same thing. If it was Dean, it would just be a matter of evolution. Jansen's operation means he wouldn't stop there."

"He wouldn't go daily."

"No, but he'd come after the weekly advertising. So, anyway, it's been quite a while since I saw you last, Pat. I remember the last time you said you felt you were always half a hair from getting lynched. Or quitting. I can't remember which."

"Both. But, no, Eddie. Not so much anymore. Things are changing slowly for me. It's not exactly peace and love up there, but people say I'm not getting half the heat the guy before me got."

Springer coughed out a laugh. "You mean Kirby? He brought it on himself."

"I don't know. It seems to have a way of happening up there."

Oldermeyer shook his head. "Nah... you can't be an idealist up in those towns."

"I see. So that's what you call anyone who isn't insane?"

Springer chuckled again, but now Oldermeyer turned and gave Feeney a serious look.

"Any damn day you want, just give me a ring."

"Thanks, Eddie," Feeney said. "But I hope no time soon. We have a pile on our plates that we need to deal with. But I mean to see this all through. If it happened these days, it would mean they'd finally really found my last straw."

Oldermeyer raised his eyebrows. "Don't worry. They will..."

The barman came back and set three drinks up. Feeney now stared at a whiskey in front of him. "I'm not sure you're doing me a favor, Ed."

"Who's doing you a favor?" Oldermeyer picked up his glass, and with a vague gesture, as though he was toasting the wall, he moved the glass towards his lips. "Here's to last straws," he said.

They all drank to that.

And then again... and maybe even again—who was counting by then—which seemed like a good idea at the time, but in fact wasn't.

It seemed a long drive, getting all the way back up through Snohomish, then Monroe, up to Sultan. But he had to get back. One reason was that he had a photo shoot, or something like that. The other he couldn't remember. But it all seemed to have to do with the high school.

When he got to Sultan High School, he parked in the far parking lot and headed towards the back door of the gym, trying to remember what he had to do, and whether it had to do with anyone in particular. He hoped not. He figured he was just presentable enough as long as no one talked to him.

Inside the gym, he sat, in a warm fog, on one set of the wooden bleachers that had been pulled out from the wall, not really registering that the class taking place in that half of the gym was one of the girls' P.E. classes. But then it did, and he sobered somewhat, realizing he was the town newspaper editor and didn't seem to be doing anything there except watching young women contorting themselves in strenuous, athletic effort.

Then he remembered he also had a camera and began pretending to be there to use that.

He still couldn't remember why he was supposed to be there.

Then: the bell.

The girls scattered for things, and then headed towards the door to the showers and lockers.

He really hadn't been paying attention. But as a group of girls went by, a figure detached itself and came towards him.

He should have noticed.

Of course, the shapeless blouse had made even bubbly, bouncy Carey blend in with the others at a distance.

"Hi," she said. Flushed and perspiring, she planted herself in front of him.

"Hi, uh..."

"Are you doing a story?"

He started nodding his head.

"Yeah," he said. "Yeah... that's right."

Suddenly a lot less drunk, he was aware that a few of the girls seemed to be deliberately taking their time leaving the gym.

Carey followed his gaze and, looking at them, made a smile.

"I've got a new story, already," she said.

"About what?"

"They're talking about getting a computer?" Carey saw him looking across the gym again and glanced around. The girls were still there.

"You have more friends now?"

"Oh, you know." She laughed. "Anyway, I've got to go. I'll see you later, huh?"

She skipped away across the gym. Giggles. And then Feeney was alone there for a while, until he realized he actually had no business being up there that day. And he realized a few other things

Something somewhere else was waiting for him. He was sure of that.

But not there. And really not there.

He was beginning to feel more clear-headed when he got back to his office. When he sat down at his desk, he pulled his appointment book across and opened it to the date.

Nothing.

But for the next day, he saw he was supposed to go talk to the Index volunteer fire department chief, and then go up to Skykomish to take a picture of the sports teams, and then back down for a Sultan council meeting.

Sports team. Skykomish High School gymnasium. Wrong school, wrong day.

Feeney slowly closed his appointment book and leaned back and looked straight up at the ceiling.

Schmucksville.

Part 4

Tragedy and Triumph

Final apologies to W.C.

Chapter 57

Dominoes

SOMETHING was up, and Warren Harrison had noticed it, too.

"I smell a lynching," he said, leaning toward Feeney. That word, Feeney thought, kept cropping up a bit too much lately.

A man in front of them turned to look at them, and Feeney and Harrison went wooden-faced.

Dick Brahnler was now standing, his finger held in the air like a schoolboy preparing to cite the Gettysburg Address.

Newton Powell scowled. "What do you want, Dick?"

"I'd like to make a statement."

"It's been a long night." The lawyer looked as tired as he sounded.

Mayor Peace nodded, raising his eyebrows as he addressed Brahnler. "Regular business is finished. Something bother you about what we did? I mean, we gotta buy paint once in a while, Dick."

"That's not what I want to talk about. It's about the way this town is getting turned into a three-ring circus, and how democracy and freedom of speech are being denied to the town's citizens."

Powell rolled his eyes. "Who has ever denied you freedom of speech?"

Brahnler took a dramatic breath, then looked straight over at Feeney. Feeney saw it coming and knew there was no way to stop the juggernaut the ex-councilman was launching. Brahnler, when he finally spoke, even pointed at him.

"When we got news coverage like this up here, with Patrick Feeney, how the hell can anyone expect free speech?"

343

Eyes turned. Feeney had no choice. For the first time ever, he knew he would have to make some sort of public statement. Unfortunately, it would have to be made to defend himself against public criticism. Yet, he thought, under what other circumstance would that ever happen? So here it was, and he was doomed to play out his part: embattled newspaper editor. A fucking cliché if there ever was one. He looked at Peace. "I guess I should respond."

"You don't have to, Patrick," said Powell. "But he now does have your name on the record."

Feeney stood up. "I never thought I'd be a part of the order of town business, down here."

"Any business," Brahnler said back, "is town business. Including your business." He looked around the room. "Especially since the big machine started up for the school bond issuance."

"We support it, yes."

"And so does the town council," Powell put in. "You know that, Dick."

"I don't care what your council supports. You're not my council."

"Well," Powell responded. "This is the democratically elected town council of someone's. And maybe it isn't your council if you don't believe in that. Democracy, I mean."

"I'm as democratic as anybody, Newt." Brahnler crossed his thick arms, jerking his head at Feeney. "I'm talking about a paper that covers nothing but the school board's side of the issue. And it's up to the rest of the town to shell out, just to tell the real story."

"It's real enough, believe me," Feeney said flatly.

"Like hell. You guys sit in here and take notes, and next week, all we see is watered down whatever."

"We quote you enough." Feeney wanted to say, we make you sound intelligent. "Anyway, what's the beef? What're we talking about? The bond issue, or you? We write about what needs doing. The only thing I hear from the opposition is that they don't want to pay taxes. Which is ridiculous. Do you have any idea how little that would amount to, compared to what they're spending right now? It's insane, Dick. No?"

He thought he saw a flicker of doubt in Brahnler's eyes, but right then Warren Harrison decided to stand up.

"I don't think you appreciate all the work we do," he said, putting his hand on Feeney's shoulder, "and all the work Patrick Feeney does."

Patrick Feeney, at that moment, was not only trying to pretend Harrison didn't exist, but was also glaring at Powell, whose face had suddenly covered itself with an exceptionally good-humored grin.

"We all know how much work Patrick Feeney does," Brahnler said, and weirdly shook his hips like he was doing a hula dance.

A few boneheads laughed, as though they knew what Brahnler was talking about. Feeney didn't give a shit about whatever cheap bullshit this innuendo consisted of, and would have been satisfied to leave it there and sit down, maybe with only a shake of his head to show he didn't agree.

But Harrison had something else in mind.

"You know, Dick," he said, "this paper is award-winning for its news coverage. Did you know that? Do any of you know that?"

"When you plaster it on your own front page, it's hard not to know."

"Well, in any case, that's a fact. And I think there is an awful lot of griping going on around here by people who are just jealous because they don't have the power right now."

A wheezing laugh burst out of Powell. Feeney had a momentary vision of dragging Harrison bodily from the council chambers.

Brahnler was nodding at his minions. "You see," he said. "There it is right there." He turned to look at Harrison. "No way we'll ever get any fair coverage from you. That's for sure."

"That's where you got it wrong," Harrison said, "no matter what I or Patrick Feeney think of you."

Feeney had been trying to make subtle face-signals at Harrison, telling him to shut up. But now Feeney's heart sank. They were dead. And Harrison was not to be stopped.

"But that doesn't make any difference. We report the news. And you can guarantee that, even if you don't think so, we, at least, make a conscious effort to tell the truth and give everybody a fair chance to have their stories fairly reported."

Brahnler looked at Harrison for a second, and then said to his friends: "Listen to this bullshit."

For once, Feeney agreed wholeheartedly with Dick Brahnler. If Feeney had had an uncomplicated part to play, he now suddenly had a very uncomplicated emotional reaction towards his colleague: strangling would have been too good for him.

Feeney was damned if he was going to say anything else to the room, if only because anything he said from there on out would be inescapably connected with Harrison's brilliant offerings. The only thing to do, therefore, was to sit down.

So he did so, with Harrison quickly following his lead.

Feeney would have liked nothing better than never to speak to Harrison again for the rest of his life. But he had to say it.

He leaned over and, trying to keep himself from hissing, said out of the side of his mouth: "People have a right to their opinions, Warren."

"Uninformed opinions."

"Most opinions are."

Harrison, evidently oblivious to any implication of criticism, was now shaking his head.

"I have to admit, I don't know how you've found the strength."

Feeney, despite his anger, had to look over at Harrison. It was the first time he had ever heard Harrison say something resembling esteem for him, at least anything which didn't have a detectable grain of self-interest in it.

"It's not a question of strength," Feeney said. "If it was that, I'd really be in trouble."

"Maybe. Anyway, I can see now why Dean says that if it wasn't for you, he doesn't know how he would have made out with Jansen."

Feeney was astonished.

"He said that?"

Harrison was glancing around the room. "Looks like the coast is clear now," he said. "I'm heading out the door."

"I'm with you," Feeney said, nodding.

They got to the front steps unscathed, but rain was now pissing down and they hesitated.

On the other end of the wide steps huddled another small group and Feeney saw they were mostly people from the PTA crowd. He had known there had been another meeting at the town hall, upstairs.

Among them, surprisingly, was lovely Faith Rockford.

While he was looking at her, she glanced back at them, and Feeney gave her a smile. She nodded at him, and then turned back to talk to her group.

"How about that," Harrison said. "She actually stoops to acknowledge the little people. I suppose all these little towns have to have their self-proclaimed prima donnas." Something suddenly caught in Harrison's mind, and he gave Feeney a little glance. "At any age."

Feeney didn't catch it, still looking at Faith. "She's a little guarded, but I don't think she thinks that much of herself."

"Think not?"

Feeney could see where Harrison might know Faith better. He spent a lot more time over at the superintendent's office than Feeney ever had. And with his looks, he had probably got on a lot better with Faith than Feeney could ever have hoped to.

Unwilling to give Harrison the slightest personal information about how he actually liked Faith, Feeney said something neutral, which on several occasions had in fact been true for a long time.

"I don't know. All I get mostly is the Marble Venus. Only the lips smile."

"You've never spent any social time with her?"

Feeney tried to imagine that, and would have loved to pretend he had, but couldn't. "No, I haven't."

"You've never talked to her? Don't talk to her?"

"Not really. And don't ever expect to," Feeney tried a grin.

"Not ever..."

Feeney laughed. "What would you think we'd ever talk about?"

For a second, Harrison nodded, but then squinted, as though something had just occurred to him. An odd smile came over his face—slightly smarmy, not especially attractive—and then it settled into a knowing leer that Feeney instinctively mistrusted.

"She's all act."

"I've never had the impression."

"More than an act." Chuckle, chuckle.

For the second time that night, Feeney had to look at Harrison, and when he did, his heart sank.

Feeney had already heard about several miscellaneous Harrison conquests.

But... her?

In the air, suddenly, black thunder rolling across a desolate wasteland of depression.

"You're kidding," he said, unable to help himself.

Harrison shook his head, his eyes conveying jaded knowledge. "One drink over the top and it all falls away. And... *man*... does she drink!" He looked back at Feeney. "Worse, though, she's a log. You barely know she's breathing."

"You got her to go out for drinks?"

"Sure, right there over at the Sky Pub. Right after the last PTA meeting, which you didn't want to go to." Another laugh. "Matter of fact, *she* dragged me in there. Must be her watering hole."

"Here in town?"

"Where else? I'm not going to blow through five gallons of gas for..." Harrison winked.

Feeney, although suspicious of what sounded like too many details—he was always suspicious of details—could only nod though, and then Harrison shrugged goodnight and sprinted off towards his car.

Feeney, remaining there, saw how Faith watched Harrison fire up all that horsepower, and drive away.

Feeney realized it really was the first time he had ever seen Faith in town after hours. He'd always thought she lived somewhere down towards Everett. A bit far away.

Feeney looked over and saw Faith give him what he could only take for a somber, almost worried look.

Difficult to read, but right then, any look from her could only take him deeper into his most parched and lonely forms of depression.

And disgust. Why the hell would anyone brag about something like that?

For a second, he almost began to walk towards her, but then he saw her turn away, and thought he saw her shoulders rise and fall a little under her jacket, as though she had let out a controlled sigh. And she stepped off across the parking lot towards her car.

And then Feeney saw Tari, over among the PTA crowd... and he took a step, but saw her walk off quickly towards the parked cars. No chance to speak.

Not really knowing why, he suddenly felt he wanted to talk to her. To anybody. Badly.

If he could get to her before she got to her car, he could...

He could what?

What the hell was he doing?

Faith's car left the lot, and nothing seemed colder than a car leaving a parking lot in the dark.

Then it began to rain. Why not? And he could tell it wasn't going to be a light one.

He turned around and headed quickly back, finding his car before the downpour started.

That evening, he thought as he threw himself into his car, had been a definite mood enhancer. A perfect set-up for finishing the evening at Bedossa's.

Which he knew was the worst thing he could do.

He drove home, put something from his album collection—or what was left of it after one of his supposed best friends in college had stolen half of it—on the turntable. Something soothing and mostly improvisational.

And sat in the dark, not really depressed.

Not really. Just... the more habitual version of something along those lines.

Chapter 58

The Merchants Associationism

THE business community was like the cherry on top of all the other madness. In this case, though, it was madness of the entirely expected kind. As it had to be, the Sultan Merchants' Association opted for unadulterated greed.

Anymore, as far as Feeney was concerned, the only redeeming feature of the Merchants' meetings, taking place on a nominally dead Wednesday night at the restaurant, was when they broke up and everybody could adjourn into the cocktail lounge.

Feeney looked around the circle of tables set up for the meeting. There was Shirley Nordstrom—no relation to the billionaires down in Seattle—who ran a Fluff-n-Blow beauty salon. Fred Baxter of the tire store, who was usually the chair. Curly Young of the hardware store. Janet Meecher, who ran the town's motel. Phil and Carol Conway, who owned the restaurant-bar they were sitting in, the Sky Pub. Gary Mills, who had a backhoe/hauling service. Tom Carlton, who ran the town's main tavern and dance hall, rivalling Monroe's Bedossa's. Frank White, who had the hardware store. And even Buck, the Barbarian Barber, was there. Laurilaure, however, had skipped the meeting that evening.

The minutes of the previous meeting were read by Janet, a stocky, strong-jawed brunette who reminded Feeney of the sort of people he remembered from high school, the types who always managed to take part in every club and organization which existed. Professionally enthusiastic. Violently cheerful.

When she had finished, Fred Baxter brought up a stubby finger as though an important point was to be made, and instead finished the gesture by stabbing it toward his own face, jabbing his glasses back up his thick nose. "Well, okay Janet. Thanks." He halted there, looking at Janet for a moment as though he was going to say something else to her. She raised her eyebrows as though expecting to respond, but then realized she'd been fooled again. Fred often stared like this at people, if only because they were, for some reason, a better place to rest his eyes while his brain slowly congealed. "Fine," he said after a while longer, looking away from Janet towards the rest of them. "Okay, here is where I'm supposed to open the floor. So somebody start talking."

For another moment, time bled to death.

Janet, still warm from fulfilling her official function as secretary, was able to lurch in to start things off.

"For myself," she said, "I was thinking how our main goal is to make Sultan a better place to live." She shrugged her broad shoulders. "For most of us, that would mean more business. Right? But there are some businesses which don't depend much on enlargement. Like Fred's."

Everyone glanced at Baxter for a second. Feeney had no idea what Janet meant. Why she had mentioned Baxter's name at all was inexplicable. But Baxter, with the innocence which only comes from the far extremes of fuzzy mindedness, looked at Janet.

"Well, I'll have you know, I sure as hell am very much for enlargement."

An inevitable, dumb laugh washed over the room. And because everyone was trying to forestall imminent and unavoidable boredom, it lasted much longer than necessary.

Janet blushed furiously.

"No, no," she almost whined. "I didn't mean... Of course, what I meant to mean... Although I didn't mean that Fred wouldn't be interested in having a more bigger business."

Janet's redness peaked, her eyes glowing bright, and where some people were evidently ready to cut her some slack, not everyone was completely scrupulous.

"Well, you know, Janet," Tom Carlton said blandly, "everybody would like to see their business get enlarged. Or at least... more bigger..."

More dumb chuckles. Feeney wondered if there was even the slightest chance of anything actually coming out of this meeting.

Janet, embarrassed and resentful, had no idea how to respond, so now just pretended she had nothing to be embarrassed about. "That's exactly what I'm getting at," she said. "The reason we don't get more business off the highway is that it doesn't look like there's any reason to stop except for essentials. I mean, what do people see going past on the highway? Other than the gas station, Tom's bar, the two restaurants and the grocery store, there is just nothing. All the other businesses face Main Street and all people see going by are the backs of them. Literally the back side of them." Janet deliberately stressed side, and glared at the rest, as though daring them to hop on that.

"There's the video store," Gary Mills said with a hopeful leer.

Mills, a going-to-fat ditch digger Feeney considered permanently stuck at the mental age of fourteen, was alluding to the minor town scandal of a recently opened video store which, besides the regular box-office fare of gore and mayhem, also offered a substantial section of hardcore porno films on the shelves in the back. Mills's was a dim attempt to keep the meeting's previous innuendo going, that being about the only thing he had found interesting.

Janet ignored Mills.

"So you know what I thought? And it would be real easy?" She swallowed gamely, and went on: "We could do something like they did over at Leavenworth, or up in Winthrop, or even Lynden. Make our town a sort of theme town. Attract tourists. Like that. I mean, you might not believe me, but I was talking once to this lady who had a shop in Leavenworth. And she told me it was really bizarre, but there are some people who will go on vacation, and when they get somewhere that even looks touristy, they go shopping for tourist souvenirs they had no plan on ever buying. A lot of them don't even look around the place they are supposed to have the souvenir from. All they want is a T-shirt, or a hat, or a table mat, or something."

Feeney expected everyone to groan at the suggestion. Leavenworth and Winthrop were two towns which had become famous all over the state for having turned themselves into theme-based tourist attractions, with a third, Lynden, straggling behind.

Leavenworth had been the first, coming up with a tenuous claim that, with mountains all around, it resembled Bavaria or Switzerland, and had passed a town ordinance requiring all businesses to build in Chalet style with long, sloping roofs and balconies. Even a gas station had to look like Heidi was just out back behind the propane tanks, churning up a fresh batch of butter. The fact was, it all just looked like a bunch of schlock being hauled to the schlock dump on the schlock truck that had somehow fallen off onto both sides of the highway.

Just too awful to contemplate.

Frank White was the first to make a suggestion. His store was a cinder block building which looked more like a blast shelter than any possible permutation of a tourist attraction.

"I think we could be like a little Dutch town, like Lynden did. I mean, we sort of look like one already, don't we?"

For half a second, Feeney contemplated asking what the hell it was about Sultan that made Frank think that, but Janet beat him to it. "They at least grow tulips up there in Lynden, and have all those Dutch immigrant families."

Janet sounded so authoritative about this that Frank looked glum. Fact was, Feeney knew, nobody grew tulips in Lynden. All that was down by Mount Vernon, which had just decided to look like... Mount Vernon.

Feeney didn't know where all this American "theme" madness had come from. It almost seemed as though Americans had now gotten so used to walking into Atmosphere, that they felt let down if a place was only clean and neat. Looking around the room again, Feeney found himself astounded to realize that the merchants weren't totally against the concept.

For the next half hour, Feeney heard first one, and then another, discuss some theme idea seriously, with the only difference coming at the choice of the theme itself.

The most outrageous idea was a sort of antebellum Southern town of white column houses and cottonwoods—they would just have to figure out a way to fake the hanging moss. Only trouble, Feeney thought, was they would have to fake the slaves as well as the moss, considering that, to his knowledge, there was exactly one person of African descent living anywhere near Sultan.

The most depressing idea was to turn the town into Bigfoot City, or something like that. It didn't take any imagination to imagine how awful it could be. Feeney easily imagined the day the town hired some engineers to create some Bigfoot monument, likened in impact to the Gateway Arch, or Statue of Liberty, or the Space Needle. Maybe even have it straddling the highway. Which would mean it would have to be a sexless monster. And from there it could stare down at cars with a menacing expression; the beetled brows concealing maybe a specialty restaurant and souvenir shop. Bigfoot Burgers.

As the talk went around the room, Feeney soon realized he was going to be expected to say something.

For a while, as his turn approached, he intended to say that because he was only a newcomer to the town, and because his was not a tourist-oriented business, and because he still didn't know enough about the area, he couldn't say anything specific but could only promise that the paper would do its best to support whatever community action was decided upon. But when his turn came, he found himself unable to dissimulate his thoughts, and actually tried to make a practical suggestion.

"I don't know," he said. "To my way of thinking, the best way to attract people is to just make the town attractive. What have you got here as far as location? A town right at the gateway to a mountain pass, and people are either getting ready to go up and over, or have just come down from the other side. What do they see right now? Just some parking lots, empty lots, a few businesses, the gas station."

"My bar," Carlton said.

"Tom's bar, which is mostly set up for an evening clientele," Feeney went on. "But what would they see if Sultan took those empty lots and grassed them over and put some picnic benches in, and planted shade trees around all the parking lots and up both sides of not only Main Street but along the highway, and every business could join in a consistent painting scheme. And what would that look like? It would look like a park, a restful place to stop and relax. Get something to eat. Go for a walk around. Have some tables and chairs up and down the sidewalks, and have a coffee. Every store could sell a few knick-knacks and souvenirs. People really do like that sort of thing. And what would it cost? Trees, grass, park benches, some sidewalk tables, and a little paint? You add it up."

Feeney had warmed to the idea now, could see Sultan transformed from a wide spot on the highway into a semi-scenic little byway. Maybe even a couple of walking bridges over the highway to link the town with the land over by the river, where a park could be created beneath the tall firs. An area that was, for the present, just a brush-covered expanse of riverfront full of litter and rusting equipment behind a few billboards and an abandoned trailer court condemned for having been built in the floodplain. Something nobody had thought much about until it had flooded. Three times.

"If you really wanted to do it up right, you could get planters everywhere and fill the sidewalks and shop windows and traffic dividers and so on. Turn the place into a "Garden Town" or something. There's a quick and easy theme for you."

He thought he'd managed to make a reasonable pitch, and he stopped there, waiting for the response. He was convinced that when the idea sank in, they would jump at it. He glanced at their faces, expecting someone to react.

Someone did.

"Flowers?" Carlton said, rolling his eyes at everyone. "That's a great idea. Who's going to plant, weed, and water a million flowers every year?" He looked at Feeney, giving him a grin for the sake of form. "You want to volunteer? Or maybe you can get some other people involved... the school board... or maybe the PTA..." He laughed.

Feeney frowned. What would the PTA have to do with anything?

A sudden paranoia swept through him, wondering for a weird second if small town gossip wasn't based on telepathy, or something. But he shook that off.

Seeing how he was being shut down with the very simple argument that nobody wanted to actually have to keep up something, Feeney did not persist with the community theme, but at least defended the idea of sprucing up the town. "Flowering shrubs would be just as good," he said.

But Carlton had got something started, and the other merchants, no surprise, were suddenly "anti-flower" as well.

Maybe because the idea was so simple, it wrecked the Big Dream. Or worse, it made a reflection on the town's, and their own, simplicity.

Feeney gave up and just dropped out of the conversation entirely, intent on just getting through the rest of the meeting without giving himself a stomach-ache. He drifted into a reverie of non-thought, knowing he would not be called upon to speak again. A self-obliviated blob of human protoplasm performing, less by sleight of hand than by sheer force of will, a disappearing act of the spirit. The meeting half over, he was already mentally gone, and happy to be so.

And that was when Carey Williams poked her head into the room.

Chapter 59

Fernweh Happens

At first, no one else noticed her. But when she spotted Feeney, waved, and came around the room to take a seat beside him, all that changed. Maybe if she'd left her coat on, it might have helped. But she'd taken it off and was all bubbles and youth.

By the time she got halfway around the room, everyone was noticing her. And Feeney too.

If she had been exactly three years older, Feeney wouldn't have given a shit. But there... he could have fallen through the floor.

"Hi," she said.

He gave her as good a smile as he could.

Mr. Natural.

The others in the room as well went back to being supposedly natural, and the talk resumed. But the air was thick with interest, glances, some of them briefly exchanged.

Carey had brought a notepad, and Feeney, finding some words somehow, nodded at it.

"Good idea," he said. "Take some notes about what's going on."

For a casual opening to a conversation, it had all the smoothness of a head-on collision, but he felt lucky even to have got that much out. What the hell was she doing?

She could not help noticing the stilted greeting, and made a lightning-fast, between-you-and-me sort of frown, and then smiled again.

"That's the idea."

He could see she had just decided this was what a reporter ought to do. The town meetings were publicly posted, and she had also decided to see what was happening. It was all perfectly explainable. And at the same time perfectly unexplainable.

But maybe he was just being paranoid. Again. Nobody could possibly know that he'd taken an interest in helping his gifted next-door neighbor. Which was, from a certain point of view, a rather gallant effort, all things considered.

But gallantry couldn't be explained, either.

A series of awful scenarios came to mind in quick succession, and he suddenly felt panic take hold of him. But caught between the unknown of doing nothing and at least having tried, he decided he could not bear being completely abandoned to the fates. It was too much like waiting to be shot. So, with as steady a voice as he could find, stifling exactly those overtones of urgency he feared might scare her, he got her full attention and glanced down again at her notebook.

"Note-taking. Yes. And start now."

She dutifully placed her notebook on the table and got out her pen, and at that Feeney decided to just take the bull by the horns.

"Everybody," he said, having little difficulty getting everybody's attention, "I'd like to introduce Carey Williams. She's one of the high school journalism interns working for the paper, and she's come to take notes and see what she can do with an article." Feeney smiled, and looked at Carey. "Unfortunately, you missed the first half hour, which was really interesting, but I'll fill you in on that. Sorry I gave you the wrong time."

Thankfully, Carey gave him a blank look and a nod, and then just looked around the table and smiled at everybody. Everybody smiled back.

From there on, the meeting dissolved into petty complaints about how the town was or wasn't doing this or that.

Feeney let himself float through all that. He suddenly was glad Carey was there. He simply had no interest in writing anything about the meeting. But that was all, and in truth he could never remember when time had seemed to creep by more slowly.

Several centuries later, the meeting came to an end. Feeney stood up, intending to head for the bar and join a few of the merchants there in a liquid effort to forget all that had just transpired.

A noble enough idea, in itself.

But Feeney also had another reason.

He badly needed to go in there, and to be seen there, alone, for the rest of the evening. If not for the rest of his life. He stood up, waiting for everyone to clear out before he would leave.

"Interesting meeting, eh?" Carlton said as he passed Feeney. "Looking forward to seeing the article." Carlton's eyes had a little gleam in them.

"Well," Feeney said, "we'll see what Carey can do. Who knows? Maybe someday she'll end up with my job."

Carlton turned his head with dramatic slowness toward Feeney, and then gave him a broad, engaging smile.

"Someday," he said, with obvious pleasure, "somebody may have to."

Feeney saw that he was unavoidably mired in the position of being the straight man to all the subterranean jokes in the world. The only way out, therefore, was to go silent.

Either that or punch the fucker.

They shared slight smiles of friendly dislike, Carlton immensely enjoying every second. But then he saw he would get no more out of Feeney, looked at Carey and gave her another smile, and deftly turned and headed into the lounge.

Feeney, warily watching him go, making sure he did not look back, kept a smile on his face. When the bar owner was finally gone, he turned to Carey, still maintaining the smile.

"So," he said casually, "how did you get up here?"

"Mom's car."

He nodded. "Um, ok," he said. And although he could have found something else to say, the deeper rumblings of paranoia and guilt pushed him forward: "so... you wanted to write about the merchants, or something?"

It took a few seconds.

Then it finally, finally, hit her. It perhaps not being exactly the same as Feeney's version of it, but close enough. She was both that smart and that quick.

"There was a game after school," Carey began, her own voice now constricted, "and I knew the merchants were having a meeting. So I thought I'd just stop in."

Feeney nodded. "No problem. But you will be doing the main story on this meeting."

She nodded.

"I suppose I should have called you. I'm sorry."

If she had called, he probably would have agreed to it. So in the end, it didn't really matter. It had just been the shock of her showing up like that. And it was only his problem.

He shook his head. "No, it was a good idea. But we'll have to work on it together since you missed the most important part of the meeting."

"When?"

"Just stop by tomorrow after school, and I'll give you the main notes. But you'll have to have something by the weekend."

"OK," she nodded, slightly cheered up.

And when she left, Feeney felt slightly cheered up, too. Except for the fact that he would now have to find articles of similar magnitude for the other three interns.

Feeney checked his wallet to make sure he had enough to go the distance, and walked into the cocktail lounge. He was relieved to find that nearly everyone was there. Even Carlton. He ordered an Americano. He didn't like soda-poppy Americanos, but he wasn't there to drink, only to be sociable. Very sociable.

He saw Phil and Carol, the owners of the Sky Pub, were sitting at a table with Janet, and that seemed the best place to go. He took a seat and smiled at them.

"So, Janet," he said, busting uncaringly in on whatever conversation might have been going on, "sorry about derailing your theme-town idea. It wasn't my intention actually to say anything."

Janet shrugged. "It doesn't matter, Pat. You know how these

meetings go. Nobody can ever agree on anyone. And I sort of liked your idea, to be honest. But to be double honest, it would only work if the town council decided to do it. The merchants, never."

Janet didn't stay long, and after a while Phil took off to check some things in the kitchen, leaving Feeney with Carol.

Carol was a member of the PTA, so it wasn't hard to find something to talk about.

"Sorry I wasn't able to be at the last PTA meeting."

"It was kind of a mess, Pat. And I told that to your reporter."

Feeney liked how she didn't use Harrison's name, and he liked the phrase "your reporter." "Yeah, well, Warren can handle that sort of thing."

Feeney suddenly thought of something. "Of course, anything he missed he could get from Faith." Feeney knew Carol and Faith were friends. He'd often seen them talking after the meetings.

"That's true," Carol said. "Faith keeps notes almost as well as you guys do." She laughed. "In fact, probably better. You know how she is."

Feeney laughed as well. Of course he did.

"Well, he would have got most of the information from her down here after the meeting."

"Down here?"

"After the meeting, when he came down here with her to have a couple drinks."

Carol gave Feeney a look.

"What?"

Feeney saw some sort of look in Carol's eyes, and went neutral. "I thought they came in here after the meeting."

"Where'd you get that information?"

"I, uh..." Feeney wasn't flustered, but he didn't have much. "He just said he'd come here after the meeting, and had notes from Faith, so I... oh, never mind."

Carol laughed. "Faith, down here? First of all, she has never been in here, ever. I can guarantee that. And certainly not after the PTA meeting. And I can tell you right now, she would never 'have a couple' drinks, with anybody. I mean, she's no prude or whatever,

she likes a glass of rosé when we're together. But 'having drinks'...
that's just not her thing."

"Never been here."

"Never."

That landed.

Feeney nodded, then looked at his Americano and frowned.

Carol followed his gaze, and then laughed again. "I never
thought you were the Americano sort, Pat."

He looked up at her and smiled. "Reckless ol' me."

Carol, despite herself, couldn't help lifting her eyebrows and
nodding. "Reckless, indeed, Pat."

Feeney just looked off across the bar and nodded to himself.

Chapter 60

Redux Redux

BUT Feeney finally got around to the second thing, and he couldn't make it work. No matter how he tried, he couldn't figure the insinuations out. Warren, Brahnler, Carlton. At one point, he was sure it had something to do with Tari, if only because that was where his thoughts had gone. People gave things away in what they were thinking, and his attraction to her had to be obvious to anyone who was paying attention whenever they were together in public.

A strange thing was happening, though, in his effort to smoke out the rumor. He had never felt more connected to the town, and some of the people, than lately. He was paying much more attention to them, and in doing so getting to know them.

Side by side at the bar, Jim Dodd and Feeney were celebrating. The judge stared gloomily at his girlfriend. Feeney stared at his glass.

Bedossa's was unusually quiet. Only a few men sat at the far end of the bar. The usual afternoon ogling of Marsha was reduced a bit by the hulking presence of Judge Dodd.

"Parker must be goddamn pleased with his sorry self," Dodd said.

"You can't deny he has the right."

Dodd's shoulders either hunched in disgust or in a shrug. "I could almost feel sorry for the local merchants, if they weren't such a bunch of grasping hyenas themselves."

"Out of curiosity, Jim, how is it, being the lovable fellow you are, that you manage to get re-elected?"

"Chickenshits."

Feeney drank off his glass, which gave him an excuse to give Marsha a prolonged look, until she noticed him. "Nothing like job security," he sighed.

"What're you worried about?"

Marsha came down and set herself in front of them, glad to take a breather from the care and feeding of the other group. She picked up Feeney's glass but did not immediately move.

"You guys are so cheerful." She looked from one to the other.

"Man wants a drink." Dodd nodded at Feeney's glass.

Marsha was nonplussed. "It's so nice to have you drop in after work, hon. That way we can both have a bad day." She looked at Feeney and smiled.

Feeney put up a mental picket fence and smiled back over it.

Marsha sighed. "All right, all right. I'll leave you two to your misery." She went, pumped a few ounces into Feeney's glass, brought it back, and then left to go down and share a little life at the other end of the bar.

"You know, Jim," Feeney said, picking up the glass, "you really ought to marry the woman one of these days."

"We don't deserve each other." The beard-shrouded features showed a rare glint of humor.

Feeney made an appreciative noise. "I'd pay good money to see you in a tux."

"Shit." Dodd nearly smiled. A frightening thing in itself. But then his face settled back into its usual state of barely concealed wrath.

"So," Feeney steered the conversation back toward the Dorin case. The dog thing—which it seemed like a million years ago they'd talked about—had been plucked from Dodd's jurisdiction by an energetic and ambitious young prosecutor named McArthur down in Everett. This was the reason for the judge's jovial, celebratory mood. No Dorin. No dog. No case. "I guess your load should drop off for a while."

"Hell no. We've got such a backlog now because of that goddamn dog, I'll be kicking juvie-offenders' asses from here 'til Christmas."

"Dorin's completely out of your docket, then."

"Let's hope so."

"McArthur wants to skin Dorin alive."

"McArthur'll make a great senator someday."

"Try to look a little happier, then. Besides, you don't even have to worry about the mutt anymore."

Dodd's eyes focused down to pinpoints. "Far as I'm concerned, whichever concerned citizen blew that piece of shit away and sent it to hell, they shot the wrong fucking one."

Feeney grinned. "Is that a quote, Judge?"

Dodd took a drink. "As long as you wait until the appeals are through."

"Christ Almighty," Feeney said. "I can see it. The A.K.C. meets the N.R.A."

"Meeting of the minds."

"It was one solution. Pretty rough justice, though."

"Trigger-happy justice. But then, what's new anymore? Anyway, I can't say I blame whoever it was too much. Who the hell in their right mind could? Poor little kid. Even though she didn't get that badly hurt, she still had to go through all that. And Dorin's lawyer made that fucking brain-fried monstrosity sound like just a pooch. I explained to that motherfucker that his Aunt Wilma's tabby could be turned into a man-eating lion if you worked on it hard enough."

Dodd shook his heavy head at the memory. "DNA. DNA. You'd think this was the answer to everything. Next thing, you'll have him trying to prove poor ol' Todd Dorin's basically a good human being, based on DNA. Poor misunderstood son-of-a-bitch. Fucking hell. I'm telling you, next asshole who walks into my court with this genetic predetermination shit, I think I'll drop the entire bookcase on him, and let the Feds grill it. That dog was mistreated into madness. Just like Todd Dorin was brought up in one of the most dysfunctional families in the county."

"You don't believe in genetic determination."

"I believe half these pinheads up here are dysgenic, yes."

"Another quote, Jim?"

"Say what you want. I could give a fuck. It's the truth. Who knows? Maybe when they were kids they all ate lead paint or something. Ninety percent of my day is spent shoveling white trash out the door. And don't tell me you think any different."

Every emotional cell in his body agreed with Jim Dodd. But Feeney knew he had no choice but to disagree. "I think differently."

"Even with all that school bond shit going on? I heard you had that moron, Brahnler, on your case one night."

"Town politics."

Dodd's gloom, if possible, seemed to deepen. "Goddamn human race. We're barely out of the trees, you know."

"I know."

"And so, what's Parker going to do with his triumph? Or would that be yours?"

Feeney contemplated his glass. "Well, he's decided there is only one mature and community-minded way he can deal with it: he figures that now that Jansen's crawled back into his hole in Snohomish, we're going to start producing a down-valley issue, bomber-style, and throw it around on doorsteps down there. It's our turn to be the assholes."

"Can he beat Jansen in his own territory?"

"He could give a flying fuck about beating Jansen," Feeney said. "Listen, Jim, if you want to understand one thing about Dean, it's not the winning that matters. It's the revenge."

Dodd's head dipped. "My sort of guy."

"Yeah, and my sort of boss."

Dodd almost smiled again. "What's the matter? Is he making you handle it?"

"Oh, no. I don't want anything to do with it. No. Dean'll take the opportunity himself. Go down there and throw his weight around with a few of the retailers. In a way, he's not in the wrong. Jansen cost us about a hundred grand all told. Not counting the school advertising. Dean's got the right to try to recoup."

"Anyhow, I'm always glad to see Don Jansen get his ass kicked once in a while."

"Hah," Feeney said, motioning Marsha for another glass. "You like to see everybody's ass get kicked once in a while."

"And it's the truth," the judge said, his hand rising towards Marsha.

They were friendly like that for another hour or so. And the whole time, Feeney never got the slightest hint from Dodd that there were any rumors going around that shouldn't be going around. Because if there was anyone who delighted in rumors, it was Jim Dodd, who would have adored telling Feeney any of that right to his face.

Maybe, in the end, it was just his imagination.

Chapter 61

Ilwaco mon amour

EXCEPT for being the place where Meriwether Lewis and William Clark had finally lurched out of the wilderness into view of the Pacific Ocean, the only other notable thing to happen in Ilwaco was when a half-mad Breton aristocrat washed up in its harbor after having rowed across the Pacific from Japan.

And the guy wouldn't even have meant to do that. He'd been hoping to end up farther south, towards San Francisco, following the dictates of a Frenchman's internal guidance in search of something that might culturally resonate in France, including higher cuisine.

Nevertheless, by fate and location, through accident or design, with the landing of Gérard d'Aboville, Ilwaco seemed to have reasserted its role as Eternal Point B for larger-than-life type navigators and explorers. And with wonderment and smug historical irony, the good folks of Ilwaco would watch as the town was descended upon by the excited and proud French media fully equipped with rented helicopters, sea-going inflatable jet-boats, and cases of imported champagne. All of it in order to record, for French national posterity, the reunification of this brave crackpot with his family, closest friends, and terra firma.

A Major Local Event, which would make up for what had been lacking in the way of a welcoming committee for the much earlier one.

But when the Gallic circus finally left, the village would go back

368

to being what it had always been: an isolated, rain-swept little coastal town looking out, from the Washington side, over the broad channel where the Columbia River dumped into the Pacific.

Of course, d'Aboville's exploit was very nearly ten years after the time Parker and Feeney visited the town. For the two newspapermen, it was six hundred or so townspeople consisting of fishermen, loggers, cranberry skimmers, and beachcombers. They were isolated and knew it, and made little attempt to encourage any more business than they got already. They belonged to one of two classes of small American town.

The first was ever engrossed in the bigger, the better, the faster. Prostrate, waiting, hoping, praying for a Wal-Mart.

The second, to which Ilwaco belonged, was the smaller, the make-do, and the slower, opting for a form of deliberate self-annihilation. Unable to join the game, they decided the game wasn't for them anyway.

Feeney did not know whether to admire or fear that crossed-arm isolationism. But one thing was certain. As mulish and ignorant as politics could get in the upper reaches of the Snohomish Valley, out in a place like Ilwaco a newspaperman could just curl up and die. There wouldn't be a tenth of a degree of difference from one end of the political spectrum to the other.

Why the hell the Washington Journalist Association had picked Ilwaco for a convention was beyond his imagination.

Just for starters, God knew everybody was aware of the precipitation records. Up and down the Puget Sound, it rained so much people forgot that this dripping wet shit constantly coming down on them was, in fact, water. And you could then politely point it out to them and they would go, oh, yeah, right, that stuff. Ilwaco made the Puget Sound seem just misty by comparison. Even a semi-rain-immune Feeney had to admit it was less than comfortable, but could handle it. As for that, he knew that the papers coming from west of the Cascades would be roughly acclimatized. But for the folks coming over from the dry side, it would seem the Forty Days and Forty Nights had been re-decreed.

It was pretty wet out there.

And yet, despite the downpours, there they all were. And Feeney, too.

Cold and windy, with a cheerless sky the color of week-old snow. At least he hadn't had to share a ride down with Parker. That really would have been misery.

For the first day, the "Seminar" day, Feeney wandered around and shared woes with his fellow editors—that is, the editors from the papers relative in size to his own. The bigger weeklies sort of strolled around being obnoxiously gracious to the smaller papers. It was hard not to do. Feeney, himself, had to struggle with not showing too patient a sympathy for papers smaller than his own.

Thus, it was a typical gathering of news people. In short, everybody, beneath the veneer of journalistic camaraderie and professional bonhomie, within a few short hours managed to turn themselves into as complete a set of asses and bores as such a get-together called for. Beneath it all, as well, surged that bloodthirsty sense of distrust and mayhem which would have been recognizable to a drunken band of marauding Vikings. And actually, several hours after the dinner events were over, anyone wandering into one of the downtown bars or cocktail lounges would have been convinced that, indeed, the Norsemen had just landed.

It was no wonder many of the women journalists had opted out of the evening festivities.

As it was, Feeney mainly killed his time by standing around and getting maudlin with a few old cronies from the good old days. Not that anyone really knew where and when those good old days had been. But it was better, at least, than standing around feeling frantic, with a bunch of other frantic guys, every one of them secretly worried about the same thing: the shape of the copy they weren't back home preparing for next week.

Parker showed up the next day just before lunch, just in time to give his speech. Feeney would always look back on the lunch in fond, if bittersweet, memory.

It all began on a promising note. With the first course barely served, and just as the first speech began, Parker started choking on a stray salmon bone.

Twenty full minutes of the lunch went by while he was back in the men's room coughing, hacking, retching and swearing. The first two speeches were gamely made to the luncheon crowd while muffled sounds of terrible agony and distress floated in through the air conditioning conduits.

One time, after a particularly alarming series of tortured bellowing—where the curious looks of nearby tables forced him to do something, if only for appearance's sake—Feeney had wandered back to see if Parker was going to live.

There, Feeney could see the publisher was in good hands, accompanied in his bulge-eyed torture by a couple of WJA committeemen, the manager of the hotel, and the cook, who seemed somewhat distraught himself. Feeney returned to his table, his duty done, and thereafter occupied himself only with looking composedly concerned whenever a particularly startling sound made its way out of the toilets.

Finally, Parker seemed to manage to clear the bone, and then after a dramatic period of silence, emerged from the bathroom and manfully made it back to his seat, ignoring the looks of sympathy thrown his way.

"Jesus Christ," he wheezed, picking up his water glass. "I thought I was going to die."

"So did everyone else."

"Fucking slophouse... might as well be a spoon."

"Pull up your tie."

Parker fumbled for the knot, and then shot an annoyed glance at Feeney. "Would you tell me something? Why is it you never comb your hair?"

"It is."

When Parker's turn to speak came, he made it up to the podium at least breathing more easily, if not still red and sweaty from his brush with death.

Feeney slumped down in his seat as the speech began, even though no one but Parker and himself knew who had written it.

"Ladies and Gentlemen," Parker began, and then in one last paroxysm, leaned over and let out a throat-rumbling, coughing hack as though he was going to heave his lower intestines onto the floor.

It was shocking and grotesque. But by a miracle, at least for Parker, that seemed to be the last manifestation of that wayward salmon bone. He straightened up, and with a now confident smile, set forth fluidly: "What an honor it is to be with you all here today. As always, it's a pleasure to have this chance to meet up again with friends and colleagues under the aegis of the WJA Yearly Convention.

"I would especially like to take this opportunity to thank the WJA Convention Committee for this opportunity to speak to you here today. Fact is, about five minutes ago, I had the impression that not only would I not be making this speech to you, but that they'd be carting me away for good."

Parker got a hearty, if here and there a perhaps slightly derisive, laugh.

"So much for salmon cutlets. I should have gone for the Stuffed Oysters. If there had been any misery attached to that, at least that would have been a little farther down the block, and later on tonight. Ha, ha, haaaaaa."

Another general guffaw swept the room, although Feeney noticed a few people were now glancing down worriedly at their plates.

Oddly enough Parker, himself, was now glancing down worriedly at the speech lying on the podium in front of him. Feeney could see that his employer was thinking of something other than the speech itself. And suddenly, Feeney was looking worried, as well.

"I know, I know," Parker started up again. "Every year we always say to ourselves, well, it's time for the WJA Convention. And every year, we're always astonished at how we actually do have the time to get together. And you know what? Every year we realize how much fun it is. And then, off we go, and then, like every year, forget all about how fun it is all over again. So I'm here to remind you, to make a point of pointing it out, that it really is important for us to get together."

So far, Parker had ad-libbed everything, and it wasn't much, but Feeney could spot something emerging, and only half wondered if any of the carefully chosen words of his text would be read.

Parker, unsurprisingly to Feeney, was following his tangent and, in fact, seemed to be warming to something.

"But not only get together, but remind us of how important it is for us to stick together."

Feeney now saw it all and knew where things were going to go. The only question now was what the odds were that Parker wasn't about to lay an egg of Little Boy proportions.

"Yes, yes," Parker went on: "It can be a rough and tumble business, and that I well know. Compete, compete, compete. We've got the electronic media, we've got the wire services, we've got the dailies, big and small, breathing down our necks. But I'm telling you, the weekly newspaper is the foundation of small-town America, the foundation of community and of democracy at its most basic level in this great country."

A gleam now began to shine in Parker's eyes:

"And we have to remember that. Always. And remember that we are brothers and sisters in this poor old, glorious, trade. We must always keep in mind the public trust comes first, the personal contact we have, the tremendous advantage we get from knowing our own readers, from having a foot firmly in our communities, and from reporting about what we know best: our closest neighbors."

Parker looked around the dining hall, scrutinizing faces, some of the people actually looking at him and not just chewing away at their lunches or gabbing with neighbors. Feeney knew, exactly, who he was looking for, and figured at least one other person might have been aware of that as well. But if Parker spotted Jansen, there was no sign any eyeball connection had been made, and Parker went on in a more down-homey way:

"Now folks, let's all imagine ourselves as being from out here in Ilwaco..."

That got a few snickers and one strange laugh that sounded like the bark of a dog.

"Who is it?" Parker asked, as if he didn't know by heart every publisher from Point Roberts to Walla Walla. "Jerry? Jerry Silverton? Where are you?" Jerry's hand shot up, and he got some applause.

"Stand up, Jerry, so people who don't know you, can see who you are."

Jerry stood up for a second, and got another round.

Parker, evangelically, now held up his own hand. "So, imagine Jerry out here. Jerry probably knows the name of every cussed thing walking around on two legs out here. Every cussed wet thing."

Another laugh.

Like most of the other people, Feeney took a glance at Silverton to see how he was taking it, but Silverton just put on the mask people wore at times like that and all anyone saw was benign amusement. Feeney felt sorry for him. Everyone knew Dean Parker, and knew how off-the-rails things could go. But it could have been worse. Parker could easily have used Feeney, himself, as a model for whatever it was he now had in mind.

"So," Parker went on, "just imagine for a moment what it would be like for good ol' Jerry, to be trying to scrape out a decent, and decently done, living out here, molding this, protecting this, nurturing this... sense... of community, without the help and encouragement of all the rest of us, his brothers in arms."

Parker smiled. Feeney cringed.

"OK, I know. I know. We forget so easy. But then, we do come along once a year to remind Jerry... to remind all of us... how much good we really are doing for our own communities. And, you're damn right, it does help. We do need to give Jerry a hand... we need to give ourselves a hand, for the honest, decent job we're getting on with. The honest, decent job people like Jerry, people like all of us, actually, are doing. Upholding American standards of decency and honesty. Looking out for our neighbors, keeping faith with them, staying aware of their needs, their hopes. Their wishes. Looking out for the children of our communities. Helping our fellow businesses. Promoting community concerns. That is to say, those communities we live in. And, needless to say," Parker paused, dramatically, "minding our own businesses."

He now smiled again, this time to make clear to everyone that this magnanimity was a genuine and natural inclination.

"Sure, I know, small towns are small towns. And there are those who might look down on the idea of living in a small pond. And not just the big city folk, you know. Not just city folk. There are some among us, I am sure, who are uncomfortable with the role of being just a responsible community leader, and spokesman, in some of our poor, podunk little burgs. Just! As if that wasn't enough."

Parker smiled, this time sadly.

"Well, I have to tell you... as far as I'm concerned... I have to tell you, I don't feel one iota of jealousy for those big dailies. Look at them, one by one, getting swallowed up by the syndicates, getting saddled with corporate direction, losing their independence not only to act, but to think. No sirree, give me my liberty, or give me death! That's what I say. And I think you all agree with me, and would all agree that, no matter what, we can all take a solemn vow that the independent local paper will always be at the forefront of that honesty and decency, the hallmark of the American small town, and way of life. And I do that by making sure my paper, and my staff of community reporters, concentrate on our community, of the community, by the community, and for the community. And not get all blown up with the idea of poaching around just for the sake of bragging rights, or whatever-to-hell other un-American, un-Community, unscrupulous, unprincipled, unethical, un-journalistic notion. Not me. Hell no. And for myself, I promise you, I will defend that to my last," Parker gave them all a sly grin, "dying breath. As I almost did. Har, har, haaar..."

Feeney thought Parker had laid it on a bit too thick there at the end, and the proof was how he didn't get as many laughs that time, with people not thinking of his joke, but what had preceded it. But Parker was beaming with pleasure. He was obviously pleased with his off-the-cuff speechmaking abilities. He'd really landed that one.

"So, on that note, I wish you all the best in your work and as always look forward to seeing how you've been doing."

Feeney had to admit, that was a subtle note in Parker's favor. Out in the reception hall, all the newspapers had brought in examples of their best issues for the year, many of which had articles and photos submitted for awards. And Parker had been one of the few publishers to actually, and carefully, look them over.

"And also later," Parker went on, "and I want to say how much I'm looking forward to it, seeing the best of the best in the results at the awards ceremony later on."

"And finally," Parker flashed them all another big grin, "I wish you all especially good luck with your desserts. Har, har, haaaaar..."

He got a pretty decent hand, and Feeney could see he was in a good mood as he made his way back to the table and even gave Feeney a smile which, for him, was a frightening thing to see on any occasion.

"Whew!" Parker dropped into his seat. "Well, that goddamn thing's over."

"You had them eating out of your hand."

"Yeah, well, maybe. And I think I got in a few good zingers concerning you-know-who."

"Dead center, Dean." Feeney saw the next speaker heading for the podium. The coffee and cake speaker. That would be the last. "Dead center."

"Where's the asshole, anyway? I thought I saw him somewhere in the back."

"Over in the corner, by the palm trees."

"Where?" Parker craned around tightly and held himself like that until he spotted Jansen. "Oh, yeah. Well, he should be hiding."

Up at the podium, a publisher from Moses Lake, named Sturp, was hesitating for a moment, reading the opening lines of Feeney's neglected and forgotten speech. Then Sturp leaned over the mike with a smile. "If Dean wouldn't mind, I'd like to buy this off of him."

"Wha...?" Parker now swiveled around the other way and looked at Sturp for a second. "Oh, that." He chuckled, realizing he was getting a few looks, and was doubly pleased at how Sturp had made it sound like he liked the speech, even though he had made everything up right on the spot. He chuckled, and then turned back to the table, muttering amiably under his breath: "Sturp always has to top you."

They listened for a minute or so, and Feeney realized Sturp was using some of his material, and getting smiles and nods.

"He is topping you."

Parker's amiability gave way to an irritated shrug.

"So," Feeney said, making a show of feigning high indifference, "just file what I wrote. Next time they ask you for a speech, which should be in about ten years, you'll have one all ready."

Parker had a benign look of innocence on his face, but then changed it to look like he was sorry. "Must have been all that coughing that got me off track."

"Bullshit."

"Don't make like a martyr. Anyway, you're going to clean up at the awards ceremony for all the school stuff, and you know it."

Feeney did know that. And he looked forward to getting recognized for what was his hardest and most determined work. He knew it was really good. And he didn't know another hack in the county, let alone the state, who could have come close.

But for a moment, as Parker went back to what was left of his lunch, Feeney looked at his employer thoughtfully, and couldn't help saying, with a slight smile, "you actually meant all that, didn't you?"

Parker didn't seem to hear him and kept picking at his plate. But then, without looking up, said: "I did."

As for the school stuff, at the awards ceremony, at least it all got an honorable mention in the "community issues" category.

Parker was sitting down in the better seats that night, but made a point of turning around and giving Feeney a look of solicitous congratulations. Feeney felt like flipping him off, but knew no one would mistake it for a joke.

And so the rest of the ceremony droned on. Publishers hop-hop-hopping up to collect prizes for newswriting, photography, self-promotion. And then they got to the main event, which covered the prizes for Feature Writing.

This was the Big Kahuna. The Cock-o'-the-Walk.

As usual, some interesting stuff did float up out of the smallest papers. The kids scrambled around down there, killing themselves with mod-trash-devo-style journalistic backflips, in the desperate attempt to be hip whilst writing about cows or the weather.

Just looking at the reporter, Feeney could guess where the

influence came from. The reference. The style. Which was not always strictly journalistic.

There goes Bob Woodward, there goes Carl Bernstein, there goes Truman Capote, there goes young Hemingway, there goes Tom Wolfe, there goes William F. Buckley, there goes Hunter S. Thompson.

Feeney was practically falling asleep, when...

"And for Category 3, Mid-Sized, the WJA First Prize Award for Excellence this year goes to Patrick Feeney, the Skykomish Register, for his piece: When the Hills Aren't High Enough, covering the Index flood. And this will also be this year's overall First Prize Award, all categories, for feature writing."

Not one of Warren Harrison's articles that Parker had submitted won a thing.

Weird irony. Added to the subtle pleasure of watching Parker slouch up to accept the award. The publisher managing even to look happy about it.

Feeney knew better than to let his face show any more than utter stoniness as Parker, making his way back to his seat, glanced up to see the expected jubilation but Feeney didn't sink that low. Much as Feeney would have loved to dance in the aisle, he knew there would come a better time to get payback.

That much, he had learned from Parker.

Chapter 62

Bad News Abby Badb

HE drove with an uncertain mood through Monroe. He didn't want to go home. Being a lone, half-drunk fool in one bar did not give him much spiritual impetus to repeat the act in another. But he still didn't want to go home, and on Main Street he pulled into an empty spot, just next to all the motorcycles, in front of the Chainsaw Tavern.

He almost never went into the Chainsaw. The name itself was enough of a reason. And then came the clientele. The sort of people who identified with the name.

But not really.

While the Chainsaw did attract a few specimens of that race which used such a machine for making a living, the bar was more the hangout for the biker crowd. People Feeney had, in a past life, come to know and didn't mind too much. But that was all. He mostly wouldn't deliberately choose to hang out with them now. Not that the guys who left their Harleys and Triumphs out front in a haphazard mess of chrome and lacquered steel were some sort of gang. But they often had all the attributes of a gang. Moving in a mass, thinking in a mass. Bold in action and word. Especially with strangers.

Throw in the hair-trigger machismo demanded by mass male etiquette, and you had a good recipe for disaster for someone who caused the mass to become aware of him. Someone who wasn't like them. Or didn't seem to be like them. Dressed in all the wrong sort of clothes, for example—Feeney, who at that moment was wearing what looked like designer jeans and a smooth leather waist-length jacket, a leftover from the disco days. Even Beebee had told him he needed to get a new wardrobe.

The Chainsaw. Normally, the rare times he ever went in there were in broad daylight, midweek.

They made good sandwiches.

He pulled open the door and walked inside, and within a minute knew he'd made a mistake. She was there at the bar. And she was looking just as lonely as he was feeling. Unfortunately, he stood there too long, and Bad Abby spotted him and although she looked momentarily surprised, she nodded at him. He sat down next to her.

"What's this?" she said. "Jilt City?"

Feeney shook his head, but he was in no way going to go into anything concerning himself. He got a beer, and they decided just to talk about life. That evening seemed, for both of them, perfect for that hopeless subject. For Abby, life had sort of happened to her. Just as marriage had sort of happened to her. She and her husband had worked very hard at it for a while. No kids. Spent all their time and the money he'd made as a logger on the ranch. But then, she said, he had suddenly just gotten tired of it.

"Did you know I was in here?" she asked.

"We barely know each other, Abby," he said, feeling empty enough to be honest.

"Well," she said. "I'm glad you came in."

She looked over at the bartender and pointed at her glass. Feeney was still working very slowly on his first beer, letting himself sober up while sitting at the bar. It was a new approach, and he could see it might be useful in the future.

"I'm glad you came in," Abby said again, taking a sip on her drink. Whatever she was doing, it wasn't involved with sobering up. "You know something? I shouldn't be so surprised to see you out and about. It's not as if you would have been stupid enough to be bringing her in here with you." She gave him an honest smile.

He froze.

Where he had been nodding and being friendly, he now looked at her with his full attention.

This is it, he thought, realizing he had come across someone who was going to tell him. And not surprisingly, it would be coming from someone who didn't really know him. It could only have been that way, he realized. Almost nobody has the courage to share rumors with the object of them. Although Abby's hazy, flirty level of drunkenness was probably helping as well.

"Yeah," he said. "Of course not."

He was in no rush. He knew that whenever it was obvious someone had information... if he wanted it, he could get it out of them. It was a newspaperman's conceit, but a real one.

"I know," she said. "I know. What a stupid idea, eh? Knowing her and all..."

"You know... her?"

He had almost said Tari, but he held back. It had to come from her, and he expected it at any moment. But it surprised him. Abby had nothing to do with Sultan or with anything else up there. And they seemed to come from such different worlds.

"Me? How would I know her? I mean, personally."

He knew within the next few questions he'd be asking her how she could know Tari, or anything concerned with the school.

"And yet, you know somehow. So how?"

She shrugged. "I don't know. Like you know about anyone. Someone always knows someone else, I guess."

"Stuff sure gets around," he said.

"Sure does," she nodded.

So it really had been getting around, and enough that it wasn't just half-guessed insinuations by Steele.

Well, if knowledge was power, Feeney thought, it could also be like a sword and cut two ways.

Rumors. For two years he'd had a front row seat to plenty of town rumors. He knew the different ways they started. But he also knew how they were very hard to trace back to a source, or even how they got started in the first place. But depending on their usefulness, whether they were true or not, he also knew they could develop a life on their own. And this one, by getting all the way to Abby, seemed to have been useful to some people.

In any case, he now had the opportunity to start a backfire, a counter rumor which would squash the first. The fact that Abby had come across the rumor meant she could also propagate one. He would just admit to her that he had found Tari attractive. Really very attractive, and for a while it had been just moth to flame stuff. Completely unconscious. But then had realized what was happening, including how it all might have looked. And that it was nothing.

He took a sip of his beer, and shrugged. "Oh, well."

"It's a shock, isn't it," Abby said, "to know how much people know. Especially something like this where you have to be so discreet. God knows, I always felt shock when I'd hear things about me."

"It's normal."

"Well, if it makes you feel any better, there's nothing else attached to it. I guess you two are being real smart. No motels. And no bars. Although that seemed pretty unlikely."

"Pretty unlikely, yeah."

"Anyway," she laughed. "Nobody really believes it, just because it's a little too much like playing with fire."

"Well," he said. "I'm not surprised, I guess. All the time we spent together working and all."

"Do you really work together?"

"Of course."

Abby nodded.

"Amazing, sometimes, how all it takes in these little towns is just a little extracurricular contact, and everybody's jumping into everybody else's bed."

"Not necessarily jumping," Feeney said, looking at the back bar and getting his Tari story ready to go.

"Nearly," she laughed. "The boredom factor. Look at that PTA president you got up there, and her little lover-boy. I don't blame her a bit though. He does look sort of like a rock star, doesn't he, with that car and all?"

Abby figured the look on Feeney's face to be little more than the usual sort people make on hearing gossip repeated for the umpteenth time.

382

Feeney had no idea what he looked like. It was like a giant comet had crashed upon him.

But what he found truly astonishing was that even that feeling could be surpassed. As it did in the next fifteen seconds.

She laughed. "Tell me one thing though, OK? I've just got to know."

"What?" he managed to get out.

"Is it true she hasn't even graduated from high school yet?"

Chapter 63

All She Wrote

COLD convenience-store bean burritos with beer made for a lousy dinner. But it was enough for a distracted Feeney, and it got him through the evening news.

The Seattle coverage was exactly what he expected. A quick rundown of the candidates from all over the state, a rundown of local issues. The defeat of the school bond issue in Sultan got exactly twenty seconds.

Bad news for Feeney had lately come in chunks of mere seconds. But as for this one, he at least knew what he could do about it. His job, for the entire week ahead, was all but completely outlined in those twenty seconds of air time.

All of it.

Not that there wouldn't be some fine tuning.

Parker would have a staff meeting to go over coverage. Diplomacy, with a sharp eye toward the subscription roll and the advertising accounts, would prevail.

Not that they would have to break their backs about it. What with Jansen's paper out of the way, Parker could relax a bit. But Feeney knew that noncontroversiality would remain the standing order.

Even though the paper had supported the bond issue, there would be no hand-wringing. If anything, it would almost sound the opposite. And this was one of the few occasions where Parker would write an editorial.

Elections, sacred symbols of democracy, were Parker's domain.

Dean would gird himself with lofty sentiments, wrap himself in Old Glory, and then pen something stirring about the Will of the People, or the Common Wisdom of the Community.

Which was just fine with Feeney.

He would not have complained otherwise, though. After all, in his role as a sort of automaton, he was paid to grind out words suitable for any occasion.

Words suitable for the consumption of a near-analphabetic public. As well as for the consumption of anyone, regardless of which side of the fence they were on.

Words. Short and suitable.

Words ready to say any goddamn thing on the face of the earth.

Words wholly unsuitable, though, were the words Feeney really felt. Very short and understandable words.

In the past few days, he'd seen himself going through all the stages of personal depression, guilt, anger, and even a half-assed attempt at denial. But it wasn't working.

That rumor took precedence over everything else.

Murder seemed the only genuinely satisfactory solution. The only one that might make him feel good again. Although, of course, he didn't know who the victim should be, and so would-be felon Feeney could only stare at the walls in frustration.

For the first time, Feeney was glad Harrison was on the staff. Feeney could slough off almost all of the reporting crap onto Superman.

With the news over, Feeney let the television drift into sitcoms while he continued his post-burrito beer fest.

He had not yet come up with a plan concerning the Carey rumor, although his reaction to Abby at the Chainsaw had been authentic, outraged and flummoxed. And when he was through, she had not doubted a single word he said. And he could see he could do the same with anyone who came his way hinting at that, and would easily blow that rumor out of the water. So he didn't care.

But right there on his sofa, having seen Tickler Steele's gamble and Ted's Folly blown out of the water, he was exhausted. As was his stock of bean burritos. But he had enough beer, and that kept him going right through the rest of the night, through to the end of some idiotic talk show, and beyond.

And for the first time in weeks, Feeney ended up having a good night's sleep.

Knowledge, even if painful, is indeed power.

Chapter 64

Beginnings and Endings

WHEN things get out of hand, it doesn't stop until it's sluiced away in a total wash.

Just inevitable.

He could have averted his eyes, at the very least, instead of staring. Let those well-bred inner manners he'd grown up with, which held that deliberately not noticing things you weren't supposed to notice was the polite way to be. But it is almost inhumanly impossible to not notice something you already knew about. And Feeney was getting tired of being polite.

Only a God could have timed it, though. No human intervention could have crafted such cruel perfection.

Ironically enough, Frank Baron enabled it. His idea was a sort of consolation rally. Baron wasn't one to give up easily. And doubling the irony, Tari had known about it. The trouble for Tari was that she hadn't figured on the depth and urgency of her husband's need to discharge his frustration.

Baron hadn't even managed to get to his office, it turned out. He was stalled in the morning rush hour down to Redmond, fuming about the election, and finally boiled over. Baron, that was. Not his car. No way he could deal with such measly things as clients and contracts. He had a message to send.

He called in and took the day off. Then he called around and managed to round up enough people to hold a sort of war council. He called Feeney as well.

"Don't you think this could be held off?" Feeney said. Years later, whenever he recalled this conversation, he would remember that suggestion pleasantly.

"The iron's hot, Feeney."

"You sure it's not just you that's hot?"

"Everybody should be upset, and not just me."

"Almost half the town wouldn't agree with that."

For a short moment, Baron seemed to be thinking. Maybe taking Feeney's advice? For once? But then... no.

"We have to do something. We don't want people to get discouraged."

"Frank, for God's sake, let it rest a little. This poor old town has been put through the wringer for half a year. Everyone's worn out. Ted's worn out. I think even Steele's worn out, although with all the blood money you guys coughed up for him, he's not likely to be suffering half as much as the rest of us. Christ, I can tell you, I'm worn out."

"I don't see why you consider yourself worn out, what with the minimal lip-service you gave."

Feeney no longer gave any effort to this sort of thing anymore.

"Frank, it's such a pleasure being on your side of the issue."

"Half the town's voters deserve to be told they are not wrong."

"Oh, shit. They don't need anyone to hold their hands for them. Maybe that's what you need. But believe me, most of the people in Sultan who voted in favor of the bond issue, disappointed as they may be, are just getting on with their lives this morning. I mean, for crying out loud, Frank, it was only a fucking bond issue. It wasn't a war."

"What do you know about war?"

"Take a couple of aspirins, Frank."

"You going to come down or not?"

Feeney shut his eyes slowly. "Yes, I'm coming down. But you'd better understand: we're not going to drape the front page in black crepe."

"Fine, fine." Baron hung up.

The meeting was for three o'clock. Feeney spent the next half hour trying to find Superman. There was the right man for the job.

But Harrison was nowhere to be found, no phone to call, and Feeney knew he would have to cover the non-event himself.

He spent the rest of the morning muttering.

The idea was to find a highly public, somewhat newsworthy place to hold a meeting. Gone mindless with desperate enthusiasm, Baron had run off somewhere and found a portable P.A. system, a podium and—had to give him credit—actual red, white and blue bunting.

At first he had wanted to hold the rally in front of the high school but Chief Spencer threw cold water on the idea. So Baron finally set up down at the Sultan River Park.

When Feeney showed up at the appointed hour, he was astonished by the size of the turnout at the park. He would never have guessed the town had so many unoccupied people hanging around during the day. Several hundred people were there, dawdling beneath the trees.

Of course, it was also a beautiful day. Actually, gorgeous. The air was drenched in sunlight and heat, and there beneath the old trees of the park the rally had more an atmosphere of carnival than of something political. Evidently, it hadn't taken much to convince people to play hooky from work. With Baron's makeshift stage, podium and bunting, it almost looked like the Fourth of July down there. Feeney, in amazement, saw a food truck selling hotdogs and all the rest. And doing a booming business.

Baron was obviously ecstatic with the results, standing on the stage with his jacket off and shirtsleeves rolled up. Ready to work.

"… and so we have to take heart," he was yelling at them over the P.A., "this is just the FIRST, the longest, and most difficult step in our efforts. For the SAKE of our CHILDREN, for our COMMUNITY, for our FAMILIES, and for the NATION, we must STAND TOGETHER AND STAND STRONG."

Feeney, carrying his small tape recorder, clicked it on.

Looking around at the crowd, he spotted a Seattle camera crew filming from beneath one of the big chestnuts and wandered over to them. Staying away from the sound man, Feeney came alongside the camera. Its operator winked at him. Newsies knew newsies.

389

Feeney, holding his tape recorder at arm's length toward Baron, squinted at the cameraman and said in a low voice, "Clint?"

The cameraman grinned. "Wow. A memory."

"How could I forget anyone named Clint? Anyway... you guys gotta be kidding," Feeney said.

"We were up at the Pass this morning, and they told us this was happening."

"They're going to run it?" Feeney didn't believe it.

Clint shrugged the shoulder that wasn't cradling the camera. "Just a public thing. You never know what might happen when you get this many people together."

"Would you like a riot?"

"That'd be nice." Clint made a slow pan of the crowd, and then went back to filming Frank Baron. Feeney knew just a few crowd shots were needed. Most of what they were looking for now were juicy sound bites.

"If I incite one, can I get a cut?"

"We're not working on spec."

"Wow. Staff," Feeney said. "I'm honored. I don't see your mouth, though."

"We weren't up here with a face. And I'm sure as hell not going to do it." Feeney and Clint looked over at the sound guy, who looked back and shook a me-neither head, and then Clint went on: "So we'll just overdub and let them play with it at the station."

They would record a few explanatory statements from Baron afterwards, and if it got picked up the anchor would do an intro and tail. Feeney envied them.

"My friends..." Baron was beginning to sound hoarse and his eyes bulged, his face getting red. It was hard work to be publicly outraged. Clint kept filming. "... just as we need to be generous in VICTORY, we must LEARN from DEFEAT. We must understand what we have done, and what we can do better. Half of our community agreed with us and voted with us. And lost. But this doesn't mean that our half of the community was WRONG. It means that half the community DID NOT UNDERSTAND THE THREAT AND THE URGENCY OF THE MESSAGE."

Clint grinned. "Who's this guy? Winston Churchill?"

Feeney wrapped his arms across his chest, and looked down at his shoes. "Just a guy who's found his mission in life."

Clint adjusted his focus. "Lucky him."

"You may be filming history," Feeney said, gave him and the mic a nod, and walked away. He looked across the crowd at Baron. Indeed, lucky him.

Baron wasn't doing too badly and was beginning to get a growing swell of appropriately timed cheers and applause. Feeney finally shut off his recorder.

Baron had probably never guessed he had it in him, Feeney thought. But he sure did now. Feeney saw how Baron himself was impressed with what he was doing.

By all rights, if you didn't know better, this little rally could have been passed off as a professional political meeting. Baron now had the tempo, the right words, the right sentiments, and he had the crowd swaying beneath him like a well-rehearsed bunch of trained seals.

Feeney had been to plenty of political rallies in his life, and he knew their smell, taste and texture. And here, right out of the blue and unbidden except by that primal facet of human nature, that magnified compulsion, that desire to control decisions, that evolutionary urge almost on par with procreation itself, Feeney was witnessing the transformation, or perhaps the rebirth, of an ordinary human being. Frank Baron, at that moment, had become a politician.

Which was both fascinating and terrifying at the same time.

Feeney figured he may as well stick around to see if anything else happened. And he did, right through the end, which was toward four o'clock.

He had taken a few notes, but that was really enough, and he did not have the curiosity in the end to hang around while the camera tandem bagged their single-face interview. Most of the crowd was gone by then. The park seemed empty. Green and sleepy. He went for a stroll across to the river, to wander there for a few minutes in the shady air.

On the other side of the river from the park, a little-used road wound back up toward the upper reaches of the Sultan River. Feeney knew the road only wound up into the trees for about five miles, and everyone knew there was nothing up on that side except a couple of old stump farms. At best, it was a good place for a picnic. But not even that, and what it got mostly used for was a convenient place for young couples to go cop a feel.

Lover's Lane.

Under normal circumstances, of course, there would have been practically no one in the park that day to notice Warren Harrison's car, with Tari Baron aboard, coming down that road out of the trees into the bright sunlight. At worst, maybe one or two mothers out walking pre-school children. A gamble, maybe. But a reasonable one.

If Tari's car was parked somewhere near the park, Harrison could normally have just let her off there and continued on over to the main road. And Tari could have just fetched her car as though she had done nothing more than walk around the park a bit.

The heavy-leafed trees and dark shadows, the beautiful sun-drenched day shining down on the little road, and whatever else was on their minds, they were in a world of their own. There was nothing really to attract their attention, the park being nearly empty. And because of that, neither Harrison nor Tari noticed a wooden-faced newspaper editor standing under the trees in the park, staring at them as they drove past on the other side of the Jackson.

Harrison brought the Porsche to a stop at the far end of the park, where a footbridge crossed the river. Tari leaned toward him for a few moments and then got out.

Feeney was thinking what a funny thing human nature was as he watched her slip through the park and then out at the exit at that end. Such a strange thing how it could so easily fail to see anything really unexpected, unannounced, or unknown.

The same way the ancient Greeks had no word for what is now known as the color blue, the same way an audience does not see the magician's trick, the same way five different people will describe the same robber in five different ways, Tari also did not recognize or see either Feeney or another man who was standing with a camera crew up in the middle of the park. Baron, up until then, had been speaking with his back toward the river, but at the sound of Harrison's turbo-charged engine, he had idly glanced back. And Tari did not see, let alone recognize, her recently jubilant but now increasingly and mindlessly distraught husband.

Feeney suddenly, and for the first time, found himself fully sympathizing with Frank Baron.

Chapter 65

Sic Transit Gloria Mundi

BACK to the office, and loose ends.

Bob Hawthorn stood inside with the door open. No one else.

"Aren't you afraid someone might steal something?" He raised his eyebrows at Feeney, who came through the door with a jelly doughnut.

"Like what, the telephone? It'd be a godsend."

Hawthorn smiled.

Feeney eyed him. "What brings you down here? Don't tell me you want to hold a rally or something, too?"

He got a frown for that. "Why would I want to do a thing like that?"

"I dunno, Bob. Why the hell not?"

"I'm not down here to gloat."

"Well, I know that," Feeney said evenly. At the end of the day, he didn't mind Bob all that much. Everyone had their world. Their row to hoe. "But you know, none of this is going to last one way or the other."

"How so?" Hawthorn gave him a genuine look of interest.

Feeney shrugged. "You know I wasn't lying about the red tags. Or at least, I hope you know that."

Hawthorn shook his head. "I guess... there'll be something."

"Bob, listen to me. This time, listen. It won't be 'something'. That's the problem. You just don't want to believe it. But, believe me, it'll be everything. The whole thing. Someday, you'll know I'm right. What Steele got going made a lot of people think all this was

394

unending, rolling noise. Insulting noise. And that had you fooled as much as anything else. And I don't blame you. I don't like to believe politicians, either. And Steele made it seem there was no middle. Everything was either all one way or the other." Feeney shrugged. "Will it be as bad as Steele said? No... there'll be a necessity to do something. But, at bottom, that school is going to be closed."

Hawthorn looked at Feeney for a long moment, and then looked down, deep in thought. Feeney knew Hawthorn was an intelligent man, and knew he had got swept up into a crusade. When that happened to people, Feeney knew, there was also an afterward, when the same people came down from all the euphoria. And began to see realities. And Hawthorn was evidently beginning to realize some things. Among them was that Feeney perhaps hadn't been just shining him on all the time.

"You make it sound like we just wasted our time and money."

Feeney laughed. "Dean doesn't consider it wasted. Far as he's concerned, it was money very well spent."

"I'd imagine so, from his point of view."

Feeney couldn't help himself. "Matter of fact, he was wondering what your group is going to do when the school does, finally, get red-tagged. If, maybe, you would launch into another crusade... maybe to have the whole school district moved down the road."

Hawthorn, for the first time, gave Feeney a careful look of speculation, gauging the truth in what he was hearing. "That's all it meant to him? He didn't consider us as rivals?"

"Rivals? No, of course not. All he cared about was your money." Feeney grinned. "You bet. As far as he was concerned, it was your decision. He didn't milk you. He just told me to write the news and let Ted and Tickler get all foamy at the mouth, and your bunch would react and do the rest."

"Jesus," Hawthorn shook his head. "When you put it that way..."

Feeney smiled. "The fact is, every newspaper publisher worth his salt has a bit of the P.T. Barnum in him."

Bob Hawthorn stood there, looking at Feeney. A long stare.

And then a tiny frown of understanding. It wasn't any one thing Feeney was saying, but the absolute confidence in the way he said it. Hawthorn noted how, despite the cynical tone coming from the editor, Feeney seemed deeply sincere and concerned. He could see he'd misjudged something.

"You're saying you saw all this right from the beginning? I mean, to your way of thinking?"

"I don't always know things. But I could feel it, yes."

"Hmmm," Hawthorn grunted. "And so, according to you, you don't think we actually won anything."

Feeney stared at Hawthorn. This was coming down. The man was finally, really, getting it. Maybe it was all the money that had been spent. Or maybe the meaning of the red tag notification had finally made him realize things. But whatever it was, the man was uneasy.

Feeney nodded, looking carefully at Hawthorn.

"That's exactly right, Bob."

"OK," Hawthorn said. "Then what is it, that you do see?"

"You actually want me to say it? Every other time I've tried, you didn't care to listen."

"Well," Hawthorn said, "since we're talking, what can it hurt?"

Feeney nodded. "Too bad you didn't say that last year. Anyway... OK... here it is. First, it's amazing how nobody is facing up to how none of this... I mean this town and this area... is going to stay the same. Look at you and your friends buying five-acre lots, looking for peace and quiet up there on the ridge. But don't tell me you haven't noticed how down lower, those rural zones are being rezoned down to urban, with sewers and all. Me, I give you another two years max."

Hawthorn said nothing. Feeney spelled it out.

"The waves of people moving up here, with that new highway spur coming up from Lake Washington, means it won't just be retired people with money, investing in old farmsteads. It'll mean housing developments with families and kids. Lots of kids. And it won't be blue collar money, at all. But all that upwardly-mobile tech money coming from the other side of the lake. People who expect their kids to have near-prep-school levels of education. Which, in turn, will put lots of pressure on the school district."

Feeney paused. "You only won a battle, Bob. You want me to go on?"

Hawthorn actually smiled. "Too bad you didn't write about this in the paper."

Feeney smiled back. "I think I did, Bob. But people see what they want to see. Do you want me to go back and pull that issue out for you?"

"And so, you think all that money was wasted..."

Feeney glanced over at the coffee maker. He thought of making a pot, seeing how nice and homey things were getting. They could have a good, down-home chat.

"Yes, Bob, I do," he sighed, moving toward the pot. "Because in the end, when the school is tagged and closed, which I'd say is only a matter of weeks, it won't be a local issue anymore and you'll find yourself battling with the county and probably even the state. Me, personally, I think you're going to find what they come up with as outlandish as you thought Ted's plan was. In fact, I think the state's proposal will simply blow you all away. I'm guessing the local levy will turn out to be twice as high." Feeney pointed at the maker. "Want some coffee?"

"No, thanks," Hawthorn said, and then laughed. "Shit...."

Feeney nodded, sighed and, giving up on the coffee, went and sat down heavily in his chair. As he did so, he saw a car pull up fast outside the office.

He looked back at Hawthorn and began trying to find something consoling to say. But that was as far as he got when Frank Baron came through the door, eyes bulging, face red, as though he were still giving his inaugural stump speech.

"So where is that son-of-a-bitch!" he yelled.

Hawthorn, confronted by his principal adversary, completely forgot about the conversation he'd just been having.

Understandably, he saw himself as the most obvious object for Baron's bad humor.

Feeney could easily rectify that impression by mentioning someone else's name, but that would be letting Baron understand that the thing had been seen. Feeney had been feeling a lot of things lately, but none of them had been suicidal.

Hawthorn yelled back. "Don't ever let anyone tell you that you're not a poor loser, Baron."

Baron turned furiously on him. "And as for you... you can go straight to FUCKING HELL!"

Baron was so loud that Claudine and another woman from next door were out on the sidewalk peeking into the newspaper office. Feeney smiled at them and they smiled back.

Some fun.

Hawthorn did not notice the "and as for you." Subtleties were not part and parcel of what was being exchanged. "You don't deserve the company," Hawthorn said.

Baron's voice rose, his face growing even redder. "Let me tell you something! That goddamn school is going to get its bond issue, and a lot faster than you, and all the other rich pigs up there on the hill, could imagine."

Hawthorn, just out of pure dislike of Baron, ignored all the realities he'd been coming to accept in his discussion with Feeney, and simply hammered back: "The town just told you it didn't want it, Baron."

"The town doesn't know fuck all, thanks to assholes like you. But you got the jump on us, this time, and got everybody so scared they followed you greedy creeps. All you care about is yourself and your goddamn property taxes. You don't give a fuck about anything!"

"Would you quit yelling, you ass."

Baron snarled. "I'll yell if I fucking feel like it, you mother fucking prick!"

Getting yelled and screamed at, by someone you deeply dislike, tends to push most of the hot buttons. Hawthorn was getting angry, his face going as red as Baron's. He shook his head in disgust, his own voice rising an octave. "Go fuck your mother...!"

Even Feeney was surprised by that. He had never heard Hawthorn say anything past the normally rude and insulting. In fact, most of the time he'd been there in that town, he'd heard very few actual insults like that except from a few drunks over at the bars.

"Guys..." he began.

But Baron exploded, lunging at Hawthorn with one arm swinging. "You fucking goddamn, son-of-a-bitch!"

Later, Feeney could never remember any blow landing. In any case, it didn't matter.

Hawthorn bellowed and threw himself back at Baron. For a few seconds it was just stupid flailing, but then Hawthorn got a nasty shot in on Baron's left ear. At that, Baron, insane with rage, reared back and threw a punch right between Hawthorn's eyes. Hawthorn staggered but remained upright.

It was a real cowboy-movie-style fight, and Feeney would have loved to watch it. Except for it taking place in his own office.

Having little else to work with, he grabbed his swivel chair and spun it toward the two men, managing to get it wedged between them. He knew it was only a momentary solution.

Out of the corner of his eye, he noticed Claudine and the other woman were grinning like it was a turkey shoot, but Claudine was also on her phone, the spiral cord stretched tight so she could talk and still watch, and he knew that Spencer or one of his cronies would soon enough be showing up.

That was good. He wouldn't have to get too mixed up in trying to stop them. Let the cops have that particular fun.

His efforts were strictly to save the furniture and especially to protect Mrs. Hagy's equipment.

His efforts, though, were short-lived and futile.

"You mother fucker!" Baron had got his arm around Hawthorn's head and was punching away at the top of it like he was trying to beat the husk off a coconut.

Hawthorn was yelling something but was muffled by Baron's shirt.

Suddenly, in a paroxysm of pain and tortured amazement, Baron flung himself away from Hawthorn and stared at the teeth marks on his arm. Then, beyond himself, he suddenly contorted as though in some weird ballet move and picked up Mrs. Hagy's aluminum chair.

"No, no...!" Feeney put his hand out.

And that was how things ended, just before the Sultan squad car rolled in front of Feeney's office: Bob Hawthorn clutching what would turn out to be a broken arm, Frank Baron in jail for the rest of the afternoon, and Mrs. Hagy in need of a new chair.

Chapter 66

5 Seconds of Fame

THAT night, Feeney saw the TV crew had managed to work up a pretty good news item, considering all that had taken place that day. As the news anchor led into the story, and before any interview with Baron was run, Feeney called Harrison and told him to tune in.

Professional coordination and all that.

It turned out Harrison was already watching it.

It was a surprisingly well-developed piece. The editors down in Seattle, having watched Baron's speech and the crowd reaction, had come to the same conclusion as Feeney. This was a political career in the making. And TV loves nothing better than politics.

For Feeney, 'pretty good' didn't come close to describing the news report, though not in any way the news crew intended.

It was almost as entertaining as the office mayhem earlier in the day.

And there on the screen was Frank doing blood, sweat, and tears.

And there was the crowd cheering.

And there was Frank, being interviewed afterwards, full of himself and spouting away like a three-term representative up for re-election.

And there, in the background, a bright red Porsche, clearly visible, with a clear view of its passengers, slinking down the road on the other side of the river.

And there was Frank, catching it in the corner of his eye.

And there was how his expression changed, mid-Winston, his

mind not wanting to believe it, but there was no room for doubt.

And there was Frank Baron heroically making a last statement.

The anchor mentioned, dryly, that Baron had been involved in some sort of later altercation. But it wasn't mentioned where, much to Feeney's disappointment.

Feeney loved the coverage, especially how the Seattle guys didn't have a clue how good it really was.

When the news show was over, Feeney thought he might call Harrison, but dropped that idea as quickly as it came. He didn't want to be the guy in the know. And he wasn't surprised at all that Harrison didn't call him. So it would wait until morning.

Feeney had a beer to celebrate.

The next morning, Harrison semi-sauntered into the office a bit late. He looked nominally all right, though there was something cagey about him.

Feeney let him settle in at his desk, and Harrison noticed Mrs. Hagy's mangled chair and looked over at Feeney.

That was when Feeney very casually mentioned to Harrison that Baron had come by looking for him after the rally in the park, but hadn't left a message.

After about twenty minutes, with Harrison, equally casually, fooling around with various things on his desk, he suddenly picked up his clippings folder, announced he had just remembered something he had to do and left the office.

Chapter 67

Alone Again

CONTRARY to what the poets say, the best source of inspiration is procrastination and a deadline.

For Feeney, years of experience had taught him to judge any given story and know, with an infallible instinct, how late he could push things before he absolutely had to panic. But this time, he was having problems.

Trying to write about that town was difficult even under the best circumstances. Trying to be fair and impartial. Trying to give people a real sense of what was at the heart of their community.

But did anyone really want to know what was at the heart of the failure of the school bond issue, or of the Baron-Hawthorn incident which, thanks to Claudine, had got around town faster than lightning?

Feeney sat there in his office, weighing options. He had no idea where Harrison was or what he was doing. And, given the way he'd gone out the door, Feeney would bet good money he wasn't coming back. So Feeney was left with the necessity of writing the entire paper himself, well past any normal deadline. It wasn't going well.

Every time he started to write a lead, he quickly ended up feeling like he was writing an obituary. He would stop. Go for a walk around the parking lot. Try again. It was now Sunday afternoon. And he had been out in that parking lot five times now.

This was getting to be true panic.

The deadline was the next morning, when Mrs. Hagy and her Flying Fingers would come in. Feeney knew he couldn't try to finish up while she blasted through the more inconsequential items. That week there wasn't even enough that was inconsequential. He had to be able to deliver the two serious stories before nine in the morning. The bond defeat and the red tag.

And after sitting there in his office for another half hour, he finally gave up.

Panic was getting him nowhere.

He flicked off his typewriter, flicked off the coffee pot, flicked off the lights, and went out to his car. And then he went to Bedossa's, where he had a couple of drinks, a couple of laughs with Marsha, and went home, literally not giving two fucks for anything.

But he did set his alarm for early, and at six in the morning, deathlike, Feeney sat typing easily, faultlessly, and bloodlessly the ghoulish account of the previous week. Numbed and uncaring, he steered his way through the tangled briar of facts, setting down those things which could be considered public knowledge, and avoiding directly, but hinting at, the things which could not.

Fortunately, the craft of journalism was a sturdy tool. Lead para: main fact with hint of cause. Second para: second fact with hint of cause. Third para: third fact. And so on, until the main facts were mopped up and then the causes were treated in descending order... quotes from proponents, quotes from opponents, the Five W's dutifully dispatched... for spice, a few official conjectures based on questions designed not so much as to clarify or inform, but to fill out the article.

And there was the first one, done by a quarter past seven— Feeney's latest offset opus: on Thursday last, gaining only a bare majority of votes and not the sixty percent required, the Sultan school bond issue went down in flames. Tears and cheers. A good-sized article, quoting almost all known participants, with photos of people queuing up for the polling booths.

He did not include too much public reaction in the bond story. Most of that, he knew, would be provided in the framing of the Baron-Hawthorn article.

Then he launched into the red tag story. Feeney didn't even need any notes to write that I-told-you-so story, and it went much quicker. Done by eight. He could have written much more, but as far as what would be down the line, what would be the fate of the school, he'd save all that for next week, with an interview with the Fire Marshal and another interview with Ted Barnwell.

And at the thought of Ted Barnwell, a thought which Feeney had been playing very surreptitiously with for several weeks made him smile. Not giving two fucks was becoming a habit.

As for Bob and Frank, simple enough—he made it a cop-shop sandwich, lead para, second para, third para all dealt with the official version of the assault and the current situation of both men. The mid-section was a rehash of details of the bond issue controversy and the council meeting confrontation, finishing with the official version of what, medically or judicially, both men could expect.

Not that Feeney felt much tolerance or sympathy towards two guys who had trashed his office, but Feeney felt no temptation to twist the knife. Although for the sake of personal integrity, he did allow a hint of the broader story concealed within the text, using a vocabulary that conveyed images, on the one hand, of distraught frustration, inadequacy, failure, embarrassment, and on the other of near-insulting obstinacy, confidence and lack of diplomacy.

But even those came as quotes from third parties, and were designed to describe the general atmosphere surrounding public opinion of late. A runic truth, and rune-smithed with all the professional ease only journalism could offer.

Mrs. Hagy, punctual as always at nine, smiled at all the fresh copy waiting for her. She smiled to see that it was actually all there. Often, he was still finishing things when she began. But he was done. She smiled at that, and at him. But mostly she smiled delightedly at her new chair. She had long wanted this special typing chair, with all sorts of adjustment knobs and fancy support cushions, had mentioned it to Feeney, and even to Dean, several times and it had been delivered at the break of dawn. As Feeney sat there at his desk, listening to the incredible rush of her typing, he gave his eyes a rest. All but finished for the day. Another week's events, entombed in ink and paper. To be spit out onto the streets tomorrow.

As usual, the real story would only make it around by word of mouth among a much smaller audience. Unless, of course, someone made an official or public complaint.

After ten minutes or so, Feeney stood up and stretched tentatively, then with growing abandon when he could trust that he would not cause himself a coronary.

Mrs. Hagy had refrained politely from looking at him too much that morning. With his work finished, he went into the bathroom to see what he could do about himself. The mirror said: not much. The corpselike pallor he could treat with another couple of cups of coffee. The red, burning eyes got a shot of eye-wash. For the puffiness around his eyes, he could do nothing except splash on some cold water. As for his hair, it just did what it did.

Back at his desk with his fourth cup of coffee, his heart pacing only a step behind a high-hurdler's, Feeney waited. As soon as she finished, he'd take all the copy down to Monroe. He was wiped out, and he knew it. But at least he was finished.

Feeney closed his eyes for a second and sighed again, hearing at the same time the office door whine open. When he opened his eyes, he saw Chief Spencer standing in front of him.

"May we talk?"

Feeney's eyebrows barely rose. "Talk?"

Spencer glanced at Mrs. Hagy, and then back at Feeney. Under different circumstances, Feeney might have amused himself with small comedy. But not that day. "We're almost finished," he said, "and I don't have time for any interviews or stories."

"Not about that, Pat."

"It's layout day, you know."

Spencer looked at him for a second, then just nodded. "I only need a few minutes. Just stop by the office."

Feeney gave him a smile, and Spencer left. It wasn't until Spencer had driven off up the highway that the smile faded from Feeney's lips. Feigned obsequiousness had stuck it there; pain had kept it there. This time, the sigh that finally escaped, as his face fell back into something more resembling absolute despair, was more than audible.

Mrs. Hagy put the last strip into the layout folder, and then swiveled to look at him from her Brand New Chair. She rarely had a word for Feeney about anything except work, but now she was looking him up and down.

Good Christ, Feeney thought. More than twenty years his senior, she could have been his mother. He tried to smile.

"Words of wisdom?"

She laughed. Another Mrs. Hagy rarity. "Good paper this morning."

"That so?"

"People don't know their good fortune to have you up here. Or else they've forgotten how bad it could be."

"Or how good, I suppose. Old Gig Shire must be spinning in his grave."

She peered over her glasses. "I wouldn't think so. Gig would just laugh."

"What was he really like?"

"I'm not that old. But I knew Arnold Bradshaw well enough. Dad and Arnie were good friends. That's how I got the job right out of high school. Not many girls got something like that in those days."

Feeney had spent many a rainy afternoon reading through back issues. "Bradshaw had a good paper. Maybe better than Gig's."

"Gig didn't print the news. He was the news. Arnie was liked. He was sort of everybody's uncle, and he was also an honest man. Gig Shire was an honest man, too. But he also ran the paper like he knew best where the town should be heading. Dad used to call him Mayor Shire."

Feeney sighed. "Sometimes I just don't know. I read the old papers and I get the feeling there was a more cohesive community up here. Not so many spats."

"There have always been spats. Gig just elbowed all that out of the way. And Arnie was too much of a gentleman."

"Which makes me...?"

"You're a gentleman, Patrick." Mrs. Hagy reached down and picked up her purse. "I don't think either Gig or Arnie would find too much to complain about the way you run the paper."

"That doesn't really sound very comforting if you're saying there was a fair bit of censorship in those days, too."

"If it was censorship," she said, "it was family censorship. You're close to the community. That's the way Arnie did it, and Gig did too, a little bit."

"I don't think they caught half what I catch."

"That is a bit different, I suppose."

"Or like Kirby caught."

"Kirby Seager came in here and within a month decided he was better than everything and everybody."

"I might be the same way."

"No, I don't believe that for a second. Kirby never connected up here, with anyone."

"You didn't like him?"

"Oh, I liked Kirby all right. I just knew the first time he came in that he was probably going to have problems up here. And then he went right on out and had them. I think he was the unhappiest editor that's ever been here. And since Arnie died, there have been quite a few."

"Don't rule me out, yet."

"That's what you say. And maybe that's what you think. But you're not really unhappy. Not in the way some of them had it. I think you just don't want to admit that you really do love this town." She stood up, then, and picked up her things.

"Love?"

She turned to look at him. "Nobody could write about this town the way you do if they didn't love it."

Feeney nodded, if only to be polite.

She smiled at him. "Maybe time for a vacation?"

"You a mind-reader?"

"Kirby had that same look on his face."

"Like you said. I'm not Kirby."

"Dean doesn't know these things."

Feeney squinted at her. "Anything else you know that I don't? About myself I mean."

Mrs. Hagy had a thoughtful look on her face. And after a moment, said, "I didn't see any copy from Warren."

"Uh, no," Feeney said. "He's working on some... bigger... things."

"Doesn't surprise me. He won't be sticking around."

"You don't like him?"

"Do you?"

Feeney laughed.

"Patrick, when I said you weren't like Kirby, what I really meant was that he turned himself into a martyr. You haven't done that."

Feeney laughed again. "You sure? I think I was a martyr before I ever heard of this place."

Mrs. Hagy settled her sweater across her arm. "You're modest in your own way. That's probably why you're so much better than he was. And for that, Gig, you know, complained more about things than anyone Dad said he ever knew. When he wasn't bullying everyone around, he spent the rest of the time just griping to high heaven. That's something even I can remember."

She then gave him a smile, and turned for the door.

Feeney sat at his desk for a few more minutes, then finally stood up, stretched, and shut down the office. He grabbed the layout copy, went to his car, and drove to the police station.

Seeing Feeney come through the door, Spencer leaned back in his chair. "Better shut the door."

Feeney stared for a second, pushed the door shut, and then turned to look at the chief of police. "Bill?"

Chapter 68

Rock Bottom, Act I

BEFORE going out the door, Feeney looked back at the Chief.

They exchanged a glance, and then Spencer nodded at him. "Now you know why I've got heartburn all the time, Pat."

Feeney nodded. "Don't worry, Bill. I won't kill anyone."

Bill looked down at his desk, and started shuffling papers. "That's nice to know."

Feeney smiled and left, but as he walked out to his car, thought he hadn't spoken the truth, and with the actual heart of a murderer, Feeney drove down the highway toward Monroe. He reached his house with Bill Spencer's warnings ringing in his ears, ignored them, and went straight onto the front porch of the house next door.

Melinda Williams opened the door. Feeney felt delighted by the look of fright on Carey's mother's face.

"I've just seen Chief Spencer. Let your husband know."

Melinda had never been anything but correct with him, and he had found her likable. But he knew perfectly well what sort of conversation had been taking place in that house. He had to admit he could admire her. The fact that she had been able to open the door to him showed that she had a certain form of native courage. A thing Feeney was convinced was lacking in Brian Williams. But as he turned to leave, something—maybe that courage of hers—made him turn back.

"You know, in all the time I've been here, if there's one thing that could make me hate this place, it would be this."

Melinda, whatever doubts she might suddenly be having, had

one simple response. "Carey's our daughter."

Feeney nodded, but wasn't going to allow even an inch of it. "This is one of the stupidest things I've run into yet. All you, or Brian, had to do was come speak to me, face to face."

Melinda frowned. "You just look down on all of us."

"Look down?"

"But we still have some morality."

"You do? Making public accusations to the police without the slightest proof—moral? You have heard of slander, haven't you? That's a serious legal liability in this state, and I have very convincing witnesses."

Melinda gave him a long look. She wanted to be tough, accusatory, angry. But Feeney's extreme calm, tinged with a bit of sadness, was too unexpected. Just the fact he'd knocked on the door now had her obviously doubting some things. But she was also stuck with that for the moment.

"I'll tell Brian."

"That's fine," Feeney said. "I'll be home in a few hours."

The door closed.

Feeney would have liked to just get in the house, get a beer, and stare at the wall. But he had other shit to deal with.

"Hi, Pat."

"Joel."

"Haven't seen you around for a while."

"Been busy, Joel. You know?"

"Sure, sure," Joel Myer, sitting as ever behind his big, messy desk, gave Feeney a smile. A just-like-old-times smile.

"I'm not going to stay here long, Joel," Feeney said. "I'm just here to pass along a message from Dean, and a piece of advice."

Joel eyed Feeney warily. "Oh, yes?"

"First, from Dean," Feeney took a rate sheet from his pocket, unfolded it and laid it softly in front of the store manager, "we did a calculation of all the money, time, and effort we lost while you were having your dalliance with Jansen."

"It was just business, Pat," Joel began to complain.

"OK, and this is just business, too," Feeney said equably. "There are the new rates."

Myer looked them over, and then looked up at Feeney.

Feeney shook his head. "Don't give me that shocked look, Joel. The rates you're looking at are just where they should have been long ago. Dean had always held off making the annual adjustments, and now he's just putting things where they should have been."

"But these rates are..." Myer was looking for some push-back, but hadn't found it yet. He had expected anger, some reprobation. But not a twenty percent rate hike. "This is outrageous."

"Is it?" Feeney pursed his lips. "You're lucky we didn't just go to what Jansen was charging you."

"Now, Pat," Myer began to bristle. "Those rates were based on circulation numbers. Which you guys don't have."

Feeney's face showed zero emotion. He shrugged. "You can take that argument and shove it wherever you want, Joel. Jansen didn't have circulation numbers, and you know it. He had print-run numbers. He had next to no subscriptions up here, although for a while he cost us some of ours because his paper was free. But he was just throwing those papers on doorsteps. Print run, Joel."

Myer looked glum. "How do you know what he was charging me?"

Feeney shook his head sadly. "Seriously?"

Myer picked up the new rate sheet. And then looked up at Feeney. "Do you guys always really know about everything?"

"Yes," Feeney said, smiling for the first time, "we do."

"You said you had some advice."

"Yeah. If you're doing something that makes you feel like maybe you're being an asshole, don't wonder about it. You are being an asshole."

"I thought you said this was just going to be about business, Pat."

Feeney nodded. "Friendly advice is always good business, Joel."

Myer looked down at the rate sheet again. "I don't suppose it would be any good to call Dean and..."

Feeney stopped him. "Don't even try."

Myer sighed. "Really?"

But Feeney had already turned and was on his way out.

Chapter 69

Rock Bottom, Act II

HE had barely had time to check his mailbox and unlock his door before an outraged mass of fatherhood, bent on mayhem, came running toward him from around the fence next door.

All right, Feeney thought, here we go.

"Feeney, I'm gonna…!" Williams started, but Feeney cut him off hard.

"What the hell were you thinking, going up to Bill Spencer? Are you out of your fucking mind? And do you actually think you can go around making accusations like that, in public?"

"I want a goddamn explanation."

Feeney tried to control the anger rising in him.

"No, you goddamn well don't. If you'd wanted an explanation, you would have been over here first, instead of going to talk to Bill."

"That's what the law's for!"

"What the FUCK are you talking about? Are you fucking nuts? You go up there telling the police chief I've been trying to play around with Carey? Do you want to get yourself sued straight into the poorhouse?"

Williams, for a moment, just stood there breathing fast, looking furious, but confused. Feeney didn't seem frightened or concerned. And certainly not guilty.

Feeney couldn't tell exactly what Brian Williams wanted. A fight? Or just to yell?

There was a frantic look about him, as though he didn't know himself and was waiting to see what Feeney would do or say.

Learning that Feeney had already spoken to Spencer had taken most of the steam out of him.

Feeney gave Williams a straight-in-the-eye look. "It's pretty serious to go talking to the police about how I'm after your daughter. Where's this shit coming from?"

"Don't act like you're so goddamn innocent."

"Why shouldn't I? I am innocent. At least of this shit. And another thing I'm innocent of is having a dirty mind. Which seems to be what way too many people around here share. Fucking losers."

"You saying I've got a dirty mind? I didn't make it up. And like we all know, where there's smoke…"

Feeney pushed his face toward Williams. "Where there's smoke… there's bullshit. I'm going to say it only once. Anyone who's going around saying it is full of shit. And whoever you got it from is a fucking liar, or just a regular moron who would spread this sort of shit around."

Williams stuck out his lip. "My friends aren't liars."

"Well, OK. Morons then." Feeney shook his head. "Anybody who told you this is no friend of yours, Brian."

Williams stuck out his lip. "Everybody knows about you, Feeney. Down at the bars every goddamn weekend, and everybody knows what you're doing, dragging women back to this fucking whorehouse."

It was so shocking and stupid that Feeney almost laughed. "Women?" And because all this was so impossible, compared to whatever actual social life he had, he just began to think out loud: "I don't know, I mean, the last girlfriend I had over here…," he thought about Beebee, "that was, man… it's been months, maybe…"

The seriously pondering look on Feeney's face caught Williams completely off guard. Feeney was just being way too real. "OK, OK, maybe not all the time. But it is a bachelor pad."

Feeney puffed out a sigh. "Well, yes, I'm not married. So that makes me a bachelor. Yes. Is that a crime? You want to see what a bachelor pad looks like? Come inside and take a look. Mirrors on the ceiling, red drapes, champagne in the fridge…"

"I don't want Carey coming over here."

"She doesn't come over here. She did borrow some of my books, actually nearly all of them. And now she gets them from the library. You've maybe noticed that, haven't you?"

Williams nodded. "Yes, yes. But... admit it, you've taken her to meetings, and you two work together."

It was falling apart. Where there had been anger, somehow it was all gone. And now there was just a mutual desire to get all this over with. Williams could just feel how nothing about this rumor seemed to fit the way Feeney was reacting. He would have known in a nanosecond if Feeney had been lying, pretending, ashamed, or guilty. But here: nothing.

Feeney turned. "I work, or try to work, with a lot of people." Somewhere, Feeney was almost tempted to tell Williams how it had started. But he knew he couldn't. If there was a real fault, it had been in his nosiness that day up at the high school office.

Williams also began to turn. "Right. Whatever. But still," he said, with some strange now-we'll-sound-reasonable voice, "This is not something she should be doing at her age."

Feeney stopped, and looked back. "What, Brian? Reading? And writing some stories for the paper?" He sighed, and saw Williams was firing up to say something else, but Feeney cut him off. "Sorry, it's been a long, long day. I'd love to discuss all this with you. Parenting problems, town rumor shit problems, public slander problems... but let's save all that for later. In the meantime, I'd suggest you talk to your daughter from time to time. And as for you..." Feeney looked off for a moment and then back at his neighbor, "If I hear any more of this, I'll see you in court, as well as anyone else spreading this garbage around."

The look on Williams's face went dark, but Feeney had said all he wanted to say, and went in his door and slammed it shut. Slamming out the world and slamming himself into the sweet, cool bliss of an empty room.

Sometimes, an empty room can seem like the sanest place in the world.

Chapter 70

Rock Bottom, Act III, or very nearly

HE went into the kitchen and rummaged around.

In the end, he thought, if he was Carey's dad, he probably would have done the same thing. He banged some cupboard doors, more out of frustration than any idea of what he was looking for. And finally, he just grabbed a beer, opened it, and poured it down his throat. And with all the banging, the mumbling, the cursing under his breath, and the beer chugging, he hadn't heard it. But when he dropped the can in the trash, the silence of the apartment brought it out from the bedroom in back: a faint whimper.

Feeney walked back and looked in his bedroom. No one. And no sound.

And then he heard a tiny sniff.

Feeney went and slid back his closet door.

Carey Williams was scrunched down onto the floor, her arms around her knees and her face wet with crying.

She shook her head. "I'm so sorry," she began, but her face twisted and she burst into a heavy spasm of desolation. Under her feet were several typewritten sheets. She picked them up, blubbering.

"I just came over to drop them off, and maybe get another book. Your back door was open, so I was going to leave them where you'd find them. Then Dad…"

Feeney nodded, as though nothing could have been more natural than having an eighteen-year-old girl sitting in his closet.

"Perfect," he said. He reached down. "Here. You'd better come out of there. For starters."

Carey took his hand, and came out of his closet. Feeney pointed at his bed.

"Sit down."

He walked out of the bedroom and went and locked his front door. Then he looked around his living room. Although his heavy drapes were open, the lighter ones were pulled closed and no one could see in. Going to the sliding door in back, the one Carey had come through, he pushed it shut and locked it as well, pulling its drapes shut.

Time, he knew, was not on his side. Carey would soon be expected home.

He went back into the bedroom and looked down at her. She sat slumped on his bed, dejected but calmer.

Of course, she couldn't have dressed herself more perfectly for the part. Her shorts were beyond short, consisting of barely more than a couple of pockets and a zipper. And a low-cut tank top.

Perfect, perfect, perfect. Feeney sighed.

"Dad's going to kill me."

"Maybe, but I think he'll do me, first."

A look of anguish passed over her face, and her chin quivered. "I'm so sorry..." Tears welled and then ran down her cheeks.

"That's okay," he said, and for one insane second actually imagined himself sitting down and putting his arm around her shoulders.

Carey got herself calmed again, and began shaking her head. "It's all so..." she looked at the papers she held in her hands, "so out of control. People get so... I don't know. Jealous, or something. You know? And worse, I'm sorry, but I thought you liked me, too."

She was too raw for lies or word games, so Feeney just went honest. "Not like what you were thinking."

A sharp cry of anguish. "Is it because I'm too young? I'm just a kid, or something?"

Feeney suddenly felt at a complete loss. He had never been in a situation like this. What does a man do with a girl with a crush? He couldn't tell if he was dealing with a tragedy of some sort, or a time bomb.

He could see she wanted and needed a response. But how could he explain the unexplainable? He knew a few things about love, and heartbreak, and disappointment. But those weren't transferrable things. Everyone had to live through their own.

"Carey, I can't explain it to you," he said. "I can barely explain things like this to myself. People get attracted to each other for different reasons, and sometimes there are elements that just don't work."

He looked at her and suddenly realized that she was no longer as plain as she used to seem. As the puffy adolescence had left her face at some point in the last year, her face now had more character, showing signs of becoming womanly and attractive.

"So, it's impossible," she said.

He had to admire her ability to be forthright. Remembering Melinda from earlier, he could see where that came from.

"Nothing's impossible, but some things..." Feeney's mind swept back to something forever bittersweet. "Sometimes it's timing, or clouds hanging over things, or misunderstandings, or assumptions, or people just not being ready. Or compatibility—age, background... fate."

Carey thought the frown was meant for her, and gave him a look that wasn't adolescent at all. "So, there could never be anything between us?"

"Not like that, Carey," he breathed out. In the face of her honesty, he could be nothing else.

She sat there for a moment, looking at him, and then she finally nodded and looked at the papers in her hand. "Here," she said, handing him the papers. "I really did want to just bring you this."

He took them. "You don't mind if I read them later?"

Carey finally smiled. But then she looked out toward Feeney's living room. "Oh, my God. How am I going to get home?"

"Good question."

Carey stared at the door. And then across her face, a shadow of a thought passed, disturbing the calm in the way a small gust of wind disturbs the seamless surface of a placid lake. "You know," she said, her voice suddenly very steady, "I could stay. I mean..."

And there it was. Yes. And then: Lolita.

Loleeeeeeeeeta...

But... no. And a big no at that.

"C'mon," he said, taking her hand and pulling her out to the living room. Then he froze. "Oh, shit."

"What?"

"What time are you supposed to be home?"

"About now."

"Your dad's going to have half the county sheriff's office out on my lawn in the next half hour."

Carey laughed at the thought of it, which caused him to give her a stern look. He went over and peeked out through his curtains. Still plenty of light outside, the windows of the neighbors gaped, like the staring eyes of zombies, up and down the street. He let the curtain fall and led Carey toward the back door. There, he peeked out across his parking lot to the alley. There were high fences there, and bushes. No one could really see anything unless they were out there in a backyard deliberately keeping an eye on things. How deep does paranoia go?

Deep.

Feeney could imagine Brian checking his back door while Melinda watched the front. Or else, to make sure Feeney couldn't catch him doing it, Brian could be standing down at the end of the alley to see what might come out there.

An amazing thing: how paranoia helped concentrate the mind.

"Listen," he said. "If things are clear, you're going to go out and go left, and go all the way up the alley, then go right to the next street over, then go left and walk all the way up to Main." He dug five dollars out of his pocket. "Buy something, a Coke, or something, and then walk home from there, on the regular streets."

"Okay." Carey was smiling. "I heard what you and Dad were saying."

"I think the whole neighborhood did, too."

He went into his kitchen and got the garbage from under the sink, went and slid open his back door, and walked out the back to the alley, dumping the sack in his garbage can. Looking up and down the alley, he could see no one and, with a wave of his hand, motioned Carey out.

Just as he had told her, she came straight out and went toward the alley. But just as she passed, she suddenly turned, leaned in, and gave him a kiss on his cheek. Then she scooted away.

Feeney backed slowly away from the alley, just lingering at the fence long enough to see her disappear around the corner before he went back into his house.

He turned on the light in his living room and opened his front door to let in the evening air. Then, for the entire fifteen minutes it took for Carey to circle up to Main Street and back again, he was glued to the tiny crack in the curtains of his dark bedroom.

Soon enough, he saw Carey coming down the street. She was drinking a can of something. First, she headed straight up the walkway to her house, and then, on reaching the porch, she stopped and looked over at Feeney's.

What in the world was she doing?

And worse, she actually turned, as though to go back down to the walkway again. But at that, the door to her house opened and Brian Williams stepped out.

"Where d'you think you're going?"

Carey, bless her heart, just turned to look at him and even took a sip of her drink. "I'll be right back," she said, "I just have to ask Patrick a question."

"The hell you will," Williams said. "You're late for dinner, as it is."

Carey went reluctantly. She went up on the front porch and crossed to the door. "Jeez," was the last thing he heard her say.

Feeney stared for a little longer, and then finally let the curtain close.

Chapter 71

How it Ended with Ted

HE could see it was going to be a long time before things settled down again. People were going to have to forget about the school bond. The bad blood. The emotions.

After the vote, people drifted back to their regular patterns, the non-newsworthy points of view and activities small communities preferred for themselves. And forgetting the passions of the issue, people were now resenting having gotten so stirred up, perhaps resenting that more than how they had felt about each other.

Looking back, it could seem that most of the shouting had been amplified by newcomers and outsiders. People like Tickler Steele, Bob Hawthorn, Frank Baron or Ted Barnwell. Feeney might have included himself in that list, but not too surprisingly, he didn't seem to be resented like the others. Because in the end he was just a reporter. But not everyone gave him a break.

Ted Barnwell hadn't even attempted to maintain professional aplomb, and hadn't been very nice about it, either. After the defeat, he had quickly applied for and been accepted at a school district over east of the Cascades. Somewhere in the Okanogan or the Palouse. Feeney, dutifully but not willingly, had gone over for what turned into a painful, blame-infused interview with the future ex-superintendent and spent most of his time fending off, with growing irritation, the more blatantly self-serving accusations.

Nerves. Disappointment. Ted's own form of embarrassment. Who knew? But with Feeney there in front of him, it was just too convenient to pass up.

"Objectivity, my ass." The superintendent's mouth twisted with sarcasm.

"Since when did objectivity have anything to do with anything?"

"I thought that's what you guys were trained for."

"So, you lost, Ted. We all lost this one. If you're going to take it personally, it's probably a good thing you are leaving."

"How else should I take it? I told these dimwits the place was going to get shut down. And it will be shut down. I told them they had little choice. And they have no choice. I didn't tell them lies. I didn't try to make them feel guilty."

"Bull."

"I didn't try to scare them."

"Double bull. The moment you threw yourself in with Steele, it was nothing but scare tactics."

"I just tried to do what I thought was right." Barnwell looked at his desk. "There's only so much you can do, though. Nobody thinks collectively anymore. Nobody has a long-term vision anymore."

Feeney smiled, or something that looked like that.

"When did they?"

"I don't know. I just don't know." Barnwell looked up at Feeney with a suddenly stubborn set to his jaw. "And I might as well tell you something. I'm pretty goddamn disappointed with you. I thought you were a friend to the school district, that you were with us heart and soul. All those big words about how the newspaper was going to support us. How you ballyhooed how you were going to do everything in your power to get the message across. And then, when it came right down to it, all we get is this mealy-mouthed sort of semi-enthusiasm. Damning us with faint praise, and all that. Christ, week in and week out, just plain shitting on us."

Feeney took a breath. "What are you talking about? We bent ourselves over backwards, Ted. Right out there on a limb. You're acting like all you wanted to see was me get up every week and fart Yankee Doodle. Because of Bob, it's true, I had to address questions or else look like an idiot. But all the rest was pure support. If you

423

ever have the guts, five years from now, go back and read what we wrote."

Barnwell's eyes shone with anger. "You'll never convince me of that. I know what happened here, I know what went down."

"Fine, fine. Think what you want, Ted. Just remember: the next time you get involved in something like this, before you go rounding up your backing, make sure you consult with a few people in the community first. They're not as fucking dumb as you think they are."

For Feeney, the interview was over now, and he put his notepad and recorder away and stood up.

"Consultation, Ted."

Feeney made his way to the door, but before opening it, he turned and looked back at the superintendent, who was sitting stiffly behind his desk giving him a blank stare.

Feeney grinned. "In the end, you know, people will understand you were trying to do the right thing. I'm sure of that. What will happen from here?" Feeney mused to himself. "They're going to red tag the ever-living daylights out of that building even before the start of the school year. Which means they'll be parking portable classrooms all over the place. Or else they'll just throw in the towel on the district and bus all the kids down to Monroe." He gave Barnwell a sympathetic look. "That is going to be shitty, and as time goes by I'm sure a majority of people will come around to thinking you tried to do your best."

He turned to leave, but Barnwell stopped him.

"Feeney?"

Feeney turned to look at the superintendent. "What?" he said, a reconciliatory smile on his face.

"Off the record," Barnwell said. "Fuck you."

Feeney nodded. "Off the record, fuck you too. But with a difference, Ted. I know what I'm talking about. And always have."

And right on cue, as always, Ted didn't know what to say.

Feeney went through the door and shut it behind himself. Quickly.

It was one of the few occasions he'd ever known when he'd had the last word.

As he passed Faith, he found her gaze following and he saw her giving him a look he had never seen her give him before. Something between sympathy and an apology. And something else. Something completely different that he couldn't quite define. But he just didn't have it in him to find out. He went out to his car.

Chapter 72

And then Tari

REGARDLESS, it wasn't one of the easier interviews to write up. The vast temptation was just to pen a headline: Soon-to-be-former superintendent says fuck you to yours truly and everybody else.

Then Tari Baron came in.

Feeney stood up.

She did not seem distraught, and even smiled. But Feeney opted for total neutrality.

"How's Frank?" he said.

"Fine. Embarrassed mostly."

"Embarrassed?"

Tari shot Feeney a sharp glance. "He can be. He's not a clown, Pat."

"Whoa. Who's saying that? Not me. I've never said anything like that."

Tari was not herself—whatever it was Feeney had always thought she was—and she wasn't listening to him. Whatever she was carrying had now triggered her into pure defensive everything. She snapped. She wanted a piece of him, and she went for it.

"Frank and I have been wondering whether we can ever get any real backing up here."

Feeney wanted to be polite about it, and had several forms of politeness offer themselves, but found that any form of politeness wasn't working much for him those days. So he just opted to be correct, even if slightly ironic.

"I'm sorry you and Frank feel that way."

Tari didn't hear the irony and just kept on. "That's not much of an apology."

"No, it certainly wasn't that, was it. And why wasn't it?" Feeney nodded. "Because it wasn't an apology. You're coming in here and telling me to my face that I somehow single-handedly blew up the school bond effort?"

"You didn't help."

Few people had ever seen Feeney get truly angry, or experienced how, when that happened, he would become shockingly cold—furiously icy and unmerciful—and completely prepared to destroy any sense of shared humanity, compassion, or sympathy. It would always surprise them, being so completely different from his usual mild and tolerant nature, quick to smile and be generous, engaged, and supportive. But the anger could happen, always for the main reason: being deliberately taken advantage of. Which was exactly what was happening.

It was completely calm, the way he said it, looking at her not with actual loathing, but a glacial dislike.

"I have had it up to here with this bullshit and," he added with a touch of admittedly ungallant cruelty, "other people's problems."

He hadn't argued with her, hadn't defended himself, hadn't tried to find common ground. He simply cut her off from any form of agreement or support.

Tari's face, formerly tight with whatever self-righteous anger or guilt or projections, now did in fact look shocked, and even a bit frightened, but he didn't care. His voice, still in that terrible, calm softness, droned on:

"One week before the vote, everything was fine. Right? Everyone was floating on... happy satisfaction. Thinking everything was dandy. And then the train wreck. And now, the main actors in the decision-making about the bond effort are looking around and trying to find people to blame. I will not accept any blame. The paper came out early, and strong, for the bond issue. I wrote thousands of words to that effect, explaining to the town the entire issue. What I didn't do is join in wholeheartedly with a plan of making people feel stupid if they had questions or concerns, treating

427

people like idiots. I voiced my opinion about Tickler Steele's approach. But I never ran one article, one word, in public disagreement. I knew Steele would look for scapegoats. His entire reputation is built on his win/loss column. And I'm not too surprised at Ted's pathetic pettiness, or even Frank's lost-the-game disappointment. But I would have thought you would have been above that, Tari. I honestly believed you were better."

He didn't give her a chance to respond, or even to see how that landed. Or in what way.

"I pounded out article after article, interviews, made telephone calls. Backing you up in every way a newspaper could, without totally crossing over into puffery. And you come in here telling me that I was playing you and everyone else false. When the truth is, it seems, just the opposite."

That last statement—he knew what he was doing. Knew that what he was saying had a deeper resonance for her. And he could see on her face that it had cut deep.

I know that you know that I know that you know...

Feeney had no way of knowing whether Tari had seen the TV news report, but even if she hadn't, he was sure she had been informed. And in this case, this wasn't just some vicious, ignoble rumor spread by despicable minds, but was a known thing. Feeney had seen that news report, Harrison had seen that news report, and God knew how many others in that town had seen it as well.

And she knew it.

He'd been through the wringer. Dealing with rumors. But in his case, there was one consolation: even at the worst, there had been doubt. But here, there was none. Or very little.

It must be awful, he thought. But even if he could accept how awful it might be for her, he was finished with it.

He could see Tari was squirming. And probably not just here in his office.

He could admit to himself that, even though he had shut down cold any feelings of attraction to her, he could feel sympathy for her. But even so, he refused to allow himself to be a human garbage can for hers.

To each, their own form of hell.

She was no longer able to speak. He now let his tone warm a bit, although he was in no way going to give her the slightest room for response.

"Week in and week out we published whatever the school board, and the PTA, and everybody else, including self-appointed ringmaster Tickler Steele, wanted. Rah-rah, sis-boom-bah. The sky is falling. And then, bam, it falls. It was put up to a vote, and the voters made a decision. They didn't like the bond proposal. That's all. What failed was the proposal. And it was clear, nearly from the beginning, there were too many questions that were not only not being answered but were being deliberately ignored or—worse— ridiculed. But... oh well, water under the bridge. Live and learn."

Tari was now looking at her feet, then his desk, then his typewriter, and there was pain on her face. "Tickler said..."

Feeney cut her off. "Tickler? Tickler said what? Tickler will only say, Tari, what serves Tickler." Feeney gave her a stern look. "All right, listen. And this is it. It's not about you, or Frank, or me, or Ted, or anybody else. What it came down to is what the town was ready to handle. The vote wasn't even close to the required sixty percent. That means the idea just wasn't there. Not enough people were convinced the plan was reasonable."

Tari gave him a stubborn look. "You thought it was reasonable."

"Fixing up that fire trap is reasonable. Improving the educational environment is reasonable. Getting more funding is reasonable. But what was unreasonable was tacking on all those dream additions, and then expecting everyone to go along. With no public input. Forcing the paper—and we went along with it, it's true—to throw its support nearly blindly behind a project that got decided behind closed doors and then shoved down everybody's throats like it was doctor's orders. That's really goddamn reasonable. And professional."

"Ted Barnwell is a professional."

Feeney felt his anger wash out of him. He no longer cared. "Ted's a fool. And it was already bad enough he was in over his head, right from the start, but then he went and let it get to his head, treating people with arrogance."

"You should know."

Feeney couldn't say he actually disliked Tari. She was an intelligent, spirited, creative, and warm-hearted person. But she was lost. And he could now picture it: where before she had held all the cards, her husband, miles behind her in intelligence, was now in possession of the moral high ground in their marriage. Normally, women held that as a sort of given, feeling they had their feet better on the ground.

"So now, I'm arrogant?" Feeney shrugged. "To my way of thinking, arrogance, in this town, is to treat people as hicks to be led around by the nose."

Tari, showing some anger come back up, shook her head. "Whatever."

Feeney was done, although he felt a bit of his own anger coming back. "OK. Never mind," he said. "So, was there actually something you wanted down here today?"

Tari looked at him, then looked around at the office. Such a bare, bureaucratic cubbyhole. And then he knew. She'd lashed out at him, she'd burbled on about her and Frank, but that wasn't why she'd come down there.

She needed to know.

And here, Feeney could feel another form of sympathy for her returning. But there was no way he could give her what she needed unless she actually asked about him. Once again, he had no desire to be known as someone who knew.

And he was enough of a gentleman to just let the facts, and the passage of time, speak for themselves. People needed, Feeney felt deeply, to be able to hold on to whatever self-respect they could find for themselves, whatever inner narrative about their personal goodness, for what it was worth. And it wasn't going to be Feeney rubbing salt in anyone's wounds.

Beyond that point, he couldn't remember anything else they said to each other. She said some damn thing. And Feeney accepted it.

And they left it at that.

Feeney watched her go. He thought she would always be attractive. But it was funny how an attractive woman could be, at the same time, something else. Or nothing at all.

He sat down. And in his office he sat for what seemed a long time. Melancholy, peaceful, and a bit lonely. And it felt like after the flood, when everything had gotten washed away, clean, down to the bone.

But if he had learned anything about floods, there would always be another.

Always.

Chapter 73

Out with the Old, In with the Old

THEN came and went the special election Charles Peace had promised to be prepared for after the bond issue.

Not surprisingly, the town turned itself upside down.

A few days later, after a heartwarmingly ironic—for him—lunch with a serenely unflappable Bill Spencer at the Delicate Egg, Feeney was down digging around at City Hall. Not that he had much to do down there; it was more the sort of morbid curiosity people have when driving past car accidents.

The town attorney, Newton Powell, wandered in from somewhere and spotted him and, with a semi-amused look, headed in his direction. Feeney stopped him before he even had a chance to open his mouth.

"No, you don't, Newt. I don't want to hear about anything. Nothing."

Powell sighed and began dangling his briefcase in a way that suggested he had nothing in it and not much to do down there, either. He gave Feeney a grin. "And you get paid for this?"

Feeney shrugged. "Today, unless I come across it myself, it doesn't exist."

"I see. Your idea of a vacation."

"Call it what you want."

It was Powell's turn to shrug, and he turned to look around the quiet office. The main secretary, behind the long counter, was busy sorting bills for the treasurer, who would be coming in later in the afternoon to sign the checks.

"You're a student of history, Pat," he said. "You can see as well as I can that we're in for the long haul now. I've watched this for years, and have seen how people are more and more turning their backs on things like community. Oh... sure... they want to feel involved. Wave the flag a bit when called upon. But they just want to sit in the privacy of their back yards and tell the world to shove it."

Feeney glanced around at the office as Powell had, eyeing the placid bureaucratic scene, silently ruled by the minute hand of the office clock as it swept in its slow circles above them. The idiocy of office routine.

"And I thought I was dismal today."

Powell shook his head.

"I'm not that. Matter of fact, I thought that'd cheer us both up."

"Thanks."

"I'm serious. Optimism is insulting. And the Heroic Epoch is dead."

Feeney eyed Powell for a moment and then suddenly realized something amazing. "Don't tell me you're staying on?"

"Can you believe it?"

Feeney couldn't. "I would have bet the farm you would have been the first one out the door."

Powell looked thoughtful. "I guess I've become part of the furniture. Nobody cares."

"Some people do. Otherwise Peace would still be in."

"Peace and Brahnler. Same thing."

"Peace," Feeney said with a grimace. "He basically erased himself, the way he was so goddamn complacent. Just couldn't believe anyone would choose anyone else but him, in comparison to a complete numbskull. Nobody would vote for a proven numbskull, would they? They not only would—they did. That was the same thinking that sank the school board. Thinking nobody would vote for something truly stupid. And now," Feeney pursed his lips, "what have we got? Brahnler's a jerk-off. Sorry. Mayor Brahnler. And we're all going to be doing that in one big circle for a couple of years."

Powell was nodding. "And when we get tired of doing that, we'll bring back Peace."

Feeney knew it, and didn't feel happy about it. But it did feel better to be honest about it. "Probably, or someone like him if he doesn't feel inclined. But getting back to what you said earlier, you know as well as I do that you wouldn't want to return to any Heroic Epoch, any more than I would."

"I don't know. I look at the ages when you could get a massing of valor. And a massing of effort."

"Well, you'd have to find a massing of evil," Feeney said. "And things may be stupid, but to get that, we'd have to drop back to a really basic level of stupidity."

Powell gave Feeney a look of good humor. "In that, Patrick, there's always a shockingly large possibility. I mean, that they'll get to that level, and maybe even beyond." He grinned. "Never underestimate what people are capable of."

Chapter 74

Dean Smooths Things Over

HE had barely gotten in the door when his phone rang.

"Where the hell have you been?"

"Hi, Dean."

"We need to talk."

"OK. What's up?"

"Not over the phone. Face-to-face."

Feeney looked at the clutter on his desk. "I appreciate that."

"Appreciate what?"

"That at least you're not going to do it over the phone."

"Do what? What the fuck are you talking about?"

Feeney managed to keep the tired sarcasm out of his voice. "Firing me." He knew that was the last thing that would ever happen, but the idea had a whimsical, almost wishful feel to it.

There was, at least to Feeney's mind, a decent, gentlemanly pause, and all he could hear was a slight wheeze. And then Parker let out a laugh somewhere between the honk of a goose and a cough. "I really should, I suppose. But no. Just get your ass down here." And, as always: click. Dead line.

Marlene stared at him when he came into the lobby.

Feeney stopped, rolled his eyes upward, and sighed. He'd been to Laurilaure's. "OK, go ahead."

"You're not..." she said, smiling. "Is this going to be the new you?"

"I doubt it," he said. "Depends on the reactions."

She smiled. "I'm sorry, Pat. You just caught me by surprise. I'm just used to... the whole look. You actually don't look too bad. Clean-cut military, or something. Serious."

"I didn't look serious before?"

"Of course, but I could kind of tell the mood you were in by how it looked."

It was Feeney's turn to stare back at her.

"What? My hair told you my mood...?"

Marlene made a face, as if telling herself to shut up. And then she shook her head.

"No, seriously, you look fine. You've always looked fine, and here's the proof. It's not every man that can look good with his hair that short."

Feeney pulled in his breath, and gave her a frown and a smile at the same time. "Yeah, okay..." he said. "While we're at it, anything else? My shirts, pants, shoes?"

Marlene laughed. "You always look good, Pat. Somehow. I don't know how. But you do."

He checked to see if she was kidding and was surprised she wasn't. It was a revelation, and he made a mental note to bring her some flowers the next time he came down.

"So, what's the deal with Dean?" he said.

"Oh, yeah. I guess Warren just leaving like that didn't sit too well. And he knows about the offers you've been getting."

Feeney looked down at his shoes. Marlene liked his shoes? "Publishers can be shitty to each other."

"I've noticed."

"I'm sure you have. But anything I should be concerned with?"

"I don't think so, Pat. He hasn't been pacing around or anything."

That was a good sign, at least. Feeney nodded at her and headed back along the corridor to the back shop.

"So, Dean, thanks for the asphalt patch," Feeney pointed down. "Dry shoes! Imagine that."

Parker waved his hand in irritation, while at the same time letting his eyes rest on Feeney's head. But then he shook his own. "Look, have a seat. Don't just stand there."

Feeney sat down and looked at his boss. Dean Parker had a strangely peaceful demeanor—at least in comparison with what he usually looked like. And Feeney thought he even looked thinner in the jowls, as though he'd lost some weight, and that his color was more normal and not just the usual fire-engine red.

"So, Pat, um... listen," Parker began. "I know you weren't happy when I hired Harrison. But I think you'll agree that the school bond created a real news bottleneck up there."

"Yes, it did."

"So you're telling me you aren't bothered by that?"

"Not anymore, Dean. I mean, he's gone."

"I see. You're telling me that if he was still around, you'd be bothered."

"What do you think?"

"He was a pretty good writer, Pat."

"If you like that sort of thing, Dean."

"Some people liked it."

Feeney suppressed a sigh. "Some people are idiots."

"So, do you want to know what happened to him?"

"You don't know?"

Parker shook his head. "In the end, he didn't even leave a note. I mean, just the day before I told him I was going to offer him a down-valley beat. I mean, I hinted at that."

"Do you watch TV, Dean?"

"Sometimes. Why?"

Feeney scrutinized his boss. It wasn't there. "Nothing, never mind."

He thought about Parker's supposed offer. Regardless of whatever else had been going on in Harrison's little world, going down valley would have meant nothing but dairy farming. And there was only so much you could write about people who spent most of their daylight hours worrying about the condition of several hundred bloated udders. But up valley, for the poor bastard, it was all just murder.

Parker shook his head. "I wouldn't have thought that would have pissed him off that much."

437

"Hard to say, Dean," Feeney gave him an innocent, perplexed look. "Hard to say."

Parker plopped his hands on his desk. "This is getting us nowhere. Like you said, he's gone. But the question is, where does this leave us? I mean, you guys had a system sort of worked out, and... now what?"

"Now what? Now... nothing. The school bond is dead. The school is dead. Ted Barnwell is dead. Peace is dead. And the news is just going to go back to usual/usual. I haven't set up any interviews with anybody, because everyone knows exactly what they voted for up there, and what they can expect. And all I'm going to do for a while is just smooth community stuff. The empty-the-newsstands photo-page stuff. For a few weeks. The town needs to breathe."

Parker nodded. "Good, yes. Exactly. Needs to breathe."

"And so do you."

"So do I?"

Feeney eyed his employer for all of ten seconds, and then said, "I have no plans to go anywhere for the moment, Dean. Nowhere. Although I'm pretty sure you're aware I could..."

Parker nodded, but not in any glum sort of way, but with a surprisingly professional appraisal of the truth of what Feeney had said. "No plans?"

"None, Dean."

Parker nodded, but now, with utter professional curiosity, lifted his eyebrows. "And, if you don't mind my asking, Pat, why not?"

Feeney nodded. On a rare occasion, a very rare occasion, he and Dean could have these honest, collegial conversations.

"It's simple," he said. "I feel like I've got shell shock. I feel like I went over the waterfall in a barrel. No—I felt like I was going over the waterfall in a barrel every day. Someday, Dean, I am going to leave. But not today. Or tomorrow. Or for quite a while. But if I do, it won't come the way Harrison did, just lighting out the door. I'd make it a process, and would make sure you were left in as solid a place as you are now."

"You've been pretty solid, Pat. That might be a hard thing to promise."

Feeney smiled, although in fact he was close to laughing. "Um… Dean… that almost sounds flattering."

Dean smiled back. "Don't get used to it."

"Oh, I never would do that."

Parker looked at his desk, and frowned. "I don't know. I just don't know if there had been any way to do things differently. I mean, we really gave that bond issue a shot, and damn, I know how you're getting treated up there. Just… such ingratitude. And also the arrogance of those idiots who won."

"That's just…" Feeney held up his hand, "what I have to deal with."

"Yeah, your part, as you call it. Well, more power to you. As for me, I was always glad to have gotten off the beat."

Feeney tried to imagine Parker as being any sort of newsman other than a publisher, and just couldn't do it.

"So… is that it?" Feeney asked.

"Is what's it?"

"Is that all you wanted to find out?"

Parker now jiggled his pen set. "Yes, I guess so, Pat. Yeah, that was it."

"OK, now you know."

"Right, so back to business as usual?"

"Yep."

"Oh, by the way, I had Joel Myer down here."

"Yeah?"

"I don't know what you said to that guy, but he agreed to everything."

Feeney laughed. "Well, I figured that. He didn't have much of a choice."

"Advertisers always have a choice. He could have gone to a half page."

Feeney had a moment of surprise. He hadn't thought of that. "Oh, Jesus. You're right."

"OK, just saying. Next time you want to scare the shit out of some advertiser, keep that in the back of your mind. And… that's all."

There could have been no clearer finish, so Feeney stood up, and actually felt better.

"See you, Dean," he said.

"See you, Pat. But just one more thing. Do your town breathing thing or whatever. But get over the mope. We've got news to print."

Chapter 75

Changing of the Guard

HE was musing about his conversation with Powell the day before. Nah, he thought, you should never underestimate people and their ability to jump completely off the rails. But Powell was right: the good old days, when people just naturally tried to do the right thing, had nearly slipped away. The stirring idea of getting all worked up for or against something, with debate and some effort at being informed, had twisted down into its poor cousin, emotion.

A mediocre age. Spawning probably something even more stupid than the sort of stupidity Newton Powell predicted.

Self-moronization. Which lent itself to boredom. And in that, there was no hope. God only knew how far the country could go with that, since the US had nearly made a cult of stupidity.

His attention drifted.

Out there in front of the office sat his poor old car.

As always, it sat exposed and naked under the pelting rain. But at least it was on high ground now, sitting like a trophy on a new patch of asphalt, three inches thick.

Feeney had shown considerable bereavement for Warren Harrison's now all but forgotten departure, and the asphalt patch he'd thanked Parker for, was Parker's consolation gift—or perhaps better: a cheap effort to appear conciliatory. Dean knew, of course, all about Ed Oldermeyer's standing offer. And about all those other offers. Publishers, as he and Marlene had discussed, love sticking knives into each other.

Feeney knew he couldn't expect that to smooth everything out.

But maybe, just maybe… he wouldn't have to do every single shit thing Dean dreamed up.

He suppressed another sigh and looked back at the mayor's wife—the new mayor's wife.

"…and he was so obviously not right for the job a blind man could see it. Peace just didn't fit in. Anyone could see that." As always, Peggy Brahnler was being as neat, prim and sincere in her opinions as the way she sat, in a jade-green business suit—it looked brand new—in the wooden swivel chair facing his desk.

Although hers was not the worst form of informal arm-twisting he had had to deal with concerning her husband's becoming mayor, her manifest hostility towards anyone who did not share her feelings made her as obnoxious, in her own small-town wifely way, as Dick was in his crude, local hero way.

Not that Mayor Brahnler had redeemed himself as a local hero, or anything near it. More like a personified public knee-jerk who thought he actually did have a mandate. Could have been worse, though. Out there, in the gathering political gloom, Feeney saw how Frank Baron was gathering support for a run for Congress. And would probably not only get that support, but would also probably win. It was strange how quickly, after the school bond failure, people had forgotten everything. Ironically, if the bond had passed, Baron's fate would have been to return quietly to his work pillaging Wall Street with relentless zeal.

Feeney tried to focus on Peggy Brahnler.

"… the sort of people," she was saying, "you know, who get to thinking they have some sort of power, and they try to rule it over you. We've seen a lot of people come and go around here who were like that."

Feeney nodded amiably and looked down at his desk. Piled with crap, as usual. But there, too, a nice little thing. A card from Carey Williams saying her first few weeks up there in Bellingham were great, and enclosing a cutting of her first article for the school paper. The subject was pretty lame, the usual school thing, but the writing was excellent.

"We aren't against Bill Spencer," Peggy went on. "Like some

people think. We're just protesting against the undemocratic way he was hired. Peace is wrong. Always onto big ideas, but never taking care of what people really need."

Feeney looked at Peggy Brahnler. It had to be some twist of nature that made it practically impossible for him to feel serious at a moment like this.

He looked back at the card. Carey's folks had been so elated at her getting accepted, they'd very nearly taken to becoming friends with him.

Well, friends… that was going a bit far. But at least they could chat. Something that, as neighbors, they'd never done before. They could even manage to laugh a bit about what had happened.

Peggy was saying something. And it seemed that he had been dissimulating well enough to convince her she had driven home her point.

"…and as for that, you understand. Nothing was personal. We think he's a fine chief of police. We'll get along perfectly fine now."

All that time, she'd held herself as immobile in the swivel chair as a short little jade Buddha. Now though, she brought her hands forward together in a clap, and stood up.

It was all so abrupt that Feeney blinked.

"Ah," he gathered himself to his feet, "yes, well, these are things which it's good to discuss, of course." He hesitated, then was relieved to discover he had nothing. "I'm so glad you came in," he finished. "So important that I get a chance to talk to people in an informal way like this. People treat me like a doctor, you know. Always the professional thing. A rare thing for people to take the time to come down here and tell me what's going on. Thank you, Peggy."

She gave him a friendly smile and made for the door, but before she got there, she turned somewhat hesitantly, and then gave him what was supposed to be a pleasant look. "By the way, I like your haircut."

Well, he was stuck, wasn't he? It had been his idea to go have it shorn down nearly to a buzz cut, abandoning himself to the urge the way a drunken sailor staggers into a tattoo parlor. Almost a tonsure. But most certainly an expiation. For… he knew not what. He did, though, think he looked even weirder without the curls than he did with them. But he had to pretend.

"Thanks, Peggy."

A nod, a tight, satisfied smile, and with the same brisk twitching of plumpish thighs that had carried her in, she was gone. Feeney had long ago noticed how the same people who spent the most time talking also made the fastest exits.

He watched the door of the newspaper office shut slowly under the pressure of the hydraulic mechanism, shutting out once again the sluicing sounds coming from the highway where the early morning rain had fallen with fury, cars kicking up such a white mist that the roadway could barely be seen.

He sat back down in his chair. He checked his watch, and then checked his stomach.

Although it was still early morning, he thought about going over and getting something at the Delicate Egg. As the name implied, they did do eggs, and had a selection of omelets. The problem was, he could also see Spencer's car parked over by the restaurant, and although no recent events had transpired lately to be any direct cause for it, Feeney felt an overpowering sense of avoidance and guilt.

Fear and guilt. Their combination: the hallmark of any journalist worth his salt.

No, that wasn't entirely true. Those were the hallmarks of any hack worth his salt. Taken further, it went deeper. And went to the place where disappointment mingled with duty, despair with hope.

Cynicism and humanity. Utterly inseparable.

If he went over there, right then, he knew Bill would be able to talk him into anything.

He looked back at Carey's note. With the chatty news was also an invitation to come up and talk to her classmates. Well, he'd think about it but one thing was for sure. He'd have to be in a better mood.

Feeney stared for a long time out of his window. Imagining…

But also, stuck in the news cycle for the week.

So quiet… but he knew it would be coming. The next thing.

He didn't actually have to be there for it, of course. He could move. Try to avoid it for a bit. Tune out. Just go. And be left alone. Just be left alone.

Maybe he could go for a drive, just drive the feeling out of himself, twenty miles down toward Everett and clear his head of this gloom. And by the time he got back, it would be there waiting for him. And he'd be ready to take it on again. His... part.

He checked his watch again, took Carey's note, folded it, and put it in his dead-center desk drawer. The one where he actually kept things he intended to keep. Then, almost unwilled, his hands came up over the desk, his fingers spread out over the keyboard of his typewriter, feeling for them down in there, waiting too. Thousands of them, ready and willing.

His words. The right words. For any occasion. Waiting.

Languishing in limbo, once again. Peeved, but professionally resigned.

Waiting for the news.

But that lasted all of two minutes, and he got up, flicked off the lights, locked the office door, and got into his car. Get over the mope, indeed.

He should have quit on the spot.

Chapter 76

Whither Feeney

FEENEY would never have *called* himself a nature boy, but it was a deep part of him, having studied and memorized all sorts of birds, plants and trees as a boy. But not to the point of overdoing it. Sometimes, though, nature boy could happen.

He was standing on the gravel scour of the Snohomish and letting himself enjoy the scenery in that state of mindless nature reverence usually reserved for tree huggers or hated anti-jobs foes up there in Loggerland. Flirting with bliss. Mountains did indeed tower. Rocky peaks did indeed rise majestically above the industrial pillage of clear-cuts. Breathtaking. Regal. Awe-inspiring. Just lovely.

All of it. Even the river, with its slash-strewn sweeps where log-jammed debris piled against flood-resisting islets, and its weedy, grass-grown banks crawled away from the smooth-stoned channels of that still-wild river, up into the trees. With the winter floods long gone, the Snohomish was smooth and placid as it plied its way down the valley through the alders and birch tangled there on the flood plain.

Next year, of course, an ugly, muddy flow of glacial melt and logging waste would churn down, roaring vengefully across the very spot he stood. Nature and man, conspiring to outdo each other in destructive effort.

But there, a quiet armistice of an early summer morning. A warming, fly-buzzed peace. An insignificant passing of insects. A butterfly. A dragonfly. A horsefly. Mosquitoes.

A fucking persistent wasp.

Across, on a distant strand of pea gravel and sand, a young bald eagle, still dark and clumsy, flopped down to peck at something flat and black. A rat, a beaver, or perhaps a raccoon, unlucky in the night.

Fact was, there were eagles up there now. They had almost been eliminated, pushed by simple expansion—human demographics—toward local extinction. Strict conservation had brought them back, and now, in growing numbers, they flapped and soared, mixing up local sentiment with patriotic self-content and nature-despising irritation.

Feeney watched the eagle feed. Picking and picking. To his eyes, the scavenging creature never seemed to be getting anything with every effort of its beak. But he figured it would eventually get what it needed.

After a while, Feeney turned and made his way back across the gravel scour, crossing through the chaos of the flood banks, the piled logs and limbs, the thickets of nettles and salmonberry, bright fields of bracken fern. And then up through the aspen and vine maple to the road and back to his car and, on a whim, continued to drive east up into the mountains.

Usually just Skykomish. Very rarely all the way up to Stevens Pass. But this time he kept going.

A little bit farther east, over the alpine meadows at the top of Stevens Pass, the tree line reappeared. But there, instead of towering Douglas fir, red cedar and western hemlock, the forest gave way to lodgepole pine, tamarack, and the ubiquitous scrunch-limbed ponderosa pine of the Dry Side.

Eastern Washington. Another world.

The beginning of the Rest of the World.

And just then, for one wild moment of happiness, he really was free. And in a sense, home.

The sky in Eastern Washington was as clear as a day in Heaven, and as he descended the gradual slopes he could see far out across the golden foothills. Out to where he knew Wenatchee sat, plopped on the west bank of the slow, fat Columbia.

Beyond all that, deeper and further into Eastern Washington,

Feeney's mind could envision the sweet, early summer wheat fields stretching endlessly over to Spokane. The leisurely old farm towns with their timeless charm, their main streets still surviving in those days with individual shops and restaurants. That is, those towns which *had* survived. Many of the original pioneer towns had practically become ghost towns, with maybe a café, and a feed and seed store, or maybe just grain elevators next to a railroad siding. But in those that were still vital, and not swallowed up by mega-farms, there could be found genuine smiles, grins, and warmth. And hard but steady and soul-satisfying work for anyone ready to do it.

Feeney rolled his window down, feeling the moisture being drawn from the air with each mile he dropped. Even Feeney's hair began to soften, fluffing lightly at the line of his forehead where his personal beauty consultant, Laurilaure, had insisted he keep at least some of it at a proper length—if not, she had warned, he'd look like a Celtic hayseed.

Feeney surveyed the countryside. Joy, having filled him, was now overflowing like an overheating radiator. He could barely take it.

He continued like that, mile after mile, dropping like a songbird through the crystalline air. Unfettered and anonymous. A nonexistence offering true liberty from the slavery of being.

And having passed through nullity, that Rubicon of non-time, and driven by the inexorable process that all movement implied, he felt a new sentiment welling in his chest, as though he was on the verge of living another life. A step toward Nirvana and an essential rebirth. Maybe not into a better condition but, if lucky, into less of a predicament.

A nearly thirty-year-old human fetus driving sixty miles an hour in a ten-year-old Chevy with a suspension problem... suddenly transported along another parallax from normal perception.

A dip, a soar, another dip and a long, sliding curve, and far below Feeney saw the first signs of Wenatchee appear.

With that, the rebirth was over, and now it was getting hot and he could smell the heavy, lethargic dust of Eastern Washington hovering finely in the air.

Down, down, down towards Wenatchee. Part of him kept saying he was wasting his time now, driving endlessly, and needing to get back. But another part of him kept saying drive, and keep driving, and just let the miles and miles pass under the wheels of the car. Going not somewhere, but anywhere else. And he went past Wenatchee and took the northern bridge across the Columbia and drove up onto those flood-scoured farmlands west of Dry Falls.

This wasn't the rich, rolling hills of the Palouse. That part of Eastern Washington he'd grown up in, with the towering wheatfield hills and small towns tucked down in the deep valleys. But the sky, with those small cotton puff clouds, and the far horizons and lazy warmth, was the same.

He'd grown up in Pullman. A college town which, in his childhood, had still been mostly a small farming community. He could remember the address, 1817 Lake Street. He knew the little house was still there, having passed through town once on some roving trip he'd taken. Growing up, all the families on the street knew each other, all the kids and their parents.

Joey Scott lived next door. He had an older brother, Gary, who taught little Patrick Feeney and Joey how to take regular car models and turn them into hot rods. Tom Buckley was across the street and he had an older, beatnik brother who, incredibly, was in high school and owned jazz and folk records and bongos. Down the street, David and Ramona Deitz had every boxed game it was possible to think of, but most of all they had a pet coatimundi. And next door to them was Laurie Hopper, the friend of Feeney's sister Aileen, who would eventually possess the first copy of Meet the Beatles on the block. And there were the Allen brothers, Johnny and Jimmy, who were supposed to be "tough" but were just older, and would fix the little kids' bikes and wash Feeney's dad's car.

Jimmy, one day, saw little Patrick on his bike and stopped him and said he had to fix something and went and got some pliers. And he came back and when he was done he pointed Patrick down the street and said, push your foot and just GO Patrick and when you get in front of your house stop and put your right foot down. And Patrick did what he said and when he stopped he saw Jimmy had raised the training wheels off the ground and Patrick had ridden the whole way on two wheels. And Patrick called back to him, "You tricked me Jimmy," and Jimmy laughed and said, "Just turn it around, put your foot on the pedal, and push," and Patrick did. And when he got back to him Jimmy took the wheels clean off. Patrick spent the rest of the afternoon riding that bike up and down the street and that night he was so proud, and showed his dad and told him what Jimmy did and his dad walked down the street and gave Jimmy a whole dollar which, in those days, could buy five gallons of gas.

And Feeney could remember how they all went running through all the back yards, and everybody went to all the school events, and swimming lessons at the park. So many events, so many memories. Adams and Edison schools. Birthday parties coming and going. The folks with their bridge parties, and Feeney's dad going pheasant hunting, and once returning with a kitten, who they named Finnegan and who lived with them for 13 years.

And all the aunts and uncles out on the farms, and family get-togethers, and the giant meals the aunts spread out for everyone in those big old farm houses. And walking "downtown" to see a matinee movie, and afterwards a real, malted milkshake at the Sears lunch counter. The feeling of a cohesive, vital community. Where people had different opinions and respected each other.

It was everyone's small town, and in those days, those small towns were the beating heart of America, and when small towns stood up, America stood up.

Feeney could envy people who grew up and stayed in those small towns. People who managed to keep it and be part of it their whole lives. Feeney's dad admitted, one day when they were out fishing on a lake near Cheney in the days Feeney had gone to school and worked on farms, that it had been the biggest mistake he'd ever made in his life, to move the family from Pullman to Tacoma. He also had loved living in Pullman, had loved the community feel, and the closeness of relatives, and the general softness of society. And in Tacoma, they lost all of that.

All of that.

Because his father had felt bad, Feeney didn't tell him his own feelings. But in truth, he had hated Tacoma, and had hated it nearly from the day they moved there. Maybe not the first year, but by the time he turned 12 he hated everything. Aileen liked to say it hadn't been that bad. But she hadn't ended up year after year back behind the school gymnasium socking it out with some jerk and coming home with sore hands and a split lip.

When Feeney left Tacoma, in the summer of 1974, he never looked back. But as much as he was a Palouse boy, and had loved Pullman, he could never find a way to get back to the small-town life he was born into. Feeney had loved Pullman, and those were the most cherished memories of his life to that point. And it was probably the deepest social reservoir of whatever good he felt he possessed, as a person, as a man. His father was his role model, but Pullman had been his cradle and his roots.

Home. The small town home, for a small town boy.

What would he have been like if he had stayed, if the family had stayed?

He knew one thing. He would have just grown up with his childhood friends, Joey, Tom, Jimmy, Johnny, David, Ramona, and all the others, in a tight, forever group. He probably would have gone to school at the university, right there. He knew he wouldn't have grown that hard Tacoma shell, not letting anything or anyone get to him, which he wasn't sure he would ever shed, unless maybe someday he could find someone he could trust, and who could find him worthy. Someone kind and generous who might actually be able to find a way to love a guy who wasn't really much more than a stray dog. Someone he could love, fully, without fear or restraint. He couldn't see now how there could be any other way he could restore anything of real worth in his life.

He drove, miles and miles, and then came to a stop.

The town's name was Mansfield. It looked nothing like Pullman, just a few buildings left of whatever downtown it might have had—most boarded up and disused—and sat on that scoured-out floodplain toward Grand Coulee that was so barren they hadn't yet figured out how to run irrigation circles on it. He had stopped next to the curb in the center of town, a town that wasn't even half a mile wide, and he bought a coffee in the only establishment of any kind in that town that could offer that. But he drank it on a sidewalk bench down by a car repair service, which seemed to be the only actual business on the street. He had no desire to sit inside some dark bar. He checked his watch. It was barely past one.

Feeney drank his coffee and stared at the street, and he knew he could be back in Sultan in three hours. There was time, he realized. That office stayed open right until six every day.

He finished his coffee, got back in his car, and headed back west. Three hours later, almost on the dot, he was parking his car outside the School Superintendent's office.

But still, he wasn't quite ready, so he pretended he needed a word or two with Ted. He got waved in, and had a word or two with Ted, which turned out not to be much different from the word or two he'd had before, and he stepped back out into the lobby.

And there he finally was.

As he approached her desk Faith gave him a smile. She politely didn't give his haircut more than a glance.

"Well," she said, "that was certainly quiet in there."

"What were you expecting?"

"Oh," she said, "that maybe something would come flying out... a paper weight or something."

"Ah," he smiled. "So, I guess he's been sharing with you his deepest, most heartfelt feelings about me."

"You could put it that way."

"Well, we're all disappointed. This last half year," Feeney almost stopped himself, this wasn't what he wanted to talk about, but something made him push on, "was a rough one."

Faith gave him a long look. Feeney realized he didn't know the slightest thing about her except how impossibly beautiful she was with those sparkling green eyes. There were no rings on her fingers, but that could mean anything.

"We'll get over it," she said, and there, he suddenly saw a slight sheen in her eyes, some emotion, a genuine smile, and something else that surprised him. A shared look of experience.

Feeney smiled back. "Yes. We will."

He could feel it. He was running out of even the slightest thing to say to her, blocked more and more by the one thing he wanted to say to her. But standing there in a wash of wondering how he could keep things going, he was suddenly astonished that it was her keeping things going.

"Are you going to stay?"

"Me?" Feeney smiled. "What makes you think I'd be leaving?"

"After all that's happened. All that's happened to you. I wouldn't be surprised if you just wanted to chuck it."

"I have to admit, it has crossed my mind."

"I'm not surprised," Faith said. "And just the fact it's crossed your mind, probably means that someday it'll happen."

Feeney laughed. "Are we projecting a bit here?"

It was Faith's turn to laugh. "I have to admit... too..."

"I know you're not originally from here."

Faith glanced at him. "Are you sure?"

"Yes," he said. "I'm sure. And don't ask. I don't want to give away all my trade secrets."

"Oh, really," she smiled. "And what else do you know?"

"Absolutely nothing."

"And me, you. It seems strange, doesn't it?"

"Strange?"

"To be in such a small town, working with each other all this time, and knowing... zero... about each other. It's just so strange, at least for me."

He looked quietly at her for a moment, and then realized she was looking right back at him. Really looking at him. And they were looking at each other. And whatever it was, all the miles and the homesickness for... something... and the fact that this moment, right here, standing in front of Faith, was exactly what he had been thinking about for hours on end... just made it all dissolve. The Tacoma shell. His doubts. Fears.

Something in her eyes said, say it. So he did. "Well, we could do something about that, if you wanted."

And the moment he said it, there came a look in Faith's eyes that made it feel to Feeney as if a wave of something from heaven or somewhere had just flowed down through him, as though his soul had been blessed. And there he saw a slight movement of her eyebrows, of a deeper emotion. And those beautiful eyes, suddenly becoming a bit misty. It had always been her. All that time.

"Let's do, Patrick," she said. "I would really like that."

Chapter 77

Through these things…

JACK Feeney had pulled out a table and sat with old newspapers spread before him, turning the pages one by one, not methodically, but almost in step with his father's telling.

Feeney, watching him, found himself saying how strange it was to talk about his life in such detail. And he realized how easy it would be to lie or embellish. Had he told Jack everything in detail? There was no way he could. It had been so rich—as everyone's life was if you began picking it apart day by day, or even hour by hour. He couldn't imagine attempting it. It would have to take up an entire, sprawling novel, an editor's nightmare, and even then he was sure an enormous amount would be left out or forgotten. But he was sure it was possible to recount it honestly, as he had done for Jack.

It was strange combing back through memories, good and bad, and discovering that the bad memories could be easily swept aside if there were enough good memories. When they were side by side, the bad ones had no real ability to cause pain, the good ones washing it over with more lasting emotion, deep and abiding. Life's true treasures, he realized, were in the memories that endured.

He hadn't hidden anything, but he knew he had let the better ones hold sway, although some of the more painful memories had changed with time, and could even be laughed at. But most of all, as he spoke, he realized he had no regrets, which was what he most wanted to tell Jack, and almost did, but Jack interrupted him.

"And you never went back there?" Jack asked.

Feeney shrugged.

"Well, I've passed through, yes. It's the only way to go up over Stevens Pass."

"But never stopped?"

"No."

"Not even to look around, to see what's changed or not?"

Feeney shook his head. "It's been a long time."

"I would have thought you'd do that. I mean, you've gone back to Pullman and other places."

"That was different. Pullman was where I grew up."

Jack looked at the pile of newspapers. "But you lived there when you were working on the paper. I mean, really lived. It was intense."

Feeney smiled. "Every day is intense if you're busy and involved in something. I've had plenty of intense experiences since then."

"Anyway, you can't tell me now that working on a small-town newspaper wouldn't be interesting."

"I never really said that. I said I didn't think they still existed. But if those types of papers are coming back, then... yes... it would be interesting. I just can't imagine it as a career, unless you actually were born in a place like that, grew up in it, had those sorts of roots deep inside you."

Jack sat back in his chair, looking off into the basement thoughtfully. "I suppose so much has changed since then. The country, everything."

"A lot has changed," Feeney agreed. "Things were done so much differently. Computers. The internet. And cell phones. The whole world just got turned upside down."

"Not just that, I mean politics, and how crazy things are."

Feeney smiled. "Things have been crazier before. And in some ways, way crazier. After the Civil War, the country was just nuts, where politics were concerned."

"Yeah, but people weren't trying to destroy democracy."

"Weren't they? You need to read more."

Jack looked at his father for a long moment, and then smiled. "You really did love that work, didn't you."

456

And there it was. The question. Feeney had lived with it for so long there were no longer any doubts, and he certainly couldn't lie. "I could have done that for the rest of my life. But no matter. Like I said, unless you were born into one of those towns like I was. . and you weren't... or were just putting a lot of other things behind you, pretty much retiring, it wouldn't be much of a career."

"Probably not, but I can't help but think I'd like to experience it like you did."

"I don't think you'd have the same experience. You might have a completely boring experience, you know? Not everyone has to deal with a newspaper war and a town civil war at the same time. Or..." Feeney smiled.

And Jack smiled back. "Right. Or. But you never know."

"Well, if you go to work in some small town, don't count on that. I got extremely lucky."

A voice suddenly came from the stairs. "Don't count on what?" They turned to see Faith standing there.

Time had been more than kind to Faith, her eyes still as brilliant, her smile just as lovely. Ever lovely. And her hair, while now gray, still framed a face that, for Feeney, hadn't aged a day since the first time he had seen her in Ted Barnwell's office.

"Nothing, honey," Feeney said. "We're just going over the Sultan days."

"Oh goodness," Faith smiled, and gave her son a look. "Those were the days indeed, when your father came up to work there."

Feeney smiled. "And how your mother saved me."

Faith shook her head. "Nonsense. Jack, don't ever believe that for a second. We saved each other."

ABOUT THE AUTHOR

Marc Lloyd Heberden was born on 20 March 1956 in Spokane, Washington. His early years were spent in Pullman and later Tacoma. After his studies at Southern Illinois University, Eastern Washington University in Cheney, Western Washington University in Bellingham, and the University of Washington in Seattle, where he earned a degree in journalism, he worked as a newspaper editor and award-winning journalist. Moving to Europe in the early 1980s he wrote for newspapers and magazines and began writing short stories, novels and screenplays. *Outside Man* was his first novel, published in 1984. Following that were *The Big Tide*, *14 Days in July*, *Feeney's Part*, *The Norman*, and *Feeney's Last*. His work has included that of being the commercial director for Paris based newspapers and magazines, a publications manager for the Organisation for Economic Co-operation and Development, and finally a program developer creating programs and teaching books for French medical personnel. He resides in a small town southwest of Paris.

www.ingramcontent.com/pod-product-compliance
Lightning Source LLC
Chambersburg PA
CBHW051534250626
47157CB00001B/43